seven deadly sins

VOL 2.

ALSO BY ROBIN WASSERMAN

Hacking Harvard

The Cold Awakening trilogy:

Frozen

Shattered

Torn

Seven Deadly Sins 1

Lust & Envy

Seven Deadly Sins 2

Pride & Wrath

Seven Deadly Sins 3

Sloth, Gluttony, & Greed

ROBIN WASSERMAN

Simon Pulse
New York London Toronto Sydney New Delhi

This book is a work of fiction. Any references to historical events, real people, or real locales are used fictitiously. Other names, characters, places, and incidents are the product of the author's imagination, and any resemblance to actual events or locales or persons, living or dead, is entirely coincidental.

SIMON PULSE
An imprint of Simon & Schuster Children's Publishing Division
1230 Avenue of the Americas, New York, NY 10020
First Simon Pulse paperback edition May 2013

For information about special discounts for bulk purchases,
please contact Simon & Schuster Special Sales at 1-866-506-1949
or business@simonandschuster.com.
The Simon & Schuster Speakers Bureau can bring authors to
your live event. For more information or to book an event contact the
Simon & Schuster Speakers Bureau at 1-866-248-3049
or visit our website at www.simonspeakers.com.
Designed by Mike Rosamilia
The text of this book was set in JansonText LT.
Manufactured in the United States of America
2 4 6 8 10 9 7 5 3 1
Library of Congress Control Number 2013931937
ISBN 978-1-4424-7506-9

seven deadly sins

PRIDE

For Mom and Dad

He that is proud eats up himself:
pride is his own glass, his own trumpet, his own chronicle.
—William Shakespeare, *Troilis and Cressida*

This world is mine for the taking.
—Eminem

chapter one

THEY WANTED HIM. ALL OF THEM. HE KNEW IT.

And he loved it.

Kane Geary had developed many gifts in his eighteen years of life, not least of which was a finely tuned radar for the appreciative stares of beautiful women. And tonight, he could feel their eyes on him, their gazes drawn to him from all over the restaurant. The luscious redhead in the back booth, stealing glances over her date's sloping shoulders; the trim blonde waiting for the bathroom, zeroing in on his chiseled pecs; their perky waitress, shamelessly grazing his shoulder as she leaned across him to lay out their food—even the age-weathered brunette up in front was joining in the fun, catching his eye with a wink every time her balding husband's back was turned.

Seated on the edge of Chez Jacques's spacious dining room, which bustled with the well-bridled enthusiasm of a small-town Saturday night, Kane was, quite simply, the center of attention. Which was exactly how he liked it. Not that Kane was an attention-grabber, one of those tedious people who talked too much, too fast, too loudly. That would be too obvious. And far too much work. Instead, he waited, knowing that his smoldering good looks and effortless grace would eventually and inevitably draw the world to him. Or, more specifically, draw the girls.

They came in all shapes, colors, and sizes, and they wanted only one thing: him. Which meant that Kane could take his pick. And he usually did.

This time, he thought, smiling at the blond beauty sitting across the table from him, *I may be onto something*. Beth Manning seemed to have it all: brains, personality, body by Barbie . . . and, as of two months ago, she had him.

She was, to put it mildly, an unlikely choice. Haven High's resident most-likely-to-succeed, a power player when it came to AP classes and extracurriculars, a nobody when it came to anything else. Beth was the world's original "nice girl," and Kane knew that, until recently, dating him had never crossed her mind. Nice girls didn't date Kane Geary. They stuck with people like Adam Morgan, Mr. All-American, earnest, good-hearted, and sweet as apple pie. But now Adam was history, and Beth was all his.

All it had taken was a little hard work, just a few surreptitious pushes in the right direction . . . and here she was. Tossed aside by her beloved boyfriend, who'd caught her cheating. With Kane. Or, at least, Adam *thought* he'd caught her. Kane smirked. You'd think that after their years of friendship, Adam would have realized that when it came to Kane, what you see is rarely what you get. But Adam hadn't bothered to look deeper; and Kane hadn't hesitated before swooping in to claim his prize.

And what a prize. Perched primly on the edge of her seat, her hand on his, his foot grazing her leg beneath the table. Gazing at him with those open, grateful eyes—as if a dinner at Chez Jacques, the overpriced "French bistro" whose chef and menu were about as French as McDonald's french fries, was proof of his boundless love. Yes, it was "the best restaurant in town"—but when your town was a dusty assortment of liquor stores and burned-out buildings like Grace, California, and when most local cuisine tasted as if a handful of desert dirt and cacti had been tossed in for "local flavor," best restaurant in town wasn't saying much. Not that Beth seemed to realize it.

Kane supposed that a lifetime in Grace—or perhaps a year with Adam—had dulled her expectations. Or at least her tastebuds.

She'd temporarily dispensed with her daily uniform, a bland T-shirt and jeans, and was instead wearing a low-cut satin dress, a pale sky blue that matched her eyes. With her long blond hair swept into a loose knot at the nape of her neck and the long silver earrings he'd given her swaying gently with her every graceful move, she looked like a model. Gorgeous, elegant—perfect. And should he expect any less?

Kane could see the question in the envious gazes of his female admirers: What does *she* have that I don't?

One thing, ladies, he responded silently, suppressing a smile. *For the moment—me.*

"What are you thinking?" she asked him, tucking a stray hair behind her ear. It had become a familiar question. Good ol' Adam was pretty much an open book—it must be somewhat unnerving for her, Kane supposed, to be dating someone with any kind of inner life, someone with secrets. And Kane didn't mind her asking—as long as he didn't have to give a real answer.

"I'm just thinking how beautiful you look tonight," Kane told her—a half-truth being the best kind of lie. "I'm thinking how incredibly lucky I am to have ended up with someone like you."

Beth giggled, her face turning a faint shade of pink. "I'm the lucky one, Kane," she protested.

He couldn't argue with that.

For Harper Grace, Saturday night traditionally meant three things: booze, boys, and boredom. She would hit a lame bar with a lame guy, flash her crappy fake ID at an apathetic bartender, and down a couple of rum and Cokes before finding a secluded spot for the inevitable not-so-hot 'n' heavy make-out session with Mr. Wrong. It had seemed a risky and adventurous formula a few years ago, but the love 'em and lose 'em act had gotten old, fast. Grace was a small town, too small—and after a few years of the same bars, the same guys, the same post-date conversation with her best friend, Miranda (usually concluding with, "Why would you ever let me go out with such a loser?"), the thrill was gone.

But, now . . . Harper glanced to her left. Adam's wholesome good looks were just barely visible in the dim light cast by the flickering movie screen. His bright eyes, his wide smile, the shock of blond hair that set off his perfect tan—it was too dark to see the details, but no matter. She knew them all by heart.

Now, things were different, Harper reminded herself, leaning against Adam's broad shoulder and twirling her fingers through his. There was no more need for cheap thrills, because she had the real thing. Adam Morgan, her next-door neighbor, her oldest friend—her soul mate, if you believed in such things. Which, of course, she didn't. But she believed in Adam—and she believed that after all the effort she'd put into winning him, she fully deserved her prize. They'd been together only a couple months, but already, he never spoke of his year with The Bland One anymore. The dreamy gaze that used to bloom across his face at the mere mention of Beth's name was gone. Knowing—or believing—that his perfect little angel had hopped into bed with someone else had had its effect. Adam had finally wised up and realized that the right person for him had been there all along, a loyal friend and next-door neighbor, just waiting for her time to come. Unlike Beth, *Harper* would never let him down, never mistreat him, never lie to him—unless, she conceded, it was for his own good.

So what if she was spending her night in a dark theater watching an endless Jackie Chan marathon rather than preening in front of the adoring masses, Haven High girls hoping that her polite acknowledgment might secure them a berth on the A-list, brawny bouncers and bartenders attracted by her billowing auburn hair like moths to a flame and hoping against hope she would ditch her date and fall into their open arms? (It had been known to happen.) So what if she had to watch what she said 24/7, to make sure none of the nasty thoughts constantly popping into her brain slipped out in Adam's presence, lest he begin to think she really was as much of a power-hungry bitch as the rest of their school believed her to be? And so what if, in order to get what she wanted, she'd had to screw over the people she loved the most, and sacrifice whatever shreds of integrity she may have had left after four years in the Haven High trenches?

None of that mattered now. Not now that she had Adam. Strong, handsome, kind, wonderful, *perfect* Adam.

She'd waited so long—but it had been worth it. All of it.

"What are you thinking?" he whispered, slinging an arm around her and drawing her close. She nestled against him, laying her head against his shoulder. He was always asking her that, and she was still delighted by the novelty of being with a guy who actually cared what she was thinking, who was focused on getting into her mind rather than into her bed.

"I'm thinking this—you, us—it's all too good to be true," she admitted. And though it was intended as a lie, the words had the ring of truth.

"It's true," he assured her, and kissed her gently on the forehead.

I'll reform, Harper decided, leaning against his warm body. No more party girl. No more shallow, superficial bitch. She would be the girl Adam wanted her to be—the girl he seemed to think, deep down, she really was. And who knew? He could even be right.

After all, anything's possible.

Miranda was bored.

She'd tried to tell herself that having all this free time on her hands was a good thing. She could use some space—a nice, long stretch of empty hours every now and then would give her a chance to do all the things that she wanted to do. She wouldn't have to accommodate anyone else—not her mother, not her little sister, not Harper, none of the people who usually saw fit to dictate the what, when, and how of Miranda's life. She'd just do her own thing. She was a strong, smart, independent woman, right? (This month's *Cosmo* quiz had confirmed it.) Enjoying your alone time was right there in the job description, and she'd been certain she was up to the task.

But it was time to face facts. These last few weeks she'd read plenty of good books, watched all her favorite movies, taken so many "relaxing" bubble baths that she was starting to grow gills—and enough was enough. She was bored. Bored out of her mind.

It's not like she needed to spend every minute of every day with Harper. Miranda was a best friend, not some parasite who needed a constant infusion of Harper's energy to thrive. They needed *each other*, equally—or so Miranda had thought. Apparently, she'd thought wrong. Because here she was, alone. *Again.* On yet another Saturday night, playing Internet solitaire while Harper lived it up with the love of her life. So much for late-night rendezvous at the bar of choice, or Sunday brunches where they dissected every moment of the lame night before. No more of the late-night distress calls Miranda had complained about so much—never admitting, even to herself, how good it felt to be needed.

Not that Miranda begrudged her best friend her happiness—not much, at least.

"You wouldn't believe it, Rand," Harper told her. Constantly. "It's better than I ever could have imagined. Having him there for me? Always? It's amazing. It's so perfect. You'll see."

Sure, Miranda would see for herself. Someday. Maybe. Until then, she was growing intimately familiar with the whole outside-looking-in thing, turning herself into an impeccable third wheel in under a week. She'd always been a quick study.

Harper refused to elaborate on how it had happened, how one day Beth and Adam were going strong, and the next, Harper was the one in his arms, Beth kicked to the curb.

Not that vapid blondes like Beth ever stayed single for long—thirty seconds later, there she was, Kane Geary's latest conquest, floating along by his side as if she'd been there all along.

No, it was girls like Miranda who stayed single—for what seemed like forever. In all the years she'd longed for Kane, had he given her a second look? Had he ever once considered that her wit and charm might be worth ten of his bimbos, despite her stringy hair and lumpy physique?

No—guys like Kane, they never did. Probably, never would.

Her computer *dinged* with the sound of a new e-mail, and she opened it warily, expecting spam. More offers to increase her girth or introduce her to some "Hot XXX Girls NUDE NUDE NUDE." Who else would be sitting in front of their computer on a Saturday night but the people trying to sell that shit—and the people who actually bought it?

LOOKING FOR LOVE IN ALL THE WRONG PLACES? read the banner headline.

Great. Even cyberspace knew how pathetic she was.

> Join **MatchMadeInHaven.com**, Grace's first teen Internet dating site! Find your true love with the click of a mouse! After all—you've been lonely too long. . . .

You can say that again, Miranda thought bitterly. And, for just a moment, she considered it. No one would ever have to know, she reasoned, and maybe, just maybe, this was her ticket to coupledom. Maybe there was someone out there, just like her, waiting for the right girl to come along. Could she really complain about being alone if she hadn't done everything in her power, *everything*, to fix the problem?

And then she caught herself, realizing the depths to which she was about to sink.

What are you thinking? she asked herself sternly, shaking her head in disgust. *You're not that desperate.*

At least, not yet.

They ate in silence.

The dining room table was large and long, too big for just the two of them. Kaia sat at one end, her father at the other, and for most of the meal, the quiet was punctuated only by the distant chattering of the maids in the kitchen and the occasional clatter of a silver Tiffany fork against the edge of Kaia's Rafaelesco plate. She saw her father wince at each clang and scrape—it didn't inspire her to be more careful.

Kaia would rather have been in the cavernous living room, eating take-out in front of the giant flat-screen TV, as usual. When you got down to it, she would have preferred to be back home in New York, eating in a chic Tribeca bistro. Even holing up in her New York bedroom with a three-day-old bag of Doritos would have been preferable to having even one more meal in Grace, CA. Good food didn't change the fact that she was in exile, a prisoner, beholden to her parents' stupid whims. She didn't want to be stuck in the desert, stuck in his pretentious, *Architectural Digest* wannabe house, and she certainly didn't want to be stuck at the hand-crafted mahogany dining room table facing the man who was keeping her there. And despite her perpetual inability to read him, she was pretty sure he didn't want to be there, either. Yet there they sat, one night a month.

And the night stretched on, interminable.

"So, how's school?" her father finally asked.

"I wouldn't know," she answered lightly.

"Kaia . . ."

The warning note in his voice was subtle, but clear. *He talks to me like I'm one of his employees*, she thought, not for the first time.

"School's fine. Delightful," she offered. "I go every day. It's a truly wonderful experience. I'm simply learning ever so much. Is that what you want to hear?"

He sighed and shook his head. "I just want to hear the truth, Kaia. And I want to hear that you're happy."

"Sorry to disappoint, *Father*, but those are two different things—and, at the moment, they're mutually exclusive. You and Mother have seen to that."

His lips tightened, and Kaia braced for an angry

response, some of that famous Keith Sellers temper, quick as lightning and just as deadly, but he kept it together. Barely. "This year isn't supposed to be a punishment, Kaia."

"Then why does it feel like one?"

"It's supposed to be a break," he continued, as if she hadn't spoken. "To give you and your mother some space. To give you some time to think about what you want your life to be."

"I want my life to be back to normal," Kaia spit out, immediately regretting it. She'd vowed not to let her guard down. Bad enough that she'd almost cried on the day he'd cut up all her credit cards—and *had* cried on the day her mother had shipped her off to the airport. She'd refused to give them the satisfaction of knowing she cared.

"Oh, Kaia. I wish I could help," he said, almost sounding like he meant it. "Maybe if I spent some more time at home. . . ."

"You really want to help?" Kaia asked, allowing a note of near sincerity to creep into her voice. She'd been waiting for the right moment for this, and there was no time like the present—right? "How about a temporary reprieve," she suggested. "Winter break's coming up, and I thought, maybe, just for a couple weeks—"

"You are *not* going back to the East Coast," he cut her

off. "Not for two weeks, not for two days—you know the terms of our agreement."

"Agreement, right," she muttered. "Like I had a choice."

"What was that?" he snapped.

"I said, if this isn't a punishment, why do I feel like I'm in prison?" she asked, loud and clear.

"Katherine, that's quite enough whining for tonight." His measured tone masked an undercurrent of tightly bottled rage. The famous Keith Sellers temper was famous for a reason.

"It's *Kaia*," she reminded him.

"I named you *Katherine*," he countered, rising from the table. "I *let* you call yourself by that ridiculous name, but you'll always be Katherine, just like I'll always be your father, whether you like it or not."

"Trust me, I know," Kaia snarled. "If I could change that, along with the name, I would have done it a long time ago."

By the time he roared at her to go to her room, she was already out of her seat and halfway up the stairs.

Just another warm and fuzzy family dinner at the Sellers house.

Bon appétit.

It was almost midnight before Kaia's father had gone to sleep and she was able to sneak out of the house. She was still fuming about the way her parents felt they could run her life. They were mistaken. They could ship her across the country and strand her in the desert, but they couldn't stop her from slipping out of the mansion, driving twenty minutes down the deserted highway, pulling to a stop in front of a squat, nondescript gray house, and scurrying up the walkway, head down to shield her face from prying eyes. They couldn't stop her from throwing open the door and falling into her lover's arms.

Her *lover*—she liked the sound of that. She'd had her share of guys, but never one she'd call a *lover*. The term was too adult, too mature for the puny prep school boys she'd toyed with back east—it was reserved for a man. And now she'd found one.

"*Je m'oublie quand je suis avec toi*," she murmured into his neck.

I forget myself when I'm with you.

He hated when she spoke French to him; it was too much of a reminder of his day job, and of their roles in the real world, beyond the walls of his cramped apartment, where he was a French teacher, she a student. He didn't want to remember—and she never wanted to forget.

The delicious scandal, the secrecy—why else was she there? It didn't hurt that he was sophisticated, worldly, movie-star handsome, that at least when they were alone in bed together, he treated her like a goddess—but really, the thrill of the forbidden had always been, and remained, the biggest draw. He was too shallow, too vain to be anything other than an object of illicit desire. She had no fairy-tale illusions of love—and knew he felt the same.

It's why they worked so well together.

"What are you thinking?" he asked idly, though she knew he didn't really care.

"I'm thinking you're a superficial, conceited, despicable human being, taking advantage of a sweet young girl like me." To Jack Powell, she could always speak some form of the truth—because the things they said to each other would never matter. Neither of them was in this for good conversation.

"And you're a callous, duplicitous, licentious girl who's out only for herself," he retorted in his clipped British accent, and kissed her roughly. "I can't get enough of you."

It was a match made in heaven—or somewhere a bit farther south.

chapter two

"THIS . . . ISN'T . . . *SO* . . . BAD . . . ," HARPER LIED, panting for breath with every word.

Miranda slammed the big red button on her treadmill and nearly toppled to the ground as the moving track stopped short beneath her feet.

"Are you kidding?" she asked, glaring at Harper. "This has got to be the worst idea you've ever had."

Harper pushed her sweaty bangs out of her face and grimaced—she would never have suggested scamming Grace's only gym into giving them a free trial workout if she'd known it would be so much *work*. After all, working, on the first day of winter vacation? It went against everything she believed in.

But it would be worth it, she reminded herself, and began pedaling the stationary bike even faster. Harper usually steered clear of physical activity (unless you counted the kind that took place behind closed bedroom doors). But she'd always told herself that an aversion to exercise was a choice, not a necessity—if the time ever came that she needed to be in shape, she'd been sure it would be a snap.

The time had come. But the only thing snapping would be her bones, if she managed to fall off the exercise bike one more time.

"Maybe it's time to throw in the towel," Miranda suggested. She made a face and gestured toward the soggy towel she'd been using to wipe away her sweat. "Literally."

"No way." Harper smiled through gritted teeth. "We're just getting into the groove." She looked hatefully at the lithe bodies effortlessly working the machines all around her. Losers, all of them, judging by their baggy T-shirts, saggy shorts, and mis-sized sports bras—and yet none of them were gasping and panting like a wounded animal. Like Harper.

"So what's with the new work ethic?" Miranda asked, turning the treadmill back on and, with a sigh, continuing her plodding jog to nowhere.

"Hello—school ski trip coming up? Need to get in shape? Remember? Are you burning off calories or brain cells?"

"Funny." Miranda didn't show a hint of a smile. "But I don't buy it. You've got us up at the buttcrack of dawn, breaking a sweat. Just to get in shape so you can *ski*? And you don't even know how to ski."

Thanks for rubbing it in.

Harper knew it was ridiculous to want to impress Adam up on the slopes—and though she hated to admit it, she knew a couple hours on a stationary bike and a *Skiing for Dummies* book wouldn't help her keep up with someone who'd been on the slopes since he was nine. But it couldn't hurt to try, right? Adam was such the all-American athlete—skiing, swimming, running, he did it all with an ease that made Harper crazy. And his previous girlfriends had been the same way—even Beth, who'd never played on a team in her life, had a natural athletic grace that made Harper sick to watch.

She just wanted to make sure she measured up. Especially this weekend. This weekend, everything had to be perfect.

"Is this all to impress Adam?" Miranda persisted. Harper winced, hating the way her best friend could read every expression that flickered across her face. "Because you've known each other half your lives. Don't you think it's probably a little late to impress him? At least, more than you already have?"

Two months of dating—two months of fearing, every moment, that Adam would find out what she'd done to get him, would find out she wasn't the person he was, she hoped, falling in love with. Harper needed to impress him, all right, every moment. Because if she wasn't perfect—if they weren't perfect together—Harper suspected there was an understudy waiting in the wings who'd be only too happy to replace her. Harper wasn't about to give Beth the chance; but she also wasn't about to admit any of her pathetic insecurities out loud. She had far too much pride to expose that part of herself—even to Miranda.

"I just want this weekend to be good, all right?" she snapped, staring resolutely at the tiny TV screen hanging on the opposite wall, and pretending to care how Dr. Phil's latest guest had managed to accidentally sleep with her transsexual cousin.

"What makes this weekend any different from . . . oh!" A triumphant grin blossomed across Miranda's face. She hopped off the machine and grabbed a handlebar on Harper's bike, forcing Harper to face her. "Are you telling me that this weekend is . . . ?"

Harper felt a tingling heat spread across her cheeks and jerked her head away. She couldn't be blushing. She never blushed.

"This is it, isn't it?" Miranda pressed on eagerly. "*WFS.* Are you kidding me? After all this time, you haven't . . ."

WFS.

Weekend For Sex. Harper and Miranda had coined the term a couple years ago, the first time Harper's parents had left her alone for the weekend. Justin Diamond, the JV lacrosse captain and her first serious boyfriend, had pulled into the driveway five minutes after her parents had left. (And about five minutes later, he'd been ready to pull out again.)

Harper gave Miranda a curt nod.

"WFS!" Miranda repeated in a hushed and wondrous tone. "I don't believe it."

"Rand, can we drop it?" Harper asked irritably, pedaling harder. Miranda was making it sound like she just hopped into bed with anything that moved—as if she had no patience, no discrimination, no self-restraint.

And, okay, it had been a long time since she'd made a guy wait so long. She knew that Beth was still a virgin, knew that sleeping with Adam would probably be the fastest and surest way to win his affection—but she wanted more than that. Adam was worth more than some guy, more than all of them put together.

Feeling like she was about to pass out, Harper sighed and stopped pedaling.

"Oh, thank God," Miranda breathed, staggering off the treadmill and taking a long gulp from her water bottle.

She tossed it over to Harper. "Here—you look even worse than I feel."

Harper bristled at the suggestion (okay, observation of the obvious) that she was a tiny bit out of shape, but gulped down half the bottle before passing it back. "I didn't *have* to stop," she boasted. "I've just got a lot of errands to run before I go to work."

Work. The word still sounded strange coming out of her mouth.

"Work?" Miranda repeated incredulously. "Work on what? Your nails?"

Harper looked away—she'd held off on telling Miranda about her little problem, but this moment would have had to come, sooner or later. "I got a job," she mumbled, staring over her shoulder as Dr. Phil's guest sobbed into a fistful of tissues.

"A what?"

"A job," Harper spit out, finally facing her. "I got a job, okay? My stupid parents wouldn't pay for the ski trip, and I needed to go, so I just—oh, forget it."

It was so humiliating. She was, after all, Harper Grace—as in, Grace, California. The town had been named for her family's mining company, and for decades they had ruled like desert royalty. And then, years before Harper had been born—no more copper. No more mines. And just like that—no more money.

At least, if you believed her parents' endless whining. But they had enough to get by. Enough for "important" things—they just didn't understand the meaning of the word. And so Harper had to carry on the Grace name, the Grace legacy, all on her own. And if that meant a few weeks of menial labor—she shivered at the thought—so be it.

Miranda frowned, knowing better than to make light of Harper's situation—not when it involved cash flow, and definitely not when it involved working hard, working for other people, working in *public*.

"Why didn't you tell me?" she asked, quietly. "Maybe I could have—"

"Don't even say it," Harper snapped. Graces didn't accept handouts. Not from anyone.

"So, where are you working?" Miranda finally asked, after a long and awkward pause.

"It doesn't matter." Like she was going to tell Miranda about her humiliating saga, traipsing from one bar to the next, only to be turned away for being too young. Not too young to drink—or too young to flirt with—but that was as far as any of these loser bartenders had been willing to go. She'd tried the Lost and Found, the Cactus Cantina, and then in desperation even Bourquin's Coffee Shop and the decrepit vintage clothing store, Classic Rags—but in the end, only one place had had any openings. And no wonder—it was the last place any sane person would have chosen to work. Which meant plenty of openings for those poor saps with no choice at all.

She made a show of checking her watch and frowned as if she had somewhere far more important to be.

"I have to get out of here, Rand," she lied, hurrying toward the locker room as fast as her weary, leaden legs could carry her.

"Is this weekend really worth that much to you?" Miranda called, scurrying to catch up.

Harper just shot her a look—the WFS look—and Miranda nodded. That said it all.

On her walk home, Miranda couldn't stop thinking about Harper—maybe that's why she didn't see him. Her brain was stuck on the fact that her best friend, who usually told her everything—usually more than she wanted to know—had started keeping secrets. There was the job thing. The WFS—did that count as a secret too? Harper had clearly gone out of her way never to mention it—but then, she'd kept unnaturally quiet on almost everything having to do with her relationship with Adam. Oh, she talked about Adam plenty. Adam was, these days, almost all she talked about. How wonderful he was. How happy he made her. How much he loved being with her. And on, and on, until it seemed like their friendship had turned into nothing more than an Adam Morgan love-fest. But they never talked about anything real, like how Harper felt about being in her first serious relationship. Or how Miranda felt like her best friend was slipping away from her. And they never, ever talked about the biggest secret of all: how Harper and Adam had gotten together in the first place.

What had happened that day, when Adam went off to a swim meet, Beth stayed in town, and Harper inexplicably showed up the next morning with Adam hanging on her arm?

To be fair, Miranda had never come right out and asked Harper what had happened—that same night, they'd had a massive fight, and Harper had left Miranda crying and alone in the middle of the woods. Left her there for no good reason—and come home with everything she'd ever wanted, while Miranda had, as always, come home alone.

Harper had never really apologized. Miranda suspected, in fact, that in the warm glow of Adam-inspired happiness, Harper had totally forgotten. Miranda forgave her anyway. Like always. But that didn't mean things had gone back to normal. Miranda and Harper had always been a twosome—but now, Harper plus Adam made two. And two plus Miranda made a crowd. There was this new part of Harper's life that Miranda couldn't have access to, couldn't really understand. She was too embarrassed to even mention any of this to Harper, didn't want to be seen as a lonely and pathetic third wheel, someone to be included out of pity. Out of obligation.

So there was another secret.

How many secrets would it take, Miranda wondered, to kill a friendship?

The question kept bouncing around in her head—it was all she could focus on. And that's why she didn't see him—not until he was, literally, on top of her.

"Can you watch where you're going?"

The boy who'd slammed past Miranda turned back at the sound of her angry snarl. He froze in the middle of the sidewalk when he realized whom he'd hit.

"I'm . . . I'm sorry," Miranda stammered, backing away. "I didn't—"

"No, *I'm sorry*," he interrupted, with exaggerated solemnity. "I didn't realize that I'd bumped into the high and mighty Miranda. What a fool I am."

"Greg . . . ," she began, then stopped herself. What could she say? *Sorry I went on a few dates with you and blew you off? Sorry that, even though you're smart and funny and liked me a lot, it just wasn't going to work?* Or how about, *Sorry that you overheard me telling my best friend that I deserve better than you?* Miranda didn't think there was a Miss Manners–prescribed etiquette for the situation, but none of the most obvious options seemed particularly appropriate.

“Sorry I yelled, Greg,” she finally continued. “I didn’t realize it was you.”

“Oh, she remembers my name,” he crowed, not meeting her eyes. “I’m so honored.”

“Greg, can we just—do you have to . . .”

“Do I have to what?” he asked loudly, drawing curious stares from two women pushing their strollers across the street. “Do I have to stand here and pretend I care what you have to say?” He paused, and pretended to think it over. “Now that you mention it—no, I don’t.”

He brushed past her and strode down the street, pausing a few feet away to shout something back to her.

“I do sincerely apologize for bumping into you—you *deserve much better* than that.”

If nothing else, the encounter—her first run-in with Greg since the “unfortunate incident”—should have proved to Miranda that her instincts had been right: She was too good for that immature jerk. But telling herself that didn’t help much. She’d been feeling guilty for weeks about the things she’d said about Greg—and the look on his face when he’d overheard.

She had hoped that maybe, since all this time had passed, he’d have cooled down, be willing to forgive her, assure her that she wasn’t such a cold and horrible person. That maybe they could even be friends.

Apparently not.

* * *

Harper had lied—not a first. She had hours to go before she officially entered the miserable ranks of the employed. But she'd needed to escape before Miranda pried more information out of her about her job, or her boyfriend. It was exhausting, trying so hard to keep her best friend out of the loop. Sometimes, it was easier to just be alone.

So here she was, hours to kill on Grace's main drag. As a general rule, the town offered only two leisure options: shopping and boozing. And since she didn't plan to show up plastered for her first day of work, those options narrowed to one.

Time to pre-spend that first paycheck. (The second one would go to her parents, to pay back the money they'd loaned her—but as far as she was concerned, the first money she'd ever earned for herself was already earmarked for a fabulous new ensemble that would make her shine up on the slopes as much as she shined on the ground.)

First stop had been the local video store. She'd snuck in, skulked around the sparse fitness section for a few minutes, and then grabbed the cheapest and most painless-looking workout videos she could find: *Sweatin' to the Oldies*, *Pilates for Beginners*, and a Paula Abdul dance aerobics tape clearly left over from 1987. After throwing a wad of cash at the clerk, she stuffed the tapes into the bottom of her gym bag and raced out of the store, hoping no one had spotted her. She wasn't about to break a sweat in public again, not after her pathetic showing this morning, but she also wasn't about to let anyone know she'd be sweating to the oldies at home with Richard Simmons. The potential humiliation factor was through the roof.

Next stop: Angie's, Grace's only "fine clothing shop." Harper usually shopped online—most Grace gear was pretty much a fashion faux pas waiting to happen—but the ski trip was fast approaching, and she had no time to waste waiting for a package that, given the incompetence of her local postal workers, might never arrive. Just one problem: Angie's was a desert clothing store, and even in the middle of winter, their cold-weather selection was limited to a shelf of thick socks, thin gloves, and a few wool sweaters covered with giant snowflakes.

"Pathetic, isn't it?"

Harper recognized the voice and turned around slowly to meet the familiar smirk.

"Fancy meeting you here," she greeted him with a smile.

"A true delight," Kane drawled sarcastically, pulling out a pack of cigarettes and lighting up—despite the prominently placed NO SMOKING sign just above his head.

If Harper was surprised to spot him in a women's clothing store, she didn't let on, nor did she reveal her true delight at running into him. They had so few chances to speak privately these days—and of course it was only in private that they could crow about the triumph of their secret plan. Harper never got tired of winning, and she never got tired of rehashing her victories. Too bad Kane and Kaia were the only ones who could ever know about this, the greatest victory of all.

"See anything you like?" Kane asked.

Harper dropped the light blue cashmere scarf she'd been fingering—it was the only worthwhile item in the store. And it was gorgeous. It also cost about as much as the entire ski trip—and thus was way out of her league. Not that she'd ever admit it to Kane.

"Nada. This place is a fashion wasteland," she complained, grabbing a cigarette from him after deciding that the clerk was too immersed in her latest trashy romance novel to notice. "So, having a good time?"

He raised an eyebrow. "Shopping? Surely you jest."

She smacked him lightly on the arm. "Not the store, Kane—the girl. You. Beth. Is it everything you'd hoped for?"

His face finally broke into a wide grin.

"And more," he confided. "She can't get enough of me. And no wonder. You should have seen the look on her face when Adam showed up raging about what she'd done. She had no idea what the hell he was talking about.

Totally crushed." He waggled his eyebrows at Harper and smirked, as he did every time he fondly recounted this point in the story. "I, of course, was there to pick up the pieces. You can imagine she'd be quite grateful."

"That's nothing," Harper claimed. "You should have seen the look on Adam's face when he saw the pictures. He . . ." But she trailed off, for there was nothing particularly amusing about the memory of her oldest friend's reaction to seeing the doctored photos of Beth and Kane. He'd collapsed in on himself, and Harper had been the cause. Knowing she could alleviate his pain with a few words—confess that the pictures were fake, that she and Kane were to blame, that Beth was, as always, pure and innocent—that had been the hardest part of the whole thing. But she couldn't do it—wouldn't do it. She wasn't proud of what she'd done, but there had been no other way.

"Come on, Grace, don't get sentimental on me now," Kane charged. "This is a time for swagger and celebration."

"Sometimes I just wonder . . ."

"What, whether we did the right thing?"

"Well, don't you?" she countered.

"Why bother?" he asked, smirking. "What's done is done. Adam and Beth were doomed—we just helped things along a bit. Think of it as a mercy killing."

"I suppose Adam is much better off now without all that dead weight," Harper mused.

"Hey, watch it," Kane cautioned her in mock anger. "That's my girlfriend you're talking about."

"Your *girlfriend*, right." Harper took a long drag on her cigarette, relishing the sharp taste of the smoke billowing out of her mouth. Adam hated it when she smoked, so she'd been trying to cut back. It had seemed a small price to pay, but God, she missed that nicotine buzz. "I guess I should congratulate you, now that we're coming up on two months. What is this, your longest relationship ever?"

"Very funny, Grace." But the smile had disappeared from his face. "Did you ever stop to think this one might be different?"

"Did I ever stop to think that the great Kane Geary, who's made a life's work of dating his way through town, who gets bored after about ten minutes of *anything*, might actually be tamed by Beth, of all people? Blond, bland, boring, *Beth*?" She finished off the cigarette and pondered the question. "No, I guess the thought never occurred to me."

"You underestimate her, Grace. You always have."

"And you *over*estimate her, Kane," she pointed out. "That's the part of this I've never understood. Why Beth, of all people? She thought you were scum, she was dating Adam, she's *so* not your type. Why her?"

Kane smiled cryptically.

"Why not?"

The most memorable moment in my life was the time when I . . .

Growing up in a small town, I always believed that someday I would . . .

If there's one thing I know in life, it's that I . . .

Pathetic!

Beth slumped against the wall of the kitchen, ignoring the sticky grease patches that quickly dampened her polyester uniform. Her college applications were due in a couple weeks, and if she wanted to make up for her horrible SAT scores . . . She shivered at the memory of filling in all those tiny bubbles as tears spattered against the test booklet. It was bad enough Adam had broken up with her without any warning, had accused her of cheating on him, had tossed her away without a second thought—but she could never forgive him for doing it all the night before the SATs. If he were trying to ruin her life, he'd made a pretty damn good start.

No, if she didn't come up with an amazing application essay, something that would blow the mind of any admissions officer who read it, she could kiss her future good-bye.

"Manning! Table seven's still waiting for their food!" her manager called. One of the other waitresses, blowing past on her way back to the main dining area, shot her a dirty look: *You may think you're better than us*, it said. *You're wrong.*

Without college, she'd have a future, all right—a long and unprosperous life of flipping burgers at the Nifty Fifties diner, smiling pathetically at all her former classmates as they breezed through on spring break before heading back to their real lives in the real world. Not like she had any time to deal with her applications, the magic ticket to a new life—she was working double shifts to pay for this ski trip that Kane was insisting on, and every spare minute was spent at home, babysitting her little brothers. *Leave it to me to get* busier *over winter break*, she thought bitterly.

Beth stood up and tried to muster enough energy to face her customers, still furiously writing and rewriting in her head.

I'm a boring girl from a boring town, but I make a mean burger and fries. . . .

"Waitress! We've been waiting for our food *forever*!"

Beth looked over to table seven—and almost turned on her heel and fled back to the kitchen. Spending her vacation at the diner, mopping up spilled milk shakes, ducking grease spatter, and taking orders from every surly, hygienically challenged customer who walked through the door, was bad enough. This was worse. It was what she hated most about this job: taking orders from her friends.

Scratch that—her *former* friends.

Christie, Nikki, Marcy, and Darcy were all dating guys from the basketball team. Which guys? Beth could never keep track—sometimes, she wondered if they could, either.

Before she'd started dating Adam, back when she was just another faceless nobody, they'd refused to acknowledge her existence. Oh, they knew her name, all right—the Haven High seniors had been trapped in one building or another together since kindergarten. There were no strangers in a small town. But you would never have known it, not from the blank stares when she crossed their path, from the way they looked right through her, as if she didn't exist. As if she were nothing.

Then she'd started dating Adam—captain of the basketball team (and every other team that mattered), perennial homecoming king, Haven High's golden boy—and suddenly, the Nikkis and the Christies of the world had welcomed her with open arms. More than that, they'd *begged* her to join them.

Come to Christie's sleepover party and home spa day!

Hang with us at Nikki's for tanning and iced Frappaccinos!

Let's all buy this super-cute pink scarf—and then wear them on the same day!

And so, despite her overstuffed schedule, despite never trusting them or her newfound status, she'd given in. Any free time she'd had that didn't go to the newspaper or to the diner or to her family or to Adam—and granted, after all that, there wasn't much left—went to the girls. It had been fun; it had also been, as she now realized, a mistake. A big one.

For as far as they knew, she'd cheated on Adam, broken his heart. So in their eyes, he was still Prince Charming, while she'd been transformed into the wicked witch.

She'd been a stranger, she'd become a friend—now, apparently, she was the enemy.

"Waitress!" Nikki called, waving her over. "Is there a problem? We're starving."

You know my name, Beth retorted—silently. Aloud, she said only, "It'll be here as soon as possible, Nikki." Through gritted teeth.

"It better be," Nikki growled.

"Or what?" The words slipped out before Beth could stop herself.

"What did you say?" Nikki asked with incredulity. She turned to her left. "Christie, is it just me, or is the waitress being rather rude?"

"I'm sure she wouldn't be rude, Nikki," Christie responded in a voice oozing with false goodwill. "Since she knows that then we'd simply have no choice but to complain to the manager."

"You're right. I'm sure I must have misheard," Nikki conceded. "You can go now, waitress," she said haughtily, flicking Beth away like a speck of dirt on her white pants. "Just bring us the food when it's ready—and try not to *cheat* us on the bill. If you can help yourself."

Beth forced a smile and walked away with a steady step. Maybe, if she pretended hard enough that the mockery didn't bother her, it would stop. Or, at the very least, her feigned indifference might eventually transform itself into something real. But for now, it was all still an act—and the show wasn't over yet. She was only steps away when she heard Marcy's intentionally loud complaint: "I just don't know *what's* wrong with the service these days."

In spite of herself, Beth hesitated, and turned around.

"Well, you know what my mother always says," Nikki replied, glaring directly at Beth. "These days, it's impossible to find good help."

Beth wanted to crawl into a dark hole. She wanted to quit her job, run home, hide under the covers, and wait there until graduation. But instead, she just strode across the restaurant to take her next order, figuring that, at the very least, her shift couldn't get any worse.

Wrong again.

"Hi, beautiful."

Kane peeked his head out from behind a menu and smiled up at her. Surprise.

Beth nibbled on the inside of her lip and hoped he wouldn't notice the tears that had formed at the edges of her eyes. She hated for him to see her like this—in uniform, serving people, being humiliated. Had he seen her with Nikki and crew? Had he heard?

"What are you doing here?" she asked, masking her distress with annoyance.

"I heard the place has the cutest waitresses in town," he deadpanned, grabbing her hand and twining her fingers through his own. "Thought I'd come check it out."

"So what's the verdict?" Beth asked, flushing.

"Jury's still out," he said, rising to give her a kiss. "But maybe you'd like to offer a bribe that would tip the scales?"

Beth wriggled out of his grasp.

"Kane, stop," she protested, backing away. She didn't want him near her. Not with grease patches dotting her shirt, not when she smelled like coleslaw and onion rings. "I asked you not to come here when I'm working," she snapped. "It's distracting."

"Your wish is my command—I'm out of here," Kane promised, a knowing smile fixed on his face. "I just wanted to give you this."

He handed her a small box, elegantly wrapped in light silver paper. Beth didn't know what to say.

"It's not my birthday, and—"

"I just saw it and thought of you," he explained, resting a hand on her lower back. "Open it."

Slightly flushed, Beth carefully pulled off the wrapping paper and lifted the lid of the box. Inside lay a beautiful sky-blue scarf. It was exactly the same shade as her eyes.

"Kane, it's beautiful!" she exclaimed. She lifted it to her cheek and sighed at the soft caress of the fabric.

"Is this—?"

"Cashmere," he confirmed.

"But it's too nice, I couldn't—"

"You'll look beautiful in it," he assured her, wrapping it softly around her neck. "And this way, you'll be nice and cozy up in the mountains this weekend." He raised an eyebrow. "Just in case *I'm* not enough to keep you warm."

Beth laughed and snuggled against him—suddenly, she didn't care what she was wearing, or how she looked or smelled. She just cared that she had a warm body to lean against, warm lips to kiss.

"Meet me back here at the end of my shift?" she whispered as they finally broke apart.

"You can count on me."

And she was beginning to wonder if it might just be true.

www.matchmadeinhaven.com

username: Spitfire

password: MStevens88

Friday's entrée at the Haven High cafeteria: meat loaf

(Miranda thought this last log-in requirement was a master stroke—how else would the website screen out all the perverts and cyberfreaks?) She hit enter, and the final version of her profile popped up on the screen.

User Profile: Spitfire

Sex: female

Age: 17

Height: 5'2"

(Okay, so she'd added an extra inch and a half—but who knows, maybe she was still growing.)

Favorite color: scarlet

Favorite food: N/A

If I were an animal, I'd be: an elephant

(It wasn't sexy, but had the virtue of being true.)

Best lie I've ever told: Mom, you look great today—have you lost weight? And can I have a raise in my allowance?

Celebrity I most look like: Scarlett Johannson

(Um . . . maybe if you squinted? While you were high?)

Three things I can't live without: 1) my iPod, 2) my best friend, 3) chocolate chip cookies

I am . . . always ready to laugh, or to make you laugh. Honest, loyal, fun (and totally willing to hold a grudge on your behalf).

You are . . . someone who thinks these questions are as stupid as I do. Someone who knows how to have a good time without making an ass of himself—and if the latter can't be helped, at least is able to laugh at himself. Someone who knows what the word "latter" means. Basically, you're smart, funny, confident, and you love that I'm all those things too.

The confident thing was a lie, of course, but she'd thought it would look good, and might attract the right kind of guy. The kind who wasn't a desperate freak too pathetic to find his own flesh-and-blood dates. If any of the guys on matchmadeinhaven.com actually fit that profile—Miranda was seriously skeptical.

But, crazy or not, she'd decided to go for it. What, other than the final shreds of her dignity, did she have to lose?

chapter three

"HERE'S YOUR UNIFORM, AND HERE'S YOUR MOP."

"My . . . mop?" Harper took the outstretched polyester hoop skirt, holding it between the tips of two fingers as if afraid of catching its germs. She just stared at the mop, however—no way was she touching that thing, much less pushing it around.

"What, did you think I was going to start you out as a waitress?" Mr. White, the Nifty Fifties manager, threw his head back and burst into mean-spirited laughter, his double chins jiggling in time with his throaty cackles. Finally he stopped, rubbing his bald spot thoughtfully. "Well, you're pretty enough to be out front, I'll give you that."

Harper held herself still as his beady eyes swept over her body. He was gross—but if it meant losing the mop, well . . . let him look.

"But you've got no experience," he continued. "You can start training as a waitress as soon as your supervisor thinks you're ready."

"My supervisor? Aren't you my supervisor?" Harper looked around the restaurant, wondering which of the crater-faced losers would be bossing her around. Maybe this was a good thing, she thought—at least she wouldn't have to humiliate herself, serving people she knew. Safe in back with the mop, she could work completely undercover.

"Me?" Mr. White expelled another hearty chuckle. "I don't supervise people at *your* level. No, I've got someone perfect for the job. In fact, you probably know her." He stuck his bulbous head out of the kitchen door, bellowing, "Manning! Get back here for a minute."

Harper's knees almost gave out, and she was forced to lean against the grimy wall for support. *Of course*, she thought. She should have known.

"Yes, Mr. White?" Beth bounded into the kitchen and stopped short when she saw Harper, looking horrified. Harper couldn't even take her usual pleasure at the sight of Beth in her tacky uniform, knowing full well that soon, she'd be sharing the same fate.

"Good news, I'm giving you a little helper," the manager said shortly. "Harper Grace, meet Beth Manning, your new boss."

"Oh, we've met," Beth said coolly.

"Yep, I figured." He thrust the mop handle into Harper's hands and kicked a rolling bucket of soapy water toward her. She squealed and squirmed away as some of it sloshed over the top and splattered onto her faux Manolos.

"I want Harper here to start with the basics: floors, toilets, spills—you know the drill. And don't be giving her any special treatment just because you two are friends—got that?"

"Oh yes, Mr. White," Beth assured him, a broad smile crossing her face. "I know exactly what to do with her."

Harper leaned back against the wall again and clenched the mop tightly.

You can handle this, she told herself sternly.

She just hoped it was true.

Adam usually counted the days until the start of basketball season. Though too modest to admit it aloud, he knew exactly how good he was at nearly every sport Haven High had to offer. Last year he'd led the league in lacrosse assists, and as captain of the swim team he'd just set a new school record in the butterfly relay—but there was nothing like basketball. It wasn't just the adulation of the town during basketball season: the cheers of the crowd, the triumphant headlines, the adoring cheerleaders—though all of that helped. It was the game itself, the rough, heavy feel of the ball cradled in his hands, the flicker of weightlessness in those moments his feet left the ground, the cool certainty of a perfect shot, when the ball flew from your fingers, sailing through the air in a perfect arc. You could close your eyes, turn away—and just wait for the soft, satisfying *swish*.

He'd woken at dawn that morning and spent the day bouncing around the house, filled with nervous energy, just waiting for nightfall, for the first practice of the season. Now that he was finally stepping into the locker room, he suddenly realized he hadn't felt so happy, so relaxed in weeks. And then, in an instant, it all went to shit.

"What are you doing here?" he asked sourly.

"I—"

"Never mind, I don't want to hear it." Adam turned away and flung open his locker, throwing his gym bag to the floor and pulling off his T-shirt in one fast, fluid motion. He wanted to get out of there as quickly as possible. He hadn't spoken to Kane since the night it had all gone down. And to run into him now—here, of all places, the site of his betrayal—

"I'm on the team," Kane said calmly. "Where else would I be?"

"You're not on the team," Adam growled. Kane had played ball for Haven High back in tenth grade. He'd lasted a month. Kane had been the best player they had, by far—but after he'd missed two practices in a row, Coach Hanford had thrown him off the squad. Now Adam was the best player they had. But only by default. "Coach Hanford would never let you back on the team."

"Hanford's out," Kane retorted. "Or didn't you get the memo? Retired to Arizona. And, lucky for me, Coach Wilson isn't such a hard ass—he seemed quite persuaded by what I had to say."

Adam pulled on his team shorts and slammed the locker shut.

"How did you—" he stopped himself. He couldn't speak to Kane, couldn't look at him, without the bile rising in his throat. Without remembering the pictures he'd seen, of Beth and Kane, in the locker room, after hours, in each other's arms.

"Could be fun, bro," Kane suggested. "Like old times, you and me—"

"I'm not your *bro*," Adam spit out, finally facing him. "I don't know what you think you're doing here, and I don't care. Just stay the hell away from me."

He brushed past Kane and headed for the door—he suddenly needed to be out on the court, to slam a basketball into the backboard. Hard.

"Now, is that any way to talk to a friend?" Kane called out after him.

We're not friends. And I guess we never were.

But out loud, Adam said nothing. Kane had thrown away any right he'd had to call himself a friend. He'd trashed their friendship; he'd trashed Adam's life. And now Kane had the nerve to speak to him? *Here?* Had the nerve to rejoin *his* team? Was he trying to destroy yet another part of Adam's life? Adam's love for basketball was pure, and it was clean, and he wasn't going to let Kane infect it, or steal it away.

Not this time.

Not again.

Beth had always been a "nice girl." She thought of the phrase just like that, in quotes, because she was so used to hearing the words in someone else's voice. "Be a nice girl," insisted her mother. "Such a nice girl!" her teachers all glowed. Other people's voices, telling her who she was, what she should be. But all she ever heard in her own, silent voice these days was a warning.

Nice girls finish last.

And here was Harper, the perfect object lesson—the antithesis of nice, and she always walked away with everything. She was beautiful, she was popular, she was *mean*—and yet still, she'd taken home the prize. Beth's boyfriend.

(*Ex*-boyfriend, she reminded herself.) And now here she was, at Beth's mercy.

Beth could do the right thing, the *nice* thing—show her all the shortcuts, the places White would never check her work, ways to take an extra-long break; Beth could get her bumped up to the waitstaff in a few days.

Or . . . she could take a cue from Harper and throw nice out the window. She could be strict. Cruel. *Mean.*

And as it turned out, she was a natural.

"Well, what are you waiting for?" Beth asked caustically, as Harper stood frozen with the mop. "A written invitation? The bathroom's that way—get to work."

Harper trudged off down the corridor. Realizing that she'd neglected to change into her uniform, Beth was about to call out after her—then decided against it. Let Harper figure out on her own why she might not want to scrub a toilet in her street clothes. Instead, she followed Harper silently down the hall. After all, she was a supervisor now. It was time to get to work.

"Are you just going to stand there all day and watch me?" Harper asked, after she'd been sweeping the mop back and forth for fifteen minutes.

"If that's what it takes," Beth answered snidely. "You're doing it all wrong—might as well just start over again."

"What?" Harper cried. "No way."

"Well, if you want me to call Mr. White and see what he thinks . . ."

Harper sighed and shrugged her shoulders. "Fine—you're the boss."

Beth was amused by how much the words thrilled her. Everywhere else in this town, Harper was in charge. Suddenly, Beth was the one with all the power. And she loved it already.

"I don't know how Adam put up with you for all that time," Harper mumbled under her breath.

"What was that?" Beth asked sharply.

"Oh, nothing," Harper replied in a poisonously sweet voice. "Just wondering to myself what I should wear on my date tonight. My *boyfriend* is taking me somewhere special. It's our two-month anniversary, you know."

Beth knew. And she knew what had happened two months ago. In one day, Adam had both hooked up with Harper and decided Beth was cheating on him. Beth had long wondered which had come first. But she wasn't about to ask.

She walked out of the bathroom without a word and back down to the kitchen, where she grabbed a fresh packet of sponges. Then she rejoined Harper and tossed her one.

"You'll want to get down on your knees and really scrub those hard-to-clean stains," she explained, pointing to a random spot at her feet. "There's one now."

Harper looked at the sponge with disdain. "My hands and knees? On *this* floor? You have got to be kidding me."

"Hey, if you can't cut it, you're welcome to quit," Beth suggested, impressed by her own icy tone. Where was all this coming from? Was this who, deep down, she really was? Whatever the answer, if felt too good to stop. "Until then," she continued, smiling as Harper slowly got down on all fours, "like you said—I'm the boss."

Kane didn't like surprises—or mysteries. So it was bad enough when Adam, totally unexpectedly, had refused to forgive him for the Beth thing even after all this time. Worse was the fact that Kane couldn't figure out why.

Yes, he'd stolen Adam's girlfriend. Obviously, he wasn't expecting a thank-you. But this? The silent treatment for two months, as if they were both ten years old again and Kane had smashed up Adam's brand-new bike? (And even back then, it had only taken Adam a week to forgive and forget.)

She was, after all, just a girl. And Kane had seen her first.

The Beth Manning they'd grown up with had been nothing; a plain, faded face in the crowd, about as exciting as an old T-shirt at the bottom of your drawer. Familiar, reliable, and not so ugly that you'd *never* wear it—but best saved until you were desperate.

Kane had known who she was, of course—he knew

all the girls. But knowing and caring are two different things—and in this case, they'd been a universe apart.

Then came sophomore year. The first day of school. And into their bio lab had walked a goddess: slim, tall, with perfect skin, a willowy figure, and glossy golden hair. It was Beth 2.0, new and improved, and from the moment she'd flowed through the door, Kane had vowed to have her.

He'd just never expected it would take so much effort.

A girl like that, a wallflower, a nobody, should have been falling all over herself in gratitude for attention from someone like him. Guys like Kane didn't speak to girls like Beth Manning—or at least, they hadn't before the Change. But there was no gratitude, and she seemed immune to his considerable charm.

So he'd enlisted Adam's help—his *best friend*, he'd thought, remembering with derision. Adam was her lab partner, and his job was simple: Pave the way, reel her in, let her see that the A-list crowd wasn't so bad, that she could trust guys like Adam. And, by extension, Adam's good buddy Kane—that she could let her guard down. It was a gambit they'd used a lot in those days, letting Adam's basic decency lure the girls in, under the assumption that Kane, too, must be a "nice guy." Even if it wasn't readily apparent. It took them a bit longer to figure out the truth—and by then, Kane had generally gotten what he needed out of them. It worked both ways: Sometimes Kane played the wingman, dazzling the ladies with his charm and then passing them along to Adam. Good old solid, reliable, dull Adam. It was a good game, and they'd worked well together, partners in crime, wading through the shallow waters of Haven hotties.

And together, they'd worked out rule #1: Any girl was fair game—as long as you saw her first.

So perhaps Kane could be forgiven for trusting his partner, for assuming that the rules of the game still applied and that Adam would work his magic and send Beth flying into his arms. Imagine his surprise, then, to find that Adam had decided to keep this one for himself.

It was a betrayal, and it had led to a loss—a public one. And that, Kane could not forget. He'd kept quiet, played along—it wouldn't do to make a fuss, to be driven to unseemly emotion, not over a *girl*—but he'd also known that it wasn't over. No girl could be allowed to choose someone over him. Not even Adam.

It had taken more than a year, but he'd gotten his way.

Beth, who had only grown more beautiful since that first sighting, had seen the light. She'd rectified her mistake, and this time, she'd made the right choice. And if ever Kane got a little bored with the whole relationship thing, he just reminded himself of his struggle. This was his rightful reward, and he was going to enjoy it. If Adam was man enough to have a relationship, to make this girl fall in love with him, then so was Kane.

And he certainly didn't need Adam's approval. Or his forgiveness. Kane didn't need anyone. But if their friendship was going to end, *Kane* would be the one to make the decision—and Kane wasn't ready for that yet. Without Adam, Grace was almost too boring to bear. So he'd talked his way back onto the team, bearing the humiliation of having to beg the new coach for a shot. If he stayed in Adam's face, reminded him of how well they'd worked together, as a team, eventually Adam would have to give up the childish grudge. In the meantime, Kane would do the diligent teammate thing: go to the practices, run the windsprints, pretend he cared. Kane would do whatever he needed to do, he resolved, except one thing: apologize.

Eventually, Beth got bored and left Harper alone with the mop and bucket.

It's like they always say, thought Harper, *ignore a bully and she'll go away*. She'd just never been on the wrong side of that equation before.

This job was, if possible, even worse than Harper had imagined. But if she kept her eye on the prize, on Adam, then maybe the time would just slip by—she'd be in his arms again soon enough.

His arms—that was good. She pictured them wrapped

around her, warm and strong. In her mind's eye, they curled up together on a soft couch, next to a giant picture window. A beautiful mountain range loomed in the distance, and snow pelted the windows, but Harper was so warm, so cozy in Adam's arms. She could, if she closed her eyes, almost feel his presence . . .

"Harper, is that you?"

Harper's eyes flew open to see those joined-at-the-hip dolts Marcy and Darcy, staring at her in horror.

"Harper, what are you doing . . . here?"

She dropped the mop in alarm and backed away, struggling to recover the blasé veneer she would need to make it through this. "I'm just, I—"

"Harper works here now," Beth said cheerfully, suddenly appearing behind the wonder twins. "I'm sorry, I must have forgotten to put up the sign saying the restroom was closed for cleaning. Oops!"

She smiled at Harper, who knew it had been no accident. Just as Beth's sudden arrival had been no coincidence. She'd come to witness Harper's humiliation; she'd come to gloat.

"Is something wrong, Harper?" she asked sweetly. "Because otherwise, you really should get back to work."

Harper drew in a sharp breath and held it for several moments.

"I'm all done in here," she finally said. "Later, ladies."

She gave them a jaunty grin and walked away, towing the bucket behind her.

It had been a humiliating encounter, but there would be no long-term fallout, she assured herself. Nobody who counted listened to anything those airheads had to say. Still, when she tried to send herself back to that comforting vision of her and Adam cuddling in the ski lodge, she was just too angry—Beth's smug face kept breaking into her reverie, hovering over her like the Cheshire Cat.

So Harper did what any good, disgruntled employee would do: She went with it. She imagined Beth coming in to check on her, ordering her around—and then she imagined herself picking up the giant bucket of hot, scummy water and dumping it over Beth's smug little head.

She kept that image fixed in her mind, varying it for fun: Beth covered in ketchup and mustard, Beth smothered in relish, Beth drowning in a vat of cole slaw and pickle juice.

The possibilities were nearly endless, and Harper mentally ran through them all. The rest of her shift raced by in a flash. Time flies when you're having fun.

Kaia's father's brand-new, mint-condition BMW had a 5-liter capacity, a 500 horsepower output, a V-10 engine, and 383 pounds per foot maximum torque.

It also, she discovered once she got out on the empty

highway, had a dead battery. Or an overheated exhaust system. Or maybe it was a torn carburetor belt.

Who knew? And, really, who cared? All that mattered was that the car wouldn't go anywhere, and she was stranded. In the middle of nowhere.

Typical, she thought, slumping down against the smooth black leather of the front seat and waiting for the tow truck she'd called. There was nothing to do now but stare out the window at the barren scenery and hope that eventually someone would show up to get her back to civilization. *What a beautifully appropriate metaphor for my life*, she thought bitterly. Trapped in desolation, forced to wait for a rescue that might never come.

She was on her way home from Jack Powell's apartment, and she was already in a foul mood. Without apology, Powell had informed her that the little love nest they'd planned for their vacation would have to be put on hold for a few days as he went off into the mountains, chaperoning the school ski trip. He'd forbidden her to come along—not that she'd wanted to. He was afraid of what she might do if they were in public together. As if she had no self-control.

Kaia had plenty of control—enough, at least, not to show him how disappointed she was. How repulsed she was by the thought of spending her winter break in Grace, sitting in her big, empty house, staring at the tasteful taupe walls. If Powell wanted to pretend he didn't need her around, she could do the same.

The sun had just dipped below the horizon, and the pink desert sunset was swiftly fading to a deep and dark night sky. Kaia shivered with a sudden chill and wondered what might be out there, in that empty stretch of land that lay beyond the road. Seventeen years in New York City had taught her an important safety lesson: Dark and isolated equals danger. Her flight instinct was difficult to suppress.

Not that she expected some drug-crazed mugger to pop out from behind the scrub brush—but still, it was dark and quiet, and she was miles away from civilization. If you could call it that. Her father had once told her there were jackals and coyotes roaming the land—and she'd seen enough cheesy horror movies to at least wonder what else might be out there, lying in wait.

Kaia could take care of herself. She'd had plenty of experience, hadn't she? It's not like anyone had ever looked out for her, or let her believe there was someone ready to catch her when she fell. But fending off a crazed pervert on the subway—or a crazed ex-boyfriend in a high school parking lot—was one thing. Being stranded, isolated, helpless? That was another.

Still, she sat motionless in the car, posing for an invisible audience, calm, cool, and collected. She didn't call someone, anyone, just for the comfort of the sound of another human voice. She didn't wrap her fingers around the steering wheel with a white-knuckled grip, and she didn't whirl her head around at the slightest sound or movement coming from just beyond her peripheral vision. And when the tow truck finally arrived, an hour later, she didn't crack a smile.

Especially not when she recognized the driver. It was that slacker from school, that scuzzy, stoned, frustratingly sexy guy who lately seemed to show up everywhere she turned. He wore a grease-stained T-shirt and oversize jeans with a gaping hole at the left knee, and as he hopped out of the truck and loped toward her, Kaia noted with disgust that his shoes were held together with duct tape. His scruffy black hair was crying out for shampoo, and his face was covered with dark stubble—five o'clock shadow, maybe, but from which day? This was her conquering hero: tall, dark, and dirty.

"Took you long enough," she grumbled as he helped her into the cab of the tow truck.

"Nice to see you again, too, Kaia," he said, checking one last time that the BMW was firmly attached to the back of the truck and then climbing into the driver's seat.

"Do I know you?" she asked, wrinkling her nose to make it clear that an acquaintanceship with his type seemed unlikely.

"You've seen me around," he grunted.

Nice of him not to bring up the time he'd rescued her from some drunken barfly looking for a new floozy for his harem. Kaia had done her best to forget. But now to be rescued yet again by the same deadbeat? It was bringing all the sordid details rushing back. Not that she was ready to offer her thanks. Or even her acknowledgment.

Instead, Kaia snapped her fingers as if she'd just made the connection.

"You're the pizza guy!" she said triumphantly. "Weed, wasn't it?"

"Reed." He shook his head and scowled. "Reed Sawyer."

"Of course, of course. Can't imagine what made me think of weed." *Could it be the stench of pot following you around everywhere you go?* she added silently.

"Maybe it's because you keep tossing me away and I just keep coming back," he suggested, seeming to take cheer from her discomfort.

"So you drive a tow truck now?" she asked. As if she cared.

"It's my dad's garage. I help him out sometimes."

A grease monkey? It figured.

They drove in silence for a while, Kaia doing her best not to admire the way his sinewy body moved beneath the grungy black T-shirt and decaying jeans. Such a shame, a prize specimen like this, buried beneath so much grime. *But if I cleaned him up a little . . .* she mused—then caught herself in horror. Now was *not* the time to be taking in a stray. No matter how his taut, tan forearm brushed her skin as he shifted gears, no matter how firmly his long, thin fingers massaged the steering wheel, no matter how—*stop*, she warned herself. *Just stop.*

"So, you okay?" he finally asked.

"Why wouldn't I be?"

"I pick up a lot of women out here," he explained. "Being alone, stranded for all that time in the middle of nowhere, it drives 'em crazy. By the time I get there, they're usually pretty shaken up."

"And I guess when they see you and that sexy smile of yours, they just fall into your arms, swooning with gratitude," she sneered. Her voice quivered as he turned his head briefly toward her. She ignored it. "Yours for the taking—is that what you're waiting for?"

"I'm waiting for a thank-you," he answered, unruffled. "But if you're in a swooning mood . . ."

"Thank you," she said grudgingly, turning to stare out the dusty window and watch the shadowy scenery fly by.

"You're welcome." There was a pause, and then, "So, I've got a sexy smile?"

Damn.

"Forget it," Kaia snapped. "I guess you desert cowboys

are as unfamiliar with sarcasm as you are with personal hygiene."

She didn't turn back to face him, and he didn't say anything, but she could imagine the superior look on his face, the mocking smile.

And, for the record, it was sexier than ever.

Adam pulled into the lot and hopped out of his car. He was late. He'd wanted to greet Harper as soon as she'd finished her first shift. But the coach had kept him after practice to work on his free throws.

"You seem off today," the coach had observed.

Wonder why.

Now he jogged toward the entrance—he hated making her wait.

But the figure standing in the entryway anxiously scanning the parking lot wasn't Harper, it was Beth. A fact that he registered only moments before sweeping her into his arms.

Instead, he stopped short, and gave a halfhearted wave.

She offered him a weak smile.

"Picking up Harper?" she asked, and he wondered whether she, too, was suddenly remembering all the moments they'd shared in this doorway, Adam rescuing her from a long night of work.

He nodded.

"She's getting changed," Beth told him, refusing to meet his eyes.

"Thanks. And . . . I guess you're waiting for . . ."

"Kane. Yeah." She looked over his shoulder into the parking lot again, as if willing the Camaro to appear. It didn't.

"So anyway, how's—"

"Adam, I wanted to—"

They spoke at once, then stopped abruptly and laughed.

"Well, this is awkward," Beth admitted.

"Tell me about it." Adam idly rubbed the back of his neck. Where was Harper? "Maybe I should just go inside and—"

"Adam, wait." She put her hand on his arm to stop him, then snatched it back—they both froze. It was the first time she'd touched him since . . . since the last time he'd pushed her away. He'd forgotten how soft her hands were. "Adam, there's something I've been really wanting to say to you. I know you think that—"

She broke off, and he waited, wondering. It was the first time in a long time he'd been able to look at her without flinching, without needing to turn away or worse, to hurt her. Did this mean he was finally getting over her? It certainly felt like he was getting over . . . something.

"Well . . . ," she began again hesitantly, "I want you to know that, even after everything that's—"

"Adam!" Pushing past Beth, Harper came flying into

his arms. "So sorry I'm late. You have no idea what kind of a day I had."

He gently extricated himself from her embrace and took her hand. "You can tell me all about it in the car, Harper. I'm sure you did great in there today."

Harper gave him a kiss on the cheek and then put a possessive arm around his shoulders.

"Oh, I couldn't have done it without Beth," she gushed, smiling at Beth, whose face had begun to pale. "I can't wait to tell you what a wonderful *help* she was today."

Adam glanced quickly over at Harper, unable to tell whether she was sincere. It wasn't like her to have anything so nice to say about anyone, much less Beth.

I never give her enough credit, he chided himself. He'd have to make sure that tonight, at least, he told her how proud he was of her. Not just for the job, but for everything.

Feeling a sudden rush of warmth and gratitude that he had someone like Harper in his life, Adam pulled her into a hug and gave her a long kiss.

"What was that for?" she asked when they finally broke apart.

"Just because," he said sheepishly, keeping his arms around her.

"He does that *all* the time," Harper explained to Beth, who couldn't even muster a smile. "Oh, but I guess you, of all people, know that!"

"Hey, were you about to say something?" Adam asked, remembering they'd been interrupted. For a moment, he'd almost forgotten Beth was there.

"No, it was nothing," Beth mumbled. "You guys have a good night."

Harper and Adam walked off toward the car together, hand in hand. Halfway there, he turned back. Beth's solitary figure seemed suddenly frail and lonely, standing in the shadows.

"You sure you'll be okay here?" he called back. "You don't need a ride or anything?"

"I'm fine," she shouted, with just a hint of a quaver in her voice. "Kane will be here any minute."

That's right—Kane. Beth was his problem now, Adam reminded himself. He knew that. It was just that looking at her there, her blond hair billowing around her head like a golden halo, it was a little too easy to forget.

It had been one of the worst days of her life—which made the night that much sweeter. After driving home, they'd come out back to lie together under the stars, on the large, flat rock between the border of their two backyards. It had been a long and painful day, and all she wanted to do was lie in his arms and breathe him in. Unfortunately, Adam had other ideas.

"Can you believe Kane? Grinning at me like that? As if nothing had ever happened?"

Harper sighed and rolled toward Adam, wrapping her arms around him.

"Maybe you should try not to think about it so much," she suggested. "I hate to see you like this."

"I can't stand it!" Adam raged. "I mean, what does she even see in him?"

Harper just clung to him tighter and tried to ignore his words and their meaning. They had never really talked about what had happened between Adam and Beth, and Harper liked it that way. Because that way she could pretend that he'd forgotten. Moved on. That he only cared about Harper and what she wanted.

"He's been with so many women," Adam continued. "He's a slut, you know? Can a guy be a slut? Because he is—and she just fell for it. Like he'll treat her any better than the rest of them." He snorted. "Someone like that will never change."

Almost unnoticeably, Harper stiffened and pulled away. It was that word. *Slut.* Not that she thought she—or that Adam—saw her as—

The thing was, Harper was no vestal virgin. She didn't regret any of the things she'd done—even if she had, she could never take them back. She'd never be Beth—and if that's what he wanted . . .

"Hey, where are you going?" Adam asked, finally noticing that she was slowly easing away from him. He placed a warm hand on her cheek and grazed his fingers down her neck. "I'm sorry, I shouldn't be talking about this. It's not fair to you."

"No." She sat up, pulling him up next to her, and took both of his hands in hers. "I want you to talk about whatever you need to. You can say anything to me. You know that."

He gave her a mischievous smile. "Does that mean I'm allowed to call you 'Gracie' as much as I want?" he asked, knowing how much she hated the childhood nickname.

"Only if I'm allowed to tickle you as much as *I* want!" she shot back, and launched herself at him, wrestling him onto his back as he shook with laughter. Finally, she took pity on him and quieted him with a long, deep kiss. It went on and on—and though she'd promised herself that she would wait just a bit longer, until they were up in the mountains, away, alone, and everything was perfect, she didn't want to pull away. His lips were so soft, his kiss so firm, and their bodies felt so right together, as if each had been designed with the other in mind.

So, after several long minutes, it was Adam who pulled away first, breathless. He brushed a lock of hair away from her face and kissed her lightly on the forehead. It was a cold, clear night, and as she lay against the cool granite, she could see her dark bedroom window. How many nights had she come home alone and gazed out at the backyard, at the rock where she and Adam used to play as children, wishing she were out there with him again? And how many of those nights had he been in his own room, only a few yards away—with Beth?

"Harper, I just want you to know," Adam murmured softly in her ear, "I love—"

Her heart stopped beating.

"—being here with you," he concluded.

She closed her eyes for a moment, then opened them slowly, gazing into his clear, trusting eyes. So he loved . . . being with her.

It wasn't everything—but it was a beginning.

chapter four

ADAM HAD BEEN WAITING DESPERATELY FOR THE chance to get away from everything, to clear his head. It had been such a confusing autumn, everything falling apart so suddenly, the world he thought he knew turning upside down. He just wanted to get away from it all: the classes, the pressure, the people. He was hoping he and Harper could have a long, quiet, romantic weekend to figure everything out, to be together, leave school and all that baggage behind.

But that's the thing about school trips: the rest of the school has a nasty habit of coming along.

"Dude, I am going to *tear* up those slopes!"

Which is, Adam supposed, how he'd ended up stuffed in the back of a school bus with a bunch of his basketball "buddies" listening to them vie for the title of BMOC (Big Moron Off Campus).

"There better be some hot honeys up there!"

"Yeah, because I'm looking for a ski bunny who knows all about going down—and I *don't* mean down the mountain!"

"Good one, man."

It's not that he didn't like hanging out with the guys—even now, as they were bragging about their nonexistent ski skills and carving their initials into the cracked leather bus seats—but he just wasn't in the mood.

"What's the matter, Morgan?" his seatmate asked, elbowing him in the ribs. "All this guy talk too rough for you? You'd rather be up front with the ladies?"

Uh—yes?

"This dude is so whipped," his first-string point guard confided to the rest of the team. They roared in approval.

"Like you'd be talking about the honeys if Nikki was back here," Adam shot back, and the point guard shut up, fast. He could intimidate 6'4" guys on the court—but 5'3" Nikki left him quivering in his Nikes, and they all knew it. When the girls were around, everyone clammed up, like perfect gentlemen.

But the girls were all the way up in the front of the bus, the guys had slipped some Baileys into their morning coffee—and the desert road stretched ahead of them with no end in sight.

"I'm gonna get so ripped tonight—you guys in?"

"Shit, yeah!"

Adam smiled weakly as his teammates cheered around him.

His inner five-year-old had only one silent, but increasingly insistent question: *Are we there yet?*

Not even close.

Winter in the desert sucked.

Kaia knew she shouldn't have been too surprised—*everything* in the desert sucked—but winter was yet another surprisingly painful disappointment.

She'd always looked forward to the season with a childlike enthusiasm: skating in Rockefeller Center, Frozen Hot Chocolate at Serendipity, the Macy's Christmas decorations, even *The Nutcracker* at Lincoln Center. By January, everyone would be tired of the biting cold, the dark skies, the ever-present slush. But in December, winter was fresh and new, the air crisp and refreshing, and it was as if the entire city came alive.

Here, on the other hand—nothing. More hot days, more cold nights. Desert wind, desert sand. No ice skating, no cozy Burberry scarves—and certainly, no snow.

She'd called Powell, hoping that even from a distance

he could liven up her night. But there'd been no answer. And he hadn't called back. Not that Kaia missed him. Not that she wished she was up there on a stupid school trip—even home was an improvement over that. (Having her teeth drilled during a Novocain shortage would have been an improvement over that.) But she was bored, and she was bitter. And she couldn't ignore the fact that while she was stuck on the couch, Powell would be whooshing his way down the slopes. And he wouldn't be alone. That handsome figure and sexy accent pretty much went to waste in a town like Grace; a ski resort, however, was a whole different story.

Not that Kaia cared. She had a life of her own—even if it wasn't a very thrilling one at the moment.

On a sudden impulse, she grabbed the phone book and flipped open to the entry for Guido's Pizza. She wasn't that hungry—especially not for the dried-out slab covered in greasy processed cheese and a watery layer of sauce that Guido had the nerve to call "pizza." But if the pizza wasn't tasty, the delivery boy definitely was—and, hungry or not, Kaia could use some good eye candy.

Let Powell do whatever he wanted up on the mountain. She was more than ready to have a little fun of her own.

"You're going down!" Harper squealed, as Adam mashed a handful of snow down the back of her jacket.

The school had done a surprisingly decent job of picking a resort. White Stone Lodge was no prize in itself. The bus was parked in front of a complex of stout reddish residential buildings all circling the three-story main lodge building, covered with faux brick and stone in a failed attempt to make it look homey. But even a run-down Motel 6 would have looked appealing in such a setting—a glistening blanket of snow covered the roofs, and delicate icicles dangled over the edge, turning the lodge into a giant gingerbread house rimmed with dripping sugar crystals. Jagged mountain peaks loomed in the background, slicing through a storybook blue sky. The endless grayish beige of the flat desert landscape had never seemed so far away.

Adam raced away as Harper scooped up an armful of snow and sent it flying in his direction.

"Face it, you suck at this, Gracie!" he called from a safe distance, pegging a snowball in her direction.

Oh, really?

She scooped up another handful and raced after him, tackling him to the ground. They tumbled into the snow together, heaving with laughter. Adam rolled over her and held a dripping snowball a few inches from her face.

"You want a piece of me?" he asked in a mock threatening voice, as icy drops spattered down on her.

She looked up at his flushed face, illuminated by a childlike joy, and suddenly lifted her head up to kiss him.

"I want *all* of you," she said sincerely—and then, before he could stop her, grabbed the hand with the snowball and smashed it into his face.

"You snooze, you lose," she crowed, exploding into laughter. He fell to the ground beside her, laughing just as hard.

The sky looked so different up here, she thought, barely noticing the chill creeping through her fingers and toes. It seemed so much closer, as if she could reach up and grab a cloud.

Adam's gloved hand took her own, and she snuggled against him, wishing that they weren't sprawled out in the open behind the resort. She wanted to be alone with him—now.

"Think your roommate's going to be around tonight?" she asked innocently. Harper hadn't actually told Adam about her WFS plan, but she figured he would see the possibilities of this weekend just as clearly as she did.

"Nah, Nikki kicked out her roommate, so he's not going to be coming back tonight."

Or ever, Harper thought—once Nikki got her claws into someone, she was unlikely to let go.

"So if you wanted to," Adam began again, tentatively.

"It would be a shame to let an empty room go to waste," she said casually. But her heart was thudding in her ears. Why was she so nervous?

"Are you sure?" he asked—and there was nothing casual about his tone.

She looked around at the sky, the mountains, the snow—his face. It was the perfect spot for a perfect moment.

"I'm sure."

Since their chaperone had disappeared within minutes of arrival, the Haven High kids were free to do whatever they wanted at White Stone Lodge. There was a party in room 17, free pot in room 32, and Miranda was pretty sure she'd heard something about skinny-dipping in the hot tub.

But Miranda wasn't in the mood. She'd brought along her new über-portable tablet in hopes there'd be some kind of wireless network she could tap into. Her dating profile had been up for a few days and, much as she hated to admit it, she was desperate to see whether anyone had responded to her. It seemed a little pathetic, to have come all this way, spent all this money, just to spend another Saturday night at home in front of the computer . . . but on the other hand, she thought, logging on to her e-mail server, Harper was likely gone for the night, so it's not like anyone would ever have to know.

Congratulations, **Spitfire**, the following **3** users have expressed interest in your profile!

User Profile: TheDude

Sex: male

Age: 17

Height: 6'1"

Favorite color: gold

Favorite food: beer

If I were an animal, I'd be: a PARTY animal

Celebrity I most look like: Brad Pitt

Best lie I've ever told: No Officer, I haven't been drinking.

Three things I can't live without: beer, sex, pot

I am . . . one wild and crazy guy, looking to party it up with one (or more) lucky ladies.

You are . . . totally hot, especially in a mini-skirt—and out of one. If you know what I mean. Wink, wink.

And then there was bachelor number two . . .

User Profile: HanSolo

Sex: male

Age: 16

Height: 5'3 1/2"

Favorite color: Martian red

Favorite food: peanuts

If I were an animal, I'd be: a Wookie

Celebrity I most look like: Mark Hamill

Best lie I've ever told: It's not a doll—it's an action figure.

Three things I can't live without: *Star Wars* boxed set, comic books, and my scale model of the Millennium Falcon (I built it myself!)

I am . . . the guy at the back of the class that you've never noticed before. The one lurking by your locker that you brush past without a word. I'm very smart, I just need some help with my people skills—at least that's what my mom says.

You are . . . friendly, nice, a *Star Wars* fan (may the Force be with you!). You like going to conventions and building models. And you would be willing to dress up like Princess Leia in the gold bikini.

And, of course, Miranda's personal favorite:

User Profile: Thrasher

Sex: Yes, please

Age: 18

Height: 11 inches

Favorite color: whatever color your thong is

Favorite food: pizza

If I were an animal, I'd be: a coyote

Celebrity I most look like: the Rock

Best lie I've ever told: Of course I remember your name.

Three things I can't live without: my bike, my booze, my band

I am . . . a guy who likes motorcycles, trucks, booze, and hard rock.

You are . . . a chick who digs guys who like motorcycles, trucks, booze, and hard rock.

Spitfire, if you would like to send a message to any of these users, click here.

Miranda snorted in disgust. What had she been thinking? Like anyone other than the freaks and the geeks would be using this stupid website. She could only imagine the look on these losers' faces if they ever saw who they'd picked. There was a horrifying thought: Even these freak shows probably wouldn't want to date her if they got the chance.

Face it, Miranda, she told herself, flicking off the computer. *You're just doomed to be alone—forever.*

"We should really get some sleep," Beth pointed out, wriggling out of Kane's grasp.

He checked the clock on the nightstand: 10:40.

"Sleep?" he asked in surprise. "It's way too early for that. Besides"—he grabbed her and pulled her down beside him—"I'm sure we can find something more interesting to do."

She stiffened beneath his grasp and, again, pulled away.

Kane issued a silent curse—pulling away was all she ever did, and this whole chase thing was beginning to lose its luster. "Fine, we'll sleep," he said irritably. "I've been looking forward to waking up next to you—"

"Actually," she interrupted, rising from the bed and pulling on her shirt (despite his best efforts, her jeans had never even made it off), "I think I should go back to my room."

"Why? We've got plenty of space, plenty of privacy. Isn't this why we—?"

She bit her lip and nervously tucked her hair behind her ears. "We'd get in a lot of trouble if we got caught," she said softly, backing away. "And I should really—besides, it's a big day tomorrow. And maybe tomorrow night . . ."

"Hey, hey, slow down," he urged her, following her to the door and taking hold of her waist before she slipped out. "What's wrong?" he asked, gently turning her to face him. "You're trembling."

He felt her muscles clench, and for a second he thought she would pull away again, but then she relaxed into the embrace and touched his face lightly with the palm of her hand. "I just need to go," she told him. "Okay?"

"Of course it's okay," he promised.

"You're not mad?"

"Not mad at all." He kissed her, softly and gently, breathing her in. "But are you sure?"

"You make it pretty hard to be sure," she told him, pressing against him and kissing him again, with more urgency this time, gripping his body as if it were a life preserver, keeping her afloat. "*Really* hard."

There was more kissing.

And then she was gone.

"Harper?" he whispered.

The room was dark, and she could see only a bare outline of his figure, carved out by a shaft of moonlight filtering through the window. She pressed herself against him, running her hands across his face, his skin, trying to memorize the shape of his body, the feel of it beneath her fingers.

"Harper, you know I—with Kaia—"

"I know," she said quietly, stopping him with a kiss. The last thing she wanted to hear about, think about, was Kaia. Adam with Kaia. Not here—not now.

"I just want you to know," he pressed on, "it was just that once—and this is the first time with . . ." He stopped and rolled over on his side, his face inches from hers. He brushed a lock of hair away from her eyes. "It's different with you."

"Adam, you don't have to do this. We can just—"

"No, I need to say this," he told her, "before we—I need you to know that . . . how much I . . . I've never known anyone like you, Harper. You're the only person in my life I can always count on—"

"You know I'll always be there for you," she reminded him. "Believe me."

"I believe everything you say, Gracie, because I know you're the one person who always tells me the truth. Promise me you always will."

"Oh, Adam . . ." She grabbed him then and kissed him, hard, wrapping his arms around her and pressing herself against his bare skin. She was done talking. And it was a good thing—because the next words out of her mouth would have been a lie.

"Yo, dude, you in there?"

The loud voice was quickly followed by a pounding on the door and some raucous laughter. Harper quickly rolled away from him, and Adam groaned in frustration. The guys. Great. Their timing was just impeccable.

"Go away!" Adam shouted, grabbing his sneaker off

the floor and throwing it toward the door. "I'm busy."

"*Getting* busy is more like it," another voice called out.

"Asses," Adam muttered. He turned toward Harper in apology. "Just give me a second and I'll deal with this," he promised, eager to get back to what they'd barely started.

"You know what?" she gave him a quick peck on the lips and hopped out of bed, pulling the sheet around herself. "Let me."

Harper strode toward the door, but froze midway there when the shouting started up again.

"You got Grace in there, dude?"

"She'll show you a *good* time—and I should know!"

"You got me to thank, bro. I taught her everything she knows."

"Just don't hog her. Leave some for the rest of us!"

Adam leaped out of bed and stormed past Harper, flinging open the door.

"Get the hell out of here," he growled, leveling a fist at the cluster of grinning idiots.

"Dude, chill, we're just having some fun with you."

"Fun's over," he said shortly, and swung the door shut in their faces. "They're drunk," he told Harper, feeling like he needed to apologize, as if this were all somehow his fault. "Come on," he urged her. She was still standing frozen in the middle of the floor. "Let's go back to bed."

They climbed onto the soft mattress and swaddled

themselves in the downy comforter, and Adam again took her in his arms.

"Ad, those things they said," Harper began hesitantly, in a tentative and unfamiliar voice.

"Shh, it doesn't matter," he promised her. "Nothing's changed—we're still here, together. I still want you."

And he did, desperately.

But he couldn't stop hearing their words, their laughter. He couldn't focus. And as he eased himself on top of her, ready to take their relationship to the next level, to start them off on a new beginning, he discovered—to his horror and humiliation—that he just couldn't.

Kane closed the door softly behind Beth—then gave it a sharp kick for good measure. What had been the point of finagling the single room? Of talking her into coming in the first place? For God's sake, it wasn't even eleven o'clock yet—was he supposed to just be a good boy and go to sleep?

Calm down, he told himself. He didn't like exposing too much of his emotions, even in private. He was nothing without his poker face, and practice made perfect.

Speaking of poker . . .

He'd overheard some of the staff talking about a weekly poker game, and had no doubt he could talk himself into it.

He weighed his options.

Sleep? Not so much an option as a failure.

Partying with his peers in some smoky, overcrowded room that, by this point, probably had sweat on the walls and vomit on the floor? Kane didn't associate with these losers when they were in town—and he saw no reason to make an exception for their change in zip code.

Poker it was.

He crept through the lounge on his way to the staff quarters, wary of running into their absentee chaperone.

Turns out his instincts were half right: Jack Powell *was* in the lounge, but judging from the blonde precariously balanced on his lap, nibbling his ear, he wasn't going to be doing much chaperoning anytime soon.

Kane shook his head in admiration—finally, a member of the Haven High teaching staff he could look up to.

Newly inspired, he went off in search of some fun of his own. Not *too* much fun, he reminded himself. After all, he had a girlfriend now—a real one. And that meant no extracurricular activities. If Adam could do it, he could do it.

As he'd suspected, his charm was more than enough to get him admitted to the back room and then to the poker game—though he supposed waving around a ready wad of cash hadn't hurt.

It had been just what he'd expected: dark room, good

Scotch, and two beautiful women facing him across the table. Those compact, svelte bodies, hard muscles only highlighting the soft curves . . . There was only one surprise. Sitting to the right of Amber and Claire was a more familiar face: Harper.

"What are you doing here?" Kane asked, taking a seat at the makeshift poker table.

Harper rolled her eyes. "Don't ask. And you?"

"I'd say that's a good policy. Don't ask and"—Kane glanced at the buxom brunette on his right and the luscious blonde on his left—"don't tell."

"Your deal," said the guy who'd let him into the game, handing him the cards. "Oh, and did Amber tell you?"

"Did Amber tell me what?" Kane asked, winking at her.

"We usually play a warm-up round before we start tossing the money around," Amber explained. "Just to get us in the mood. Strip poker." She looked him up and down. "I hope you don't mind."

"Mind?" He glanced toward Harper, who only smiled and raised an eyebrow. "Trust me, I don't mind at all."

Was she crazy?

Kaia stared out the dusty window of the pickup truck, wondering if she'd lost her mind. What other excuse could there be for her agreeing to this ridiculous plan?

A few hours earlier, as she'd half hoped and half feared,

Reed had shown up with her cold, greasy pizza. After trading yet another round of insults, she'd challenged him to find some way to alleviate her Grace-induced boredom. He, in turn, had shown up at the end of his shift with a dirty pickup truck and a challenge of his own: Drive off into the middle of nowhere with a skuzzy stranger and hope that his definition of "something interesting to do" wouldn't land her in the morgue.

She didn't even know why she'd called him. So he was hot. Fine. There was no point in denying that. Nor could she deny the fact that when he looked at her, when his eyes burned into her, she trembled.

But that was irrelevant. It had to be. Kaia Sellers could *not* involve herself with someone like this *Weed*, poor, stupid, aimless, and completely unacceptable. Couldn't, and wouldn't. And yet . . .

And yet, she'd made the call. And when he'd shown up at her door, she'd welcomed him in, hadn't she? Leaned toward him, so he would smell her perfume. Favored him with a sultry smile.

And now here she was in the old truck, Reed by her side, speeding through the darkened landscape, the lights of civilization (if Grace qualified) fading into the distance behind them.

I must be crazy, Kaia thought, unsure whether to be appalled or amused. It was the only possible explanation.

Crazy was fine—for a night. But whatever happened, Kaia promised herself, one night was all it would ever be. Reed Sawyer could not be allowed into her life. He didn't fit. And never would.

They drove in silence, and when the truck suddenly came to a stop, Reed turned off the engine and got out without a word. Kaia climbed out as well (once it became painfully clear he wasn't planning on opening the door for her) and looked around in dismay. If this wasn't the *middle* of nowhere, surely it was only a stone's throw away.

That's it—he brought me here to kill me, she thought in sudden alarm.

They were parked on the shoulder of a dusty road that stretched across the flat land until it disappeared into the darkness. Ahead of them sat the massive, hulking frame of a gutted industrial complex, long since abandoned.

"We're *here*?" she asked, masking her increasing panic with the comfortably familiar cloak of disdain.

He nodded, and hopped up on the hood of the truck.

"And where is 'here,' exactly?"

"This is Grace Mines," he explained. "Or used to be. It closed down—then it burned down."

"And then what?" she asked, intrigued in spite of herself. She hopped up onto the hood of the truck next to him, looking more closely at the shattered remains of the mine, gleaming in the light of the full moon.

"Then nothing. Who has the money to do anything about it?" he asked rhetorically. "It's been like this ever since I can remember. I guess it always will be."

Kaia tried to imagine the empty husk before her as it had been in the boom times, teeming with workers, young men seeking their fortune, fathers struggling to support their families, the air filled with the clicking and whirring of machinery. This place had been alive once. And now? Weeds sprouted amid the fallen beams, empty beer cans lay strewn in piles of ash, the jagged glass of the shattered windows splintered the moonlight—now, it was just a corpse. A fallen giant, a dead zone, soon to be reclaimed by the wilderness around it.

"You come here often?" she asked, her tone more serious than she'd intended.

He nodded. "Something about it—" He looked over at her, then looked away. "We can go, if you want."

"No, I want to stay for a while."

And she was surprised to discover it was true.

They sat there side by side, not talking, not touching. They sat for a long time, just staring at the old building, at the desert that lay beyond it. Kaia shivered once and, wordlessly, Reed tucked his jacket around her shoulders. It was heavy and warm—and smelled like him. Not pot this time, but a deep, rich scent, like dark coffee by an open fire. It fit here—*he* fit here—strange and dark, like the ruins, with a quiet dignity.

She was about to take his hand when she felt the first spatter of rain.

Rain? In the desert?

Before she had time to be confused, the skies opened up. It was as if bucket after bucket of icy water were being dumped from above—the rain fell fast and hard, pelting their skin, turning the desert dirt around them into rivers of mud.

"What the hell is this?" Kaia complained as they both scrambled back into the truck. "It's not supposed to rain in the desert!"

"Sometimes it does," he said simply, hoisting her into the passenger seat, then rushing around to the driver's side, finally throwing himself in and slamming the door.

They looked at each other—both sopping wet, their hair and clothes plastered to their bodies—and burst into laughter.

"This is, by far, the weirdest date I've ever had," Kaia said, wringing out the edge of her shirt as best she could.

"Who says it's a date?" he retorted, but with a smile.

"We should probably wait for it to let up before we drive home," Kaia said, gesturing toward the opaque sheet of water flooding down the windshield.

"I guess we should," he agreed. "Cold?"

"What?"

"You're shivering."

She was cold, she realized. She hadn't noticed. She nodded and, hesitantly, he put an arm around her. She inched to the left, resting herself against him. It wasn't much warmer—but she stayed.

She leaned her head against his shoulder and they listened to the rain pelting the truck, spattering against the soft ground. She shivered again, and he held her tighter. His wet hair was still dripping, and she watched the drops of water trace their way down his face. They looked like tears.

They sat there together, motionless, for a long time.

And then the rain stopped. And they drove away.

chapter five

"BETH, DID YOU REALLY THINK I'D BE COMING TO ski school with you?" Kane asked, laughing.

She blushed and shook her head. "That was silly. I guess I thought maybe you'd teach me—"

He snapped her ski boot shut and helped her latch it to the ski, then grabbed his board and began guiding her toward the bunny slope.

Kane laughed again. "Me? Only if you want to land in the hospital. Trust me, you don't want to pick up any of my bad habits."

The hospital?

Beth's heart plummeted as she pictured herself in a

broken heap at the bottom of a snow-covered cliff.

"It's going to be fine," Kane assured her, catching her look of terror. "I just want you to learn from the best. This way, I can get some good boarding in—and then we'll have all afternoon to spend together."

"Okay," she agreed. She leaned over to try to give him a quick kiss through his ski mask, and practically toppled over into the snow. "And Kane?" she asked as he steadied her. "I'm sorry again about last night."

"No apology necessary. And I'm glad I got the chance to go to bed early, for once. You were right—we have a big day ahead of us!" he said heartily, and with that, he grinned and glided away, waving in farewell as he careened down the slope.

Beth took a deep breath and inched her way toward the sign marked WHITE STONE SKI SCHOOL: BUNNY BEGINNERS. If she was having this much trouble on flat land, she wasn't too eager to find out how she would fare on the slopes. But she supposed she didn't really have another option.

Beth took a place next to Miranda, the only person in the lesson she recognized. They exchanged a quick glance—the disappointed *Oh, it's you* vibe was palpable.

But there was little time for disappointment or hostility, not when the instructor, a chipper young woman in a fluorescent orange ski suit and matching skis, had already started rattling off instructions at lightning speed.

Knees locked, knees bent. Shift your weight. But not too much. Hold your balance. Ski poles down. Arms out—

It was far more than Beth could take in, and by the time the instructor began offering tips for slowing down, Beth was half ready to throw her ski poles off the mountain and spend the rest of the day reading in the lodge. Somehow, the instructor's suggestions—"Line up your skis like french fries to go fast"; "Angle your skis like a slice of pizza to go slow"—didn't inspire her with much confidence that, when plummeting down the hill toward a giant tree, she'd be able to avoid it.

"Okay, bunnies, time for our first run!" the instructor cheered. "Just push off—and . . . go!"

As the students around her launched themselves into motion, Beth looked dubiously over the lip of the so-called bunny slope. It suddenly looked like a ninety-degree angle.

"You have *got* to be kidding me," Miranda muttered under her breath. She looked about as confident in her abilities as Beth felt.

After a moment, they were the only two students left at the top of the hill. Miranda gave Beth a half smile.

"It's going to be pretty embarrassing if we give up now, isn't it?" she asked sheepishly.

"Embarrassment never killed anyone," Beth pointed out, "whereas skiing . . ." It was a *long* way down.

"On the count of three?" Miranda suggested.

Beth nodded and, hesitantly, quietly, they counted off together.

One.

Two.

Threeeeeeee . . .

I'm not going to die, Beth repeated to herself aloud as she hurtled uncontrollably down the hill. The wind whipped past her face, the bumpy ground skidding beneath her feet.

French fries. Pizza. French fries—no, pizza, she mumbled to herself, trying to force her skis into the proper angle, whatever that was. But it was no use—her skis were going wherever they wanted to go. She was just along for the ride.

It seemed to take forever—then, suddenly, miraculously, she was zooming toward the bottom of the slope, toward a crowd of waiting skiers, unable to stop or turn, snow flying from her wake, until finally, in desperation, she spread her skis into the widest angle she could and slowed to a stop, tumbling over into a blessedly soft mound of snow.

Alive. And safe. And totally ready to do it all over again.

"What a rush!" Miranda cried from a few feet away. She too was flat on her back in the snow, one ski lying by her side, but her face was flushed with happiness.

"A few more runs and we'll be ready for the Olympics," Beth boasted in a still shaky voice.

Miranda, having picked herself up, offered Beth a hand. "A few *thousand* more runs, maybe," Miranda corrected her. "I don't know about you, but I thought I was going to die pretty much the whole way down."

"I've never been so happy to stop moving in my life," Beth admitted.

"So . . . you ready to go again?"

"Again?" Beth brushed some snow off her face and planted her ski poles defiantly into the snow as if staking a flag into the ground of a newly discovered land. "What are we waiting for!"

"Are you *sure* you don't want to try a lesson first?" Adam asked again.

At least he's talking to me, Harper thought. It was a small but crucial step in the right direction, given that their morning had consisted largely of Adam refusing to meet her gaze. When he'd had to ask her to pass the salt over the cafeteria breakfast table, he'd first turned bright red, stuttered a few incoherent syllables, and finally spit the words out only by looking fixedly down at his lap. Suffice it to say, they hadn't spoken yet about the equipment malfunction of the night before. Fine with Harper. She was more than happy to put the episode far behind her. And judging from the look on his face after it had happened, when she'd tried comforting him ("Don't worry, it happens to everyone"), he was eager to do the same.

The thing was: It didn't happen to everyone. Or, at least, not everyone who was with Harper. No one had ever had any problems in that department when it came to her—so what was going on with Adam? Was there some part of him, deep down, that didn't want to be with her?

Stop obsessing, she told herself. Once they'd gotten out of the lodge and onto the slopes, Adam had relaxed, grateful for the chance to focus on something other than their nonexistent sex life. Harper forced herself to do the same. Unfortunately, that meant focusing on skiing . . . and for Harper, that was proving to be almost as unpleasant a topic.

"Who needs lessons when I've got you?" Harper asked, trying to ignore her clenched stomach and rapid pulse. Their chairlift swung gently in the wind, and Harper grabbed the metal guardrail a little tighter, refusing to look down to the ground below. *Way* below. Instead, she focused on how good the two of them must look together in their ski gear. Harper's shopping expedition had paid off, and she was sporting a svelte dark-green ski jacket with matching ski pants. She looked *good.*

In all her fantasizing about this trip, she'd almost forgotten about the whole skiing component—athletic endeavors were so not her thing. But really, how hard could it be? You just point your skis in the right direction and let gravity do the work. Any idiot could figure that out. She wasn't about to be one of those wimpy bunny slopers that the *real* skiers just laughed at. No one laughed at Harper Grace. Besides, Harper planned to spend the entire day by Adam's side—especially after last night. She didn't want him to spend any time off by himself. Thinking.

The ride ended far too soon, and Adam pushed her off the lift just in time. They paused at the top of the slope. Harper tightened her grip on her ski poles and focused on the little kids zipping back and forth across the mountain—if they could do it, so could she.

"You ready?" Adam asked dubiously.

She nodded.

"You sure?"

She nodded again.

"Just remember what I taught you, okay? And I'll be right behind you the whole way down."

"Don't worry," she assured him. "I'll be fine. . . ."

She pushed herself off down the hill and, suddenly, she was flying through the snow, her hair streaming out behind her, faster and faster. She shifted her weight to the left, to the right, to avoid crashing into someone, veered around an icy patch, and still, faster and faster—

I'm skiing, she marveled, *and I'm* awesome.

And that's when she hit the bump.

And her skis flew up off the ground, taking her with them. She soared through the air, her arms and legs waving wildly, helplessly, and for a moment she felt weightless—and then the ground returned.

With a crash.

A clatter.

A thud.

Silence.

Kane was practically asleep on his feet. Riding down the same beginner trail again and again would have been enough to put anyone into a coma of boredom. And feigning enthusiasm every time Beth made it twenty feet without falling was wearing him out.

"You're doing great," he lied, when they'd landed at the bottom once again. "Think maybe it's time for you to try a more difficult slope?"

"Oh, I don't know." She bit her lip and looked up at the mountain peaks in the distance. "I don't think I'm ready for that yet."

"You're better than you think you are," he prodded her.

She shook her head. "Not that much better."

He shrugged and began maneuvering his snowboard back toward the chairlift. "Whatever—we'll just go again."

She grabbed him and pulled him to a stop, slightly off the trail.

"Kane, if *you* want to go hit some harder slopes for a while, it's okay."

"I'm not going to just leave you here," he protested, imagining himself shooting down a black diamond trail, chasing the wind. It killed him to be out here in such fresh powder, stuck gliding down the same bunny hill over and over again, at snail speed. "But why don't you come along—you're really getting good now."

She laughed. "And what definition of good are you using? No, I'm staying here. But really, you go—have some fun. We'll meet up later."

She was lying, that much was clear. She wanted him with her, and was terrified to ski by herself. He should stay. That would be the good boyfriend move. It would have been Adam's move. *But she's not with Adam*, he reminded himself. And who knew *what* she really wanted, if she wasn't going to admit it. Why not take her at face value, enjoy himself? It was fresh powder, after all, and a new board. You don't waste that. Not if you're Kane Geary.

"Have I mentioned how beautiful you look out here?" he told her. "Like a snow goddess."

She pushed him playfully. "You don't have to butter me up, Kane. I'm not going to be mad if you go—you came up here to board. You should do it."

"That's not all I came for," he reminded her, pulling

her scarf away from her face so he could warm her chilled lips with a kiss.

"Well then, you'd better take care of yourself up there and make sure you stay in one piece . . . so you can meet me later," she told him, with an uncharacteristically mischievous note in her voice. This was working out better than he could have hoped.

"Wouldn't miss it," he assured her.

"And remember—" she called after him as he slid away.

"I'll be careful!" he promised.

But really, what was the fun in that?

Harper didn't know what had been more humiliating. Lying on the ground, snow seeping through her clothes, as more and more curious skiers gathered to gawk? Being strapped to the back of a rescue mobile like a couch strapped to the hood of a car and then unceremoniously unloaded in front of half her school? Or maybe it was the fact that after thoroughly examining her, the doctor at the first aid station had concluded there was nothing wrong with her other than a few bruises and a twisted knee.

Not that she wasn't grateful. Imagine if she'd broken her neck—or, almost as bad, her nose. But the injury was just minor enough to make her feel like an idiot for making such a scene—and just major enough to keep her off her feet for the rest of the weekend.

Adam had tended to her for a while. He was guilt stricken over his abject failure as a ski instructor, and she was only too happy to play his damsel in distress, letting him prop her leg up with pillows, bring her hot chocolate, and kiss her bruises until she had to smile. (And, if nothing else, at least all the commotion had taken his mind off their little "problem.")

He'd been so sweet, in fact, that she'd felt guilty about spoiling his fun. She'd told him to go back out on the slopes—he'd refused, she'd insisted. And finally, he'd given in.

It was only when he'd gone, and she was left alone in the empty lodge, her hot chocolate turned cold, her knee throbbing, the cozy fire burned out, that she realized her stupidity. She was trapped in here, in pain, while Adam was out there alone, easy prey for all those desperate girls who would love nothing more than to steal him away from her.

Easy prey for Beth.

She could see it now.

"Oh, Adam, you look so handsome on your skis!" In that simpering voice. "I'm so sweet and helpless—won't you help me get down the mountain?"

Harper would have been pleased to help her—right over the edge. But Adam, on the other hand, would be nothing but a gentleman, only too happy to lend his services. And once she'd sucked him back in with the needy routine, she'd never let him go.

Kane was nothing, no one, she'd claim. A horrible mistake. Adam was her one, true love.

It was nauseating, even as a hypothetical.

Adam would resist at first. He was nothing if not loyal.

But Beth would beg and Beth would plead—and then, Harper knew, Beth would cry. And she'd look so beautiful and so fragile standing out in the snow, throwing herself on Adam's mercy, that eventually, he would just give in. After all, he would surely reason, Harper's tough, she can handle it. Beth is the one who really needs me.

If only he knew.

It was crazy, she told herself. Totally unlikely—certainly no more likely than a chance meeting in the halls of the high school or the cramped streets of their tiny town. But still, she couldn't stand the idea of Beth out there having *Harper's* dream vacation.

Harper whipped out her phone, determined to get her mind off the whole horrible thing. But who to call? Even Miranda was out on the slopes, having fun. Harper was alone. There was only one person she could think of who might have time to talk, distract Harper from her living nightmare—and it wouldn't have been her first choice. Or her fifth. But she was out of options, and sometimes you just had to play the hand you were dealt.

She hit call.

"Hey, Kaia—yes, it's Harper. Just thought I'd check in, give you the download on the trip so far . . . what? No, nothing too exciting—wait, I *do* have some hot gossip. You'll never guess what our trusty chaperone's been up to. Let's just say he's got his hands full. Or should I say, his lap. . . ."

He didn't notice her until he'd sat down beside her on the chairlift—and by then, it was too late.

This *really* wasn't his day.

They recognized each other at the same time, just as the lift swept their feet off the ground. Now there was no turning back—they were trapped together until they reached the top.

"Hey," Adam grunted.

Beth nodded and looked down. Most of her face was hidden by a thick blue scarf—only her eyes were visible, and he couldn't decipher their expression. Once, he'd been able to read her thoughts, just from the look in her eyes. It felt like a long time ago.

They rode in silence for several long minutes, watching the skiers dart around beneath them. Adam swung his skis, gently rocking them back and forth.

"Could you not do that?" Beth asked. Adam looked over and noticed how tightly she was gripping the guide bar. For a moment, he considered swinging his legs wildly, just to see her face fill with fear. But he suppressed the impulse—and hated himself for it.

"Sorry," he said awkwardly, and stopped. "So, uh, how's the skiing?" *And where's your boyfriend?* he added silently. Nice of Kane to send her off by herself. Typical. But no more than she deserved, he supposed. And she was a big girl. She could handle it.

"It's fine," she responded unconvincingly. "It's great. Kane and I are having a great time."

"It doesn't look it," Adam snapped.

"What?"

"If you two are having such a *great* time together, where is he?"

She looked away. "That's really none of your business," she said bluntly. "Did I ask you where Harper was?"

"She's—"

"I don't care," Beth cut in. "That was my point."

"Fine. Sorry I said anything at all," he retorted.

"Me too."

Beth hopped off the chairlift as soon as her skis could reach the ground. She couldn't get away from Adam fast enough. She hated what being around him did to her. Half the time she was an emotional wreck, ready to throw herself at his feet and beg him to take her back, the other half she was this cold, sarcastic monster she barely recognized.

He deserved it, of course—what right had he to comment on her relationship, act so wise and superior, as if he were just waiting for her and Kane to fall apart? He didn't know anything about them—or anything about her, not anymore.

She was so angry that she forgot to be afraid as she launched herself down the trail. So busy fuming about Adam that she failed to notice the icy patch until it was too late—her legs went skidding out from under her—one ski off to the right, the other off to the left, and just when it felt as if she would snap in half, her skis snapped off instead, and she landed, facefirst, in a pile of snow.

Ouch.

It took her a moment to catch her breath and make sure all her limbs were still attached and in working order. Yes on both counts. She sat up and brushed the snow out of her face, taking stock. One ski lay a few feet away, and there were her two ski poles, but the other ski . . .

Beth's heart sank. It was nowhere in sight. Had it slid down the mountain without her? She wondered how much it would cost to replace a rental ski—and how in the world she'd make it down without it.

"Lose something?"

Adam skied to a stop just in front of her—and he was holding her missing ski.

“I saw it go flying,” he explained, “and figured . . . are you okay?”

She nodded and, with some hesitation, took his hand and let him help her up.

“I saw you go flying too,” he told her, “and I thought . . .”

“It looked pretty bad, I guess?” she asked with a wry smile.

“No, no,” he assured her as she snapped her boots back into the skis. “You were doing great until you fell. You’re a natural.”

He’d been watching her? Beth felt her face warm, and was glad her scarf would hide the blush. The scarf made her think of Kane—and that made her think it was time to go.

“Well, I guess I should get back on the horse,” she said, taking a tentative step forward on the skis, only to topple over once again—and this time, she pulled him down with her.

“I take it back,” Adam said, rolling over and spitting out a mouthful of snow. “You totally suck.”

He burst into laughter and, after a moment, Beth broke out in giggles.

“I’m so sorry,” she gasped, trying to get hold of herself. “Let me help you up.”

“No, don’t touch me,” he warned, but he said it with

a warm smile on his face. "I don't want to risk another human avalanche."

He picked himself up and then, again, hoisted her to her feet.

"I guess I should have paid more attention in ski school," Beth admitted ruefully.

Adam flicked a clump of snow off her shoulder, and Beth realized how long it had been since he'd touched her. But just a moment ago he'd grabbed her hand and pulled her upright as if it were nothing.

Which, she supposed, it was.

"I could—I could help you out a little," he suddenly suggested, looking surprised to hear the words pop out of his mouth. He couldn't have been as surprised as Beth.

If he'd asked her ten minutes earlier, she would have laughed in his face. Accept help from Adam? As if.

Suddenly, it didn't seem like such a bad idea. "I guess we could do that," she accepted shyly. "If you want."

"Okay, then," he said, in his can-do voice. She knew it well. But then, she knew everything about him, every inch of him, well. Or, at least, she had. "The first thing we need to do is work on your stopping skills. Did they tell you in your lesson about 'making a pizza'?"

Beth rolled her eyes. "Not you too! I still don't understand what skiing has to do with fast food. It's so ridiculous."

He gave her a playful shove. "Now I *know* you're not mocking the pizza—not the very bedrock of our skiing society!" He looked so stricken that she burst into laughter again.

"I wouldn't dare," she promised. "Bring on the pizza."

He positioned her on the skis, and they practiced stopping and slowing down and, eventually, "french fries," for when she wanted to speed up, and soon, Beth was no longer terrified by the out-of-control flight down the mountain—she was exhilarated.

Despite all that was unspoken between them, and all the horrible words that had been said and could never be forgotten, things could still be easy between the two of them. She felt she was rediscovering something, or someone, that she hadn't even realized she'd missed. Not Adam—or not just Adam—but herself. The person she had been—before. She thought she'd lost that person forever. Maybe, just maybe, she'd been wrong.

By the time Adam returned, flushed and sunkissed from his day in the snow, Harper was seriously bored—and seriously cranky.

She'd gossiped with Kaia, made small talk with the steady stream of losers who'd returned to the lodge with bumps and bruises of their own, read through this month's *Vogue*, twice—at one point she'd gotten so desperate for something to do that she'd actually called her *mother*. In short: It had been a painfully long afternoon—made even longer by the fact that Adam showed up twenty-three minutes later than he was supposed to. (And yes, she'd been counting.)

But she played the good girlfriend—she put on a happy face.

"How are you doing?" Adam asked, greeting her with a kiss and laying a gentle hand on her wounded knee.

"Much better, now that you're here," she said truthfully. "So how was your afternoon?"

"Awesome!" he beamed—then looked down at her and quickly corrected himself. "I mean, it was okay. You didn't miss much."

He was so adorable when he tried—and failed—to be a smooth operator.

"It's okay, Ad, I want you to have fun," she assured him. It sounded like the right thing to say . . . even if it wasn't quite true. "So you didn't get too bored, skiing all by yourself? Or did you hook up with one of the guys?"

"No . . ." He stepped behind her, beginning to rub her shoulders. "Actually, I spent most of the day . . ."

His voice trailed off, and Harper tipped her head up to catch a glimpse of his face. What was he thinking?

"Spent most of the day doing what?" she prodded him.

"You know, skiing, just enjoying the outdoors," he

said quickly. Too quickly? "But I missed you—how's your knee?"

"It's a little better," Harper said, easing herself up off the couch and balancing on her good leg. "I think if I can lean on you, I should be able to . . . make it back to your room." She hadn't intended for her voice to rise at the end of the sentence, as if it were a question—but then, she didn't know what to expect. Not after last night.

"You can always lean on me, Gracie," he teased, hurrying to her side and slinging an arm around her waist. "Let's just take this one step at a time."

They hobbled out of the lounge and back toward the rooms. Harper smiled. It was so nice to be cradled in Adam's arms, letting him guide her and support her, that the pain in her knee was almost worth it. Almost.

And then Beth crossed their path—and her smile disappeared.

"Hi, Adam," The Blond One said shyly, ignoring Harper. "You ran off so quickly before . . . when Kane came over . . . well, I just wanted to say thank you for helping me today."

Harper looked sharply over at Adam, whose normally open face was shut up tight. She couldn't read him at all. And she didn't like it.

"And what did this wonderful guy do for you today?" Harper asked, in a sugary sweet tone. She leaned her head against Adam's chest. His heart was pounding.

"He didn't tell you?" Beth's oh-so-innocent smile widened. "He spent his whole afternoon teaching me how to ski. I'm sure you would much rather have been off on the black diamonds or something."

"No, I—" Adam looked down at Harper and cut himself off. He continued in a much more formal, measured tone. "I was happy to help, Beth. Now, we should really get Harper back to the room."

Beth gave Harper a weak smile. It wasn't returned.

"Okay, well—thanks again," she said, offering Adam an awkward little wave. "It was . . . good to catch up."

"Yeah." Adam tugged Harper away, and they began shuffling down the hall as fast as Harper could hobble.

"That was very sweet of you," Harper said carefully, anger and fear simmering in her chest.

"I didn't plan it—," he began.

"Oh, of course not."

"But you should have seen her out there." He chuckled at the memory. "She had no idea what she was doing."

And that was your problem how?

But Harper stopped herself before the words could pop out of her mouth. She had a choice. She could follow her territorial instincts and make sure Adam knew just how wrong he'd been to spend the day with the enemy. And then *lie* about it. She could pick a fight with him that would probably end up with her limping back to her room, alone. She could leave him secure in the knowledge that she was a jealous, unforgiving harpy—and leave him free to chase after the sweet and innocent princess of his dreams. *What would Beth do?* she wondered. It was galling to even ask herself the question—but, given the starry look in Adam's eyes every time that blond hair crossed his field of vision, maybe it was also her smartest move.

Beth, the doormat, the good girl would likely just bite her tongue. Smile. Tell Adam she was happy to see him move on from his anger. Beth wouldn't care if Adam befriended an old girlfriend—or if she did, she'd know it wasn't her place to say anything. It was the kind of behavior that made Beth into such a limp dishrag, at least in Harper's estimation, but it was also the kind of behavior that made Adam love her. And if that's really what he wanted, maybe it was worth a try.

"Well, she's lucky she had you around to help her," Harper said finally, with as much sincerity as she could muster.

"You mean that?" Adam asked, giving her a searching look. "I thought you'd be mad. That's, uh, why I didn't say anything before."

"Of course I'm not mad, Ad—you can hang out with whoever you want. And"—she paused, choking the words out was actually inflicting physical pain—"I'm really glad to see you and Beth getting along better. I'm really happy for you."

Adam pulled her closer to him and kissed the top of her head. "Do you know how amazing you are?" he asked.

Great. Just one problem, Harper thought sourly, beaming up at him. *That wasn't me.*

chapter six

KAIA PULLED HER CAR INTO THE LOT OF THE LOST and Found and switched off the ignition, slamming a fist into the steering wheel. It had been hours since Harper's phone call, but she was just as angry.

He'd wanted her to pity him, stuck in the mountains with a bunch of high schoolers.

"I'd so much rather be with you," he'd sworn.

Right. Me—or the first blonde who crosses his path. Same difference.

Kaia didn't even know *why* she was so angry. It's not like she and Jack Powell were "going steady" or something pathetically absurd like that. You couldn't cheat on someone if you weren't in a relationship, right? Yes, he'd forbidden her to see other guys, and she'd accepted it, for the sake of keeping their secret. He was right: High school boys *did* get jealous—and, eventually, curious. But, she now realized, *he'd* never promised not to see other women. And she had never thought to ask.

And why would she? Wasn't that their thing? No obligations, no attachments, no messy emotions screwing things up and getting in the way.

So she had no right to be mad, no right to be jealous. And if her ego had taken a hit, realizing that, apparently, she wasn't enough for him—well, her ego was pretty tough. It would survive.

And meanwhile . . .

She picked up the flyer she'd tossed on the passenger seat: BLIND MONKEYS! ONE NIGHT ONLY AT THE LOST AND FOUND!

Reed was the lead singer, and had told her about the concert—and though she'd tried her best to forget about it, to forget about *him*, here she was. Their date—or whatever it had been—made less and less sense, the more she thought about it. And for the past twenty-four hours, she'd thought about little else.

Still, she'd promised herself she wouldn't pursue anything. For one thing, he was way beneath her. For another, she had Powell—or at least she would, when he finally returned to town. Besides: garage bands, dive bars, and Kaia didn't mix.

But tonight, after Harper's call, she'd suddenly changed her tune.

Not that she had a sudden craving for smoky air and off-key covers. And she certainly wasn't willing to admit that the thought of Powell with another girl—another woman—had driven her so crazy with jealousy that she'd hopped in the car and driven to this dead-end pit of a bar to throw herself at a pizza-boy-cum-tow-truck-driver-cum high-school-dropout-to-be.

So what the hell am I doing here? she thought irritably. *I should just turn around and go.* Now.

But, instead, she opened the door, got out of the BMW, and headed toward the bar.

She didn't know why she was there, or what she was getting herself into—but there was only one way to find out.

Maybe she was just a glutton for punishment.

After a long, hard, and too often painful day of skiing, Miranda was safely back in her room. She could plop down on the bed, pull out her iPod, let some good music wash her tension away. . . . But, instead, she pulled out her computer. She no longer had any delusions that anything good could come from matchmadeinhaven.com—and yet she couldn't squelch that last ounce of hope. She just couldn't stop herself. So she logged on.

> Congratulations, **Spitfire**, the following 1 user has expressed interest in your profile. Click here to learn more!

She was sure this latest candidate would be just as much of a loser as the rest, but there was no harm in finding out—just for the sake of curiosity, of course.

> User Profile: ReadItAndWeep
>
> Sex: male
>
> Age: 17
>
> Height: 5'9"
>
> Favorite color: the desert sky, just after sunrise
>
> Favorite food: chocolate chip cookies
>
> If I were an animal, I'd be: a lab rat—plenty of nervous energy and nowhere to go. Just like your typical Grace teenager.
>
> Celebrity I most look like: Brad Pitt
>
> Best lie I've ever told: I look a lot like Brad Pitt.
>
> Three things I can't live without: 1—Woody Allen movies, 2—my copy of *The Fountainhead,* 3—someone to talk to
>
> I am . . . counting down the days of high

school like a prisoner waiting for parole. Sick of everyone telling me, "You're such a great guy, why aren't you dating anyone?" And a little embarrassed to be on this website.

You are . . . smart, funny, ambitious, and love to laugh. You hate dating for the sake of dating and are looking for something real. Good-hearted, loyal, and not afraid of a challenge.

It seemed too good to be true. A smart, funny, sensitive guy? Looking for love? And drawn to *Miranda*? She allowed herself a small smile. Maybe there was hope for her yet.

"Oh, that feels *so* good," Kane moaned. He leaned his head back against the rim of the hot tub and closed his eyes. "I could stay here forever."

"Mmm, I know what you mean." Beth stretched out along her side, reveling in the jets of hot water pummeling her sore muscles. Her face tingled in the cold night air.

It was an almost perfect end to an almost perfect day.

Kane hadn't asked anything about her afternoon, and she wasn't about to volunteer the fact that she'd spent the whole time with Adam, skiing and laughing. It had felt almost like old times, the two of them together, anticipating each other's every move, the easy ebb and flow of conversation. As if he'd let himself forget everything that had happened—at least until the end of the day, when they'd parted. They had stayed on safe topics all afternoon, meaningless chatter about the snow, about college applications—but in the end, it had seemed as if he was finally about to say something that mattered. And then he'd spotted Kane in the distance—and his whole face had frozen. And that was it. He'd waved a brusque good-bye and skied away. As if the whole day had never happened. They were right back where they'd started.

But it's a beginning, Beth thought hopefully. *And maybe now we can . . .*

She cut herself off. Can what? Get back together? It's not like she was still in love with him, or even wanted him back. *Friendship*, she assured herself. That's all she wanted. To reach a point where they wouldn't have to ignore each other in the halls. To know something about what was going on in his life. To have him care what was going on in hers.

That was it—nothing more.

She was with Kane now, exactly where she wanted to be.

He floated lazily across the hot tub to join her and playfully flicked some of the churning water in her face.

She giggled, but before she could splash him back, he grabbed her hands and kissed her.

"You look pretty spectacular in a bikini," he commented when they broke for air, giving her an appreciative glance. "Anyone ever told you that?"

Beth blushed and sank a bit deeper into the water, suddenly very aware of how much of her was exposed.

When she didn't reply, he grinned and flexed a bicep. "Traditionally, now's the time when you tell me how handsome and sexy I look," he pointed out.

Now she splashed him. "Yes, you're a total hottie, babe," she gushed in her best Barbie voice.

He leaned back and closed his eyes again, his face plastered with a smug smile. "Mock me all you want, but you know you wish I was wearing a Speedo."

Beth laughed and nestled herself against him, relaxing into the delicious warmth of the water, the brittle sting of the winter air, the solid body beside her. She suddenly felt very tired—and very content.

So tired and so content that she let her guard down for a moment—and the question she'd been holding in for so long just slipped out.

"Kane?"

"Mmm?"

"Why are you with me?"

He began idly rubbing his hand up and down her arm. "I thought we just established that," he said lightly, without opening his eyes. "You're one hot babe, I'm one hot babe—makes perfect sense to me."

"Seriously, Kane—we've got nothing in common."

"We both like hot tubs," he pointed out. "And bikinis . . ."

She rolled her eyes.

"Come on," she said, exasperated. "I mean it. We're totally different. And I'm nothing like any of the girls you dated before."

He opened his eyes then, and sat up and took her hand. "Have I ever made you think that's a bad thing?" he asked gently.

"No, I just—"

"You're right. You're nothing like them, Beth. And *that's* why I'm with you."

"I just think people must look at us and wonder." Beth sighed. "We don't seem to make any sense." She didn't know why she was saying all these things, not now, but it was as if once she'd started, she couldn't stop herself.

"We make sense to *me*," he insisted. "Who cares what other people think? They don't know us—they don't know me."

Beth touched her hand to his cheek. "Sometimes . . ." She paused—but she'd come so far already, why stop? "Sometimes, I feel like *I* don't know you."

She could feel him tense beneath her fingers, and he shifted away.

"You know me," he countered. "This is me—what you see is what you get. I'm easy."

Beth shook her head. "That's got to be the biggest lie you've ever told me. Easy?" She smiled fondly. "Not so much."

"What do you want from me?" he asked petulantly.

Beth draped an arm around him, wishing he hadn't gotten so defensive—she didn't want to fight. She just wanted to talk. They didn't do much of that, she realized.

"I guess I just want—more," she told him honestly. Spending time with Adam today had reminded her of what it was like to *really* know someone—and she wanted that again, somehow. "I really like you, Kane, and I just want more of you—I want to know all of you."

He perked up suddenly. "Something else we have in common," he pointed out. "I want to know all of you, too. Your lips." He kissed her gently. "Your neck." He kissed her again, soft, brief kisses that grazed her chin and ran down the length of her long neck. "Your beautiful—"

"Kane!" She squirmed away. "We're in public!"

"You're right," he replied, gaping at the surroundings as if he'd only just noticed. "What are we doing here? Come on." He stood and extended a hand to her. "Let's go back to my room. We can start this whole getting to know each other thing."

She stood, without his help, and grabbed a towel as

she stepped out of the hot tub and onto the steamy patio. "That's not what I mean, and you know it."

"Hey, get your mind out of the gutter. I meant we should go back to my room and talk . . . for a while." He draped another towel around her shoulders and pulled her close to him, rubbing her shivering body to warm her up. "I really like you, too, Beth," he whispered in her ear. "You're not the only one who wants more."

Beth took a deep breath and closed her eyes, resting her head against his dripping chest. Part of her wanted to go with him—*all* of her wanted to go with him, in fact. Why not? He was handsome and charming, his smile made her tremble, they were in this beautiful, romantic resort, and for whatever reason, he wanted to be with her. And, she realized, she wanted to be with him.

So what was the problem? Why did the thought of stepping into his room and closing the door behind her make her heart race and her muscles tense? She knew what he was expecting out of this weekend. She'd known it from the start. So why did the thought make her hyperventilate?

What is wrong *with me?* she thought in frustration. She'd let her fears torpedo her relationship with Adam. Was she going to be alone the rest of her life because of her stupid issues? Kane wasn't Adam—he'd been patient with her so far, but patience wasn't in his nature, she could tell. How long would he wait?

She opened her mouth to tell him, *Yes, let's go back to your room*—but couldn't choke out the words.

"I've got to go back to my room and dry off, take a shower," she said lamely. She gave him a long kiss, then extricated herself from his embrace.

"You can shower in my—"

"I'll come over later, when I'm done," she promised.

And she so wanted it to be the truth.

But she knew herself.

And so she knew better.

It was like a scene out of a movie, and it couldn't have been more perfect. Adam had lit a fire in the fireplace, and the low flames popped and crackled, filling the room with a fresh woodsy scent and a warm glow. Harper lay on the bed, her swollen knee elevated, sipping a steaming cup of coffee (with some Baileys poured in for good measure). And the pièce de résistance: Adam, stripped down to his boxers, his tan, taut body lit by the glow of the fire, as if bathed in a golden aura. He was fiddling with the radio, searching for a suitably romantic station—but Harper, tired of waiting, waved him back into bed. A crackling Carrie Underwood song on the local country-western station would just have to do.

As Adam climbed onto the mattress next to her, Harper closed her eyes and was finally able to forget about her throbbing knee, Adam's afternoon with Beth, the horror of the night before—it was all erased by the gentle pressure of his body against hers.

"I've been waiting all day for this." Harper sighed as Adam kissed her, first on the lips, then dotting the skin of her exposed breastbone. "I'm just—ouch!"

"Sorry—your knee?" Adam pulled away hastily but, wincing, Harper rolled over and leaned back into him.

"Forget it. Just—" She kissed his bare chest, rubbing her hands up and down his biceps, his rippled stomach muscles. Everything about him was incredible. "Just relax." She rolled over onto her back and he kissed her again, running his hands through her wild mess of hair. Every inch of her skin was tingling, alive at his touch. She could feel him trembling, and she smiled, knowing that, this time, she could be the teacher and he the student—that she was about to show him things he could never have imagined. His soft breath tickled the side of her neck and she giggled, then caught her breath as, ever so slightly, his lips played their way across her body.

She'd never felt this way, exhilarated, bright with anticipation—not since the first time. Maybe not even then. She'd done it all before, but with Adam, everything was new, everything was—

"Harper?"

"Oh, Adam," she moaned. "You're—"

"Harper?" He pulled away from her and sat up abruptly, his face tense and red. "I . . . can't. I'm sorry, it's—"

"Again?" she asked in disbelief, before she could stop the word from slipping out. She put a hand on his shoulder, but he shrugged it off.

"I want to. I just . . ."

Harper came up behind him and put her arms around him, teasing her fingers through the soft blond hair on his chest.

"It's okay," she assured him. "It's—this happens." Did it? Certainly never to her. Not before. And not twice in a row.

"It's *not* okay," he exploded in frustration, pushing her away. He rose and began to pace around the room. He was so vibrant, glowing with anger and frustration—she wanted him even more. "Goddamnit! This is just so . . . humiliating."

"Adam," Harper began plaintively, unsure what to say. She got out of bed and went to him, grabbed him, forced him to stand still. "Adam, look at me."

But he refused, and when she lightly grabbed his chin and tried to turn his face in her direction, he squirmed away. It was like talking to a petulant little boy who knew he was about to get in trouble and didn't want to face up to what he'd done.

Or, in this case—hadn't done.

"It's not you," he muttered, staring fixedly at the crackling fire.

Right. What else could it be? After last night with those losers from the basketball team . . . and then he'd spent all day with sweet, virginal Beth. Harper held her breath for a moment, trying to get her emotions under control. Adam was with *her* now—he wanted her. This was all just a fluke. Bad luck, bad timing. It had to be. And they'd get through it.

"Adam, do you want to try—"

"Maybe you should just go," he interrupted her in a rough, husky voice. "It's late, and—"

"Sure. Yeah." Harper backed away from him and hastily began pulling on her clothes. She'd hoped they would at least sleep there together, curled up in each other's arms. Awkward as it was, it was better than . . . nothing.

Don't make a big deal out of it, she instructed herself, *and maybe it doesn't have to be a big deal.*

"We have to get up early tomorrow, anyway, to drive back and"—she faked a yawn—"I'm really tired." She slipped into her heavy coat and zipped it up. Even though she wouldn't actually have to step outside to get back to her room, she was suddenly cold, and wanted something warm and heavy wrapped around her.

"Harper, I—" Adam paused, and finally turned to face

her. Standing there in the middle of the room, still half naked, he looked so vulnerable, Harper just wanted to rush to him and assure him everything would be all right. And make him assure her that it didn't mean anything, that he wanted to be with her, as much as ever.

"I guess I'll see you tomorrow," she said instead, affecting a cheerful voice.

"Tomorrow," he agreed. He gave her a lame little wave and took a step toward her, then stopped. "Good night."

Harper forced herself to smile, then limped out the door. None of it meant anything, she assured herself. Sex, no sex, whatever. Adam was falling in love with her, and it didn't matter what his friends said, or how much his pretty princess ex-girlfriend wanted him back—Adam was hers, for good.

She wasn't worried. Of course not. If there was one thing Harper was sure of, it was the power she had over men.

All men. Hadn't she proven that by snagging Adam in the first place? So whatever was going on in Adam's head, it was minor. It was temporary.

It had to be.

Miranda was already in bed and nearly asleep when she heard the door open and saw Harper's shadowy figure tiptoe across the room.

"Wasn't expecting to see you tonight," Miranda said, flipping on the lamp by her bed.

Startled, Harper nearly tripped over herself.

"Let's just say Adam and I wore each other out," she said, giving Miranda a meaningful grin as she began changing into her pajamas.

Miranda laughed—there was nothing she loved more than Harper's post-date epics, although since she'd started dating Adam, the juicy stories had been few and far between.

"So? Spill," Miranda pressed. "Was it worth the wait?"

Harper blushed, and Miranda almost choked. She'd seen Harper's face turn red after a few too many hours in the sun—or a few too many margaritas—but never out of embarrassment. And *never* about a guy.

"A lady doesn't kiss and tell," Harper protested, climbing into bed and tucking herself beneath the garish flowered comforter.

"And that applies to you how?" Miranda asked, ducking as Harper tossed a pillow at her head. "Come on, was it everything you expected?"

"And more," Harper allowed, a secretive smile playing across her lips. "It is *Adam*, after all."

"That's all you're going to tell me?" Miranda shrieked, throwing the pillow back at her best friend.

Harper just laughed. "Come on, Rand, I'm tired. Can

we just say it was amazing and incredible, and leave it at that? Dirty details in the morning, I promise."

"Yeah, yeah, fine," Miranda agreed grudgingly. "It's not like I'm living vicariously through you or anything."

"Speaking of which," Harper asked, turning to face Miranda and propping herself up on her elbow, "what did you do tonight? I figured you'd still be out partying."

Decision time. Miranda could admit to Harper, her best friend, who knew everything about her down to the name of her third-grade imaginary friend, what she'd done with her night. That is—nothing. Or, more specifically, nothing, followed by an hour of trolling for dates on the Internet, followed by more nothing. She could confess everything about matchmadeinhaven.com and spend the next two hours sitting up and speculating about the charming and mysterious ReadItAndWeep, and plotting out her next move.

And for a second, it seemed like a fabulous idea. Miranda opened her mouth to spill all—and then caught herself, just in time. Because there was Harper, exhausted from a night of wild, passionate—whatever—with the love of her life. And all Miranda had to offer was an empty bag of Oreos and a new crush on a cybergeek? She could already see the look of patronizing encouragement—or worse, ridicule—that was sure to follow her confession.

No, thank you. Not tonight. She was too tired—and,

to be honest, too secretly excited about ReadItAndWeep—to bear the humiliation. Besides, what were a few more secrets between friends?

"Big party in some kid's room," Miranda said truthfully, avoiding the small fact that she hadn't bothered to attend. "You're right, though, it's late. I'll tell you all about it in the morning." She quickly flipped off her light so that Harper couldn't read the lie on her face. A moment later, the light over Harper's bed went out too, casting them both in darkness.

"Miranda?" Harper suddenly asked, her disembodied voice sounding strangely hesitant.

"Yes?"

There was a long pause, then—

"Nothing. I'm just . . . glad you had such a great night."

Miranda sighed. Little did she know.

"Not as great as yours," she chirped. Also true. "You're so lucky to have someone like Adam."

"That's me," Harper said drily. "The luckiest girl in the world."

Reed's band sucked.

Kaia didn't know too much about music—but then, she didn't have to, because whatever the band was playing didn't really qualify.

It was loud, all right, and did seem to somehow involve

instruments. But the guitarist's screeching solos sounded like a drowning cat, and the drummer, off in a world of his own, had abandoned any kind of rhythm for the random clanging and pounding you might expect from a three-year-old left alone with a pile of pots and pans. The overall effect was slightly less than melodic.

As for the bar . . . Kaia's short time in Grace had quickly revealed to her that the nightlife options were rather lacking—but this place topped the list of dumps. It was overwhelmingly brown, from the padded imitation leather walls to the bartender's cigarette-stained teeth. A couple of arcade games were tucked into the corner, along with a jukebox and what looked—at least from a safe distance away—like a coin-operated porn viewer. The walls were covered with the tattered remnants of holiday decorations—a year's worth of holidays, from sagging and faded Fourth of July flags to ripped four-leaf clovers. A handful of surly loners nursed their drinks at rickety tables, and a group of burly middle-aged men, apparent escapees from a Teamsters' convention, roared with drunken laughter by the beer-stained pool table.

If there had been a stack of comment cards, Kaia would have recommended that the management erect a new sign on the fake saloon doors out front: ABANDON ALL HOPE, YE WHO ENTER HERE. It would be both an appropriate sentiment and a public service.

After her first sip of flat beer and the opening chords of the Blind Monkeys' first "song," she'd almost walked out.

And then Reed had begun to sing.

The song was horrible, the original lyrics lamely unoriginal, and the backup band worthless. But Reed's voice . . . it was like barbed wire draped in velvet. Low and hoarse, but warm, and with an intensity that scared her—and drew her in. He leaned in toward the mike and gazed out at the audience, and his eyes seemed to meet hers, then flicker past. Kaia couldn't look away.

He wore a tight-fitting navy T-shirt and black jeans, and his face was framed by a tangled halo of jet-black curls that kept flopping down over his eyes.

He'd clean up nicely, she mused—but the idea of Reed Sawyer in a Hugo Boss suit and Bruno Magli loafers seemed laughable, and wrong. His look fit him—just as the bar fit him, the town fit him. She was repelled by all of it—so why couldn't she tear herself away?

The band played for an hour, driving most of the regulars out of the bar in search of a quieter hole in which to hide. But Kaia stayed. When the set finally ended, Reed stepped off the stage, obviously exhausted. She knew he had seen her—but he didn't smile, didn't wave, didn't come over. Instead, he walked slowly to the bar, where the bartender—an overweight brunette in a low-cut top—had a drink waiting for him. He sat down on a stool with his back to Kaia.

No one turned his back on Kaia.

And she wasn't about to go up to him. She didn't even want to, not really—what would be the point?

So, instead, she sat there for a few minutes, sipping some water and refusing to look in his direction. Then she made a decision: enough. She got up from her seat, grimacing as her heel sank into something suspiciously soft and moist on the sticky floor, and walked out of the bar.

The parking lot was shadowy and half empty—and when she got to her car, there was a dark figure leaning against it. Her heart leaped into her throat—and then she recognized his silhouette. It was Reed.

"Where did you—?"

"There's a back exit," he explained, jerking his head toward the bar. "I saw you go. Leaving without saying good-bye?"

"Without saying *hello*," Kaia corrected him. "But it's unfortunately too late for that." He somehow brought out the nasty in her, just by breathing. And he just stood there and took it—almost as if he knew her, could recognize the feeble attempt to drive him away. Maybe she was glad it hadn't worked.

"Did you like the show?"

"It . . . had its moments."

"Yeah, we suck," he acknowledged. "I didn't expect to see you here."

"I'm not very predictable," Kaia said, taking a step toward him. In the dim orange glow of the flickering streetlight, she could barely make out his features, and his eyes were only pools of darkness—unreadable. "I'm rarely what you'd expect."

"I know," he told her, and took a step closer as well.

They were almost touching, and she could feel a shiver of electricity pass between them, as if the air itself were charged with tension. Possibility.

"I should get back inside," he said, but didn't move.

"I should get home," she agreed, but she, too, kept still.

"I wish it would rain again," she said suddenly, nonsensically. And it was true.

"It will," he promised. And he took one more step and the space between them disappeared. Her lips met his hungrily and she sucked in the taste of him, sweet and sharp at the same time. She thrust herself against him and pushed him against the side of the car, drinking in the feel of his hands roaming across her body.

He pulled away first, her skin still craving his touch.

"I'm going now," he said simply, with the mocking smile she loved to hate. "I'll see you around."

And he was gone.

chapter seven

IT'S TOUGH TO HAVE A BAD TIME WHEN YOU'RE nestled amid the ice-covered peaks with nothing to do but frolic in the snow and bring your wildest romantic fantasies to life. Opportunity is everywhere. You have to really work to avoid it.

They'd managed.

A waste, Adam thought as he unpacked his duffel bag and came across the unused pack of condoms. *A total, fucking waste.* He threw them across the room toward the wastebasket. Missed.

A disaster, Harper thought, pressed up against her window, watching Adam's bedroom window a few yards away.

All those hopes and all those expectations—and they'd all come to nothing. He turned out the light and then, almost as an afterthought, pulled down the shade. Almost as if he knew she was watching.

A mess, Beth thought, as Kane dropped her off at home and, with barely a peck good-bye, sped away into the night. The trip had started out so well—and then it had just fallen apart. Why did she always make everything so complicated? Why couldn't it just be simple, for once? Easy. Straightforward. Clean.

A miscalculation, Kane thought, speeding down the dark, empty highway. He'd pushed too hard, been too obvious. Not a problem. He could do slow. He could do subtle. He could do whatever was needed to get the job done.

A mistake, Kaia thought, lying in bed and wondering whether Powell was home yet, when he would call. That's all it had been. All *he* had been. A terrible mistake. A moment of weakness. She'd indulged temptation, no harm done. But it was back to reality now. Reed Sawyer was nothing but a mistake—one that could never happen again.

* * *

Although one in ten men suffer from impotence at some point in their lives, the disorder remains

> largely misunderstood, due to the persistent shroud of embarrassment and shame that accompanies the condition.

You can say that again, Adam thought bitterly. It had taken him a full hour to even work up the nerve to type "impotence" into the search engine—and as he read through the numerous and mostly unhelpful websites, he couldn't stop looking over his shoulder every ten seconds, even though he knew there was no one home to catch him.

> Impotency can be attributed to psychological or physical causes. But fear not! Whatever the root of your condition, there are answers, if you're willing to look for them. There's no need to suffer in silence any longer!

Condition. It was such a harsh, clinical term. But then, most of the websites Adam had managed to find were exactly that: harsh. Clinical. And thoroughly depressing. Somehow, reading about surgical procedures and hydraulic penile implants was not improving his mood.

This wasn't for him. He wasn't some graying, middle-aged guy who needed a fistful of Viagra to get it up—he was a healthy, athletic, eighteen-year-old guy in his sexual prime. Tomorrow night was the first basketball game of the season, and everyone watching him sprint across the court would assume he was just as strong and virile as he looked—young, fit, with all his parts in working order. They'd never guess what was really going on—and, while he was on the subject, what the hell *was* going on?

Psychological causes can include stress, guilt, depression, and relationship problems.

Adam sighed, and pushed himself away from the computer. So he was messed up—like that was a surprise. A month ago, he'd been happy, relaxed, confident—then Beth and Kane had bashed the hell out of him, and now he didn't know who he was or what he could rely on.

The worst part was, in the past, Adam might have been able to swallow his pride and gone to Kane for help on this one. But now, he had no one to ask—no older brother, no trusted friend, and he hadn't talked to his father in years. And the Web was obviously useless.

No, he was on his own. There wasn't much he could do about his stress level, but he could at least reassure himself that the cause wasn't physical. He pulled an old *Playboy* out from beneath his mattress. It couldn't hurt to remind his body of what it was supposed to do.

After all—practice makes perfect.

"Yo, Gracie, this slaw isn't going to clean itself up!"

Harper winced. It was one thing when Adam called her "Gracie"—hearing the nickname in his lilting Southern accent reminded her of all those lazy summer afternoons they'd spent chasing each other around the backyard during childhood. Calling Harper "Gracie" had been the surest way for Adam to end the afternoon flat on his back with a wad of dirt stuffed in his mouth. (Though, even then, Harper had secretly loved it.) But when Mr. White, the diner manager, adopted his little pet name for her, it made her skin crawl—and it usually meant she had a particularly disgusting task awaiting her.

There was one week left of winter break, and Harper had planned to spend every spare minute at the diner, in hopes she could pay back her parents and quit by New Year's. It had seemed like a good idea in theory—but, in practice, it sucked. Especially today. *Merry Christmas to me*, she thought bitterly. *Ho, ho, ho.*

The laughter was appropriate—her life was a joke.

"And when you're done in there, Gracie, come back here and see me. I've got a little holiday treat for you."

"Yes, Mr. White," she called out as sweetly as she could, still determined to demonstrate that she could be a model employee even under the most heinous of circumstances.

White had promised to try her out on table service

today, since she was the only waitress forced to be there. But surprise, surprise, there were no customers. And so Harper was stuck spending Christmas with her new best friends, Mr. Mop and Mr. Bucket.

All this so she could pay her parents back for the ski trip? *WFS.* Right. She and Adam were supposed to be closer than ever by now—instead? They'd barely seen each other since getting back. Harper had, of course, been stuck at the diner. And she suspected that Adam was hiding out.

"Any day now, Gracie!"

Harper sighed and slogged toward White's "office," expecting to find him, as usual, with his feet kicked up on the desk, watching TV and picking his nose.

"Yes, Mr. White?" she said, affecting a subservient tone—it didn't come easy—and poking her head in. "What did you—ew!" Harper stopped short in the doorway. There was White. Way too much of him. As she'd expected, he was leaned back in his chair, his tree-trunk legs propped up on the desk, and the local public-access Christmas show blaring in the background. Just one problem. He was wearing a half-unbuttoned, cream-colored (or at least it looked like it used to be cream colored) shirt with sweat stains rimming his pits and a forest of chest hair poking through—and barely anything else. His thick, hairy legs were totally bare.

"What's your problem?" Mr. White growled.

"I—I—" Harper wasn't struck speechless very often, but then, how often was one trapped in a dingy back room with your hairy half-naked boss?

Still, she had an image to protect.

"What did you want, Mr. White?" she asked, maintaining a neutral tone. "I'm kind of busy out there."

"Just thought I'd give you your Christmas treat," White said, standing up.

A Christmas bonus? Dare she hope?

"You don't mind the *ensemble*, do you?" he asked with a sly grin that said he knew exactly how much she minded and was loving every minute of it. "I figured, since it was just the two of us . . ."

He approached her, shirt flapping against his bare legs, and Harper forced herself to stand her ground. *Is he really stupid enough to try something?* she wondered, swiftly calculating her options. He was big, yes—but also fat, slow, and stupid. She'd kick him in the balls, she decided, and then sue him for everything he had. This whole sordid episode could turn out to be a blessing in disguise.

"You see, round this time of year, I like to do a little something extra for my *special* employees," White explained, leering at her. "And you're one of my special employees, Gracie, aren't you?"

Steady, Harper prepared herself. *Wait for your moment.*

He lumbered toward her.

Closer, closer—

And then he was past her—bending down to get something in the corner. Harper watched in confusion. If she wasn't getting a bonus, and she wasn't getting sexually harassed, what the hell was she doing there?

"Here ya go!" White said triumphantly, standing up and tossing her a huge cloth sack. "Merry Christmas! Ho, ho, ho!"

"And this would be?" Harper wrinkled her nose and carefully set the bag on the ground. It smelled even worse than she did, and after a full day of mopping up the diner's bathrooms, that was saying a lot.

"It's laundry day, sweetie. As you can see—" He gestured toward his lower half. "I'm fresh outta pants. And—" here he leaned toward her and winked. "I'm *almost* out of unmentionables. If you know what I mean."

Harper recoiled from his hot, musty breath—and left the bag on the ground.

"I'll give you ten bucks to take care of this today. And if you do a good job, you can do it every week." He turned away from her and sat down at his desk again. "You're welcome."

"You want *me* to . . . do your laundry?" Harper could feel her good employee routine slipping through her fingers. "Are you kidding me?"

"Don't play coy with me, sweetie," White said, gazing

at the TV. "You may have a fancy name, but I know you need the cash." He chuckled. His laugh sounded like a garbage disposal. "Otherwise, why the hell would you be working here?"

Harper looked down at her feet. She could see a dirty gray piece of cotton peeking out of the top of the bag, but didn't want to think too hard about what it might be.

As she saw it, she had two options.

She could suck it up and take the laundry, prove to herself and the world that, contrary to popular opinion, Harper Grace didn't mind a little hard work once in a while. More importantly, she could pay back her parents that much faster, hastening the blessed day when she could finally walk out of the Nifty Fifties and never come back.

Or she could throw the bag of dirty underwear in his face and remind this loser that class and money were two separate things. He may have her beat on the latter, but where the former was concerned, he wasn't even worthy enough to shine her shoes.

"Oh, what, did I offend you?" he snarled. "*Bethie* never had a problem with it."

Harper rolled her eyes. Of course not. Little Miss Perfect let White walk all over her. Watching Beth get bawled out by the manager on a daily basis had been the only glimmer of pleasure in Harper's dark diner days.

What would Beth do?

Beth would probably accept the laundry gratefully, like a dog begging for scraps. *Beth* would smile sweetly and thank White for his Christmas "bonus." *Beth* would hold her nose, wash the underwear, and come back eager for more torture.

But Harper wasn't Beth—thank God. And it was about time people started to appreciate it.

She gave the bag of laundry a sharp kick, pretending her foot was connecting with something far more satisfying. It skidded across the room, strewing pants and underwear all over the office floor.

"Did you forget who you're dealing with here?" White growled, standing up. His face had turned a deep, purplish red.

"No—I forgot who *you* were dealing with," Harper corrected him. "But now I remember. And just in time."

"What's that supposed to mean?"

"It means I used to think your burgers were the nastiest thing in town—and then I met you. I quit."

Kaia was having a bad day. And the text didn't help.

Merry X-Mas! New Year's at Smash. Be there!—L

P.S. J's been asking about you. . . .

Lauren was the only one of her New York "friends" who kept in touch with regular—if brief—texts, tantalizing missives about the life Kaia had left behind. She was also the only one who didn't rub Kaia's face in the fact that she was missing everything. And "J" was, of course, Joshua Selznick, an ex-boyfriend with a model's build and a mogul's wallet.

Kaia fantasized for a moment about making a grand re-entry to New York for New Year's Eve. A private party at Smash, one of the hottest clubs in the city (and, conveniently, owned by a friend's father). A wild, all-night adventure filled with glitz and glamour, just like the old days . . .

New Year's had always been Kaia's favorite day of the year, but her father had all the power—and all the credit cards. Which meant she was stuck.

Unless . . .

Kaia was pretty sure her mother hated her, but there was one person she hated more: Kaia's father. Motherly affection might not be enough to win her approval for a trip back east—but maybe divorcée disgust would.

Such a strategy would, of course, mean contacting her mother—but sometimes it was necessary to make a small sacrifice for the greater good. Five minutes later, she was calling, half hoping there would be no answer.

"What is it?" came the harsh greeting.

"Mother?" Kaia asked tentatively.

"Oh, darling, it's you. I thought it was your *father*. similar numbers, you know. What is it, darling? I'm running out."

Kaia always marveled at the way her mother was able to take a word of apparent affection, like "darling," and somehow drain it of all warmth.

"It's been a while since we've talked," Kaia began.

"Oh, has it?" her mother asked distractedly.

"Four months, Mother," she pointed out.

"Oh no, I'm sure it hasn't been that long. Don't be melodramatic, darling. Well, it was nice to hear from you, but—"

"It's Christmas, Mother. Don't you even want to know how I am?" Kaia asked through gritted teeth.

"You sound lovely, darling. I assume your father's taking proper care of you."

"That's the thing—"

"I can only hope he's managing to be a better father than he was a husband. That bottom-feeding, scum-sucking . . . well, it's all in the past now. You're an angel for putting up with him."

"He's not around very much," Kaia admitted.

"Oh, then lucky you!" her mother exclaimed. "Now Kaia, I really must go, so—"

"I want to come home for a visit," Kaia blurted out.

"Dad won't let me—he's trying to keep me away from you. I—" Could she really get the words out with a straight face? "I miss you."

"Oh. Well, that won't do at all," Kaia's mother said calmly. "Who does your father think he is? Of course we'll plan a visit. Sometime soon, darling. Don't worry."

"I was thinking next weekend," Kaia said, hope rising.

Her mother laughed, a brittle, glassy trill that contained no real amusement or joy. "The weekend? Oh no, I'm far too busy. It's New Year's, you know."

She knew.

"And, of course, the rest of winter is just a mess—so many benefits to attend, you know how it is. But don't worry, we'll find some time—maybe in the spring. Or definitely in the summer."

"I'm moving back in the summer," Kaia pointed out coolly.

"Of course, of course—well, that's perfect, then. It's been lovely hearing from you, darling."

"But—"

"Let's chat again soon, shall we?"

And the line went dead.

Once upon a time, there was a shy young girl who wanted nothing more than to get out of her small-town life and see the world. She thought she'd be trapped in her tiny, boring house forever—and then one magical day, she opened a book. And the whole world changed.

Beth crumpled up the paper in disgust. It was so melodramatic, so cheesy—so lame. Almost as bad as her first effort:

My name is Beth Manning and I would love to attend (Your School Here). I am bright and energetic, the editor of my school newspaper, and I think I could make an excellent addition to (Your School Here).

Yeah, that was great. She might as well just submit a blank page with the heading "I am so boring, I have literally nothing to say for myself. Please admit me, anyway."

Out of desperation, she'd checked out *How to Write a Winning College Essay* from the Grace local library—hoping that even though it was written in 1987, it would still help her get over her writer's block. But so far? Nothing.

Be creative, the book urged. *Be yourself.* Unless "yourself" is weird or just totally bland, Beth thought dispiritedly. Then maybe it was best to be someone else.

She wondered if Harper was even bothering to fill out her applications (the way things were going, maybe she'd just steal Beth's). How might her essay read? "I'm Harper Grace, and I'll be attending your school next year, because I want to—and, let's be honest, I always get what I want."

But Beth was too sickened by the thought of Harper to continue down that road—because that led to Harper-and-Adam, and *that* usually led to her leaning over the toilet, waiting for a wave of nausea to pass.

Be honest, the book kept saying. *Talk about what you want, what you're proud of. Why you're special.*

But how was she supposed to do that in an essay when she couldn't do it in real life? She didn't seem to know how to be honest about what she wanted anymore—not with Kane, not with Adam, not with herself. And she had no idea who she was anymore. Before, it had been easy. Beth, the good girl. Everyone knew it. But now? She smiled, thinking of how much she'd enjoyed tormenting Harper at the diner, how she'd managed to convince Mr. White to saddle her with the dreaded Christmas shift. Was that the work of a good girl?

Maybe honesty was the answer after all.

> *I used to be the perfect student, the perfect daughter, the perfect girlfriend. Then my boyfriend dumped me, I tanked the SATs—and now I don't know who I am or what I'm doing. I do know that I still want a future, and I want it away from here—and that if you take a chance on me, it just might pay off.*

Well . . . it was a start.

Just not a good one.

Mercifully, the phone rang, and although Beth had promised herself no breaks until she'd finished a draft, she leaped to answer it.

"Hey—what are you doing?"

Beth wondered—was it strange that she'd been dating Kane for over a month and a part of her still found it a little bizarre that he was a part of her life. Something about the casual intimacy still threw her off. She just wished she knew why. "Working." She sighed. "Sort of."

"It's Christmas," he pointed out.

"Don't remind me. My brothers are on a massive sugar high from all the candy canes. From the sound of it, they're having some kind of shouting contest."

"I know, I can hear it."

"What? Where—" Beth went over to her window and looked out. Sure enough, Kane was lounging against a tree. He smirked at the sight of her and gave her a languid wave. "What are you doing out there?" she asked, laughing. "Do you want to come in?"

"Actually . . ." And in that pause, Beth was reminded of how much Kane hated her house. He'd never said anything, of course, but whenever he stepped inside, she could tell it got to him—the noise, the clutter, the size (or lack thereof). It didn't usually bother her, but when Kane was there, it felt like a zoo—she was just glad he didn't think of her as one of the animals.

"I was hoping you could come out and play," he said, affecting an innocent little-boy voice.

Beth giggled.

"I've got all this stuff to do, my essay—"

"Just for a little break? I'm booooored," he whined.

"Well . . . I do have to give you your Christmas present," she mused. "And maybe if it were just a quick break."

"You can't resist me," Kane boasted and, giving her another wave, ended the call. Beth shook her head. For whatever reason, it was true.

Victory. He'd gotten her away from her work and out of the house—but was it normal that those be such major triumphs? Never having had a real girlfriend before, Kane didn't really have any idea how often you were supposed to see her or what you were supposed to do when you did—and with Adam still pouting, he didn't have anyone to ask.

While he hadn't gotten everything—or really, anything—he'd wanted out of Beth up in the mountains, Kane was no quitter, not when it came to beautiful women. And then there was the disconcerting fact that he was actually enjoying her company—fully clothed, out of bed, inches of space between them, and he still wanted her around. It didn't make any sense.

Not that there weren't a few occasional perks.

"Mmm," he breathed when they broke from a long kiss hello. "You smell amazing. What is that?"

"Um." She blushed and tucked her hair behind her ears—a nervous habit that, Kane was ashamed to admit, he was beginning to find adorable. "Shampoo?"

"So what's this I hear about a present?" he asked, taking her hand and leading her down the sidewalk.

She gave him a playful shove. "You're such a little kid sometimes—can't you wait?"

"I'm nothing if not patient," he pointed out, only half joking. After all, she had no idea how long he'd waited around for her. Was still waiting.

"It's just something little," she said hesitantly, pulling a small wrapped box from her coat pocket. "I hope you like it."

"You've got nothing to worry about, babe," he said, slinging an arm around her. "I'll love it."

He unwrapped the gift. Inside the box lay a CD case, with a picture of the two of them together taped to the cover.

Old-fashioned and total cheese.

"I . . . I put together some songs I thought you'd like," she explained. "You know, music that made me think of you."

"Oh, Beth." He slipped the CD into his pocket and gave her a kiss. It was so hokey, so painfully sincere, so . . . Beth. "I love it." And it wasn't a *total* lie. "I can't wait to get home and listen to it." Except for that part. Kane shuddered to think what kind of lovey-dovey crap Beth might have included.

"Your present isn't quite ready yet," Kane explained, though the truth was, he'd forgotten. It had been a long time since he'd needed to buy someone a Christmas present.

"Kane, you don't need to get me anything else," she complained, fondling the blue cashmere tucked around her neck. "This scarf is so beautiful, and so expensive—"

He cut her off with a kiss. "Your gift is coming," he said firmly, "and you'll love it." Whatever it turned out to be. "So, what are you up to for the rest of the day?"

"Kane, it's Christmas. I've got all this family stuff."

"Of course you do," he said heartily. "I knew that." Though, actually, the idea hadn't occurred to him. Family. Another stupid tradition he'd forgotten. Along with Christmas lights and presents.

"What about you? Are you and your father . . . ? Or do you want to come home with me?"

"No," he said hastily. "I've got family stuff of my own." If "family stuff" meant beer and cold pizza alone, wondering if his father would remember it was Christmas and actually come home that night.

For a second, Kane was tempted. He hadn't had a real Christmas, a family Christmas, since his mother died. After that, it had been just him and his brother, getting drunk, laughing at the loser carolers, and then, when Aaron went off to college, it was just him. Beth's Christmas, on the other hand, was probably straight out of a Hallmark commercial: stockings hanging from the mantel, wrapping paper all over the floor, disgusting displays of Christmas spirit. And for a second, Kane was tempted. Why not let Beth play Tiny Tim to his Scrooge, teach him the true meaning of blah, blah, blah.

The fact that he was getting bored just imagining it? Probably not a great sign.

Maybe he was too old for Christmas. Maybe he was just over it.

"Are you sure?" Beth asked dubiously. "Because we'd love to have you. I'd love for you to be there."

Kane sighed. Whenever he was around her, he felt like letting down his guard. It was dangerous—and yet strangely appealing. Like a drug he couldn't stay away from.

"I'm sure," he told her, cupping her chin in his hands and tipping her face up toward his for a farewell kiss. Kane believed in drugs—but he didn't believe in losing control. Which meant it was time to go.

She had known the bar would be open on Christmas. It was just that kind of place. Dingy, graying, scattered with familiar faces, the faithful pilgrims who came in almost every night, looking for—something. They never found it. But they kept coming back.

It was a bar for people who had nowhere else to go—especially on Christmas.

And it was Powell's favorite.

After the pleasant chat with her mother, Kaia had needed to get out of the house. Have some fun. And she'd known just where to go. She hadn't heard from Powell since he'd returned from the ski trip, but she was sure it didn't mean anything. So he'd had a little fun, and a little ski bunny, while he was away. It's a free country. It's not like she hadn't had a little fun of her own. That night with Reed might have been an aberration, a freakish fluke that could never be repeated—but it had definitely been hot.

Playtime was over. And Kaia had no doubt that Powell was just waiting for the perfect moment to summon her. The bunny was—must be—history. After all, you don't trade in caviar for tuna fish, and Kaia was caviar all the way.

Still, Kaia decided, it couldn't hurt to show her face, remind him of what he should have been missing. Besides, it was Christmas, and he deserved a holiday treat. Whoever said "'tis better to give than to receive" had obviously never met Kaia Sellers.

She'd dressed herself in red and green from head to toe: red backless top, green peasant skirt, red kitten heels, and, to top it off, a red velvet ribbon tied around her waist.

Aren't you going to unwrap your present? She rehearsed the line in her head, loving the way the words sounded, and could already see the look on his face. He'd feign annoyance, of course—she was supposed to wait for him to beckon her, that's what they'd agreed on. Those were the rules. No speaking in public, no dating other guys, no obligations, and, most of all, no surprises.

According to the rules, she should be sitting home, biding her time, waiting for him to call.

But Kaia had never been too good with rules.

She almost walked by the bar—from the outside, it was nothing but a narrow gray cement block with a small, dark, unmarked door. She swung it open and stood in the doorway, waiting for her eyes to adjust.

He wasn't at his normal stool at the end of the bar, nose buried in a book. Instead, he was tucked into one of the few booths lining the wall. He was sipping a glass of red wine. And he wasn't alone.

The ski bunny, Kaia thought with disgust. It had to be. She was blond, lithe, limber, her face radiating a gentle, trusting imbecility—and she was perched on Powell's lap, nuzzling his neck.

Other girls might have confronted him, or started to cry—or just slunk away into the night. But Kaia was better than that. So she just stood there and watched. Waited.

Until, finally, he noticed her. While the ski bunny

gave his ear a tongue massage, Powell's eyes met Kaia's, his expression unreadable. Was that guilt in his eyes? Anger? Dismissal? Fear?

Kaia didn't know—and didn't really care. What Jack Powell felt, what he wanted, was beside the point. She'd let him think he was in charge of their little "relationship"—a nice power trip for him that didn't cost her anything. But that was over now.

Powell liked rules so much? Maybe it was time to give him a new set—show him whose game they were really playing. Kaia gave Powell—who hadn't taken his eyes off her, despite the squirming blonde in his lap—a slow, cruel smile. Then turned around and left the bar.

Calm down, she instructed herself, taking a few deep breaths and forcing the anger away. She couldn't get emotionally involved, not if she was going to win this little battle of the wills.

And she was going to win.

She always did.

chapter eight

THE PHONE RANG TWICE BEFORE HE PICKED IT UP—just enough time for Harper to change her mind, almost hang up, then reconsider once again. She'd been over and over this in her head and had concluded that, humiliating as it was, she just had no other choice.

If she was careful, and lucky, her parents would never find out that she'd quit her job—but she still owed them $300, and there were no job openings anywhere in town. So unless she wanted to sell off all her possessions—or her organs—she was stuck. Trapped. With only one very unappealing escape route.

"Grace—to what do I owe this pleasure?"

Kane. Supercilious, haughty, but loaded. All she needed to do was ask him—

But Harper found she couldn't quite get the words out. Maybe if she did it fast, like a Band-Aid. "I need . . . a . . . favor."

Or painfully slow could work, too.

"I'm listening."

Harper silently cursed her parents for sticking her in this position. If they'd only given her the money for the ski trip in the first place, no strings attached, she wouldn't be stuck groveling like this.

Things could be worse, she reminded herself—she could be abasing herself in front of Kaia. Or worse, Beth. Kane was an ass, and he would probably hold this over her head until graduation, but on the plus side, she didn't really care what he thought of her. After all, it was Kane. She'd helped him steal his best friend's girlfriend—so who was he to judge?

"I need to borrow some money," she said flatly. "Three hundred dollars."

"Whoa," he whistled. "Dare I ask why?"

"No."

"And when will I be getting this loan repaid, with interest?"

Good question.

"I don't know."

Bad answer.

"Now Grace, pray tell, why would I possibly do this for you?"

"Because you've got no reason not to?" Harper suggested, knowing that, for Kane, it was usually as good a reason as any. And certainly more palatable than throwing herself on his mercy. "Because you might find it amusing to have me in your debt?"

"Ah, Grace, you know me so well," he marveled, and Harper breathed a silent sigh of relief. "So when should I deliver this windfall?" Kane asked. "Tonight?"

"Only if you're going to be at the basketball game," Harper said, rolling her eyes. "I have to be there to 'support my man.'" Vomit. Beth had always been Adam's eager good luck charm and one-woman cheering section. So Harper was forcing herself to play along—but lame high school sporting events were so not her thing.

"Just save some of that school spirit for me," Kane requested.

"You?"

"Haven't you heard? I'm back, baby. Starting point guard, making my varsity debut."

"*You?*" Harper repeated.

"What? Can't I lend my many talents to our school's proudest team? Besides, have you seen those cheerleaders?"

"What are you really up to, Kane?"

"What's the money for, Grace?"

"Point taken." She knew it was stupid, but being too poor to pay for the ski trip was just too embarrassing. Better Kane should think she had some dark, nefarious purposes. Keeping up an image was hard work. "So, you can give me a check tonight?"

"I'll be there," Kane promised. "And so will my money. Just one thing, Harper."

"What's that?" she asked, suddenly wary. Kane never called her by her first name.

"This is a lot of money."

"I know, and I'll pay it back when—"

"In the meantime," Kane said, "you owe me."

"I just said, I'll pay you—"

"No, not money," he corrected her. "A favor. Quid pro quo. And when I call it in, you'd better be ready to deliver."

Miranda answered the phone with a weary sigh. "No," she said, before Harper could speak.

"It'll be fun, Rand, I swear."

"Now, where have I heard that before?" But Miranda was smiling. She loved those rare occasions when Harper was forced to beg, and she had to admit, it was good to feel needed again, special . . . but that didn't mean she was giving in. "Like I told you the last time you called, and the time before that, I'm not going. Do you know how boring basketball is?"

"Um, yes," Harper replied in a "duh" voice. "Why do you think I need you to come with me? Besides, you know that's not the real reason you won't go."

"Nice of you to throw that back in my face, Harper," Miranda said in annoyance. She picked up her tablet so she could check her e-mail. See if *he* had written. "You *know* why I can't go."

"Maybe if you're nice to him, he'll let you try on his costume," Harper suggested, choking back laughter.

Miranda groaned, but had to laugh along. It was funny, when you thought about it, that the only guy who'd been interested in her all year had turned out to be the school mascot, a bumbling loser who hadn't minded dressing up like a big green cactus as the whole school jeered at him.

Although . . . it had been kind of nice, having someone like Greg dote on her for a week or two. And he hadn't been *that* big a loser. At least, not until she'd blown him off and he'd turned into the king of the assholes. Miranda shook her head, trying to knock all thoughts of Greg out of her brain. This was *exactly* why she couldn't go to the game.

Besides, she thought, opening up her e-mail, she had other things on her mind. Better things—better guys.

"Kane will be there," Harper wheedled. "He's on the team now."

Kane Geary, running up and down the court in those tight gym shorts . . .

"I don't care," Miranda lied. "Besides, what happened to your whole 'forget about Kane' mantra?"

The tablet *dinged.*

You have new mail.

It was him.

"I know what I said, Rand, but you never know, and—"

"I know you're desperate, Harper, but this is just pathetic," Miranda told her, distractedly scanning the e-mail. ReadItAndWeep was online—and wanted her IM name so they could chat. The e-mail had been sent only a few minutes earlier—would he still be there? Could she risk a live chat? Could she risk missing it? "Look, I've got to go, I have stuff to do."

"What stuff? It's winter break! Come on, for me?"

"Bye, Harper. Have fun at the game!"

"But—"

Miranda hung up on her. It was rude, she knew—but she also knew Harper, and this was the only way to get her to shut up. Besides, she was in a hurry.

Spitfire: Hey, U still there?

ReadItAndWeep: Thought you'd never ask. How goes it?

Spitfire: You live here—how do you think?

ReadItAndWeep: B.O.R.I.N.G.

Spitfire: Bingo.

But she was lying—she was far from bored. "Talking" to ReadItAndWeep was, in fact, the highlight of her day. His e-mails had been so witty and articulate—and as they frantically typed back and forth to each other, she was pleased to discover that his real-time persona was even better.

ReadItAndWeep: NEVER seen Annie Hall? Unbelievable!

Spitfire: YOU've never seen Bring It On.

ReadItAndWeep: Not the same thing.

Spitfire: Right—your movie sucks. Mine = a modern classic.

ReadItAndWeep: You dare to insult the master? Blasphemy! You ready to dodge the lightning bolts?

Miranda laughed out loud. She felt like she could talk to him for hours—even if he did worship at the altar of Woody Allen.

Spitfire: I think I'll risk it.

ReadItAndWeep: A risk-taker. I'm impressed. You up for another one?

Spitfire: ???

ReadItAndWeep: I think we should meet. Face-to-face. What do you think?

ReadItAndWeep: Spitfire?

ReadItAndWeep: Hello?

ReadItAndWeep: Anyone out there?

Miranda stared at the keyboard, frozen with fear. She couldn't bring herself to answer.

But she couldn't bring herself to log off.

Kaia winced at the booming, off-key "music" emerging from the marching band, which had just wound its way around the court and was now dispersing its members through the bleachers. The better to deafen the audience, apparently.

It was her first public school sporting event—and it was just as loud, tedious, and tacky as it always looked in the movies. Cheerleaders stumbling all over themselves, crazed fans with their faces painted in the school colors—rust and mud—and down on the court, a bunch of beautiful boys running aimlessly up and down the hardwood floor, getting all hot and bothered about a stupid ball going through a stupid hoop. Pretty to watch—but such a waste of all that sweaty exertion.

So what was she doing there?

It had seemed unlikely enough for Harper to invite her along—even Harper seemed surprised when Kaia actually agreed to go.

But Harper had said those magic words: "Everyone will be there." And, when pushed to clarify, had explained that "everyone" included all the Haven High students—*and* all the teachers. Which meant everyone's favorite British bachelor would be in attendance—thus so would Kaia.

Unfortunately, they were ten minutes into the game, Powell was nowhere in sight, and Kaia could already tell this night was going to drag on forever. To her credit, Harper seemed none too riveted to her boyfriend's pyrotechnic display of athletic prowess. She could barely keep her eyes on the court.

Then both girls yawned at the same instant and, catching sight of each other, burst into grateful laughter. Boredom loves company.

"Want to take a little break?" Harper suggested. "I could really use a cigarette."

At this point, Kaia could really use a lobotomy. But a cigarette would do.

"I'm already out the door," she said, climbing down off her bleacher seat and leading the way through the crowd.

Harper had been right: It seemed everyone in town was there. And there, in the front row, looking bored out of his mind, was Powell. Briefly, she considered crossing the room and spicing things up for him—certainly an embarrassing scene in front of this crowd would go a small way toward paying him back for Ski-ette. But it would also spell the end of them—and Kaia wasn't ready to say goodbye just yet. Even from a distance, he stood out, a splash of wild color against the dullness of the crowd, sex appeal radiating off him in visible waves. Harper caught her staring and sighed appreciatively.

"I know exactly what you're thinking," she said.

If only she did. Snagging a guy as fine as Powell should at the very least have secured Kaia some bragging rights.

"Let's go," Kaia urged her, forcing her gaze away from Powell's sculpted face and broad chest. She'd deal with him later.

They ducked out a side door and found a dark, empty spot against the side of the gym, lounging in the shadows between two flickering streetlamps.

"Your boyfriend won't miss you in there?" Kaia asked, lighting up and offering Harper a cigarette.

"God, no. This game's been all he could talk about for days. I'm the last thing on his mind."

"You don't look too happy about it," Kaia observed. "That newlywed glow wearing off so soon?"

"Adam and I are *fine*. Perfect, in fact."

Yeah, right. But no way was Kaia letting Harper walk off to pout, leaving her alone without a companion—or a car. What would she do then? Watch the game?

"Whatever," she said agreeably, backing off. "Glad I could help you get what you wanted." It couldn't hurt to remind Harper just whose idea the whole thing had been—without Kaia, Harper and Kane would still be standing with their noses pressed up against the window, watching Adam and Beth's nauseating displays of affection. "And, you know, that it all worked out. Happily ever after and all that. Personally, I'd be a little bored."

"Well, maybe that's because you—" Harper began hotly, then, looking thoughtful, stopped and leaned back against the wall. "Maybe it's this town," she admitted, taking a long drag from the cigarette. "It's enough to drain the life out of anything."

She could say it was the town, but Kaia suspected that the real problem lay a little closer to home, even if Harper didn't realize it. Adam, after all, *was* the town—Grace's good ol' boy, one of those guys whose life would peak in high school. He'd spend the rest of his life reminiscing about the good old days, not noticing that his beer belly was growing at exactly the same rate that his hair was falling out. Harper didn't look the type to be satisfied with being the good little wifey to a has-been local hero, serving chips 'n' dip to his poker buddies. Why else was she out in the parking lot smoking when she should have been inside, cheering on her man?

But now wasn't the time to bring all that up. Harper wanted to blame her existential angst on the town, and Kaia was only too happy to play along.

"Tell me about it," she complained. "You would think having time off from school would be a good thing, but it just makes it all the more obvious that there's *nothing* to do. I thought I'd be getting out of here for New Year's, but no such luck. Looks like I'll be ringing in the New Year with some hillbillies and flat beer."

Harper laughed. "I'm officially offended by that—but God, what I wouldn't give for a real New Year's, for once. The best we usually get is some illegal firecrackers down at the town dump."

"Pathetic," they said together, rolling their eyes in unison.

"You know what?" Harper asked, spinning to face Kaia, her eyes wide with excitement. "You have a fabulous house. You should have a party."

"Me? I don't know anyone around here."

"But I know everyone—I could help."

"You don't even like me," Kaia pointed out. "And the feeling is mutual."

"True. But you have to admit," Harper said, giving Kaia a sly grin, "we've made a damn good team."

"I'll think about it." The idea of a horde of drunken high schoolers invading Daddy dearest's pristine mansion did have a certain appeal. *Architectural Digest* would likely be somewhat less interested in a feature profile once Kaia had turned the Sellers house into Animal House.

"I'm starving," Harper complained suddenly, breaking into Kaia's reverie of filial delinquency. "How much longer do you think this is going to take?"

"You're the one dating the quarterback."

"Center. I think."

"Whatever—go in there and get him to speed it up a little."

"I don't think that's how it works . . . but I wonder if anyone would notice if we left for a while and found something to eat. . . ."

"Hold that thought," Kaia said, getting the glimmerings of a brilliant idea. "I think I can do you one better."

She whipped out her phone and, taking a few steps away, dialed the number she now had programmed in. "Hello, Guido's? I need to place an order for delivery."

Done. In twenty minutes, their steaming hot pizza would arrive—along with one steaming hot delivery boy.

Now for step two. She dialed again.

"What?" That British accent was so sexy, even when he was sounding annoyed. Especially then.

"I'm outside the gym," Kaia said tersely, knowing he'd be fuming. And knowing he wouldn't hang up. "We need to talk."

Adam cursed under his breath as the ball failed to so much as graze the basket. Airball. He was playing like shit tonight. And he knew exactly why.

"Yo, Kane, good one!" the power forward yelled as Kane stole the ball and landed an easy layup. Another one. There was only one star on the court tonight—and Adam wanted more than anything to bash his cocky, preening face in. It was, to say the least, hurting his concentration.

"Morgan, take a break for a while!" the new coach shouted, sending Lubowski, a lumbering second stringer out in his place. Adam slouched down on the bench with a sigh. If even *Lubowski* was playing better than him, things were worse than he'd thought.

"Dude, looks like you've got some competition this year," the guy next to him on the bench observed. He gestured to the cheerleaders, who were obviously slobbering all over Kane's every move. "Usually they're all about you, man."

"Thanks for the heads up," Adam snapped.

"Hey, take it easy," the guy—Bill, or maybe Will—

said cheerfully. "It's not so bad on the bench. I should know, I've been here for years."

So Kane was out there winning the game and Adam was stuck on the bench with some guy who'd never actually touched the ball. He knew it shouldn't matter—he'd always claimed that it didn't matter, the trophies, the news clippings, the girls—but who was he kidding?

He ignored Bill/Will and turned around to scan the crowd, searching for Harper, hoping that the sight of her would remind him of something real, something important, remind him that the game was just that, and nothing more.

But Harper was lost in the crowd somewhere, and the only familiar face he saw was Beth's. He watched her until her wandering eyes met his, then quickly looked away. Back to the court. Back to Kane, who was passing by the bench in a slow jog up the court.

"Nice try tonight," he called in a low voice. "Maybe this weekend I can give you some pointers."

Adam knew he should fight it, should *make* the coach put him back in the game, show Kane he was unfazed. Show Kane that he couldn't have everything, that he didn't always win.

But, instead, he stayed quiet, stayed seated.

The thing was, Kane *did* always win—and Adam was so tired of losing. Maybe it was just better not to fight.

Harper didn't know how they'd had such good fortune, but she was only too happy to enjoy it. When Jack Powell had come storming out of the gym, his face clouded with irritation and a barely contained rage, Harper had been grateful for the quick peek, but assumed he would just walk on by. Instead, inexplicably, he'd stopped to chat with Harper and Kaia—and, just like that, their long and boring night began looking up.

Not that Harper cared about the next lesson in French class or the long-delayed plans to renovate the cafeteria, or whatever it was Kaia was so cheerfully babbling about. Harper was just content to enjoy the scenery. Then again, maybe that was Mr. Powell's motive as well, since he seemed even more disenchanted with the topics of conversation than she was. And he kept sneaking sidelong glances at Harper as if waiting for her to say something. Do something.

Mr. Powell was the first new teacher Haven High had seen in years—and, thanks to his age and obvious sex appeal, rumors had been flying for months. Could they be true? Could the dashing young teacher have his eye on one of his students? Could it be that he was waiting, plotting, hoping to get Harper alone, for a very special student-teacher conference?

Not that she'd ever do anything about it, of course.

There was Adam, for one thing—and, for another, hooking up with a teacher was definitely on the wrong side of the sexy/sleazy divide. But that didn't mean she couldn't preen a little under his surreptitious attention, right? Flirt a little, give him the full Harper Grace treatment? You certainly couldn't fault his taste.

"I should be getting back," he finally said, aiming his piercing stare at Kaia. (*Probably wishing she'd go away and leave us alone*, Harper thought smugly.) "Unless there's anything else you ladies need."

"Oh, Mr. Powell, please stay," Kaia simpered, "I really need to talk to you about these new textbook standards you were telling us about. It's so fascinating."

Pathetic, Harper thought. Could she be any more obvious, throwing herself at him like that?

"Well, maybe I didn't mention it before," Mr. Powell began after a pause, "but it's very important that these textbooks follow the *rules*. Otherwise, the school board will just toss them out. After all, one textbook's just as good as another. Don't you think, Harper?"

"What?" Like she was listening. Who could pay attention when he had such adorable dimples? "Uh, sure."

"Oh, I don't know about that," Kaia countered. "I would think that if a textbook were something really new and different, it might be able to make its own rules. And you know, if one school district didn't want it, another one would be sure to snatch it up."

"And I suppose that in this charming little scenario, the first school board would be sorry?" Mr. Powell asked drily.

"It would feel like quite the fool," Kaia said, imitating his British accent. "It would probably want the textbook back, but, sadly, it would be too late."

Suddenly, Kaia peered into the darkness and waved at an approaching figure who'd just gotten out of his car. "There's our pizza!" she chirped.

"You ordered a pizza?" Harper and Mr. Powell asked together, equally incredulous.

"You *said* you were hungry," Kaia reminded her. "I'll go reel him in," she added, skipping off toward the pizza guy, who was wandering aimlessly in the darkness.

As Kaia's silhouette faded briefly out of sight, Harper turned toward Mr. Powell and realized he was looking intently at her, as if trying to figure something out.

"Well, well, well," she said, her heart pounding in her chest, but her voice steady and light. "Alone at last."

Kaia approached Reed and greeted him with a silent wave. She took the pizza in one hand and, ignoring his confused look, slipped a possessive arm around his waist and led him back toward Harper and Powell.

The pizza had been late, but no matter—she'd been amusing herself by torturing Powell with meaningless small talk, knowing how it made his skin crawl to be seen with her.

"Hi, guys!" she said perkily as she and Reed approached. "Look who brought us the pizza."

Reed—who, despite his greasy GUIDO's T-shirt and baggy jeans, was looking incredibly tasty—extended a hand toward Harper. Kaia forced herself not to notice the way his unruly long hair brushed the lids of his dark, bottomless eyes. After all, this was business.

"I'm Reed," he said slowly, as if every word had to battle its way through the haze of pot lying between his brain and his mouth. "I think we—"

"They don't care who you are," Kaia interrupted him. She handed the pizza off to Harper, then put her arms around Reed's waist. He was so trim—but so firm. "But *I'm* glad you came," she said, gazing up at Reed—every inch of her attuned to Powell, a few steps away.

"I, uh, didn't know you two knew each other," Harper stuttered.

Kaia touched her hand to Reed's stubbly cheek and glanced over her shoulder.

"Oh, we've gotten to know each other really well these last few days," she said, narrowing her eyes at Powell. "We've gotten very *close*."

"I should go," Reed said, disengaging himself. He pocketed the money Kaia had given him for the pizza and took a step backward.

What's wrong with him? Kaia thought angrily. *Can't he see that I'm throwing myself at him? What is this, performance anxiety? He's only into me when we're in some freakish, secluded spot all by ourselves?*

She shivered at the memory. She'd promised herself she wouldn't think of those nights again.

Focus, she reminded herself. *And don't let him go.*

"Reed," she called sweetly, and he turned around again to face her. "You forgot your tip."

She stepped toward him and gave him a soft, chaste kiss on the lips.

Behind her, she heard a gasp. And knew without looking that it wasn't Harper. Perfect.

Then Reed put his arms around her and pulled her closer, and their chaste kiss turned into something else. Long, deep, his fingers crawling down her back, their bodies fusing—and then it was over.

Reed walked away, into the shadows, and Kaia watched him go. Watched long after his figure had disappeared.

Eventually, behind her, Jack Powell cleared his throat.

Kaia had almost forgotten he was there.

chapter nine

"COME ON, KANE, WHERE ARE WE GOING?" BETH peered out the window at the desert landscape speeding by as if the bumpy, arid land on either side would offer some kind of clue. But there was nothing out there but scraggly Joshua trees, distant hills, and the occasional billboard for an XXX strip club a mere fifty miles away.

"How many times have you asked me that?" Kane asked, glancing over at her with bemusement and then turning back to the road.

Counting this morning, when he'd begged her to ditch her applications for the day and take a road trip? Counting the hour in the grocery store buying water and picnic preparations, and then the hour and a half on the road?

"About thirty," she guessed, blushing.

"Add another zero and you'll be closer," Kane said, shaking his head. "And what have I told you each and every time?"

"'It's a surprise,'" she quoted dutifully.

"So? Can't you come up with a new question?"

"Okay." Beth smiled mischievously. "Are we there yet?"

As the sound of laughter filled the car, Beth leaned her head back against the leather seat and closed her eyes. Maybe Kane was right and she should just relax, see where the day took them. She'd never been very good with surprises—but, thanks to Kane, she was learning.

"Patience," Kane counseled. "All good things come to those who wait. At least . . ." he put his hand on her leg and began rubbing her inner thigh. "You did."

Powell's apartment was worth about what he was paying for it. Which meant it was slightly cozier than a soggy cardboard box, with better insulation. The rusted aluminum siding covering the face of the house was slathered with peeling grayish-yellow paint—and the inside wasn't much more appealing. Powell's tiny monthly rent check paid for a bedroom about twice the size of his bed, a bathroom (leaky shower, no tub), and a living room/dining room/entry hall/kitchenette area that offered slightly more elbow room than the front seat of a car.

In only a few short weeks, Kaia had memorized the shape and position of every water stain on the avocado-green wallpaper, and every crack in the vomit-colored ceiling. The only thing she wasn't sick of yet was the view, and that was only because she'd never seen it—Powell made her stay away from the windows.

Or, at least, he had in the past. Lying back on his bed and watching him pace angrily back and forth across the small room, Kaia could almost feel the balance of power shifting in her direction.

"A pizza boy, Kaia?"

He couldn't get over it. Not just the idea of her in someone else's arms, but the idea that he'd been sharing her with a delivery boy, of all people. Powell was a snob at heart. It was something they had in common.

"A ski bunny, *Jack*?"

"So this is revenge, then? A little juvenile, don't you think?"

Kaia just shrugged. "Not everything I do is about you," she pointed out. "Sometimes I like to have a little fun."

"I told you, no high school boys," Powell snapped. "We agreed on that at the outset."

Kaia sat up and leaned forward, and in spite of himself, Powell's eyes followed her cleavage.

"You want me to go?" she asked, pretending to gather her belongings. "Fine with me."

"I suppose"—Powell sat down beside her—"I could be persuaded to give you a second chance." He began kneading his hands against her bare shoulders, exploring the contours of her neck, her back. "Provided you give up your pizza boy."

"And you?" Kaia asked, walking her fingers lightly up his bare arm. "Will you be giving up Snow White?"

"That wasn't part of our deal," Powell said.

Kaia slowly unbuttoned her shirt, revealing a lacy red bra. "New deal. You play, I play."

"I don't like to share," Powell said in a low, dangerous voice. He wrapped his arms around her from behind and squeezed tight. Almost too tight.

"What a coincidence," Kaia whispered, leaning her head back against him so that her lips were nearly pressed against his face. "Neither do I."

Harper didn't believe in failure. So when her parents took off for a day of antiquing (read: spending too much for other people's discarded clutter at roadside flea markets), she was ready. Without a job to stand in her way, she had all the time in the world to set things up—and when Adam finally showed up, she knew he'd be blown away.

"Uh, Harper?" he asked, hesitating in her doorway. "What's going on?"

"Do you like it?" she asked eagerly, stepping aside so he could get the full view. "I did it for you. Well . . . for us."

"It's, uh . . . wow."

With only a few hours of hard work (Harper's least favorite kind), the living room had been transformed into a winter wonderland. The electric fireplace roared and crackled as if it held a real pile of logs, the walls were dotted with crudely cut paper snowflakes, and Bing Crosby's "White Christmas" blared from the stereo. (Good thing her parents were addicted to cheesy holiday music—they had a whole shelf of this crap.)

"But . . . why?" Adam asked as Harper guided him to a couch piled high with blankets. She'd turned the air conditioner on full blast, and offered him a steaming cup of hot chocolate.

"I thought we were just hanging out, Harper—you know, low-key. After last night at the game—"

"Oh, don't think about that," Harper said quickly, ruffling his hair. The last thing he needed now was to dwell on his inadequacy.

"I thought we could both use a little treat," Harper explained. "After all, the ski trip"—how to put it delicately?—"didn't really go as planned. So I thought we could have a 'do-over.'"

"A 'do-over'?"

"You remember, when we used to play four-square in the driveway, and you'd try to cheat—"

"I never cheated," he protested indignantly.

"Whatever you say," she said, leaning against him. "Anyway, if something, or *someone*, interrupted normal play, we'd just forget it ever happened and start that turn all over again. A do-over."

"Have I ever told you you're adorable?" Adam asked, and she knew she had him.

"Not nearly enough."

It was the romantic getaway from hell. Or rather, *to* hell, if hell was anything like the dark, cluttered space with half-empty pizza boxes dotting the floor, also known as Kane's brother's apartment. Aaron Geary and a few of his friends sat around the room on makeshift chairs—mostly milk crates and rusty lawn furniture—while Kane and Beth shared a sagging beanbag that was leaking tiny white plastic beads all over the floor.

What more could a girl ask for?

"No thanks," she said firmly as a giant bong—the first she'd ever seen in person—was again passed around the circle. Beth had been trying all afternoon to breathe shallowly so as to ingest as little of the pot fumes as possible. Still, the smoke was giving her a raging headache. And her patience was wearing thin.

"Can I talk to you for a second?" she hissed at Kane, who was bopping his head along to the Jimmy Buffett sound track—on an endless loop—totally oblivious to her discomfort.

She pulled him up off the beanbag chair and led him down a dark hallway into Aaron's bedroom.

"Have fun, lovebirds!" Aaron shouted. "I just changed the sheets!"

What luck.

Beth grimaced and tried not to touch anything in the room—a thick layer of dust covered everything, from the rickety futon to the dilapidated dresser. A few empty vodka bottles served as the only decoration.

"Having a good time, babe?" Kane asked, leaning in to her. Unsteady on his feet from an afternoon overflowing with beer and pot, he almost toppled over.

Beth recoiled from his touch and turned her head away from his foul pot breath. "No, I'm not having fun," she informed him testily. "Why did you bring me here?"

"What do you mean?" Kane sat down on the futon and tried, unsuccessfully, to pull her down onto his lap. "It's a road trip—it was supposed to be fun."

"Kane, you dragged me out here into the middle of nowhere to waste the day in your brother's pit of an apartment with his burnout friends. How, exactly, was that supposed to be fun?"

"Lighten up, Manning—do you always have to be so uptight?"

From the look in his bloodshot eyes, she could tell that it had just slipped out—but she could also tell that he'd meant it.

Kane stood and tried to put his arms around her, but she pushed him away.

"I'm leaving," Beth said, with as much dignity as she could muster. "It's obvious you'll have more *fun* without me." She meant it to sound cruel, angry—but maybe it was true. Maybe she *was* uptight. Hadn't Adam always implied as much, even if he'd never come right out and said it? Why couldn't she just hang out and enjoy herself for a few hours, turn her brain off, relax?

"Beth, wait," he begged, grabbing her arms and pulling her toward him. "Don't—I shouldn't have said that. I didn't mean it."

"Yes, you did," she said quietly, not meeting his eyes.

"I *didn't.* I love spending time with you. Of course you're fun."

"Yeah, right." Kane was a champion sweet-talker, but it was going to take more than charisma to fix this.

"Look, to be honest, I knew this wasn't your thing," he finally admitted, sitting down again. "You can go, if you want. I wouldn't blame you. I never should have brought you out here."

It wasn't the words so much as the uncharacteristic note of sincerity—and, more than that, vulnerability—that gave her pause. Made her stay. She sat down beside him. "So why did you bring me here?"

He looked down at his hands, which were playing aimlessly with the fraying edge of his brother's comforter. "It's stupid."

"Too bad," she said, relishing the rare sensation of having control over the conversation. "What's going on?"

"I just . . . wanted you to meet my brother," Kane mumbled. "I wanted to show you off to him," he added, putting an arm around her. Beth didn't resist. "To show him . . ." His voice drifted off.

"What?" Beth asked gently. She took his hand.

"You're the first girl I've ever introduced to my family. I'm . . . proud of myself, I guess you could say, for dating such an amazing girl. That someone like you would be with me."

"Kane . . ."

"I sound like a total loser."

"No!" she protested. It was possibly the sweetest thing anyone had ever said to her—and to think she'd almost walked out before giving him a chance. It was just like her, Beth berated herself—always judging, always planning, never willing to take things at face value, to just relax into the moment. The only good news was that it was never too late to change.

"We should get back out there," Kane suggested, obviously embarrassed.

"What's your hurry?" Beth asked, pulling him toward her into a kiss. Suddenly she didn't care about the dirty comforter or the sagging futon, the spiderwebs in the corner of the room or the deadbeats eavesdropping on the other side of the door. She only cared about Kane—and she was ready to show him just how much.

Adam tried to remember what the website had cautioned him about calming down, releasing his stress.

Relax, he told himself. *Enjoy the moment. Enjoy Harper.*

So he tried. He kissed her, rubbed her back, closed his eyes, and pulled off her shirt. She was beautiful, she had an amazing body—but it just wasn't . . . it just wasn't happening. The whole thing felt so fake and scripted: put this hand here, that hand there, think sexy thoughts. And the damn Christmas music in the background wasn't helping.

"Mmm, Adam, I love the smell of your hair," Harper mumbled, her face buried in his neck.

It was the same thing Beth always used to say.

And that was all it took—her face, unbidden, swam up in his mind's eye, smiling mockingly at him. And there was Kane, suddenly next to her, kissing her, both of them laughing at Adam, at his stupidity, his weakness. His inadequacy.

Get out of my head, he wanted to scream, feeling like the walls were closing in. He hadn't slept the night before, going over and over the game in his head, seeing Kane's face as he scored the winning shot while Adam rode the bench. All he'd wanted to do today was get away, forget all his problems. But here was Harper, pushing him, reminding him of everything he couldn't do, couldn't be . . . it was all too much—

"Stop!" he finally said harshly, pushing her away, feeling like his head was going to explode.

"What is it?" she asked, lightly touching his cheek. "What's wrong?"

"It's all this, this shit," Adam said, throwing wide his arms to encompass the decorations, the music, all of it. "This is the last thing I want to think about, Harper—I thought we agreed to just forget that night ever happened. And then you go and throw it in my face?"

"I just thought, if we tried again . . ."

He wasn't angry at her, he knew that. But he was too ashamed to admit it—too ashamed to admit that he'd failed her once again. What kind of teenage guy was he? Where were all those raging hormones when you needed them? Instead, here he was, stuck with a horny girlfriend, lukewarm hot chocolate, and a limp dick.

"I have to go," he said quickly—and it was, suddenly, a physical need not to be there anymore, not to have her look at him with those pitying eyes. He was too proud to accept her pity—and too terrified of what would happen when her pity turned to scorn. What if, after a few days of this, a week, she got sick of it? Of him? What if she told her friends?

This is Harper, he reminded himself. *You can trust her.*

"I'm sorry," he said sincerely. But he couldn't touch her. "I really am. I'm not mad. I'm just—" He stood up and backed away. "I just need to go. I'll call you."

He was out the door before she could say anything.

True, it was Harper, and he could trust her more than anyone—but how much was that?

After Beth, after Kane, he wasn't sure he believed in trust anymore. And if betrayal was inevitable, maybe it was just better to be alone.

She'd bought it. He'd known the family card was just the right one to play—and once again, his instincts had proven infallible. Poor Kane, so reluctant to open up, so eager to show off his beloved girl to his beloved brother. All they'd done in Aaron's room was kiss, but Kane wondered. If only he'd thought of the teary-eyed routine back on the ski trip, when they'd had a room to themselves and all the time in the world.

And yet—it hadn't been a total lie, had it? Why else had he brought Beth along on this little excursion, knowing ahead of time it would likely be more trouble than it was worth. Wasn't he trying to show her off to his brother, prove that Kane had managed to get something Aaron never had?

Kane shrugged it off—he didn't care to plumb the depths of his subconscious. Leave that to the ladies.

"We can take off in a minute," he whispered to her. She was pretending to be deeply engrossed in his brother's explanation of the differing merits of Grand Theft Auto and Trials Evolution. What a girl.

She nodded slightly, and Kane patted her on the shoulder before standing up and catching the eye of one of the guys across the room—a lanky, scraggly haired college dropout who went only by the name of "C." He jerked his head slightly toward the door and headed outside, knowing C would follow. Time to accomplish what he'd come for.

"Yo, Kane, good to see you," C said in a raspy voice, once they were alone. He bumped fists with Kane, then frowned. "I'm just sorry you came all this way for nothing."

"What are you talking about?" Kane had, after much thought, come up with the perfect present for Beth—something to make their New Year's Eve a night neither would soon forget. And C had promised that, as always, he'd be able to hook Kane up.

"Man, sorry, I thought I had enough, but you know how it is."

"No, I don't know how it is. You couldn't tell me this before I drove all the way up here?"

"Forgot." C shrugged. "What can you do?"

"You've got *nothing*?" Kane asked in frustration. "Absolutely nothing?"

"Well"—C's mouth widened into a rat-like grin—"you gotta keep a little something, just in case."

"I'll take it."

"No way, man, that's my emergency supply."

"Double the usual price," Kane suggested. This was an emergency.

"No deal. It's not about the money, bro. It's not for sale."

"Everything's for sale," Kane countered, a philosophy that had yet to fail him. "There must be something you want, something only I can get for you."

"Actually . . ." C chewed the corner of his lip. "There may be something—but you're not going to like it."

C spit it out—and under other circumstances, Kane might have laughed in his face and walked away. But today was C's lucky day.

"It just so happens that you've named the one thing

I'm able to deliver," Kane said triumphantly. He could already see all the details falling into place. It was amoral, it was underhanded, and it was going to make someone *very* unhappy, but it would get Kane what he needed.

And in the end, what else mattered?

chapter ten

"DO YOU KNOW WHAT TIME IT IS?" HARPER ASKED groggily, slumping back against her pillow.

"Did I wake you, princess?" Even through the phone, Harper could hear the false note in Kane's syrupy sympathetic voice. And after the week she'd been having, she wasn't in the mood.

"Yes."

"Good—because you've got to get going or you'll be late."

"Late for what?" Harper was on the verge of hanging up. It was way too early in the morning for one of Kane's mind games.

"You've got a date."

"Trust me, I don't." Not that she wanted to think about that. She hadn't heard from Adam since he'd run off from her ill-conceived winter extravaganza.

"You do now. His name is C. And you're going to love him." Kane laughed. "Actually, you're going to hate him—but you're going, anyway."

"I'm hanging up now," Harper warned him impatiently.

"Look, he graduated a couple years ago from Haven and apparently he had a huge crush on you. God knows why."

"I'll ignore that," Harper snapped.

"You blew him off."

"Imagine that."

"But for some reason, he's been longing for you ever since . . . kind of sweet, when you think about it. You know, in a crazed-stalker kind of way."

"Charming," Harper drawled—a bit intrigued, in spite of herself.

"Since the poor guy's been pining away for you so pitifully, I told him you'd drive up there and have lunch with him today."

Harper almost dropped the phone. "You did *what*? Why would I possibly do that?"

"Out of the goodness of your heart?" Kane suggested.

"Funny, I seem to have misplaced that."

"Then need I remind you of the favor you owe me?" Harper gripped the phone tightly—she should have known that nothing from Kane came without strings attached. "I'm calling it in."

"Kane, lending me money doesn't give you the right to pimp me out to your deadbeat friends," she pointed out.

"Oh, get off it, Grace, it's lunch, not an afternoon rendezvous at the Whore Hotel. All you need to do is drive up there, let the guy buy you lunch and pay you a few compliments, then drive home again. And, oh yeah," he added, affecting a casual tone, "he has something for me, a package, so if you can bring it back with you, that'd be great."

"And if I say no?" Harper asked.

"Have you cashed the check yet?"

Damn.

No.

"I can always stop payment."

Harper wanted to throw the phone across the room. He could be such an asshole sometimes. All the time.

"But hey, I wouldn't do that to a friend," he smarmed. "I'm more than happy to do you a favor, because that's what friends do for each other. *Right?*"

"His name is C?" Harper asked. "What's it stand for?"

"Nothing—just C."

Of course.

"And he's in college with your brother?"

"He *was* . . . ," Kane clarified.

"He graduated already?" she asked—a prodigy wouldn't be too bad.

"He . . . moved on."

No name and no future—this just kept getting better and better. Still . . . he was an older guy, and he found her desirable, which was more than she could say for the other man in her life. And it's not like it would be a *real* date or anything, so Adam would have nothing to complain about. (Not that he would ever find out.)

"And you won't have to pay interest on the loan," Kane added hopefully.

Free lunch and an interest-free loan, all for spending a few hours letting some guy tell her how beautiful she was?

"Gotta go, Kane—looks like I've got myself a date."

"I have a proposition for you, *mon chérie*," Powell said, dipping his Oreo in a glass of milk and taking a bite. Their first night together, they had dined on fine wine and imported cheeses, Kaia remembered with a sweet pang of nostalgia. Now they'd been reduced to early morning milk and cookies. When did things go from scandalous to seedy to suburban?

"I'm listening."

"What are you up to on New Year's Eve?" he asked.

Kaia maintained a neutral expression, but inside, she was beaming. He wanted to spend New Year's with her? It looked like her little power play was already taking off.

"I've got this party to go to," he began, and she looked at him in surprise. A couple weeks ago he'd chastised her for smiling at him in the high school hallway. Now he wanted to take her out in public?

"I can't get out of it," he complained, "but I should be home by one or two, and I thought—"

"What?" she snapped, comprehension dawning. "That I'd have nothing better to do on New Year's Eve than sit around and wait for your booty call? Just how pathetic do you think I am?"

"You didn't seem to have a problem with it tonight," he pointed out, "or any other night, that I can recall."

"Well, it just so happens that on *that* night, I've got something else to do."

Powell sat up in bed and looked at her suspiciously. "Something else—or *someone* else?"

His jealous tone was confirmation enough that her little show with Reed had done the trick. But it looked like he hadn't quite learned his lesson—not if he still expected her to be sitting by the phone at all hours, waiting for his call. She'd stay faithful to their pact—but that didn't mean he owned her.

"I'm having a party of my own," she explained, deciding in that instant to make it true. "But if I get bored, later, maybe *I'll* call *you.* But don't count on it—my parties aren't often boring."

"Well then, all the more reason to get my fill of you while I can," he said, tugging her close.

"I'm leaving now," she informed him. Time to make him beg.

"Now, now, don't go away mad. *J'ai besoin de toi, mon amoureuse. Reste avec moi—je t'implore.*"

I need you, lover. Stay with me—I beg of you.

He knew she couldn't resist him when he spoke to her in French, his British accent submerged in the soft syllables of longing.

The language of love, they called it. But there was nothing pure and nothing loving in his tone—only naked desire. Need.

And nothing appealed to Kaia more than that.

"*Je suis ici,*" she whispered, falling into his arms. "*Et je suis tout tiens.*"

I'm here.

And I'm all yours.

Forty miles was a long way to drive for lunch. She made a mental note to have Kane repay her for the gas.

Harper had a lot of time to make mental to-do lists,

since it's not like she was listening to C prattle on about his Jay-Z playlist or the garage band he and his friends were planning to start . . . any day now. (C had a lot of plans, apparently—and not a whole lot to show for them except a few tattoos and a thriving business in supplying illegal substances to desperate high school kids.)

She remembered him now. Back in Grace, C had been Charles Dallas, aka "Chuckie D," who'd bounced around from group to group looking for his niche. He'd dropped his junior high Dungeons and Dragons clan, washed out of the rapper wannabes, and finally settled in with a bunch of deadbeat dealers who spent most of high school in the parking lot, swapping stories about what they'd do when they escaped from Grace. Most of them never had.

"You want dessert?" C asked, appearing not to notice the fact that Harper's plate—piled high with a rancid "buffalo" burger and stale chips—was untouched. She wasn't about to eat anything in this dive, a dingy roadside diner decorated with old license plates and populated by a few locals who were drinking their lunch before heading home to watch the game and work on their trucks. They'd agreed to meet here, halfway between their two towns, but Harper realized now that she should have sucked it up and driven the full eighty miles—at least C lived in a college town, with other people, other buildings, anything other than the dusty gray emptiness that surrounded them on all sides.

"Thanks, anyway," she said, in the same monotonous tone she'd been using the whole meal. "I'm full."

"I had in mind a little something *off* the menu," C said, tapping his jacket pocket and giving her a toothy grin. Harper so did not want to know what was in there.

"Raincheck?" she requested wearily. "I'm good. Really."

"You sure are," he agreed, looking her up and down with appreciation. "I still can't believe I'm here with you. I mean, it's fucking Harper Grace! In a dump like this, with a loser like me. I must be dreaming."

Harper allowed herself a small smile. A compliment was a compliment, no matter who delivered it.

"The guys are never going to believe this," he crowed, tossing a wad of cash down on the table.

"The guys?" Harper asked as C pulled out her chair and helped her up—so chivalrous for a deadbeat.

"Oh, yeah. There's a bunch of us up there from Haven, and we all remember you. I mean, dude, you're *Harper Grace.*"

Harper pushed a stray hair out of her eyes, preening under his longing gaze. So she had a little fan club up there, did she? Feeling a sudden burst of goodwill for C, she laced her arm through his as they strolled the gravelly path toward the parking lot. "So, C," she said sweetly, "what is it, exactly, that makes me so memorable?"

As C began rhapsodizing—in his admittedly limited vocabulary—about her many divine attributes, Harper's mood lifted. So this is what it felt like to be worshipped. She'd almost forgotten.

". . . and, you know, you're just totally sexy. I mean, *hot.*"

"My boyfriend doesn't seem to think so," Harper muttered—then stopped walking, appalled she had said it aloud.

"Any guy who doesn't think you're the hottest thing he's ever seen is fucking crazy," C exclaimed.

Harper turned to look at C, really look at him. He wasn't *so* bad looking, if you ignored the crooked smile and the way one eye seemed to wander off when he tried to meet your gaze. And the bad skin. And the greasy hair.

Okay, he was a dog. But he was looking at her like a hungry puppy who'd just spotted a Salisbury steak. And Harper decided to put him out of his misery.

"You think 'the guys' won't believe we had lunch together?" Harper asked, putting a hand on each of his shoulders and pulling him toward her. "Wait until they hear about this."

It was a wet, sloppy kiss, short on romance, overly long on bad breath and C's thrusting tongue. But as he pressed himself against her and Hoovered his way across her face, sucking and slobbering like an animal, Harper could feel just how much he wanted her. At least someone did.

❧ ❧ ❧

Adam skimmed through the Facebook gallery without paying much attention. He'd almost deleted the e-mail without opening it. Some guy on the team was dating a girl who was obsessed with photographically documenting every moment of their senior year, which meant periodic mass e-mails filled with memories Adam would just as soon forget. And the ski trip was at the top of the list.

But something had made him save the link. And this afternoon, something had made him open it. Most were pictures of people he barely knew, didn't care about—he and Harper had done their best to stay away from the crowd, and that meant away from the camera. But there were a few shots that made him pause. Harper, bundled in her thick green coat, leaning against Adam's shoulder. Adam, tossing a snowball at Harper, grabbing her hand as she tried to escape.

There'd been some good moments, he reminded himself.

And so he was smiling when he clicked open the next photo. When the picture of Beth and Kane, tangled in each other's arms, exploded across the screen.

Adam slammed his fist down on the keyboard and shut off the monitor. But the image stayed with him, burned into his brain, like those other images, two months earlier. Every time he saw them together, it was as if it were the first time, and he was hit with the same blast of shock, disgust, and fury.

And every time, there was only one thought that calmed him down, one person who could remind him that not everything in his life was ugly and twisted. No matter how awkward things were between them, she was still the only one he could talk to. The only one he wanted to talk to.

He called her, and waited.

The phone rang and rang.

He didn't leave a message.

It was a long drive home, and Harper had plenty of time to think. Too much.

She'd kissed another guy, she realized, the gritty, sour taste of C still in her mouth. No wonder Adam didn't want her—deep inside, he could tell what kind of person she was. A quitter. A cheater. Adam had no idea what she was really like—but some part of him must sense it, Harper realized, must know that she wasn't good enough for him.

She'd never felt so low—and then she got home. And things got worse.

"I'm skipping dinner," Harper mumbled to her mother, blowing by her on the way upstairs to her room.

"Hon, wait a second. Your father and I have something we want to say to you."

Uh-oh.

In the history of Grace family relations, that had never been good.

Already halfway up the stairs, Harper slunk back down and followed her mother into the parlor. Her father was already there, perched stiffly on an overstuffed blue chair he only used to entertain guests. The whole room was, in fact, used only under special circumstances—the Graces' large house, left over from boom times, had far more space than their small family could use. Often, Harper felt like the house was mocking her, reminding her of the life she was supposed to have.

"Sit down, Harper," her father requested sternly.

She did as he said, stomach sinking, mind racing to figure out what it was she might have done.

"Harper, as you know, the family's been going through some tough times lately," her father began.

As if she needed a reminder. "And, as you know, we decided that this ski trip stretched our budget too much, and that if you really wanted to go—"

"I'd have to pay for it myself," Harper finished with him. Old news. Unless—what if they had somehow found out that she'd quit her job?

"We've been watching you very carefully these last few weeks, and we want to tell you—"

Here it came.

"We're so very proud of you, Harper."

"What?"

"We know how much you hated the idea of having a

job, honey," her mother explained. "And to see you going off to work every day—"

"On your winter vacation, no less!" her father chimed in.

"We just want you to know, sweetie, that we really respect what you've shown you can do."

"Your mother and I have talked it over and we've decided that, as a reward, if you make enough to pay us back for half the ski trip, we'll cover the other half."

"I-I don't know what to say," Harper stuttered, feeling her lies bubbling up inside of her, along with her lunch. "Thank you?"

"You don't have to thank us, honey." Her mother came over to offer her a warm hug. "We're just so happy to have a daughter who's not afraid of a little hard work. I always knew that if you really put your mind to something, you'd be able to accomplish anything."

Harper felt like shit. Lower than shit. Her parents were treating her like a superhero. Some hero—what were her special powers: the ability to destroy relationships in a single bound? The power to make her real, lying, cheating self disappear?

Her parents had certainly bought in to her secret identity—and, for the moment, so had Adam. But it was a small town, and she wasn't invincible. How long would it be, Harper wondered, before the truth came out?

* * *

"I can't wait to see who you really are."

Miranda couldn't forget his words, couldn't stop repeating them to herself. They were so exciting—and terrifying. What if he took one look and ran away in the other direction? What if he was expecting someone totally different: someone tall, skinny, confident? And instead he ended up with Miranda. Who wouldn't be disappointed? Who wouldn't feel cheated?

Beneath all the self-deprecation, Miranda still found time to wonder—what was *he* really like? What kind of guy needed to pick up girls on the Internet? Was there such a thing as a cool, artsy, intelligent, single guy? Or was ReadItAndWeep just a troll—a pale, gawky weirdo just looking to get laid?

What were the odds that he would be good enough for her—and if he was, that she would be good enough for him?

A million to one seemed a cautious guess.

And yet—sometimes, Miranda reminded herself, you've got to take a chance. So she'd made the date. She'd gotten dressed in her best casual—but hopefully hot—outfit: slimming dark jeans, with a lacy, see-through black top; brushed her long, lank hair into something approximating silky sheen; dug out her tallest pair of high heels; and taken one last look in the mirror. Two days on the slopes had failed to tan her pale skin, but in certain lights, she had an arguably healthy glow. Good enough.

She took a deep breath and set off for Bourquin's Coffee Shop to meet the man of her dreams. Or, at least, of her e-mails.

She'd just left her house when the phone rang. Miranda almost didn't answer. If it was him, backing out at the last minute, did she really want to know? And then she remembered: They hadn't exchanged phone numbers. She was safe. Or so she thought.

"Harper?"

"Rand . . . Rand, I need you."

"Are you—what's going on?"

Harper's voice sounded strange, muffled, her words broken by hiccuping pauses.

"I don't know what's wrong with me, Rand, I just—I'm a terrible person, my life is shit, I'm—"

"Slow down, Harper, please, just—calm down." Was she crying? Impossible. "What's wrong?"

"I can't tell you. . . . It doesn't matter. I just—I can't be alone right now. Rand—can I come over?"

"Uh . . . I'm kind of . . . out, right now, Harper."

"Oh." She said it in such a small, pitiful voice, Miranda cringed. "Okay, I guess I'll just talk to you"—she sniffed and, Miranda thought, might even have whimpered—"later. Bye."

"Harper, wait!" Miranda sighed, weighing her options.

She could hang up. This was probably just another Harper Grace melodrama—it would blow over in a few hours. And, given the number of times Harper had ditched her in her time of need, there would be a certain poetic justice in leaving her hanging. Maybe it was time to put her own life first, for once.

On the other hand . . . this was Harper, her best friend. And that had to mean something, right? She'd never heard Harper like this before, vulnerable, needy. And, Miranda had to admit, it felt pretty good. Like Harper had finally figured out how desperately she needed the kind of friendship that only Miranda could provide.

"I'm about five minutes from home, Harper," she said, hoping she wouldn't regret this. "You can come over whenever you need to."

"Thanks, Rand, you're the best. Really. I don't know what I'd do without you."

It felt so good to hear those words—almost good enough to make Miranda forget about the mystery man who was sitting in the back of the coffee shop waiting for the girl with red hair and a spunky sense of humor. The girl who would never show up, who didn't have a number to call. She'd e-mail him to explain, she promised herself. And he'd understand. He would have to.

* * *

Four hours later, holding Harper's hair as she leaned over the toilet, puking up a night's worth of Screwdrivers, Miranda was no longer so sure she wanted this best friend gig after all.

Harper had shown up half drunk and, after an hour or so at Miranda's, had gone the rest of the way. Her parents were, thankfully, out for the night and her sister was sleeping over at a friend's house—so there was no one but Miranda to witness Harper's meltdown, and no one but Miranda to clean up the mess.

The most frustrating thing was that Harper wouldn't tell her anything about what was wrong. Their conversations wandered around in lazy circles, as unable to walk a straight line as Harper was.

"He doesn't love me," Harper would sob.

"Who?"

"Adam. He thinks I'm a slut. I *am* a slut. He hates me."

"What are you talking about? Of course he doesn't—"

"Everyone hates me. I'm going to be all alone. When they find out what I did."

"Who?"

"My parents. Adam. Beth. You. Everyone. You'll all hate me. You should hate me. I'm horrible."

"But what did you do?" Miranda asked, again and again, mystified.

"Nothing. Everything. I don't know—it doesn't matter.

Nothing matters, because he doesn't want me. He doesn't love me."

And then the whole thing started all over again.

Until the puking began. All that vodka on an empty stomach—Harper should have known better. Or Miranda should have known better for her.

Finally, Harper stood up. Slow, unsteady on her feet, and stumbling back to Miranda's room, flopping down, facefirst, on the bed. Miranda forced her to turn over on her side, forced her to drink a little water.

"What will I do without you, Rand?" Harper asked, moaning with the effort of having to move.

"You'll never have to find out," Miranda said soothingly, taking off Harper's shoes and covering her with a light blanket. She settled into a chair by the bed, planning to stay up and watch Harper breathe. Just to make sure everything was all right.

"No, you'll leave me, when you find out," Harper whimpered. "You all will."

"Never," Miranda swore.

"No." Harper sighed, and closed her eyes. "Soon."

chapter eleven

In 500 words or less, describe something about yourself that makes you proud.

I never knew I was afraid of heights until I was standing at the top of the mountain, looking down. The hill looked like a ninety-degree angle—and it looked bottomless. I didn't want to admit it at the time, but I was scared. I was terrified. I didn't know what I was getting myself into. I just knew I had to do it. No matter what, I had to try. So I pushed myself to the very edge, I counted to three, and then I tipped my skis forward—and I was flying!

I'm proud of myself for making it down the hill in one piece, but that's not what this essay's about. I'm proud of myself for going back up to the top and trying all over again, even though I was just as terrified the second time around, and the third. But that's not what this essay is about either.

Because what I'm most proud of is the fact that I went down at all, that first time. I looked over the edge, and I was scared out of my mind. But I did it anyway.

I'm a quiet girl, and I live a quiet life. Not boring, not dull—just quiet. "She's a nice girl"—people say that a lot. Also: "She always does the right thing." "Always does what she's supposed to do." And I'm proud of that, too.

But that's not me, or at least, not all of me. Because somewhere in me, there's someone else, someone loud and exciting. Someone looking for mountains to ski down, for all kinds of new experiences, no matter how scary they may seem at first. Every once in a while, something inside of me wants to take a chance, and do something that no one would ever expect. Trying new things, facing your fears, taking a risk—it's not always easy. I'm still finding my way. But I know that college will be the perfect place to learn. The way I see it, going to college is like the ultimate ski slope. It's terrifying, the great unknown—but you know that if you can just make that first jump off the edge, you'll have an amazing ride.

I'm ready to jump.

Kane looked up from the page, and Beth watched him expectantly, her heart in her throat.

"So? What do you think?" she asked, not sure she wanted to hear the answer. After days of being totally blocked, she'd been suddenly inspired and had stayed up all night writing. Kane was the first person to read it. And if he thought it was stupid—and, reading it over for the hundredth time, it sounded stupider and stupider to her—she didn't know what she would do.

"You're a genius!" he exclaimed, taking her in his arms. "It's brilliant."

"Really? You're not just saying that? If it's terrible, I'd rather know now and—"

"It's amazing," he insisted, cutting her off with a kiss. "You're amazing. This is exactly the kind of corny bullshit colleges love to hear. You're going to have them eating out of your hand."

"It's not—" Beth stopped, unsure how to explain that she'd meant every word, cheesy as it may seem. But she didn't want Kane to think less of her, and wipe that admiring look off his face. And it didn't really matter if he'd totally misunderstood her intentions, if he believed the essay or not. He *liked* it—that was the important thing.

Right?

Kaia read over the invitation a few times and then clicked send, fully satisfied. Harper had supplied her with a list of e-mail addresses and assured her she'd put the word out that all the right people should show up—and all the wrong ones should stay home.

It had been easier than she'd expected to snag her father's permission for the party (sneaking out of the house was one thing—sneaking one hundred people *in* might have proven somewhat more difficult, so she'd gone the more official route). Of course, she'd billed it as an elegant cocktail hour, something to keep her and her "friends" out of trouble on the big night. But after threatening him with her other suggestion—spending some quality time together, just the two of them—she suspected he would have agreed to anything. Keith Sellers cancel his annual New Year's trip to Cabo to spend the night doing the "Father Knows Best" thing with his delinquent daughter? It was about as likely as her mother popping in for a surprise visit.

No, Kaia was on her own—as usual—and, courtesy of Daddy, had a nice chunk of change with which to make this party worthy of Harper's hype. The servants were holding on to the cash, of course. Kaia's father had figured that with his credit card in hand, she'd be on the next plane back to New York. (And he was right.) Besides, better that the help hold on to the purchasing power, since they'd be the ones doing all the purchasing.

She'd hit only one snag so far in the planning process: the list of invitees. True, Harper had supplied most of the names, but there was a wild card: Reed Sawyer. Kaia had toyed with the idea of inviting him—after all, it would be nice to have someone to kiss at midnight. Someone dark, mysterious, and handsome, whose lips lit her on fire. . . .

And that's where she'd cut herself off. Reed was a toy, a plaything, something to use and discard once she'd gotten what she needed out of him. Seeing him again, thinking about him any longer, would just tempt her to forget all that—and if she wanted to keep Powell around, she couldn't afford to forget.

Reed didn't know it yet, but his new year was going to be Kaia-free.

Lucky thing, Kane supposed, that Adam's mother had answered the door. Adam probably would have slammed it shut before Kane could get a word out. Mrs. Morgan—like most women—was far more accommodating.

Maybe he'd been inspired by Beth's corny essay. Or maybe, much as he hated to admit it, by Beth herself, those clear, shining eyes, trusting, open, always ready for a challenge. If she was willing to try something new, to take a chance—and Kane was hoping that he'd correctly interpreted her words to mean she was finally willing to take a real chance on him—so could he.

So after leaving her house, he'd gone to Adam's—and since Adam's mother had pulled a Benedict Arnold, Kane now knew exactly where to find him.

It was the first place he would have looked.

It was a cool day, but Adam was playing shirtless, sweaty enough that Kane knew he'd been on the court all day.

"Practice makes perfect, eh?" he called out as he approached, wincing at the sarcastic note in his voice. He could never stop himself from goading Adam on—it was so easy and, it was, after all, the only way he knew how to speak. But even he could tell it wasn't helping. He'd joined the basketball team in hopes of reminding Adam of the good times they'd had together, thinking that the easy jock banter would help them gloss over the past. But Adam seemed to get angrier with every passing day—and, much as Kane hated to admit it to himself, the whole situation made him uncomfortable. He still didn't think he had any reason to feel guilty, but he'd feel much better if he could persuade Adam to feel the same way.

"What are you doing here?" Adam asked gruffly,

breaking into a run, dribbling the ball downcourt, away from Kane.

"Thought I might give you some help with your little problem," Kane called, running after him.

"What problem?" Adam bristled, shoving Kane away.

"Whatever you want to call it—'performance anxiety'?"

Adam suddenly tripped over the ball and fell flat on his ass. Kane tried hard—if not hard enough—not to laugh. Performance anxiety indeed.

"Who told you about that?" Adam asked hotly, standing up, grabbing the ball, and walking it back up court.

Kane slipped it out of his hands and began dribbling away.

"Everyone knows," he pointed out. "Or have you already forgotten that the whole town saw you choke the other night?"

"You're talking about basketball?" Adam asked, visibly relieved.

Kane launched the ball up for a perfect three-pointer and glanced over at Adam. "What did you think I was talking about?"

"Nothing," he muttered, chasing the ball out of bounds. "It doesn't matter. What do you want?"

"Like I said, I want to help." Kane had no trouble with fake sincerity—but the real kind always came out sounding forced. Mocking.

"I don't need your help. And you don't believe in it. So really, what do you want?"

Kane steeled himself. What he was about to do, he'd never done before—but how hard could it be, right? Other guys—lesser guys—did it all the time, and Kane knew he was as tough as any of them. "I just wanted to say—" He stopped, struggling to choke out the words. It was like Beth said: You had to close your eyes. And jump. "I'm sorry."

Adam whipped his head around. "You're *sorry*?" he said incredulously.

"Yeah." Kane grinned, proud of himself for making the effort—and Adam, of all people, should know exactly how much of an effort it had been. But he'd done it—and, you know? It hadn't been all that bad. "I'm sorry," he repeated, just because he could.

"Gosh, Kane, I've never heard you apologize before," Adam marveled. "That must have been really difficult for you."

"It wasn't all that bad, really. But, you know, our friendship's worth more than my stupid pride."

"Yeah, coming here, humbling yourself—that's real love," Adam said, and Kane suddenly gave him a closer look. Sarcasm was rare for Adam—and it showed. "I mean, you betray me, steal my girlfriend, humiliate me in front of the whole school, *destroy* me—but hey, you're sorry. Do you know how much that means to me?"

Kane said nothing.

"It means *shit*!" Adam yelled, hurling the ball toward Kane's head—who ducked just in time. "You think you can come here, say, 'I'm sorry, bro,' and I'm supposed to laugh it off? Now what—you, me, and Beth all go out and get drunk together? Like it's no big deal?"

"It doesn't have to be a big deal," Kane pointed out. "You're just making it into one. She's just a girl—"

"You *would* say that." Adam shook his head and jogged over to the side of the court to grab his T-shirt and his car keys, and began stalking toward the parking lot. "I'm sorry too," he called over his shoulder. "Sorry I was ever stupid enough to think we were friends. Sorry I ever let you into my life just so you could piss all over it. Guess what, Kane? Some mistakes you don't make twice."

Kane picked up the ball that Adam had left behind and slammed it angrily into the ground. Adam wanted to sulk, Adam wanted to hate him forever? Let him. Kane had violated his own policy, had opened himself up, put himself out there for someone else—and look how he'd been rewarded. He'd tried, he'd failed—and that was it.

Adam had at least been right about one thing, Kane thought: Some mistakes, you don't make twice.

"Can you believe it?" Adam asked, still fuming, hours after he'd left Kane on the basketball court.

Harper sat in the corner of his bedroom, knees hugged to her chest. She shook her head. "No, Ad, I can't believe it, any more than I could believe it the last ten times you told me the story."

Adam ignored the undercurrent of irritation in her voice—he was still too upset to give Harper's mood much thought. He'd called her as soon as he got home, needing some solace, a sympathetic ear—and whatever had, or hadn't, happened between them, she was always the person he turned to when he needed a friend. But here they were, sitting across the room from each other, this huge distance between them. And it was only making him feel worse.

"Like he could just say 'sorry' and I'd forgive him," Adam raged. "Like I could ever forgive him for what he did."

"I know. It was horrible," Harper said mechanically.

"Though at least he did apologize. You know what I can't get over? *Beth* has never apologized! Never even admitted what she did. I mean, if she could just accept some responsibility—"

"Adam!" Harper shouted suddenly. "Stop!"

"What?" He looked over at her, suddenly noticing her red-rimmed eyes, the lines of tension around her mouth. "What's wrong?"

"What's wrong is, I'm tired, and hung over, and sick of hearing this."

"Excuse me if I'm boring you," he said hotly. "I just thought—"

"Ad, I'm your best friend," Harper said, standing up. "And as your best friend, I'm happy to listen to anything you need to say. . . . But as your *girlfriend*, I can't listen to another word about how Kane and Beth broke your heart. If you want her back so bad, why don't you just go and get her? What the hell are you doing here with me?"

Adam hopped up and strode over to her, but she pushed him away.

"I know you're just with me as . . . a fallback," Harper said, her voice breaking. "Could you make it any more obvious? I can't be Beth for you, Adam," she cried, hitting at his chest as he tried to pull her into an embrace. "I tried . . . but I just can't."

"Who said I wanted you to be?" Adam asked quietly.

"You didn't have to say it. I'm not an idiot."

"Could have fooled me." He led her over to the edge of his bed. "Harper, sit down. Please. There's something I want to show you."

She sat down grudgingly, a scowl masking the tears straining at the corners of her eyes. Adam opened the closet door and began digging through a pile of junk in the back—it had to be here somewhere. He would never have thrown it away. Finally, he found it—at the bottom of an old shoe box, tucked beneath a fraying stack of baseball cards and an old Lakers cap.

He turned back to Harper and placed it in her hands, sitting down on the bed beside her and putting an arm around her shoulders.

"What is this supposed to be?" Harper asked, holding the graying, chewed-leather leash between two fingers with a look of distaste. "If this is your way of telling me you need a girlfriend you can control, I already told you, I'm not Beth and—"

"Harper, just stop for a minute," Adam said, taking one end of the leash and running his hands across it. He'd forgotten the feel of the worn leather beneath his fingers, how comforting it could be.

"Did I ever tell you I used to have a dog?" he asked, closing his eyes for a moment to picture the scrappy terrier he'd had to leave behind. "We left Calvin in South Carolina when we moved." Adam could still see Calvin's droopy face, watching Adam walk out the door one last time, as if, somehow, he knew his owner was never coming back. His ears and tail stuck straight out at right angles, he hadn't barked, hadn't whimpered, hadn't run after the car—he'd just stood there and watched as Adam had abandoned him. His father had promised to look out for Calvin, but Adam knew that would never happen. And so he hadn't been surprised, a few months later, to get the call. It had been a big truck. Fast. Unavoidable. A painless way to go. So his father had said.

"When I moved here, I didn't know anyone," he continued, shaking off the memory. "Didn't have any friends, the house was this strange place, and my mother, well, you know . . ."

Harper didn't say anything, but she nodded, and her face had softened into a pensive frown.

"I brought this leash with me and, I guess I was so desperate for a friend that—" Adam paused. This was more embarrassing than he'd expected it to be. He looked over at Harper, semi-patiently waiting for him to get to the point. He'd keep going—she was worth it. "I pretended like Calvin was still here. I'd walk that leash all over town, talking to Calvin, telling him everything, how I hated my mother for bringing me here, how I was lonely, how I missed home and wanted to go back, even if—well, I told him everything. It sounds pretty ridiculous now," he admitted, blushing at the memory, "walking all over town, talking to myself. But I couldn't have made it here without him. Not at first."

Harper sighed and dropped her end of the leash. "It's a nice story, Ad, but I don't get it. Why haven't I ever heard about this before? And why tell me now? What's the point?"

"That *is* the point, Harper." He dropped the leash on

the floor and put his arms around her. "You never heard about Calvin because, once I met you, I didn't need him anymore. I had something real I could count on. I put this leash away in a box and never looked at it again. I didn't need some imaginary friend to keep me from feeling lonely. When I met you, Harper, I knew I'd never be alone again."

"That's sweet, Ad, but—"

"No, not 'but'—you need to hear this, and you need to believe it." He'd never spoken to her, or anyone, this honestly before, had never even said these words in his own mind, but knew suddenly that they were true, and that this was something he should have said a long time ago. "You are the most important person in my life, Harper. Not Beth, *you.* I know it took me a while to figure things out—"

"A long while," she teased him, but she was finally smiling, though her eyes still shone with tears.

"But now I know, and I'm sure, it's always been you, Gracie. I don't want you to be like anyone else. I don't want you to change, or to doubt me. I just want you. I—" He'd only said this to one other girl in his life, and it had ended in disaster. He'd vowed to be more careful, to go slow, to guard himself against more pain. But he couldn't hold back. Not when it felt so right. "I think I love you, Harper."

"I love you, too, Adam," she whispered, and melted into him, her lips meeting his in a warm kiss. He laid her back against the bed, her wild hair splayed out against his pillows, and he thought idly that it was a good thing he'd changed his sheets the day before—and then the stray thought was knocked out of his head by an overwhelming rush of desire as she stripped off her shirt and he fell upon her perfect body. As he ran his fingers across her arms, her back, her chest, she wrapped herself around him.

It's happening, he thought in wonder. This time, it was really going to happen. It wasn't like with Kaia, the intoxication of passion mixed with guilt and bewilderment, or with Beth, a battle, a physical debate in which he always needed to prove himself worthy of her, and always failed to make his case. This was easy. This was right.

As he wriggled out of his jeans and groped in his nightstand for a condom, he felt a flash of panic—what if he failed once again? If he just wasn't capable?

But then, just as suddenly, the terror passed—and all it took was a look at her face, her eyes closed, the edges of her lips pulled into a blissed-out grin. This was Harper—and with the same warm certainty that all those years ago had allowed him to banish his imaginary friend, Adam relaxed. This was Harper—and nothing bad could ever happen to him with her by his side. Together, they could take on the world. Together, they made sense.

Together forever. It was the kind of promise children made to each other, he thought, before they knew anything about a world that could tear them apart. It was such a naive vision of the future—pure, innocent. And maybe that was okay, maybe that was right—because he and Harper had been children together for so long.

Today, together, it was finally time to grow up.

chapter twelve

Have you been good this year?

Very, very good?

Too bad.

Reality check: Santa doesn't care if you're naughty or nice.

So you might as well have a little fun. And there's still time.

New Year's Eve

512 Red Rock Road

9 p.m. to dawn

Start your New Year off right—or,

even better, very, very wrong.

—K

Adam locked the front door behind him and walked across the lawn to Harper's house. He put his finger on the doorbell, but stopped, suddenly, before pressing down.

In all the years he'd known her, Harper had never been on time. She would never notice if he took a moment for himself, to think.

New Year's Eve—and look how things had ended up, he thought, sitting down on the front stoop. Last year at this time, he and Beth had driven out to an empty spot in the desert—the same place that, months before, they'd shared their first kiss. They'd huddled together on a blanket spread out across the uneven ground, their faces flickering in candlelight. He had never wanted anyone so much—and never been so sure of anything. He'd believed in Beth, believed she was the last girl, the only girl, he'd ever want to be with. He would have done anything for her, he'd realized that night.

She'd destroyed all that—and he had thought he would never move on. That things would never be the same.

And they weren't—they were better. Adam looked up at Harper's window, wondering what she was doing, what she was thinking. He was thinking about her, and only her—and about the way her body had felt against his. There was no one to clap Adam on the back, to tell him job well done, but he beamed with pride nonetheless—after all, he'd proven to himself, to the world, that he was a real man. Had taken Harper in his arms and shown her how he really felt. How much he needed her—and discovered how much she needed him.

All the pain, all the resentment, all the anger he'd carried around with him these last several weeks—he was done with it, he decided. A real man didn't need to hold a grudge. Didn't need closure, or revenge. He resolved that, this year, he would treat himself to a fresh start. He would truly, finally move on, whatever it took. He was big enough to move on—maybe even, with the new strength Harper had given him, big enough to forgive and forget.

Forget it, Kane told himself, again. Just forget. Move on. It's done.

But Adam's jeering face kept swimming back into focus in his mind's eye. Kane had exposed himself—and failed. And he didn't like it.

Winning came easy to Kane. But then, he usually chose his contests well. After all, any game you couldn't win wasn't worth the effort. That was his first rule: Pick your battles, and pick them wisely. His second? It's not over until *you* say it's over—and Beth was a case in point. Adam thought he'd won, had sat back and enjoyed his illusion of victory, and only Kane had understood that the game was still afoot. He'd bided his time; then, when the moment was just right, had played his hand. And he'd won in the end, as usual. As always.

And that was it, Kane had finally realized. Adam couldn't stand to lose. Too bad—who could? Was Kane supposed to restrain himself, refrain from pursuing his own desires, just because Adam wasn't able to protect his own turf?

Not a chance. And with that, Kane felt the annoying tendrils of guilt release their tight grip around his neck. He'd done what was needed to win. And since life itself was nothing more than competition, how could that be wrong? Kane based all his actions on cool logic, on strategy—and it always led to victory. Let your emotions get involved, and things just got messy. This episode with Adam was proof enough of that.

No more, Kane resolved, ducking into a convenience store to pick up a few essential items for the big party. (Noisemakers, confetti, and condoms—after all, hope springs eternal.) Emotional attachment and clear thinking didn't mix—and it was only by holding on to the latter that he could survive. Thrive.

As for Beth . . . he'd just have to be careful not to get too close. Kane had proven to himself, to her, to everyone, that he was the better man, that he could win her heart. Now he just needed to decide what he wanted to do with it.

What do you want? Beth asked herself, sitting down on the curb in front of her house, waiting for Kane to arrive. Better to wait outside, in the crisp, quiet night, than in the noisy, claustrophobic house, dodging nosy parents and sugar-crazed siblings. She needed her space. And time to think.

Last year, it had seemed like such an easy question. She wanted Adam. He wanted her. And for so long, they were happy.

The first words I heard this year were I love you, Beth thought in wonder. *From Adam.* He'd said it at midnight, and they'd greeted the New Year with a soft kiss that felt like it could last until spring. *Everything began with him.*

"I love you, too," she had whispered, believing it to be true. But maybe she'd been wrong. Maybe Adam had just been easy. Safe. She'd never worried about what he really wanted, or why he wanted her around. She'd just accepted him, and everything he said—and look what had happened.

So maybe, just maybe, she was better off. Adam had cast her aside—but had she crumbled? Had she given up? Not Beth. Never. She'd moved forward, moved past Adam, found herself a new guy, a new life. And Kane wasn't easy. He wasn't safe. Life with him was a risk, every day a new challenge.

For so long she'd questioned that, wondered if it was a sign that she'd made the wrong decisions, that her life had run off the tracks. But now? Beth meant everything she'd said in her essay—truly wanted to be that person, someone who took chances, someone who embraced the new, the different, the difficult. And she finally knew she was strong enough to do it.

She'd proven to herself that she could handle anything—and so, she resolved, this year she'd put aside her doubts and her fear. She'd try to loosen the reins a bit and embrace uncertainty. Maybe her life was headed off the track she'd set for herself—and maybe she didn't care.

I don't care what he thinks of me, Miranda told herself, over and over again. He was just a guy from the Internet—she didn't know him, might never see him again after tonight, so none of it really mattered. She had nothing to lose. So why was she short of breath, and so nervous she felt ready to pass out?

She hadn't eaten anything all day. Could you lose weight just by skipping lunch and dinner? she wondered. It was too late to worry about that now, and definitely too late to try on yet another outfit in a desperate search for one that didn't make her look frumpy. At any other party it wouldn't have mattered. How many parties had she spent hours preparing for meeting Mr. Right only to spend her night trapped between Mr. Wrong and the punch bowl? But this party was different. Because this time, she knew Mr. Right would be there—and he'd be waiting for her.

ReadItAndWeep had forgiven her for standing him up and had agreed to try again. They would meet at 11:30 on

Kaia's back deck—and if things went well, Miranda might finally get her New Year's Eve midnight kiss.

Miranda had read dozens of self-help articles, all promising that confidence was the key to attracting a mate. Believe you look good, they claimed, and *he'll* believe it too. Take pride in yourself—and gain his undying respect and admiration.

This year, Miranda resolved, she was going to give it a try. Starting tonight.

I look great.

I am smart, funny, and fabulous.

Any guy would be lucky to have me.

The words rang empty in her ears, but she said them aloud, over and over again. Conviction through repetition. She hoped.

Every year on this night, with no one to turn to at the stroke of midnight, she vowed that *next* year would be different. Next year, she'd find the right person, someone who would live up to her standards—and, as an added bonus, notice that she was alive. Next year she wouldn't be alone.

This is the year, she told herself with gritty determination, every January first.

Maybe this year, she'd finally been right.

Everything was right with the world. Finally. Adam loved her—he *loved* her. Harper couldn't stop repeating the words to herself. She adored the way they sounded.

He loves me.

Tonight, they would be admired, envied, the center of attention—and why not? They were the perfect couple. Every girl at that party would wish she could take Harper's place. But none of them ever would. Adam had made that clear—and Harper finally believed him.

She wrapped the glittery purple scarf around her neck—brand-new purchase, courtesy of Mom and Dad, though they didn't know it—and applied one last layer of raspberry lip gloss. Adam was due any minute, and she was running late—it had taken her far too long to decide what to wear. But the perfect outfit was essential: Everyone who was anyone would be at Kaia's tonight. Harper had seen to that.

A last-minute party wasn't the easiest thing to pull off, but Harper had plenty of connections—and, fortunately, the town of Grace wasn't about to offer much competition when it came to exciting nightlife. Even on New Year's Eve.

Harper had been happy to help. These days, she was happy to do pretty much anything. Being in love could do that to you. And not only was she happier than she'd ever been, but for the first time, it was a happiness that didn't depend on seeing others miserable.

Not completely, at least.

She slid on a pair of strappy silver heels that went perfectly with her silvery halter top, and checked herself out in the mirror.

I look hot, she thought approvingly. *I look like the kind of girl who* should *be dating the hottest guy in town.*

Officially, it was Kaia's party, she supposed. But it would be *Harper's* night. And, in a few more hours, the beginning of *Harper's* year. She'd wasted so much time worrying that Adam didn't want her, worrying that she should be a better person—screw that. Adam loved her just the way she was. He'd proven that much last night. And then again this afternoon. And Harper had proven to herself that she was every bit as incredible as she'd always thought.

It was New Year's Eve, a time for resolutions, and this year, Harper had only one: No more second-guessing herself, no more feeling guilty about how she might have acted, regretful about what she might have done. She deserved everything she had—and she had it all.

They say you can't have it all. But what did they know?

And what better way to celebrate her good fortune, Kaia decided, than to open her house to the peons and show off her remarkable house and her remarkable life?

She'd slipped into a dusty rose Miu Miu top, with deliciously expensive fabric and a plunging neckline, and paired it with a suede skirt she'd picked up at a Betsey

Johnson sample sale last year. The color looked fabulous against her deep tan—which, she had to admit, was even better than the one she'd picked up last winter break, sipping Margaritas on a yacht off the coast of Turks and Caicos.

Too bad that, along with her perfect wardrobe and her perfect tan, she couldn't show off her perfect man. Jack Powell was considered such a prize—Grace's bachelor #1—it was a shame Kaia couldn't broadcast their relationship to the world. Powell had his choice of any girl, any woman he wanted—and he wanted Kaia.

To think she'd almost let herself get distracted, by Reed, of all people. Pizza boy had something, that was clear. But it wasn't anything she wanted. Not while she had a man like Jack Powell at her beck and call. Living in New York City had taught Kaia a few things, and she knew that you didn't trade in your penthouse for a tenement. First-class apartments were hard to come by—almost as hard as first-class guys. *Especially* in a place like this.

Kaia and Jack Powell, together? That was a power couple, a pair who would turn heads.

Kaia and Reed Whoever? An image like that could only turn stomachs—starting with Kaia's own.

So what if she found Reed intriguing, if her heart pounded a little faster, a little louder when he was around? All that was in the past—and, she resolved, it was going to stay that way. The New Year meant no more Reed. No more playing with fire—and no more digging through the trash.

Kaia was strict about her New Year's resolutions, stricter than most—she usually lasted well into February.

This year, she lasted about five minutes. And then the doorbell rang.

She checked her watch—8:30—still far too early for even the most overeager of guests. And Kaia was pretty sure Harper wouldn't have invited anyone clueless enough to even show up on time. Or did they not do fashionably late out here in hicksville?

She opened the door—and there he was, the same ratty T-shirt, the same smoldering eyes, and suddenly she was right back where she'd started.

On the brink of disaster.

"I heard you're having a party," Reed said by way of greeting. "My invitation must have gotten lost in the mail."

"You weren't—" Kaia cut herself off, torn between wanting to slam the door in his face and wanting to rip his clothes off. Telling him he purposely hadn't been invited didn't seem like the right move, but what if he wanted to stay? *That* could never be allowed. Your guest list defined you, and she refused to be known as the type of girl who invited—or even acknowledged the existence of—his type of guy.

"I don't do parties," he informed her.

She struggled not to look too relieved. On the other

hand, she wasn't quite ready for him to leave. And she definitely wasn't ready for the realization that a part of her wanted to leave with him. "So why are you here?" she asked, trying to sound as if she didn't care.

Which, she assured herself, she didn't.

"I figured we'd start the New Year together," he explained.

"It's eight thirty," she pointed out caustically.

"I thought you could just pretend," he said, flashing a knowing grin. "You're good at that."

He pulled out a paper noisemaker and gave it a half-hearted toot. Then, tossing it aside, he pulled her into his arms.

"Happy New Year," he whispered, his breath hot against her cheek, and then kissed her, sucking deeply on her lower lip, digging his hands into her flesh. She tore at him with urgency, at first, and then something shifted—the rough and raw energy between them softened, deepened. As his hands cupped her face, she opened her eyes, and he was watching her, his bottomless brown eyes only centimeters away. She could see herself reflected in them. She closed her eyes again and shut in the darkness, her world narrowed to the taste of his lips, the touch of his fingers, the sound of his breathing.

Happy New Year? She mused. *Just maybe.*

chapter thirteen

"YOU'RE THE ONLY ONE I WANT, THE ONLY ONE I need. . . ."

Adam let the lyrics wash over him and pulled Harper in tighter as they swayed slowly back and forth to the music. She leaned her head on his shoulder, her auburn waves cascading down his chest.

Kaia's house, even more impressive than he'd remembered, was filled with people—some lounging in the hot tub, some picking their way through the gourmet spread, and a few couples off on the fringes, lost in their own world, like Harper and Adam.

A cool, bluish light lit the oversize room, giving the

stark white furniture and walls an icy sheen.

"I could never live here," Harper murmured, voicing his thoughts. "It's too . . ."

"Cold," he finished for her. And it was true. Living like this, like Kaia, you could freeze to death.

"But it's a great party," she continued. "Don't you think?"

"Definitely." Also true. "But any party would be great—with you." Adam had already had a couple drinks, and, with a little alcohol poured into him, his cheesiness factor skyrocketed.

Harper raised her head from his shoulder and looked him in the eye. "Ad, you don't need to butter me up. You've already got me," she pointed out, giving him a quick kiss on the cheek.

"What?" he asked defensively. "It's true!"

She laughed and shook her head, her hair whipping across his face. "You're a little drunk, my friend. But you're also pretty damn sweet, so I guess it's okay."

"Well, as long as I have your permission," he blustered.

She laid her head back against his shoulder. "I love this song," she said softly.

"All I ever needed, here in your arms . . ."

More couples had joined them on the impromptu dance floor—but only one of them caught Adam's eye.

Kane had his back turned, but Adam could see her face, peeking over Kane's shoulder. Her blond hair was down, falling across her cheek like a golden curtain. And her clear blue eyes met his.

"*. . . the only one I want, the only one I need . . .*"

He closed his eyes—but he still saw her face.

Beth jerked her head away.

Stop watching him, she instructed herself sternly, knowing it was no use. She'd been following him with her eyes all night, catching a glimpse of him embracing Harper by the doorway, holding hands on the stairs, kissing on the back deck. They were everywhere—and Beth couldn't force herself to stay away.

"What's wrong?" Kane asked, peering down at her in concern.

"Nothing," she said quietly, thinking fast. "I was just looking . . . at all these couples dancing. It's kind of sad, isn't it, how no one really dances anymore?"

"We're dancing," he pointed out.

"No, that's not what I mean. We're just standing in one place, rocking back and forth. That's not dancing—not *really*. In the old days . . ."

"Let me guess: women in fancy ball gowns, men in tuxedos sweeping them around the dance floor?" he suggested.

"Waltzing the night away," she added, with a dreamy, faraway smile.

"Don't forget the 'forbidden dance,'" he put in with a smirk.

She gave him a teasing push. "Kane, I'm serious!"

"And like I always say, your wish is my command." He grabbed her hand in his, placing her other hand firmly at his waist. "Let's go."

"Go where—?"

Without answering, he swept her feet off the floor and, in classic ballroom form, began leading her around the room, weaving through couples and crowds of people, twirling her out and then reeling her back in.

"People are staring at us!" she gasped through her laughter.

"Let them stare," he crowed. "They're just jealous."

The whole room had, indeed, gradually stopped talking and turned to gape at the couple whirling through the room as if clumsy extras in a remake of *Cinderella.* But for once, Beth didn't care. She was having too much fun, breathless with laughter, flying in Kane's arms, feeling suddenly, wildly alive. He was right: Who cared what anyone thought?

Finally the song ended, and he dipped her with an exaggerated flourish and then swept her back up into a deep kiss. "Happy New Year," he whispered.

"I've never—that was unbelievable," she babbled, still flushed and giggling.

"I promised you I'd show you a good time," he reminded her. "You just have to trust me."

"I guess I've learned my lesson," she agreed, unable to stop smiling. She kissed him again. "So, what's next on the agenda?"

"Funny you should ask." He pulled a small box out of his pocket and handed it to her. "I've got a little surprise for you—Merry belated Christmas."

"What is it?" she asked in delight, tearing off the wrapping paper. Her smile faded as she opened the box and saw what lay inside.

Two small yellow tablets. And that was it.

"Kane, what is this?" she asked in a dull, flat voice.

"Just something to make our New Year's *ex*-tra special," he explained, putting an arm around her.

She shrugged it off.

"I don't do drugs," she snapped. "You know that."

"It's not like this would make you a junkie," he wheedled. "It's just something special, a one-time deal. And you won't *believe* how it will make you feel."

Beth suddenly felt like she was in the middle of one of those horrible after-school specials they forced on you in junior high health class, where the heroine almost bows to peer pressure but, in the end, wises up and decides to "just say no!" Or maybe this was one of those where the heroine decides to throw caution to the wind . . . and ends up living in a cardboard box with needle tracks tracing across her arms.

No, I don't do drugs, she'd assured her parents the one time they'd gotten up the nerve to ask. *Trust me, even if I wanted to, I wouldn't know where to find them.*

It had been true—for seventeen years—and now, suddenly, it wasn't.

Beth looked at the small open box, the innocuous-looking tablets. How much harm could they do, just this one time? What about all her talk about trying new things, taking risks—was it just that? Talk? She was always so predictable, so *good*, always doing the right thing. She looked across the room and there he was again, Adam—her gaze drawn to him no matter how hard she tried to avoid it. He kissed Harper, and Beth shivered. She'd done the right thing with him, and where had it gotten her? He still thought she was a cheater. A traitor. Everyone did. So why not actually *do* something, for once? It's not like she had a reputation to protect, not anymore. Was she going to go through her life too afraid of consequences to ever really *live*?

She picked up one of the pills between her thumb and index finger and looked at it thoughtfully.

"You said you wanted some excitement in your life, a thrill," Kane pointed out. "This is it—it's like nothing you've ever felt before."

"I don't know, Kane . . . it's not . . . is it safe?"

"As safe as can be," he promised. "Would I be willing to take them myself if it weren't safe?"

She raised an eyebrow, and he gave her a rueful grin.

"You have a point," he admitted. "But I would never put you in danger." He grabbed her and kissed her, lifting her off the ground, and then, slowly, eased her back down to earth. "I just want to show you something that's almost as amazing as you are."

It was tempting—and it would be so easy to say yes. But skiing down a mountain was one thing, Beth decided. Throwing yourself off a cliff was another. "I don't think so," she said, wishing she sounded more resolute.

"Come on," Kane urged. "You know you want to."

Beth looked at him and, suddenly, snapped back to reality. *You know you want to?* This wasn't even *creative* peer pressure—it was absurdly textbook, as if he'd lifted the line from a drug pusher's manual: *How to Drug Friends and Influence People.* She might be naive, but not naive enough to fall for this.

Beth put the tablet back into the box, replaced the lid, and tried to hand it back to Kane, but he refused.

"Take it," he said irritably. "I went to a lot of trouble to get these. I promise nothing will happen to you. Don't you want to have some fun, for once in your life?"

Without a word, she slipped the box into her purse,

shook her head, and began to turn away. She needed—well, she didn't know what she needed, exactly, other than to be somewhere else, away.

"Don't you trust me?" he asked plaintively.

And that's when she finally figured it out.

No. I don't.

It was 11:29, and Miranda pushed her way out to the back deck, her heart pounding in her chest. He was out there, somewhere, her mystery man. He'd told her he would be wearing a gray-and-green-striped shirt, and she'd told him she would be wearing a pale blue, off-the-shoulder top. She still hadn't told him that she was mousy and flat-chested, with rust-colored hair and a big mouth—but he'd find all that out soon enough. She hoped he wouldn't care.

She saw the shirt first.

Normal build, normal height, no extra limbs—so far, so good.

Then she saw his face.

She raised her eyes to the ceiling. Was it too much to ask that she not be the punch line of *every* cosmic joke?

Introducing Bachelor #1: Greg. Of course. The Greg she'd dated a couple of times and then blown off, the Greg who reamed her out every time he saw her, then raced off in the opposite direction. Miranda choked back a spurt of crazed laughter and resisted the impulse to offer up a feeble request: Can I see what's behind door number two?

But then, maybe because of the champagne, maybe because of the holiday spirit, maybe because she was just tired of being alone, Miranda took a moment. And reconsidered. After all, she remembered another Greg, the one who had been so good to her, before everything went down. A guy it had been so easy for her to talk to, and who, back in the beginning, at least, had seemed to like her so much.

Maybe this wasn't such a disaster. Maybe it was actually the universe's way of giving her a second chance.

"Miranda?" he asked in disbelief. "Please tell me *you're* not Spitfire?"

"Guilty," she replied with a weak smile.

The look on his face mirrored her own expression of a moment before: a mixture of disappointment, incredulity, and disgust.

"It figures," he mumbled under his breath, and turned to walk away.

"Greg, wait," Miranda said, grabbing his arm. "I know this seems—"

"Pathetic? Like a cruel joke?"

"Weird," she said firmly. "But think about it. This kind of makes sense. We have a lot in common, we get along . . . we used to get along. . . . Maybe this is a sign? That we should give it another shot?"

"A sign?" He shot her a look of disbelief, then shook his head. "It's a sign, all right—a sign that I should have listened to my instincts, that I should have known better than to try to meet someone on a website. What was I thinking—what kind of girl could I really have expected to find on the *Internet*?"

"Could you lower your voice?" Miranda begged, edging away from him as the people nearby turned to stare.

"I told myself they wouldn't all be desperate and pathetic," he continued, just as loudly. "I lied to myself. I should have known, they would all be just like *you*."

Kane took another gulp of vodka from his trusty silver flask.

She'd walked away from him. Again. On New Year's.

This was getting old.

And what had he done wrong this time? Just tried to show her how to have a little fun. But she was too good for that, wasn't she? Too trapped by her narrow-minded view of the world to even notice when someone offered her an escape route.

Kane reached in his pocket and pulled out another of the little yellow pills. Good thing he'd kept an extra supply on hand, just in case. He had hoped they could share this experience, that it would loosen her up and bring them closer—and isn't that what she was always whining about?

Wishing he would open up, let her get close? She'd had her chance—and she'd blown it.

He popped the pill in his mouth and let it dissolve on his tongue, washing it down with another swig of vodka.

He hated to take this stuff on his own, it was such a waste—but soon the drug would sweep over him and take him away, and then he wouldn't care. Besides, he was used to alone. Alone was how he lived. It had never stopped him before, and it wouldn't stop him tonight.

He wouldn't let it.

She'd been a fool. Made an enormous mistake. That much was clear. But so much was still muddy and confusing.

Beth threaded her way through the crowd and found her way out to the back deck, taking a deep gulp of fresh air. Turning her back on the noise of the party and the revelers in the hot tub, she leaned against the railing and looked out into the night. She'd made a mistake, yes. But what was it? Walking away from Kane? Or walking toward him in the first place?

Half of her wanted to run back into the party and apologize; the other half wanted to leave and never look back. And, much as she hated to admit it, there was a small, small part of her conscious of the pills lodged in her purse, wondering: What if . . . ?

Too many options; too many decisions. So instead, she

stayed at the railing, still, willing herself to think about something other than herself, than her bad choices. If she could clear her mind completely, maybe she could start over, start fresh. But before she could reboot, she'd need to shut down her mind, shut off her thoughts—and they were racing too quickly to be caught.

She heard the footsteps, getting closer and closer, then stop, just behind her.

She heard her name spoken, softly, hesitantly.

But she didn't turn around—not yet. She didn't know what she was going to say. And as long as she kept her back to him, she wouldn't have to decide.

"How many rooms does this place have?" Harper asked in astonishment as she stumbled into the study after Kaia.

"I'm still trying to figure that out," Kaia giggled.

Harper goggled at the room as they stepped inside—it was about eight by eight and, as far as she could tell, seemed to serve mainly as a closet for the Sellers' elaborate computer and media set-up. "This is unbelievable," she gushed.

Under normal circumstances she might not have been so eager to expose her awe at Kaia's starring role in *Lifestyles of the Rich and Bitchy*, preferring to mask her longing for the other girl's clothes, car, house . . . life. But these weren't normal circumstances. It was New Year's Eve, she was at a party, her life was nearly perfect—and she'd already had maybe a little too much of the fluorescent pink punch sitting in a Waterford crystal bowl by the door of the kitchen. She was totally buzzed—but was it the alcohol? she wondered. Or was it Adam?

Kaia, a few miles away from sober herself, was clicking frantically through the music files. "I know it's in here somewhere," she insisted. "You have got to hear this song."

"I can hear it later," Harper pointed out. "We can't spend the whole night in here while you look." But she wasn't annoyed—her umbrella of goodwill was large enough to cover Kaia. Especially since Kaia was, after all, the one who'd delivered Adam to her doorstep. She felt a wave of friendship toward her former rival and, just as Kaia found the right song and clicked play, pulled her into the center of the room, and began twirling her around. An intense driving beat burst from the speakers, matched by a pumping base line. Harper and Kaia whirled around, throwing themselves into the music, the moment.

Suddenly, the door swung open, and Kane stumbled into the room, grabbing Harper away from Kaia and swinging her into his arms. "Can I cut in?" he asked gruffly and belatedly, his breath hot and stinking of vodka.

Harper pushed him away. "Get off, Kane. You're drunk," she complained in disgust.

"Oh, and you're not?" he countered, grabbing her again and trying to kiss her.

She veered away, and his lips smeared across her cheek. She'd never seen him like this—so *sloppy.* Beneath his lackadaisical front, Harper knew, lay a total control freak—and yet, at the moment, he was most definitely out of control.

"What's the matter, you don't think I'm sexy?" he slurred, flexing a bicep.

"Yeah, Kane, you're really sexy," she agreed sarcastically. "Especially now."

"Oh, I'm not good enough for you now?" he asked hostilely, lurching backward.

"Why do you care?" she snapped. "You're with Beth now, *remember*? Where is she, anyway?" Harper looked around in mock confusion. "Having a little trouble keeping track of your date?"

"Apparently no more than you are," he shot back, his voice suddenly clear and steady. "Or has Adam's personality finally faded so much that he's turned invisible?"

Harper ignored the insult and immediately poked her head out into the main party area, ready to prove Kane wrong.

But Adam was nowhere to be seen.

And neither was Beth.

"Lose something?" Kane asked sardonically.

She barely heard him—she was too busy asking herself the same question.

chapter fourteen

HE FOUND BETH OUT ON THE DECK, HER BACK TO the party, staring aimlessly out at the dark desert expanse stretching beneath her.

"Beth?" he said quietly—no answer.

Tentatively, he touched her shoulder, and she whirled around. But her face relaxed as soon as she recognized him.

"Oh, it's just you." She sighed.

"Are you okay out here?" he asked, noticing that her eyes were red and glassy with unshed tears.

"I'm fine," she assured him. "Just . . . thinking."

"Yeah, I've been doing a lot of that lately," he commiserated, leaning up against the rail that encircled the deck. "And there's something I want to talk to you about."

She ran a weary hand through her hair.

"Adam, I don't really have the energy right now for—"

"Then just listen," he begged her. "I need to say this. It's New Year's, you know."

"Yes, I'd noticed," she said dryly.

"I don't want to start the new year like this," he told her. With us—like this."

She wrinkled her face in confusion. "Are you saying you want us to get back—"

"No, no, no," he cut her off hastily. Was that relief in her eyes? Or disappointment? "No—I just hate it that we can't even talk anymore." *Except for that afternoon in the mountains*, he didn't say, though he wanted to. *That day when it seemed like things could be . . . different. Better.*

"We're talking now," she pointed out.

Just be direct, he coached himself. Beth had hurt him, badly—but he had to let it go. He couldn't move on if he was still trying to punish her, he'd realized. And also . . . he just couldn't stand to hurt her anymore. No matter what she'd done to him.

"I want to apologize," he finally blurted out. "I've treated you like shit. I've been horrible to you, and I realize now I was wrong."

"Well, that's nice of you, but . . ."

"We all make mistakes, Beth," he pressed on, "and I

should never have expected you to be perfect. So I want you to know"—he took a deep breath, for this was an incredibly difficult sentiment for him to express—"I forgive you."

"You forgive me?" she asked incredulously. "*You* forgive *me*?"

He'd expected tears of gratitude, an outpouring of shame, or even just a wordless hug—but he hadn't been prepared for the wave of anger flooding her face.

"You forgive me for what?" she snapped.

She had to ask?

"You know for what—for *Kane*," he hissed.

"How many times do I have to tell you that nothing *happened*?" she cried.

Adam felt his muscles clench and he tried to stay calm. He couldn't believe it. He'd worked so hard to do the mature thing, swallow his pride, offer his forgiveness—and she still couldn't even admit what she'd done to him?

"You can tell me as many times as you want," he retorted, his voice rising, "but it won't help. I know what you did. Why can't you just admit it?"

"There's nothing to admit!" she exclaimed.

"I can't—" He started to turn away, then stopped. He couldn't keep doing this to himself. He couldn't start the year off like this. It wasn't fair—to anyone. "Look, I didn't come out here to start a fight with you," he said softly, turning back around.

"I don't want to fight anymore either," she admitted, the tension visibly leaching out of her body.

"Can we call a truce?" he asked hopefully. "Agree to disagree?"

She nodded. "I'd like that."

They stood facing each other in silence for a moment, and then Adam broke the wall of distance with a hug, sweeping her into his arms. Her hair still smelled like lilacs, fresh and sweet. It felt so right to hold her, to remember the way her body had fit snugly against his. And she clung to him, her arms wrapped tightly around his neck, her face buried in his shoulder, and he could feel her crying—but when she finally looked up at him, her eyes were dry.

"Remember last New Year's?" she asked, her arms still wrapped loosely around him, his arms lightly encircling her waist. When Adam was with Harper, pushing Beth out of his mind seemed so easy. But now, facing her, holding her, the past seemed more real than the present.

He nodded ruefully. "This isn't the way I thought things would end up."

She sighed. "I know. I guess I thought we would . . ."

"So did I," he said softly, brushing a tear from her cheek. Her skin was like silk. It would be so easy to lean forward just a bit, to close his eyes and forget where he was and what had happened between them, just to feel the tender touch of her lips again. He caught his breath for a moment, and all he could see were her lips, glossy and slightly parted, and all he could feel was his desperate need—

"We should really get back inside," she said awkwardly, breaking away from him.

He dropped his hands to his sides abruptly. What the hell had he been thinking?

"I should—go find Harper," he stammered.

"And Kane." She sighed. "I guess I should . . ." She shook her head. "Let's just go back inside." They threaded their way back toward the sliding-glass door to the living room, but before they stepped through, Adam stopped her.

"I'm glad we talked," he told her, leaning close. "I really want things to be better between us."

"They will," she promised, and took his hand.

They stood at the threshold, and Adam knew he had to step inside, rejoin the party, find Harper. But Beth's hand was still tightly wrapped around his, comforting and warm.

And he really didn't want to let go.

"I can't believe you let him out of your sight," Kane taunted her. "You really think that's safe?"

"Would you just shut up?" Harper snapped irritably. She was so sick of Kane's overblown ego, his superiority complex—as if he were really so much better than the rest of them. "Adam loves me," she maintained. "*I've* got nothing to worry about. You, on the other hand . . ."

She turned away to join Kaia, who was lying low and clicking through music files in the back corner, obviously trying to stay out of the line of fire, but too curious to slip out of the room.

"And what's that supposed to mean?" Kane asked, flinging himself onto a small leather couch pressed against the wall. "Beth and I are just fine."

Harper just snorted.

"Got something you want to share with the rest of the class, Grace?"

"You and Beth are a walking disaster," she informed him. "A ticking time bomb, a train wreck, a—oh, pick whatever tired cliché you want. The whole relationship is a joke."

"I'm not laughing," he said in a dangerous voice.

"But everyone else is," Harper countered. "It's so obvious she'd never be with you if Adam hadn't broken up with her. She never would have even looked at you."

"What about you?" Kane asked, rising from the sofa and striding toward her. "Like Adam would ever have dropped Beth for the town *slut*?"

"You can insult me all you want," Harper said, feeling the bile rise in her throat. Sticks and stones may break your bones—but names seeped inside and killed you slowly from within. Not that she'd ever admit it. "But I know the truth," she insisted. "Adam *wants* to be with me."

"Only because he thinks Beth cheated on him," Kane pointed out.

"So?"

"*So?* So she *didn't*—or have you forgotten that little detail? In this delusional world you've created for yourself, have you forgotten that we just made him *think* she cheated on him?" He grabbed Harper by the shoulders and gave her a rough shake. "Snap out of it. He's not with you because he wants to be. He's with you because you tricked him. You lied to him."

"*We* lied," Harper corrected him. "And it doesn't matter." She pulled herself away and turned her back on him, hugging herself in an effort to hold it together. "He would have come to me eventually. We just sped things up a little."

"No, *Beth* would have come to *me* eventually," Kane countered. "They always do. You, on the other hand, would still be alone."

"Why are you doing this to me?" Harper asked in a tight and muffled voice.

"Why are *you* trying to pretend you're so much better than me, that your relationship with Adam is oh-so-perfect, while Beth and I are—" He turned Harper around to face him, and she met his gaze fiercely. "We're the same, you and I."

"We are *not*," she insisted.

She glared at Kane, at his smug, superior face. He didn't care about anyone, about whom he lied to, whom he hurt. That wasn't her, she assured herself. She only did what she did because she had to. It wasn't her fault. That person, cold and calculating, heartless—she could act the part, but it wasn't real. It wasn't *her*.

"We are, Harper," he pressed on. "Looking at you, it's like looking in a mirror. Why don't you just admit it? For once in your life, why don't you just tell the truth?"

"She doesn't know how."

Kane glanced up at the sound of the cold, thin voice—but Harper didn't need to. She'd recognized it. She'd know his voice anywhere. But finally she couldn't stand it anymore. She had to turn around, had to see his face—and Adam was frozen in the doorway, Beth by his side.

The world went dark for a moment, and Harper thought she would pass out—longed for unconsciousness. But then everything swam back into focus, and it was real. He was there. And from the look on his face, she could tell.

He'd heard everything.

⁂

At first, their angry voices hadn't really registered. Adam hadn't processed what they were saying, what it meant. It was only when Beth, standing beside him just outside the doorway of the small study, issued a quiet moan, that he had understood.

He had blundered in here looking for Harper, and he'd found her, he realized. The *real* Harper.

The four of them stood frozen in silence for a moment, just staring at one another in disbelief. Beth broke first.

"How could you?" she cried, her eyes whipping back and forth from Harper to Kane. "Did you really think you'd get away with this?"

Kane shrugged his shoulders and flopped down on the couch. "Sure, I did," he admitted, his hands propped casually behind his head. "Don't tell me you're surprised."

"I-I-" Beth stopped stuttering and burst into tears, fleeing the room. Adam wanted to chase after her, but it was as if his feet were stuck to the floor. He couldn't move—couldn't take his eyes off Harper.

"Adam—" She rushed up to him, put her hands on his shoulders, "Adam, please, you have to understand."

Gently but firmly, he took her hands off his body and returned them to her sides.

"Don't touch me," he warned her in a low monotone.

He felt a dull, hard anger spreading over his body. Not the burning rage that had swept over him when he'd found out about Beth. This was something different, something new. He felt calm and cold, as if his veins had turned to ice, as if something inside of him had died.

"You were my oldest friend, my best friend," he told her slowly. "I trusted you." Past tense. "I thought I *loved* you."

"Adam, please," Harper begged, tears streaming down her face. In all the years he'd known her, he had never seen her cry. He wondered idly whether he should be feeling surprise, or pity. He felt—nothing. Hollow. Spent.

"I love you, Adam!" Harper cried, throwing herself against his chest, clinging to him. "You mean everything to me."

"And you mean nothing to me," he spit out, pulling himself away. "*You're nothing.*"

She flinched at his words, but he had moved beyond caring. He wasn't even trying to hurt her. He was just stating a truth. Everything he'd believed in, everything he'd trusted in, it had disappeared. There was nothing left but emptiness. The Harper he had known—the Harper he may have loved—just didn't exist. Smoke and mirrors, a pretty illusion. That was all.

"I have to go now," he said mechanically. "I have to find Beth."

"Then go," Harper said, slumping down to her knees

as if she'd lost the strength to stand. "Just go. But you know you won't be happy with her, Adam. You know it won't be like what we had. What we had was real."

"And you killed it." Adam pointed out. "Maybe you can forgive yourself for that," he added, stepping around her and out the door, "but I can't."

chapter fifteen

BETH NEEDED TO GET OUT, TO GET AWAY. SHE FELT like the walls were closing in on her, as if everyone were staring at her—the clamor of the party rose in her ears and hammered at her, crushing her. She just needed to go, to think.

She slipped out the front door and then paused, drawing in deep and desperate breaths of the dry night air. She supposed she should be worried about finding a way to get home, but that seemed like a remote problem, something that would take care of itself, somehow, sometime. Right now she just breathed in the peace and quiet, and waited.

Because deep down, she knew he would come.

And he did.

"I thought I'd find you out here," he said from behind her.

Beth didn't turn around.

Adam touched her back for an instant and then pulled his hand away.

"I don't know what to say," he admitted.

Beth hugged her arms to her chest. She could think of plenty of things for him to say: how he should have trusted her instead of throwing her away; how stupid he'd been to be duped by Harper's sadistic game . . . but then, hadn't she been just as stupid? Hadn't she fallen blindly into Kane's arms? Or worse, not so blindly. She'd seen what he was, she'd known it deep down, and she'd ignored it. She'd wanted so badly for it to work, for Kane to be the guy she needed him to be—for her new relationship to somehow *best* Adam's. It had all been more important to her than the truth.

She turned to face Adam, and almost gasped. He looked wrecked. Literally, as if a sudden storm had swept through his life and cast him on a barren shore. His eyes were hooded, his shoulders slumped.

"I—I'm sorry," he said, raising his hands from his sides, palms up in supplication. "I don't know what I'm supposed to do."

"You should never have trusted her word over mine," Beth pointed out.

Adam shook his head.

"No. But . . ." He looked up at her, his eyes welling with tears. "She was my best friend."

It was a sentiment Beth would be happy never to hear again, even in the past tense.

"And I was your girlfriend," she retorted angrily. "Why was it so hard for you to remember that part? *I* loved you too. *I* was always there for you—how could you think I could ever do anything like that?"

"I don't know!" he cried, his mouth twisting into a gash of pain. "I don't know."

He looked so miserable, so lonely, so bereft, she couldn't stand it.

"It's not all your fault," she offered, a note of sympathy entering her voice. "They played you. They played us both. How were you supposed to know?"

"I should have—" His voice faltered, and she took a few steps toward him, put her hands lightly on his shoulders.

"You should have trusted me," she said firmly. "But you didn't."

"Because I'm an idiot."

"Because something was wrong between us, Adam," she reminded him softly. "That's why you believed them. Because you and I, we were already—"

"Don't say that," he protested. "Please. I . . ." He

closed his eyes for a moment. "I loved you. And you . . . I thought . . ."

"I loved you, too." It still hurt to say the words.

He tensed beneath her fingers.

"I still can't believe it," he said, his voice tight with anger. "How could anyone be so—" he choked himself off, shaking with rage.

"Adam, forget it," she advised him.

"Forget it?" he repeated incredulously. "And how the hell am I supposed to do that?"

"You just do." She turned him around to face her. "It was horrible, what they did," she agreed, shivering at the memory of Kane's arms cradling her as she cried and cried, and all the while, he'd been the cause of all her pain. "It was unspeakable, but in the end, they didn't get away with it," she pointed out. "We're here, now, together. Maybe this is . . ." She hesitated. "A second chance."

He grabbed her hands and pulled them to his chest. "You mean . . . ?"

"We've both done some things we regret," Beth told him. And it was true. She had shut him out, long before Kane and Harper broke into their lives. She'd stopped trusting him, picked fights over nothing. Harper and Kane had shoved them over a cliff—but they'd made it to the edge all by themselves. Maybe this was their do-over. "But maybe if we start off slow, forget the past . . . that is, if you still want to."

He brought her hands to his mouth and kissed them softly. "More than anything." He suddenly looked at his watch. "It's midnight," he told her with surprise. "Happy New Year."

She looked up at him and smiled. "I think it will be."

And then he kissed her.

"Happy New Year!" the roomful of drunken revelers shouted, throwing confetti and flinging themselves into one another's arms.

Miranda spotted Greg across the room, making out with some random girl. She couldn't pull her eyes away from them, Greg's hands running through her hair, their bodies wound together. That used to be her—could have been her.

She had hated kissing Greg, she reminded herself. It had been a total drag, long and wet and boring.

But standing there alone on yet another New Year's Eve, watching all these couples start off their year together, she wondered: Maybe her standards were too high, unrealistic. Maybe settling was better than being alone.

"There you are, Stevens!"

Miranda whirled around to see Kane, a wide grin stretched across his face, lurching toward her. He flung his arms around her and whirled her off the ground, and then, before she knew what was happening, gave her a wet and sloppy kiss. On the lips.

He had kissed her.

Kane's lips had just touched hers.

"Happy New Year!" he shouted, slinging an arm around her shoulders. Miranda barely heard him.

He'd kissed her.

And now, she was standing there, nestled beneath his arm, leaning against him, breathing in his familiar cologne.

He was obviously drunk or high—maybe both—it was the only time he ever showed any genuine affection to anyone. But Miranda didn't care. The alcohol, the drugs, whatever, they'd just loosened him up, cracked through that impenetrable veneer and dragged his real feelings to the surface.

He'd come to find her, at midnight—he'd kissed her. Not Beth, not any of his double-D ditzes. Her.

So he was drunk. So it had probably been a "just friends" kiss. So what? She was starting out the new year in Kane Geary's arms, and whatever happened next, she would always have this moment, this night.

And for right now, that was enough.

Harper watched Kane and Miranda celebrate together and smiled sadly. Miranda would be so pathetically happy at even the tiny, drunken show of affection. The next day she'd call Harper and they would spend hours dissecting the single moment. And the day after that? When she found out, as she inevitably would, that Harper had betrayed her, had pushed her "one true love" into the arms of their worst enemy?

Then she'd be gone from Harper's life, just like everyone else.

She'd just lost Miranda, even if Miranda didn't know it yet. But she couldn't muster up the strength to care. How could she focus on a trivial pain like that when her entire body, her whole being, was throbbing with the agony of having lost Adam? When he'd turned his back on her and walked away, she'd felt like a piece of herself had died.

If he'd only gotten angry. If he'd yelled, screamed, kicked something—anything but that cold, dead voice, those empty eyes. As if anything that had ever been between them was just—gone.

Her life was in ruins. Reduced to rubble.

Harper stood in the middle of the party, the crowd surging around her. She didn't cry. She didn't scream or tear at her hair or fall to the floor or do anything that might betray the searing pain within, that might show the world she'd been torn in two.

That wasn't her way—and, after all, what would people think?

So she stood there, still, a frozen smile fixed on her face, and watched the celebration. All around her, people were laughing, hugging, starting their New Year off right, together.

And still she stood, unseen, unmoving—unloved.

And maybe that was exactly what she deserved.

Under other circumstances, Kaia supposed she would have enjoyed the little show put on by Haven High's resident star-crossed lovers. But for some reason, she hadn't. Maybe because she hated to see her carefully crafted plans laid to waste, or maybe because her brief alliance with Harper had inspired a twisted kind of loyalty. Maybe it was just because, with two hot guys in her pocket—the sexy prince and the equally sexy pauper—she was feeling unusually charitable. Whatever the reason, she was displeased to see Harper take such a blow—and while Harper had tried her best to play it off, grin and bear it, Kaia wasn't buying. She could see beneath Harper's surface.

And she didn't like what she saw.

She suspected that when she found Adam and Beth—who had quietly and conveniently disappeared—she would like *that* sight even less. Why should Mr. And Mrs. Holier Than Thou get to ride off into the sunset together, no harm, no foul?

Kaia hadn't given anyone any gifts this year. She

hadn't felt there was anyone in her life who deserved an act of generosity. But, suddenly, she changed her mind. Harper could use a little pick-me-up—and Kaia knew just what to get her.

This one's for you, Harper, she thought, heading off in search of her prey. *You'd better appreciate it.*

Beth didn't know how much time had passed—a minute, an hour—she knew only that she was back in Adam's arms, and she felt so happy, so safe. She felt like she'd come home. From out here on the front lawn, you could barely hear the party raging inside. It was as if they were all alone. Together.

"Well, well, well, so this is what 'happily ever after' looks like."

Beth and Adam sprang apart at the sound of Kaia's caustic voice. Beth glanced over at their unwanted trespasser with disgust, but just smiled tightly and said nothing.

Adam wasn't so polite. "Do you mind?" he snarled. "We're busy."

"So I can see," Kaia said with a smile. "Don't mind me. I just wanted to congratulate the happy couple."

Adam put a possessive arm around Beth and glared at Kaia. "Now you've done it," he said. "So go."

"Okay," she agreed cheerfully. "Good night—and

good luck. I hope you actually manage to get her into bed this time."

Beth flinched, but the warm pressure of Adam's hands kept her still.

Ignore her, Beth instructed herself.

"And as for you." Kaia turned to Beth, who steeled herself and promised she wouldn't reward Kaia with a reaction, no matter what the other girl said. "I hope *you'll* be more satisfied by him than I was."

And she walked away.

Adam's face had turned white, all the blood drained away.

"What did she mean by that?" Beth asked, turning to him in hope—and desperation. "What's she talking about?"

Adam was silent. He opened his mouth, but no words came out, and he finally closed it again.

"Adam, what does she *mean*?" Beth asked again, her voice taking on a tinge of panic because, already, she knew. The look on Adam's face, the look on Kaia's—maybe Beth had always known. Maybe that's why she hadn't asked, hadn't let herself wonder why Kaia had suddenly appeared in—and, just as inexplicably, disappeared from—his life.

"You slept with her, didn't you?" Beth asked harshly, her tone brittle. *She* felt brittle—as if a single touch could shatter her into a million pieces.

He said nothing.

"You slept with her while we were still together," Beth insisted now, with less of a question in her voice.

Still, Adam stood there infuriatingly mute.

"Say something!"

He grabbed her hands, but this time she whipped them away, covering her face. "Just tell me it's not true."

"I can't," he finally admitted.

Her body turned to stone—starting with her heart.

"Beth, can't we just—you said we could make a fresh start—"

"Get away from me," she told him in a husky voice.

"I can't just leave you, not like this," he protested, approaching her. She backed away, almost tumbling backward over the uneven ground.

"I said, get away from me!" She closed her eyes and took a deep breath, trying to stop herself from exploding. Not from yelling or flying at him in a rage, both of which she would have been happy to do if she'd been able, but from literally exploding, from letting the hurt and anger rip her to shreds from the inside out.

"Now, Adam. *Go.*"

And so he did.

Beth stumbled blindly down the long driveway toward the dark, empty street below. She supposed that she could find someone to give her a ride home, but she preferred to walk. It would take her all night, trudging for miles along the empty highway, but that was all right. She needed the time to think, to plan.

Because this wasn't like before, Beth realized, when Adam had tossed her out with the garbage in what she now realized was a hypocritical fit of jealous rage. She wasn't broken. She wasn't distraught.

She was angry. And the anger made everything clear.

Harper. Kane. Kaia. Adam. They'd all betrayed her. They'd played their little games with her life, kicked her back and forth like a soccer ball, destroyed her, again and again.

So what was she supposed to do now? Go home and cry? Gorge herself on ice cream and whine about how the world was ever so unfair? Blunder through life finding someone else to trust, only to be crushed and stomped on once again?

She didn't think so.

The old Beth might have cried her way home. And, like a nice girl, a good girl, she would have wept, and waited, and wept, until finally, she'd moved on. She'd get past it.

But not this time—not this Beth.

She walked home dry-eyed, her fists clenched, her mind racing.

Because this time, she wasn't going to get past it.

She wasn't going to get over it.

She was going to get even.

seven deadly sins

WRATH

For Michelle Nagler and Bethany Buck,
extraordinary editors who have given me an
extraordinary opportunity

. . . let grief convert to anger; blunt not the heart, enrage it.
—William Shakespeare, *Macbeth*

And I really want is some patience
A way to calm the angry voice
And all I really want is deliverance.
—Alanis Morissette, "All I Really Want"

preface

IT WAS A MISTAKE.

It had to be.

She'd heard wrong. Or it was a lie.

A dream. A nightmare. Something.

Because if it was true—

If it was true, and this was reality, there was no going back to the person she'd been. Before.

She remembered that person. Hard. Angry. Fury coursing through her veins. It had consumed her, until her focus narrowed to a single point, a single goal: vengeance.

It had been the perfect plan, every detail seamlessly falling into place. She had lain awake imagining how it would play out—wondering whether it would still the howling voice inside her, not that she'd finally given in to what it most desired.

Vengeance.

The plan had worked. Everything had unfolded as she'd imagined it. She'd gotten exactly what she'd wanted. But . . .

She'd made a mistake. A fatal error. Because it hadn't gone exactly *as planned, had it?*

There was supposed to be humiliation—and there was.

There was supposed to be suffering—and there was.

Everything had gone the way it was supposed to. Except—

No one was supposed to die.

two weeks earlier . . .

chapter one

HARPER BURROWED DEEPER BENEATH THE COVERS. How was she supposed to sleep with all that banging?

"Come on, Grace, open up."

Damn her parents. Which part of "I don't want to see anyone" did they not understand?

"We're bored," Kaia complained through the door.

"Come out and play with us!" Kane added, in that little-boy voice most girls found irresistible.

Harper Grace wasn't most girls.

"Go away," she shouted, her voice muffled by the pillow pressed over her head. "Please!"

With that, the door opened—and the covers flew off the bed.

"Time's up, Grace," Kane said, flinging away the comforter. "No more feeling sorry for yourself."

"Screw you. I could have been naked under here!" Harper said indignantly, suddenly realizing that the ratty sweatpants and faded gray Lakers T-shirt was an even more embarrassing ensemble.

"Why else do you think I did it?" Kane asked, chuckling.

How could he laugh?

The three of them had worked so hard to split up Beth and Adam and, for an all too brief moment, they'd finally gotten everything they'd wanted. Kane got Beth. Harper got Adam. And Kaia . . . got to stir up some trouble, which seemed to be all she needed. But now? Everything had come to light, and gone to shit. They were alone. How could Kane laugh, when Harper could barely stand?

"What are *you* looking at?" Harper snapped at Kaia as she climbed out of bed and wrapped a faux silk robe around herself. She hated the idea of Kaia seeing her bedroom, all the shoddy, mismatched furniture and cheap throw pillows; compared with Kaia's surely elegant and unbearably expensive digs, it probably looked like the pathetic "before" shot on one of those lame home-makeover shows.

Harper sighed. Even the prospect of trading insults with her former rival didn't deliver the jolt of energy it should have—not now that Kaia was one of only two friends that Harper had left. Some friends.

A heartless playboy. A soulless bitch. And me, Harper thought sourly.

Not quite the Three Musketeers.

"We're here to cheer you up," Kane said. "So cheer."

"Like it's that easy," Harper grumbled. Though, obviously, it had been for him.

"We even brought reinforcements," he added, pulling a bottle of Absolut from his pocket with a magician-like flourish.

"What, is that your answer to everything?" Harper asked harshly. "If you hadn't been so drunk last week, and opened your big mouth—"

"Children, children," Kaia cut in, placing a perfectly manicured hand on Kane's broad shoulder. "I thought we agreed we were going to move past all that unpleasantness, kiss and make up. Her voice was soft and light, with a razor's edge—that was Kaia. Beautiful and dangerous.

As if Harper was scared of her.

"I don't care what we agreed," she shot back. "If Kane hadn't opened his big, stupid mouth . . . if Beth and Adam hadn't overheard his stupid bragging . . ." She couldn't finish.

"And if I hadn't opened *my* big, stupid mouth, the two lovebirds would be back together right now instead of at each other's throats," Kaia reminded her. "But no need to thank me, and no need to blame him. Even if he's an idiot."

"Hey!" Kane protested. But he was smiling—the infamous Kane smirk, which not even heartbreak could wipe off his face.

"Thanks for the pick-me-up, guys," Harper said, "but I'm not interested. You're dismissed."

"Are you just going to wallow here forever?" Kane asked in disgust. "Doesn't sound like the Grace I know and love."

"As if," she snorted. "I *meant*, I've got better things to do than play guest of honor at your little pity party."

"Like what?" Kaia asked skeptically.

"Like getting ready for my date," Harper lied. She rolled her eyes. "Did you really think I was going to spend Saturday night in bed? Or at least, in *my* bed? Please." She shook her head as if pitying their poor reasoning skills. "I'm just resting up for the main event."

"Now that's more like it," Kane said, his smirk widening into a grin. Kaia just narrowed her eyes, unconvinced.

"So I mean it. Get out," Harper told them. "Or I'll be late."

"Whatever you say, Grace," Kane agreed, grabbing

Kaia and backing out of the room. "Who am I to stand in the path of true lust?"

Harper sighed, and waited for the door to close so she could crawl back into bed, blissfully undisturbed. On second thought—

"Kane?" she called, just as he was about to disappear down the hall. He popped his head back in, and Harper forced herself to smile. "Leave the vodka."

"I can't wait to see the look on her face when she reads this," Miranda Stevens crowed, putting the finishing touches on their masterpiece. "She'll be out for blood."

"Too bad she already sucked us dry," Beth Manning pointed out. She laughed bitterly.

The flyer had been Miranda's idea. She'd been thirsty for revenge against Harper. Beth still had no idea why Miranda was so eager to take down her former best friend, and she didn't really care—Beth had more than enough reasons of her own to go after Haven High's reigning bitch.

And Harper was only the first name on a long list of enemies.

There was Adam Morgan, who was supposed to be the love of her life. Too bad he'd turned out to be a lying hypocrite, accusing her of cheating when he was the one who'd slept with another girl.

Then there was Kaia Sellers . . . the other girl.

Last—and least—there was Kane Geary, whose lies she'd been dumb enough to believe and whose kisses she'd been weak enough to accept.

Sweet, innocent Beth, who rescued spiders and cried at the sappy Hallmark commercials, now hated them all, and none more than Harper Grace, the one pulling the strings.

"All they care about is what people think of them," Miranda had pointed out, "so we flush their reputations and that's it—they're finished."

"Any chance you want to tell me why you're doing this?" Beth asked now.

"Now why would I do that," Miranda replied, pulling her chair up to the computer, "when I could tell you about the time in eighth grade when Harper laughed so hard at the movies, she wet her pants?" Miranda shook her head, almost fondly, and began to type. "I had to call her mother on a pay phone to tell her to bring a new pair of underwear when she picked us up. And meanwhile . . ." Miranda's voice trailed off as she concentrated on typing up the story.

"Meanwhile what?" Beth urged her, choking back laughter.

"Meanwhile, Harper was inside the theater, crawling around on the floor so that the usher wouldn't spot her and throw her out. Eventually I had to fake an asthma attack—you know, create a diversion so she could get out without anyone spotting her."

"Lucky for her you were there," Beth marveled.

"Yeah?" The fond smile faded from Miranda's face. She turned away from Beth and stared at the screen, her fingers clattering loudly against the keyboard. "Yeah, I guess it was."

Cool.

Reed Sawyer hung up the phone and kicked his feet up on the rickety coffee table—really a row of old milk crates held together with superglue and chewing gum. He brought the joint to his lips and drew in a deep breath, closing his eyes as the searing sensation filled his lungs.

She couldn't stay away from him, that was clear.

Very cool.

"Dude, who was it?" his drummer asked, leaning his head back against the threadbare couch. "You look weird."

"Blissed out," the bass player agreed, taking the joint from Reed's outstretched fingertips. "Who's the chick?"

"No one," Reed mumbled.

"It was *her*," the drummer guessed, eyes gaping, and now he leaned forward on the couch. "Wasn't it? The rich bitch?"

"Don't call her that," Reed snapped, the words slipping out before he could stop them.

Damn.

Now they would all know.

"What are you doing with her, dude?" the bass player asked, shaking his head. "Girl like that? She's out of your league."

Let's see: silky jet-black hair, long lashes, designer clothes perfectly tailored to her willowy physique, the smoothest skin he'd ever touched . . . yeah, as if he needed a reminder that she was out of his league.

"What the hell do you know?" Reed asked, his voice lazy and resigned. It wasn't just the foggy halo clouding his mind or the buzz still tingling in his fingers that kept his anger at bay. It was the fact that the guys were right. As if it wasn't obvious that a grungy high school dropout-to-be and the pretty East Coast princess didn't belong together. Not to mention the fact that she *was* a bitch. She treated him like he was scum and obviously thought his friends were a waste of oxygen. But still—

They fit.

"Whatever," he said, standing up. Slowly. "I'm out of here."

"We've got rehearsal," the bass player reminded him.

"Do it without me," Reed said shortly, knowing it didn't matter. Every week, they got together to "rehearse." And every week, their instruments remained piled in the corner, untouched.

Reed had resolved that tonight, they would actually play a set. But that was hours ago, before things got fuzzy—and before she had called. He threaded his way through the ramshackle living room the guys had set up, filled with furniture snagged from the town dump and empty pizza boxes no one could be bothered to throw out.

"Just forget her, dude!" one of the guys called after him. "She'll mess you up!"

Reed just shrugged. Everything in his life was a mess; this thing with Kaia, whatever it was, would fit right in.

"I never . . ." Kaia paused, trying to come up with something suitably exotic. That was the problem with this game. Once you'd done everything, there was nothing left to say. "I never got arrested."

She wasn't surprised when Reed took a drink. That was the rule: If you'd done it, drink up. And of course he'd been arrested. He was that kind of guy.

"For what?" she asked, leaning toward him.

They were perched on the back of his father's tow truck, at the fringe of a deserted mining complex. It was the place they'd come on their first date . . . if you could call it that.

Reed just pressed his lips together and shook his head.

"You're not going to tell me?"

He shook his head again. Big surprise. He didn't talk

much. In fact, he didn't seem to do much of anything besides smoke up, hang out with his grease monkey friends, and stare at Kaia with an intense gaze that stole her breath.

He was beneath her—just like the rest of this town, this hellhole she'd been exiled to for the year. He was nothing. Dull. Deadbeat. Disposable. Or at least he should have been.

They rarely talked. Sometimes they kissed. Often, they just sat together in the dark, breathing each other in.

It was crazy.

And it was fast becoming her only compelling reason to make it through the day.

"I never," he began, putting down his shot glass. "I never kissed you here."

"Liar." Kaia caught her breath as he put his arms around her waist and kissed the long curve of her neck.

"How about here?" he murmured, lightly grazing his tongue along her skin and nibbling her earlobe.

She closed her eyes and sighed heavily.

As if from a great distance, she could hear her phone ringing and knew who it would be. Was it only a few weeks ago that Jack Powell had seemed the consummate prize? The handsome, mysterious French teacher who was totally off limits and totally unable to resist her—he had it all, just as Reed had nothing. So why let the phone ring and ring? Why let Powell sit in his squalid bachelor pad, wondering and waiting, while she hooked up on the back of a pickup truck?

Kaia didn't know.

But with Reed's arms wrapped tightly around her, his curly black hair brushing her cheek, she also didn't care.

Dear Adam, I know you said you never wanted to hear from me again.

Adam Morgan held the match over the letter and paused for a moment, mesmerized by the dancing orange flame. It burned so brightly in the desert night. He dropped the flame into the darkness—and watched it spread.

I'm sorry. I know I've said it before, and you won't listen—but I'm not going to stop. I can't, not until . . .

The envelope had arrived on his doorstep after dinner. She hadn't even had the courage to stick around. Probably too afraid of what he'd say. But Adam had promised himself that he wouldn't say anything at all. Not ever.

I know you think I betrayed you—betrayed what we had. But you have to understand, it's only because I love you. And you love me, I know you do.

He hadn't bothered to read it. He wouldn't give her the satisfaction. Instead, he'd climbed into his car and driven out of town, down a long stretch of deserted highway. He'd pulled over to the side of the road and climbed out. Scrambled over pebbles and spiny cactus brush, with nothing to light his way but the crescent moon. Fifty yards into the wilderness, he'd stopped. Crushed the letter and flung it to the ground.

Lit the match.

If you would just let me explain, Adam. I had *to get you away from her. She wasn't right for you. She couldn't give you what I could. She couldn't love you like I did. Like I do. We've been friends forever—more than friends. You can't give up on us. I can't. I* won't.

The flame was slow, almost deliberate. It ate into the letter, blackening the edges. The pages curled in the heat. The letters swam in front of his eyes, nothing more than meaningless black crawls. None of her words meant anything now; everything she'd told him over all these years had added up to nothing but lies.

For a moment, Adam was tempted to stick his hand in the flame. Maybe a physical pain, torn and blistering flesh, would steal his attention from the other, deeper pain that refused to go away. But he kept his hand still. And the letter burned.

I'll keep apologizing until you hear me. Until I can make you understand. I can be a better person. I can be anyone you need me to be. But I can't do it without you.

The letter was almost fully consumed. Adam was getting cold, and knew he could stop now, stomp out the fire, and leave the remaining fragments for the animals and the elements.

But he waited, and the fire burned on.

I miss you—don't you miss me?

And on.

I need you. We need each other.

And on.

Please.

And then there was just one smoldering fragment left, curling into the flame.

Love forever,

Harper

Adam stamped out the glowing pile of ashes and walked away.

chapter two

BETH HELD HERSELF PERFECTLY STILL, HOPING HE would change his mind and disappear. She didn't want to have to speak, but doubted she'd be able to force herself to stay silent. She didn't want to cry, or give him any indication whatsoever that she still cared, because, of course, she did. And more than anything, she wanted to stop.

"Hi," Adam said softly, sliding into the empty seat to her left.

If only the assembly would begin. Then there would be no chance for conversation, and Beth could pretend he wasn't there.

She hadn't looked in his direction yet, but she'd felt

him hovering, wondering whether or not to sit down. Despite everything he'd done, it was as if a part of them was still connected. And maybe that was why she couldn't resist sneaking a glance at him out of the corner of her eye, longing to smooth down the windblown tufts of blond hair.

With a few words, she could have him back. "I forgive you." That's all it would take, and she could curl up against him again, his arms warm and strong around her. She could be a "we" again.

But she'd promised herself she would never forgive him—and unlike Adam, she kept her promises.

"You're not going to talk to me?" he asked.

Let him figure that one out for himself.

"At least *look* at me!"

Her lip trembled. *I will* not *cry*, she told herself.

"Fine," he spit out. She could tell he was struggling against his temper. "Then just listen." It's not like she had much of a choice—but it was a long time before he spoke again.

"I don't know what I'm supposed to say," he whispered as he reached for her hand. She whipped it away, afraid that if she let him touch her, or if she looked into his clear blue eyes, her anger might drain away.

She willed the principal to take the stage and begin the assembly; it was her only escape.

"What do you want from me?" Adam pleaded. "I said I'm sorry. I told you it wasn't my fault—"

"And whose fault was it?" she snapped. This was good. The more he denied, the more he evaded his responsibility, avoided how much he'd hurt her, the angrier she got. And that made things so much easier.

"Kane's," he pleaded. "Kaia's . . . Harper's."

Beth flinched at the name. It was true, Harper had manipulated him—Adam had just been stupid enough to let her. It was Harper who'd convinced Adam that Beth was cheating on him. Harper who'd enlisted Kane to prey on Beth's weakness and dupe her into a relationship based on lies. And, of course, it was Harper who'd swooped in to collect her prize—Adam—after he'd dumped Beth.

But even Harper couldn't be blamed for the most painful betrayal of all. No one had forced Adam to sleep with Kaia. He had no excuse—he and Beth had been together, they'd been *happy*, and he'd knowingly destroyed it in one stupid night.

"Is that supposed to fix everything?" she finally asked. She still couldn't bring herself to look at him.

"I don't know. I just . . . I wanted you to know that I'm . . . I mean, if we could just—" He suddenly stopped, and then she did turn to face him. He was doubled over in his seat, his head plunged into his hands.

"Just stop," she begged, forcing herself not to lay her hand against his broad back.

"I can't."

"Why?"

"Because I still love you."

He said it in a pained, strangled voice, without lifting his head. Beth didn't know whether to laugh or cry. Once, those words had been able to fix anything. Now they just left her feeling emptier than before.

"I love you," he said again.

And now Beth did something she'd once vowed never to do, not to Adam.

"I don't care."

She lied.

In the old days, Miranda and Harper would have skipped the assembly, taking it as a good excuse to sneak off to the parking lot for a smoke-and-bitch session about their least favorite people (Meaning: 90 percent of the student body).

But these weren't the old days. Too bad Harper didn't seem to notice.

"Rand, let's get out of here, what do you say?"

Harper had popped up from behind her seat, and Miranda stifled the impulse to swat her away like a mosquito she'd just caught draining her blood.

"I'd say forget it," she replied wearily, wishing she had

the discipline to keep her mouth shut. The silent treatment had never been her thing. It was hard enough to just stand her ground with Harper—she'd been forgiving her for years, like a bad habit. But this time . . .

All she had to do was picture Kane—his tall, lean body, his knowing grin, his silky voice—and after all those years of fantasizing, his image sprang easily to mind. As did the echo of Harper's promise: "You and Kane—it's a done deal. I swear."

And what had she done instead? Pushed him on Beth, all to serve her own agenda. It was all about Harper, and always had been.

Harper couldn't even be bothered to deliver a real apology. Sure, she'd groveled for a couple days, but when Miranda stood firm, she'd resorted to a bravado that was as insulting as it was ineffective. Miranda could barely stand to watch her, putting on this gruesome show as if nothing had ever happened.

"Go find someone else to screw over," Miranda snapped. "I'm done."

"That's great," Harper said. "Very nice way to treat your best friend. What ever happened to 'forgive and forget'?"

"Not my style," Miranda muttered.

"Right—as if you have any style."

Inside, Miranda cringed, and glanced down at her outfit, a plain white T-shirt and cheap Walmart jeans. Same as yesterday, same as the day before. Five years as sidekick to Haven's alpha girl and Miranda had somehow remained, to the end, cool by association, and association only. But Harper had never before flung the bitter truth in her face.

"I'd rather have no style than no class," Miranda replied pointedly. Harper wanted to jab at a soft spot? Two could play that game. And Harper, who still longed for the days when her family had ruled the town, and still chafed at the humiliating turn the Graces had taken, from princely robber barons to penny-pinching dry cleaners—Harper was nothing if not class conscious.

"I have more class—"

"All *you've* got," Miranda interrupted, "is a reputation. For now."

"Is that a threat?" Harper sneered, and for the first time, Miranda knew how it felt to be on the other end of Harper's poisonous gaze. But it only strengthened her resolve. She'd been wondering whether the little revenge plot hatched with Beth was too much, had gone too far—what a waste of worry. Obviously, Harper had put their friendship behind her. Miranda could—and would—do the same.

"Give me a break," Harper continued, rolling her eyes. "As if anyone in this school would listen to anything you have to say."

Oh, they would listen.

And then Harper would pay.

"I'm proud and pleased today to make a supremely important announcement that will affect all of you in the student body of our fair Haven High."

Kaia wasn't paying much attention to the principal and her pompous speech. Principals were always going on about "supremely important"—aka supremely irrelevant—announcements. It was part of the job description, and Kaia was content to hold up the students' end of the bargain: ignoring every word that came out of the principal's mouth.

But today she was putting on a good show of listening raptly—it was the best way to avoid Jack Powell's wandering eye.

"I have just learned that Haven High will be receiving a great honor. The governor of the esteemed state of California is setting off on a tour of the region's finest educational institutions, and he has decided to visit Haven High! Yes, the governor himself is arriving in two weeks for a *personal* inspection of our facilities."

Kaia would have snorted, were it ladylike to do so. The only state inspection this place deserved was the one that would condemn it. Peeling paint, creaky stairs, the mysterious stench that refused to dissipate—Haven High was a toxic waste dump masquerading as a high school.

With a few shining exceptions . . .

He was startlingly handsome, she'd give him that, she thought, watching Powell mingle with his balding, paunchy, middle-aged coworkers. He didn't belong here, not with his rakish smile, thick, wavy, chestnut hair, that arrogant smile and Jude Law accent. It had been such a turn-on, watching the other girls pathetically slobbering over him, and knowing that *she* was the one he'd chosen. Although technically, *she'd* chosen *him*—and, with a little prodding, he'd finally embraced his good fortune.

"In honor of the governor's arrival, one senior will be chosen by his or her peers to represent our fine school. He or she will deliver a speech on the subject of education—and I know he or she will do us all proud."

Kaia was proud of her catch, and would have loved to put it on display. But Jack Powell's policy was strict and unforgiving: In public, they ignored each other, without exception.

And yet, there he was, twenty rows ahead, craning his neck around and obviously searching for something—for Kaia. The irritated expression on his haughty face gave it away. She knew he hated the idea of chasing after anyone, but apparently he'd overcome his aversion: He'd left four messages on her voice mail since she'd ditched out on their last rendezvous, each one more incensed than the last.

"In preparation for the governor's arrival, I will be instituting a *no-tolerance* policy for all violations of school regulations. I expect you all will honor the rules as you always have, and *not* embarrass the administration or yourselves through any juvenile misbehavior."

Kaia, on the other hand, had always enjoyed the hunt. Extra points if she could break some rules in the process. Powell had been a special challenge, a cold, aloof trophy, whose acquisition had been fraught with the potential for scandal. Who'd have thought she'd be bored so quickly, willing to trade it all in for a greasy slacker in torn jeans, who reeked of pot and mediocrity?

"I look forward to reading your submitted speeches, and I know all of you at Haven High will look forward to this opportunity to shine for our state leadership. You'll do me, and yourselves, proud."

As the principal stepped down to a smattering of lackluster applause, Kaia grabbed her bag and slipped out the back of the auditorium. She knew Powell would never dare confront her on school grounds, much less in front of his boss—but why take a chance? She hadn't decided quite what to do with him yet, and didn't want to be forced into a decision. If the Reed thing blew over, it would be nice to have Powell ready and waiting on the back burner.

And if not . . . she'd let him down in her own time, and her own way. Gently.

Or, come to think of it, maybe not. After all, he liked it rough.

When the assembly ended, Beth zoned out for a moment, allowing herself to hope that her luck was about to change. If she was selected to deliver the speech to the governor, it could bulk up her college applications, and maybe even make up for her dismal SAT scores.

It was the first good news she'd gotten in weeks, and it gave her the strength to think about the future. She had to find a way to rebuild her life, without some guy to lean on. She'd done it before, but the prospect was still terrifying. Now, with this little kernel of confidence growing inside of her, maybe it was time to take the first step.

As the students filtered out of the auditorium, she followed a few feet behind a quiet, nondescript group of girls, careful not to let them notice her—but almost hoping they would. At least that would take the decision out of her hands.

She'd put this off for as long as she could, but being alone was just too hard. Miranda was useful, but she wasn't a friend. *Adam* had been a friend. As had the rest of his crowd, she'd thought, all the guys on the team, their girlfriends. Turns out, it was a package deal. Lose Adam, lose them all.

"Hey, guys. What's up?" She tried to make her voice sound nonchalant, smiling as if it had been only days since she'd last spoken to them and not—had it been weeks? Months?

"Beth?" Claire spoke first, as she always did. The other girls just stared at her with a mixture of hostility and confusion Beth recognized instantly. It was the look Beth had always flashed when one of the Haven elite had deigned to speak to her, inevitably with some kind of demand disguised as a not-so-polite request: *Let me borrow your history notes. Let me copy your physics homework. Let me have the key to the newspaper office so I can hook up with my boyfriend.* Those people only talked to you when they needed you, she and her friends had agreed. *Those* people. She'd never imagined that she would be one of them.

"What do you want?" Claire added, already half turned away.

"I just thought—" Beth hesitated. What did she want? To go back in time? Back before she'd skipped Claire's Halloween party to hang with her boyfriend, before she'd partnered up with Adam on the American history project, leaving Abbie to fend for herself? Before she'd abandoned their lunch table, skipped the annual anti–Valentine's Day moviefest, forgotten Claire's birthday even though they'd celebrated it together since sixth grade? "I thought maybe we could . . ." But she couldn't make herself finish the thought.

"Is it true you broke up with Adam because he slept with someone else?" Abbie suddenly asked. Beth took a sharp breath, and her eyes met Claire's briefly—she looked equally shocked. Then Claire looked away.

"That's so rude," Claire snapped at Abbie, who, Beth remembered, always did what Claire told her to. "You can't just ask incredibly personal questions like that to someone you *barely know*."

Beth had known Abbie since they were parked in neighboring strollers at the Sun 'n' Fun Day Care Center fifteen years ago, and Claire knew it.

"That's okay," Beth mumbled. "I don't mind talking about it." A lie.

"I heard you dumped him for Kane," another girl piped up. She had mousy brown hair and a hideous orange sweater. *My replacement?* Beth wondered.

"No, she dumped him, too," Abbie corrected her, then looked over at Beth. "Uh, right?"

"I can tell you guys about it at lunch today," Beth offered tentatively. "If you want."

"We don't want to bother you—" Claire began.

"Awesome," Abbie and the mousy girl chorused over her. "We'll see you then."

Beth sighed, hoping Claire's frosty attitude would thaw by the time they hit the cafeteria. Otherwise, it was going to be a long and painful hour, rehashing her failed love life while squirming under Claire's hostile glare.

It wouldn't do much for Beth's appetite.

But then, neither would eating alone.

"Don't do that, Kane, it tickles!"

Ignoring her pleas, Kane picked up the wriggling brunette and hoisted her over his shoulder as she kicked her legs with mock distress.

"Put her down, Kane!" her little friend, a dainty redhead, shrieked. Kane knew it was only because she was eager for her turn.

"Calm down, ladies," he urged them, depositing the brunette back on the ground. He slung an arm around each of them, admiring the way his muscles bulged beneath his tight sleeves. The new weights were working already. "You know you love it."

"Whatever." The brunette giggled, shoving him. Once their bodies made contact, she didn't pull away.

"Say what you want," he allowed, "but I know you're thrilled to have me back on the market."

The redhead—or, more accurately, the *air*head—stood on her toes to give him a kiss on the cheek. "I just don't know why you stayed away for so long," she whispered, her breath hot against his neck.

Good question.

"So what happened?" the brunette asked, tickling the

back of his neck. He jerked away. "We thought you were reformed."

"Player no more," her friend chimed in. "Beauty tamed the beast. What gives?"

So what now, the truth?

Right.

Like he'd ever admit that he'd been the one rejected by a nonentity like Beth, or that losing her had cost him something more than his reputation. He knew that with a few easy words he could turn this around and make it into a win, trashing Beth's rep and redeeming his own.

But he couldn't do it.

He had no regrets, he insisted to himself. He'd just done what was needed to get what he wanted, same as always. Beth was a big girl who could make her own choices—and, if only briefly, she'd chosen him.

"You can't fool me," she'd said once, kissing him on the cheek. "I know who you really are."

He'd almost been sorry to prove her wrong.

"Come on, Kane," the redhead pushed. "Dish us some dirt!"

But Kane just smiled mysteriously and tugged her toward him, wishing her hair was blond, her eyes blue and knowing. "What's the difference what happened?" he asked. "I'm here now—and so are you, which means everyone wins. Right?"

The girls exchanged a glance, then shrugged.

"We're happy if you're happy," the brunette concluded, rising on her tiptoes to kiss him on the cheek.

Kane forced a grin. He certainly *looked* happy—and isn't that what counts?

Harper didn't have the nerve to face Adam. But she couldn't stay away. She was too used to seeing him every day, telling him everything, depending on him. Now that he wasn't speaking to her, the days were incomplete. Harper felt as if she'd lost a piece of herself that only came alive in his presence.

And she had no one to blame but herself.

She'd positioned herself in a small alcove across from his locker, knowing he'd stop by on his way to basketball practice. She just wanted to see him. And if she watched from afar, she wouldn't have to face that accusing look in his eyes.

She just hadn't counted on him spotting her.

"So what, you're following me now?" he growled, turning his back on her and throwing his stuff into the locker.

And there it was, that look in his eyes, as if she were a stranger, someone he wished he'd never met. Harper had tried to bluff her way through her encounter with Miranda, pretend that she didn't care about what happened between them—but when it came to Adam, she didn't have the strength for that kind of lie.

"Ad, I know you don't want to talk to me—"

"So why the hell are you here?" He slammed the locker shut, but kept his back to her. She took a small step in his direction, then another.

Because I can't stay away.

Because I need you.

Because you need me.

"Because I have to tell you I'm sorry."

"Trust me," Adam said gruffly. "You've said enough."

No. She'd begged him to stay. She'd left him unanswered voice mails, written letter after letter, but she'd never stood across from him and apologized for what she'd done. She'd never had the nerve. Harper Grace, who could say anything to anyone, had been too afraid to speak.

Was she sorry for what she'd done?

The elaborate plan had given her Adam, opening his eyes to the possibility of the two of them being more than friends. It had pried him away from his bland, blond girlfriend and made him realize that puppy love was no substitute for the real thing.

And when it all came crashing down, it had guaranteed that he would never trust her again.

"I *am* sorry," she said, hoping to convince herself as much as him.

He kept his back to her, placing both hands flat against the wall of lockers. His shoulders rose and fell as he took several deep, slow breaths. Harper couldn't tear her eyes from the fuzzy blond hair at the nape of his neck—she used to love to run her finger across it, making him shiver.

"I'm sorry," she said again. She came closer, but even as she stood just behind him, close enough to touch, he didn't turn. He must have known she was there, but he didn't move away. "Adam." She put her hand on his back, ran it lightly up toward his bare neck. It felt so good to touch him again. "Please . . ."

"Harper, *don't*," he said, a low current of anger running through his voice. His fingertips turned white as he pressed them against the wall. "Just walk away." He slammed his right palm flat against the locker, and a sharp crack echoed through the empty hall. "Go. Please."

Adam would never hurt her—but, suddenly, Harper was afraid. She put her hand down and watched his frozen form for a moment.

Then she walked away.

Harper didn't lose. She got what she wanted, without exception. She didn't give up, ever.

But maybe this time, she had no choice.

❧ ❧ ❧

"And what are *you* wearing?" Kaia asked, trying to keep the phone from slipping through her wet fingers as she sank lower into the hot tub. "Oooh, sexy."

She'd cancelled yet another rendezvous with Powell, but the man was insatiable—and so she'd given in to a little foreplay by phone. Thirty seconds in and she was already bored out of her mind; even that sexy British accent, describing where he would touch her and how, had lost its ability to thrill.

Kaia stretched a long, bare leg up into the air, enjoying the bite of the cool wind against her skin. She closed her eyes, straining to pay attention, wishing she could just tune out Powell's prattling and enjoy the silence of twilight.

Though she would never admit it to her father—and he would never bother to ask—there was one thing she appreciated about this desert hellhole: sunsets. Spectacular splashes of pink and orange, a blazing ball of reddish yellow sinking beneath the haze, lighting up the open sky. Best of all were the moments just after the sun disappeared beneath the horizon, and the sky gradually darkened, pinks fading to purples and blues until the first stars broke through the dark fabric of the sky.

"What? Oh yes, it feels good. Great," she said quickly, trying to sound enthused (though not trying too hard). "And if you just moved your hands down, and then I—"

She sighed. "You know what? I'm just not feeling it."

Powell grumbled, but Kaia was done with him for the night. And finally, after she'd agreed to model her new Malizia bikini for him in person sometime soon, he let her go.

She hung up the phone, but before laying it down on the deck, had a better idea. She called Reed and held her breath, surprised by how much she suddenly wanted him to answer.

But the phone rang and rang, and eventually Kaia gave up. She slid down farther and farther into the water, until only the tip of her nose and her dark eyes hovered above it. Kaia never let herself depend on anyone, and so she wouldn't let it bother her that Reed was unavailable. Still she couldn't help wondering where he was . . . and whether he was thinking of her.

Adam blew off practice.

He had to.

Once, basketball had been an escape, a way to get out of his own head and relax into the rhythm of running, leaping, throwing, pushing himself to the limit. It had been a refuge.

And then Kane joined the team.

These days, Adam didn't have the energy to sink many shots or work on his passing. Every ounce of strength was devoted to resisting the temptation to bash in Kane's smug face, and pay him back for ruining Adam's life.

Only, after the encounter with Harper, Adam didn't have much strength left.

So he ditched practice, seeking a new refuge from the mess he'd made of his life. He needed to turn off his brain, and the 8 Ball, a dank pool hall at the edge of town, was the perfect place to do it.

It was dark, even during the day—black boards over the windows ensured that no afternoon light would slip in and disturb the handful of surly regulars. It was a place to hide. And, with five-dollar pitchers, a place to forget.

He'd come here with Harper once, and she'd put on a disgusting show, throwing herself at the sleazy goth bartender. Maybe it should have been a sign. But Adam had ignored the warning, and instead dumped a pitcher of beer on the bartender's head in a jealous rage. The bartender had vowed to make him sorry if he ever returned—and so, since then, Adam had known to stay away.

But Adam was tired of doing what was good for him—things managed to blow up in his face, anyway. So why bother?

"Can I get a Sam Adams?" he asked the bartender. It was the same guy. Good.

"Don't I know you?" the loser asked, pushing his greasy hair out of his eyes to get a better look.

"Is that supposed to be a pickup line?" Adam asked sarcastically. "Because trust me, I'm not interested."

"You're the asshole," the bartender exclaimed. As if, in a place like this, that was a distinguishing characteristic.

"Who are you calling an asshole?" Adam stood up and gripped the edge of the bar. All the emotion that had been simmering within him finally rose to the surface—and in a moment, he knew, he could give it permission to explode.

"I thought I told you never to come back here," the scrawny weasel complained. He turned away. "I'm not serving you. Get out."

"Or what?" Adam growled.

"Or I'll call the cops on your underage ass. In fact, maybe I'll do it, anyway, just for fun."

Adam flexed his muscles.

Made a fist.

Pulled back, and—

Stopped.

If he let himself lose control, he might never get it back again.

So instead of smashing in the bartender's face, he grabbed a glass from the bar and threw it, hard as he could, to the ground.

"What the hell are you doing?" the bartender cried, as glass sprayed across the floor.

"I have no fucking idea," Adam said honestly, and walked out. There were plenty of other bars in town, plenty of cheap drinks. Plenty of ways to forget.

And that was exactly what he needed.

If it was too dangerous to let himself react, then—at least for one night—he could let himself drown.

She was like a statue in the moonlight, pale, graceful, glowing in the night. He sucked in a sharp breath, forcing his body to stay calm. He couldn't afford to give himself away.

She was so close—and it was so hard not to reveal himself, and take possession of her. As was his right.

He'd been with her before; he would be again. But nothing was more delicious than watching from a distance, knowing that she belonged to him.

She climbed out of the hot tub, and he held his breath. This was the moment he'd been waiting for. Her perfect, glistening body, slicing through the air, every step precise, premeditated. As she toweled herself off, shivering, she suddenly froze, staring out into the darkness.

He froze, too, and it felt as if their eyes had locked. Had she sensed his invisible presence? His heart slammed in his chest, and his fingers tightened against the fence post he'd crouched behind. Moments like this—the threat of being caught, the chill of a near miss—made the game worth playing.

But he'd learned well how to minimize the risks, and knew she would never catch on. Nothing was sweeter than facing her day in and day out, knowing that she could never imagine what lay behind his mask.

She liked to think she didn't trust anyone, but she trusted him. She underestimated him, and he allowed it.

For now.

chapter three

THEY'D DECIDED TO GO OLD SCHOOL.

A Facebook invite or e-mail would have been more efficient, and a website might have been snazzier, but after serious consideration, Beth and Miranda had decided that neither had the technical prowess to put something like that together undetected. And plausible deniability was key.

E-mails could be traced. Circuits always led back to their source. But paper was untraceable—and as editor in chief of the school paper, Beth had access to all the printing equipment she needed.

She pulled the stack of flyers out of the printer as Miranda ejected their flash drive and wiped their work from the computer's memory.

"Behold," said Beth, holding up the crimson sheet crammed with dirty little secrets. "Our masterpiece."

Miranda grabbed a copy and quickly scanned the elegantly designed layout.

"Unbelievable, isn't it, that they were able to accomplish so much in their short, sordid lives?"

"I'm not sure '*accomplish*' is the right word," Beth said, reading out a few of her favorites. "'HG used to steal money from the collection plate. AM is impotent. KG is afraid of the dark.' I'm not sure what it is they've accomplished."

"Other than making asses of themselves," Miranda said, and laughed. "Well, thanks to us."

They'd included some gossip about a bunch of randoms, too, just for cover. But that was a diversion. Soon everyone would know that KG was so desperate, he had to trick girls into sleeping with him; that sometimes HG still stuffed her bra. Neither Miranda nor Beth knew much about the mysterious new girl from the East Coast, but before everything came down, Harper had passed along a bit of juicy info about Kaia and Haven High's resident pothead that was too weird not to be true.

"Are we really doing this?" Beth asked, as she split the

pile in half and handed one stack to Miranda. It was almost 6 a.m., which meant there'd be plenty of time to spread them all over school before even the most diligent early bird appeared for his worm.

"Definitely." Miranda swung her long, reddish hair over her shoulder and looked defiantly up at Beth. "It's exactly what they deserve."

"I guess . . ."

"No second thoughts," Miranda ordered. "They screwed us. Both of us. Because they thought we'd put up with it."

And Beth remembered the surprise in Kane's eyes when she'd pushed him away for the last time. The mocking look in Harper's every time Beth dared confront her, as if knowing that sweet, quiet Beth would always be the one to back down first. And she remembered the way Adam had treated her when he'd thought she was the cheater, his cold, unrelenting cruelty, the unwillingness to bend, to trust, to forgive.

Now *she* was supposed to just get over it? Because betraying Beth, well, that didn't really count?

"You take the science wing, I'll hit the lockers by the cafeteria," Beth said determinedly. Forget moving on. Forget backing down.

"That's better," Miranda cheered, locking up behind them. "Let's get this done."

❧ ❧ ❧

Did you see?

Is it true?

I heard he was a virgin *when he slept with Kaia.*

And when she blew him off, he cried.

Well, I *heard Kane wanted Beth so much he posed naked with Harper and they doctored the photos.*

They didn't just pose—he and Harper totally did it on the locker room floor.

No, I heard it was on the soccer field, and Kaia was in it too. Threesome, baby.

So who was taking the pictures?

Could Kaia really be hooking up with that skeezy stoner?

Don't you know? She's a total nympho.

Why do you think they threw her out of her last school?

Did he really—?

And then she—?

How could they—?

I don't believe it, but . . .

You won't believe it, but . . .

It doesn't make any sense, but . . .

Trust me.

It's true.

"Oooh, Harper, you must be soooo humiliated!"

Harper rolled her eyes. She'd been (barely) tolerating her lame sophomore wannabe-clone for months now, but the Mini-Me act was getting old. Especially now that the girl had dug up the nerve to speak to her in public. As if Harper was going to dent her own reputation by acknowledging Mini-Me's existence—or, worse, giving people the impression that they were actually *friends.*

"We just want you to know we're *there* for you," Mini-Me's best friend gushed. Harper couldn't be bothered to remember her name, either, and since the girl was decked out in the same faux BCBG skirt and sweater set that Harper had ditched last season, Mini-She would suffice.

"What are you talking about?" she hissed, through gritted teeth. Under normal circumstances she would have just closed her locker and walked away. But something strange was going on today. She'd been getting weird looks all morning, and once, difficult as it was to believe, it had almost seemed like someone was laughing—at *her.*

"Oh, Harper, we don't believe any of it," Mini-Me assured her.

"Of course not," Mini-She simpered, her head bouncing up and down like a bobblehead doll. "Well, except that thing about—"

"None of it," Mini-Me said firmly, giving Mini-She an obvious *shut your mouth* glare.

"None of what?" Harper was getting increasingly irritated by the twin twits—and by the sensation that something very bad was about to happen. Or had already happened, without her knowing it, which was worse. Harper owned this school, and *nothing* happened without her say-so.

"You mean you haven't . . ." Mini-Me's eyes lit up. She tried to force a concerned look, but her eagerness was painfully clear. "Oh, I *hate* to be the one to show you this, but . . ." She pulled a folded red flyer out of her back pocket. Harper had seen them floating around that morning, but assumed it was just another lame announcement about the next chess club tournament or some charity drive for the community service club. "Maybe I shouldn't show it to you," Mini-Me said, waving the folded flyer out of Harper's reach.

"But at least we can be there for her, when she sees it." Mini-She patted Harper's shoulder, and Harper squirmed away with a grimace. "We'll *always* be there for you, Harper, no matter what anyone else says."

"You've always got us," Mini-Me agreed. "I mean, we don't care if you wet your pants or slept with a million guys or—"

"Give me that," Harper snarled, snatching the flyer out of Mini-Me's hand. She unfolded it slowly, forcing her hands not to shake.

The words leaped off the page.

All her darkest secrets, all her most embarrassing moments, her deepest fears, all laid out in black print, stretching across the page for anyone to see. It had been published anonymously—the coward's way—but Harper didn't need a byline to know whom to blame. There was only one person who knew all her secrets—the one person she had trusted never to betray her.

Harper smiled, though it felt more like a grimace of horror. Hopefully the Minis would be too dim to tell the difference. Then she shrugged. "Is this all?"

"*All?*" Mini-Me squealed. "Don't you get it? 'HG'—Harper Grace. That's *you.*"

Harper rolled her eyes, almost thankful for the Minis' presence; the familiar sense of disgust was helping her suppress all those less desirable emotions. Helplessness. Humiliation. Despair.

Focus on something more constructive, she warned herself. *People can only hurt you if you let them. Don't be a victim.*

"See?" Mini-She chirped. "Like it says right here, 'HG was so desperate for AM that she . . .'"

Harper tuned her out—after all, she already knew the story. It was more important to regain her focus and start working on damage control. But cool, calculating strategy was impossible when one unquestionable fact kept drilling into her brain.

Miranda had betrayed her. No one else knew what she knew.

She wouldn't have done it on her own, Harper was

certain of that. She didn't have this kind of nastiness in her. She would have been goaded into it by someone else, someone so pure and innocent that no one would ever suspect her of spewing such poison.

"What are we going to do?" Mini-Me moaned. As if there were a "we."

"Who needs to do something?" Harper asked, crumpling the flyer into a ball and tossing it over her shoulder like the trash it was. "You know what they say, there's no such thing as bad publicity."

"You don't even care?" Mini-She asked, eyes wide and adoring. From the expression on the Minis' faces—impressed and totally devoid of pity—Harper grew certain that she'd be able to fix this.

These last few weeks had been the most lonely and miserable of Harper's life—something like this could have been a fatal blow. And yet, she marveled, perhaps Beth had done her a favor. Because she suddenly felt invigorated. She felt offended and insulted, righteous and wronged, empowered and enraged.

She felt like herself again.

And it felt good.

Beth and Miranda met up in the second-floor girls' bathroom after third period to compare notes. The school was buzzing about the already legendary flyer—half the student body had memorized it, and the other half had used it as a springboard to create and pass along wildly unlikely rumors of their own.

"I can't believe we actually did it," Miranda whispered, checking under the stalls to make sure they were really alone.

"You should have—" Beth quickly stopped talking as two babbling juniors burst through the door. Miranda turned on the faucet, pretending to wash her hands, while Beth peered into the streaked mirror, applying a new coat of transparent lip gloss.

"You think she, like, did it to herself?" the tall brunette asked, smoothing down her hair and using her pinkie to rub in some garish blue eye shadow. "But, like, why?" She dug through her overstuffed silver purse and pulled out a large gold hoop, wide enough to fit around her wrist, and clamped it onto her earlobe.

"Oh, puh-leeze," the shorter, pudgier one said, locking herself inside an empty stall. Her bright yellow platform shoes tapped against the linoleum. "She's mad crazy for attention, you know she'd do anything."

"But we're talking total humiliation hot zone—"

"Massive meltdown territory, but does she seem upset? Negative. You know she's, like, loving every minute of it."

"I don't know," the tall one said, now perched on the sink, fiddling with her nails, which were painted cotton candy pink and so long that they almost curled back toward her fingertips. "Maybe it was some nobody, like, you know, some bitter loser who wanted—"

"As if." A laugh floated out of the stall. "How would some loser know all of that? No, it had to be—"

Finally, Miranda couldn't help herself. "Did you ever think that maybe—"

"Uh, excuse me?" the brunette said, glaring. "Were we talking to you?"

The shorter girl burst out of the stall and quickly slathered on a layer of hot pink lipstick. She didn't bother to look in Miranda's direction—or make a move toward the sink. "Was she, like, eavesdropping on our conversation?"

"Whatever. Forget her."

"Her who?" the other girl cackled as she pushed through the girls' room door, the brunette following close behind.

Miranda and Beth stared at each other for a moment, then burst into laughter. "Were they for real?" Beth asked in wonderment.

"Oh, yeah, like, totally, I mean, you know, whatever," Miranda said, giggling. "For reals, dude."

"And that makes *us* the losers?" Beth asked, grinning.

"Apparently." Miranda stuck out her hand to shake. "Nice to meet you, I'm nobody. And who are you?"

"Someone who would *never* walk out of this bathroom without washing her hands," Beth joked.

"I think we're missing the key point here," Miranda said, trying to stop laughing. "Did you hear the way *they* were talking about '*her*'?"

"Harper," Beth filled in.

"Right. Obviously. Like she was this pathetic nonentity, desperate for attention. . . ."

"Humiliated," Beth said, raising her eyebrows.

"Pitiful," Miranda added, shaking her head.

"Defeated."

Miranda grinned and slung an arm around Beth's shoulders. "And all by a pair of bitter nobodies. Who would've thought?"

The curiosity-seekers had been swarming Kane all morning—and by lunchtime, it seemed half the school had surrounded him, desperate for insider information and some notoriety-by-association. Outwardly, he smiled, preening under the attention. But underneath, he was fuming. It was Beth. It had to be. No one else could know some of the things she'd printed, the few secrets he'd been foolish enough to share.

That was the worst of it: the realization that he'd brought this on himself. After swearing to protect himself, he'd left himself raw and exposed.

Not again—never again.

After spotting the flyer, Kane had quickly started his own campaign of disinformation; judging from Kaia's and Harper's animated smiles and the naked curiosity of their eager disciples, it seemed the girls had chosen to do the same. They sat at separate tables, each the center of a small whirlpool of people, flowing past to catch a moment with the stars. The horde surrounding Kane was, of course, the largest.

"She begged me to take her back," he confided to the second-string point guard. "It was getting pathetic. I mean, tears is one thing—you know girls. But when she started showing up at my house in the middle of the night? It's not like I *wanted* to call the cops. . . ."

"Let's just say, I now have a pretty good idea of what it must feel like to kiss a cold, dead fish," he confided to the sympathetic blonde from the cheerleading squad.

"And the smell . . . you know, she works at that diner, and all the onions, the grease, the sweat . . ." He shook his head, and the busty freshman patted him sweetly on the shoulder. "It was nauseating. I have a very delicate stomach, you know, and sometimes . . ."

"Sure, *she* couldn't get enough of it," he bragged to the gawky junior who managed the basketball team. "But what was I supposed to do? She was—well, let's just say Adam's pretty lucky he never made it to home base."

He almost felt sorry for Beth. She was like a dolphin, playing at being a shark. Which was a dangerous game: You were likely to get eaten.

The note the teacher had handed her had been short and sweet: *Report to my classroom. Now.*

Okay, maybe not so sweet.

"Jack," Kaia said simply, stepping into his empty classroom and closing the door behind her. "Bonjour."

Powell was perched on the edge of his desk, fingering a red sheet of paper. Kaia recognized it immediately, with little surprise.

"You said you'd stopped seeing him," Powell said coldly, placing the flyer carefully down on the desk. "I thought I'd made my position perfectly clear: I don't like to share."

Kaia strode toward him and took a seat at one of the desks in the front row, aware that his gaze was glued to her long, tan legs, barely covered by a green suede miniskirt.

"Do you really want to discuss this *here*, Jack?" It was a violation of every rule he'd set for them, and it stank of desperation.

"There's nothing to discuss. You told me you'd stopped. You told me you wouldn't, with—*that.* And now I read . . ."

Kaia laughed. "Are you going to believe some piece of trash you probably confiscated from one of your clueless freshmen? Just how gullible are you?"

Powell's skin turned slightly red, whether in anger or embarrassment, Kaia couldn't be sure. She could put him out of his misery right now, confess to the dalliance with Reed, and suggest he find himself another student to play with—or maybe even pick on someone his own age. But Kaia wasn't quite ready to finish things, and she *certainly* wasn't going to let some loser with a printer and a grudge force her hand.

She got up and walked slowly to the door, as if to leave, then paused with her hand on the knob. "Do I really need to defend myself?" Kaia asked. "Or can we stop this game and play another . . . ?"

Powell hopped off the desk, walked toward her, and then did something he'd never done before on school grounds. He touched her.

Placing his hand over hers on the doorknob, he turned the lock.

"We can table this for now," he told her, his lips inches from the nape of her neck, his fingers digging into her skin. "You're a smart girl, Kaia. You know better than to screw this up. Take this as a warning."

He pulled her roughly toward him, and she let him, hyperaware of the people in the hallway, just on the other side of the door. Only a few inches separated them from discovery, a thought that turned her on far more than Powell's hands roaming across her body.

Yes, Kaia was a smart girl, and she almost always knew better. She just never acted on it.

Where was the fun in that?

The whispers flew back and forth over Miranda's head. No one thought to ask her what was true—most likely, no one thought of her at all.

Without Harper, I'm invisible, she thought, pushing around the soggy food on her tray. She had no appetite. Not when Harper was at the center of an admiring crowd, soaking in the attention. Miranda had just given her more of what she loved the most. From across the room, Miranda couldn't see the self-satisfied grin on Harper's face, but knew it was there. And she couldn't hear the spin Harper would put on everything to cast herself in a good light—but she knew Harper would. A spotlight. It all seemed so obvious now, that this was how their feeble plot was doomed to end.

Teaming up with Beth, blandest of the bland, to take on Haven High's dark queen? What had she been thinking?

Beth wasn't as bad as Miranda had always thought, and was probably undeserving of all the hours she and Harper had put into mocking her behind her back. (Miranda had long ago perfected her Beth imitation, which never failed to send Harper into uncontrollable gales of laughter.)

But "not that bad"? What good was that, when you were going up against someone who had It? Someone who could mold minds, bend wills, make the world into exactly what she wanted it to be. Harper had It, and Beth didn't. Neither did Miranda.

Together, they made one big, fat nothing, and Miranda was beginning to wonder if she might have been better off alone.

Spin control only took a small portion of Harper's attention, and she devoted the rest of it to watching Miranda, pathetically slumped over a table on the other side of the cafeteria. They'd fought before; their friendship was built on fights. But this was different.

Miranda could never hold a grudge—and so Harper had never had to worry that, eventually, all would be forgiven. She'd learned that lesson in sixth grade, when the two of them had their first huge fight while rehearsing their sixth-grade performance of *Macbeth* (suitably abridged for attention-deficit-disordered twelve-year-olds). It had started small: an argument over who got to use the "real" (plastic) sword and who would be stuck wielding a wrapping-paper tube covered with aluminum foil.

Harper won, of course, bringing up the unassailable point that the whole show was named after her character. It seemed only logical that she, as the star, get the best of everything—lines, costumes, makeup, and, of course, *swords*. But Miranda had given in grudgingly, and only after hours of endless argument; by the time Harper finally took the stage, plastic sword in hand, she and Miranda hadn't spoken for a week.

When the climactic scene arrived, Miranda had the first good line. "Turn, hellhound, turn!" she cried as Macduff, the one man destined to take down Macbeth.

Harper spun to face her challenger. They stared at each other across the stage, readying themselves for the sword fight, gritting their teeth and narrowing their eyes as if the fate of the kingdom truly lay on their shoulders. Their teacher had been very specific: Cross "swords" three times, and then Miranda would slice off Harper's head. In a manner of speaking, of course.

Miranda swung, Harper parried, jumped back, sliced her sword toward Miranda, who blocked the blow with her wrapping-paper tube and danced around the stage, taunting Harper under her breath.

And Harper, who'd been planning to lie down and deliver the greatest death scene Grace Elementary had ever seen, couldn't bring herself to lose the fight—and, by definition, her dignity—in front of all those people.

She swung wildly, and Miranda's flimsy sword bent in two—at which point Miranda screeched in frustration and launched herself at Harper. The two of them stumbled to the ground, writhing and rolling across the stage, pinching and poking, tickling and tugging hair . . . until their eyes met and, simultaneously, they burst into uncontrollable giggles.

Harper and Miranda had spent that weekend in an intense, forty-eight-hour catch-up session, sharing every detail of the painful hours they'd spent not speaking to each other.

"I was sooooo bored," Miranda had complained.

"You were bored? I fell asleep standing up," Harper countered.

"I had to play Jeopardy Home Edition all night with my parents."

"I spelled out the names of everyone I know in alphabet soup."

"I missed you," Miranda had confessed, laughing.

Even then, Harper had known better than to confess that she'd missed Miranda more. They'd laughed about it for years, and sometimes even now when Harper was being particularly bitchy, Miranda would call her a "hellhound"; Harper always replied with her own favorite line: "Lay on, Macduff, and damn'd be he that first cries, 'Hold, enough!'" It was the code of their friendship, and its meaning was simple. They would never turn into their characters; they would fight—but never to the death. They would always stop in time, just before landing the final blow.

But here she was, watching Miranda pick at her food, scared to go over to her, scared not to. If Harper stood over her pleading, "Lay on, Macduff"—meaning, *Yell at me, hit me, hate me, and then, please, forgive me*—would it fix anything?

Not likely, Harper decided—not if Miranda had been behind the gossip flyer. That was a death blow. Harper may not have seen it coming, but she knew when it was time to lay down her sword and leave the stage.

chapter four

"OKAY GIRLS, TIME FOR A VOTE: *CRAZY STUPID LOVE* or *The Princess Bride*?"

As *Crazy Stupid Love* won by general acclamation, Beth tried to will herself to care. A few days ago, she would have said this was all she wanted—to be accepted back into the fold, to regress to the good ol' days of sleepover parties and road trips to the mall, popcorn and girl talk.

"Beth, can you grab us another bag of Hershey's Kisses?" Claire asked, and Beth traipsed upstairs, fighting against the suspicion that they'd start talking about her as soon as she was gone. They'd invited her, which was a step in the right direction—but no one seemed to particularly want her around.

"Have no fear, the chocolate's here," she said gamely, returning downstairs and pouring the Hershey's Kisses into a bowl.

"Great, let's stick in the movie," Claire suggested. Beth couldn't wait. As soon as the lights went out, she could drop the fake smile and stop trying to force perky conversation. She could let her mind wander and try to figure out exactly how she was going to make it through to graduation.

"Before we watch, I want to ask Beth something," one of the girls said eagerly. It was Leslie, the one Beth had come to think of as her replacement. Though had she ever been that timid and sallow? Claire rolled her eyes, but plopped down on the couch, defeated. "So . . . ," the girl continued. "What was it like?"

"What was *what* like?"

"*You* know," Abbie said. "*It.*"

"You and Kane," Leslie pressed, "what was it like when you . . ."

"What was it like to have a boyfriend?" Beth asked incredulously. Yes, when she'd been part of this group, they'd all been single—but almost two years had passed. Since then, surely at least one of them had—

"Sex," Claire said harshly. "They want to know what it was like to have sex." She scowled at Beth, as if daring her to respond.

"But I—" Beth had been embarrassed by her virginal status for so long that she'd almost forgotten what it could be like, to be part of a group where there was no pressure to be someone you weren't or go somewhere you weren't ready to go. For the first time all night, she smiled a real smile. "I haven't," she explained, feeling a surge of relief that she could say the words without worrying that anyone would judge her. She'd forgotten what it was like to have girl friends—*real* friends. "I mean, Kane and I never—and neither did Adam and I, so I'm still a . . ."

"Virgin?" Claire snorted. "Yeah, right."

"I *am*," Beth insisted, trying to ignore her.

"But, Beth," Abbie began hesitantly, "we've all heard . . . Kane said . . ."

"Kane's lying," Beth protested hotly. "Whatever he said, we never—"

"And *I* heard that you were the one who talked him into it," Leslie said. "That he wanted to take it slow, but—not that there's anything wrong with that," she added hastily, catching sight of Beth's expression.

"Leave her alone," Claire decreed, and Beth felt a brief stab of gratitude. Very brief, as Claire continued, "Obviously, she doesn't want to talk about it, not with *us*. No need to lie anymore, Beth. We'll just stop asking."

Beth kept the smile frozen on her face as Claire popped in the movie and the lights went out. It was only then, under the cover of laughter and music and inane dialogue, that Beth was able to move. She crept over their sprawled bodies, and up the stairs to the guest bathroom. Once inside, the door shut and locked behind her, she sat down on the toilet seat, put her head in her hands, and let the tears leak out.

She was losing control.

There were so many people she needed to be. With Adam, the bitter, unforgiving ex; with Harper, the tough rival; with her family, the reliable caretaker. She'd thought that with her old friends she could relax and just be herself, but they didn't want that. They wanted yet another Beth, a world weary refuge from the popular crowd who could give them the inside scoop on a world they'd never inhabit.

So many masks to wear, and none of them fit, not really. She didn't know who she was anymore—and she no longer had the energy to figure it out.

Harper was back. So much for skulking in the shadows and hiding under the covers. That wasn't going to get her anything. It wasn't going to get her Adam. And it wasn't going to get her revenge.

So Friday night, she'd whipped out her phone and called Kaia and Kane. It was time for a council of war, and these two were battle-tested.

"Nice to see you out of bed, Grace," Kane commented as they settled into a booth in the back of Bourquin's Coffee Shop.

"It's even nicer to see me in it," Harper quipped, "not that you'll ever know."

Kane grinned, and Kaia set down a tray of frothy iced coffees.

"And the plan is . . . ?" she began, arching an eyebrow.

"I thought that was your department," Harper joked—and then the smile faded from her face. After all, the last plan Kaia'd come up with had led to disaster. It had, ultimately, led them here.

"We all agree it was Beth?" Kane asked, delicately holding the notorious flyer between two fingers as if afraid to get his hands dirty.

"I still say she couldn't have done it alone," Kaia pointed out.

"She's very resourceful," Harper put in quickly. She'd deal with Miranda—her own way, in her own time.

"You're the one who always told me she was a waste of space," Kane reminded her.

"And *you're* the one who always told me I underestimated her," Harper argued. "Obviously you were right."

Kane closed his eyes and took a deep breath, as if inhaling her words. "Music to my ears. But you sound surprised—when are you going to learn that I'm always right?"

"So, Mr. Right," Kaia said, leaning forward eagerly. "You know her best—how do we take her down?"

Silence fell over the table.

"If we had proof, we could just turn her in," Harper mused. But there was no proof—and, besides, ratting her out to the authorities seemed such an inelegant solution. Why pass the buck to the administration when they could handle the problem themselves?

Kane put down his coffee and looked up at the girls, his lips pulling back into a cold smile. "I can tell you what her pretty little heart desires the most this week—"

"Not you," Kaia and Harper quipped at the same time. Their eyes met, and they burst into laughter. Kane's expression didn't change.

"If you two are done . . ."

The girls nodded, adopting identical *we'll be good* expressions.

"As I was *saying*, if I know Beth, there's only one thing she wants this week: something flashy that would impress colleges and cement her goody-goody rep once and for all . . ."

"She could prove to the whole school that she's the best," Kaia said thoughtfully.

"All the teachers would love her," Kane pointed out.

"And she'd get to feel like a VIP, superior to the rest of us," Kaia added, with a knowing smile.

"Well?" Harper asked in confusion, growing tired of the game. The two of them were having way too much fun stringing this out. "*What?*"

"That speech for the governor," Kane explained. "I hear she's going for it, and she hasn't got any real competition. Unless . . ."

"Wouldn't it be a shame," Kaia picked up, "if someone stole it out from under her? Someone prettier, more popular, someone *she* probably thinks can't string two words together?"

"And maybe she finds out that she can't just flutter those blue eyes and get everything she wants," Kane concluded.

"Especially"—Kaia grabbed the flyer from him and tore it in two—"if she's going to play with fire."

"And exactly who do you—" Harper stopped as the obvious sunk in. "You want *me* to write the damn speech? Put on a show for the governor like the principal's trained monkey?"

"Who better to beat her out than her sworn enemy?" Kaia pointed out. "The one who already stole everything worth having?"

It did have a certain beauty to it.

And Harper did so love to win.

"Are you guys sure about this?" Harper asked.

"Second thoughts, Grace?" Kane asked, arching an eyebrow. "This was your idea."

"She tried to trash our lives," Kaia pointed out. "Yours, most of all."

Harper didn't want to say what she was thinking—that maybe Beth had lost enough.

"You know Adam would go back to her in a second," Kaia reminded her. "All she'd have to do is say the word. He thinks she's so pure, so innocent. . . ."

Beth had brought the fight to them, Harper reminded herself, and after all, what had she really lost? Kane was right: She could have Adam back whenever she wanted. *Harper* was the one left alone, groveling for forgiveness that might never come.

Didn't Beth expect a little payback for that? More to the point, didn't she deserve it?

"All right," Harper conceded. "I'm in. All in."

"Good decision," Kaia said, clinking her mug against Harper's. "To revenge."

"To winning," Kane added, clinking their glasses with his own.

Harper paused just before taking a sip, and added one more toast. "To justice."

Kaia checked her watch on the way out of the coffee shop. She had just enough time to head home and change, before meeting Reed. Or she could stop by Guido's Pizza early and see if he was ready for her. If not, she could at least sit there as he worked. She loved watching his sure movements behind the counter, tossing the dough, smearing the sauce across a fresh crust, sprinkling the cheese. She'd never thought fast-food preparation could be so hot.

She slid in behind the wheel of the BMW, but before she could decide which way to turn out of the lot, her phone rang.

"Good news. My dinner engagement has been cancelled. I'm free for the night. Be here in half an hour."

Kaia chewed on the corner of her lip and tapped her index finger against the phone. Powell liked to order her around. It gave him the illusion he was in control.

"Can't—plans," she said quickly.

"Forget them," he suggested. "I have a special treat for you."

For a moment, Kaia was tempted—but as she thought of Reed's lopsided grin, and the way his rumpled, curly hair always made it look like he'd just climbed out of bed, the temptation passed.

"Sorry," she told him, her flat tone making it clear that, as usual, she wasn't.

"What could be more important than a night with me?" Powell asked.

"What's the difference?" Kaia snapped, suddenly

unwilling to make up a lie. This wasn't a relationship, after all—they were under no obligation to each other. That was the beauty of it, at least until he'd turned into the amazing human jellyfish, wrapping his tentacles around her at any opportunity for fear she'd slip away. "I'm not coming."

"Tu me manques," Powell said. *I miss you. "Mon amour." My love.* He knew very well that she couldn't resist when he spoke to her in French.

"I'll come now," she said with a sigh, regretting it almost as soon as the words were out of her mouth. "You've got twenty minutes."

"You say that now, but you know you won't want to leave." She could hear the smug grin behind his words and, as always, it repulsed her—and turned her on. "You know you can't say no to me."

"Twenty minutes. That's it."

Kaia clicked the phone shut, cutting off his laughter. So, new plan: two guys in one night. She'd double-dipped in the dating pool before, but this time felt different.

Kaia pulled out onto the road, turning toward Powell's dingy side of town. She refused to let herself slip into some kind of juvenile relationship, imagining that she and Reed were "going steady"—it was a slippery slope and, before you knew it, she'd likely be sucked into a downward spiral of gooey love poems, Valentine's Day candy, pathetic pop songs, and dithering about whether "he loves me" or "he loves me not."

That was unacceptable, and even if she didn't particularly *want* to see Powell tonight or suffer through his groping fingers and pompous Brit wit, she would, anyway, just as a reminder that she was free. Kaia had never let herself be obligated to anyone—as far as she was concerned, it was a step away from ownership, and no one owned her. No one ever would.

"Now *that* is a fine piece of ass!" The second-string point guard leaped out of his chair and pushed his way to the edge of the stage, waving a wad of dollar bills in the air.

Adam looked around the table searching for a bemused expression to match his own, but saw only naked desire in his teammates' eyes. So what was wrong with Adam? Three half-naked women dancing onstage a few feet away, their perfect bodies gyrating to a hard, driving beat—and all he could do was stare into his glass and wallow in his own pain?

"You're pathetic, man!" one of the guys complained, clapping him hard on the back. "Stop sulking and look where we are. This is *heaven.*"

Heaven, or Mugs 'n' Jugs, a triple-X strip club on Route 47 that promised Live! Nude! Girls! and failed to card even its most obvious underage patrons. Adam had made the traditional pilgrimage out here for his sixteenth birthday, but hadn't been back since.

Now he remembered why. Sure, a few of the girls were hot, parading across the stage in their barely-there costumes, this one a tiger-lady, that one a vampiress, all of them flashing the same *fuck me* look at their loser clientele. But once you tore your eyes away from all that bare skin, you couldn't help but notice all the depressing details: the worn-out speaker system, piping the same five songs on a maddening continuous loop; the overpriced drinks and underpaid waitresses; the middle-aged businessmen who'd snuck away from their dreary lives to spend a few hours pretending that the strippers were performing just for them, that their bored *come hither* expressions were more than just business.

"Why'd you drag me here?" he complained, shouting to be heard over the loud techno beat. "I thought we were just going to shoot some pool."

"What are you complaining about?" the center asked. "Look around you and tell me this isn't better than pool." He looked up at the waitress, who'd stopped at their table to clear their drinks, and was leaning so low across Adam that her bare midriff brushed his shoulder. "Hey, baby," the center leered, and pointed toward the stage. "Why aren't you up there with the rest of the hotties?"

Adam cringed, but thankfully, the waitress ignored the

idiot. She turned to Adam instead. He cringed again.

"Hey, sweetie, why so glum?" she asked, stroking her finger across his jawline. "Don't see anything you like?"

Adam took a deep breath, almost choking on the heady mix of smoke and cheap perfume.

"It's not that," he stuttered. "I'm . . . uh . . ."

"Distracted," the waitress guessed. She slapped a small glass down on the table and poured him a shot. "It's a girl, isn't it?"

"No, it's—" How to answer that? He couldn't get his mind off a girl, yes, but which girl? The one he wanted to kiss, or the one he wanted to throttle?

"It's always a girl," the waitress said knowingly. She poured a second shot, then lifted the glass herself. "She's not worth it, kid. You're too young for that face." She squeezed his cheeks together and gave his face a gentle shake, like a grandmother doting on her angelic little boy. Then, in a decidedly un-grandmotherly move, she wrapped his fingers around his glass, clinking hers against it.

"To forgetting," she toasted, and downed the shot. She looked at him expectantly, and so he tipped his head back and dumped the drink into his mouth, trying not to choke as the cheap tequila lit a fire down his throat.

"You're still frowning, kid."

"I—"

"Let's try this." And the waitress put down her tray,

grabbed his face with both hands, pulled it toward hers, and kissed him. Hard. Fast. Wet. Sloppy. And incredible.

She pulled away, and Adam just gaped at her, dazed, as the warm tequila buzz spread through his body and the cheers and hoots of his buddies beat dimly against his ears.

"There, that should do it," she said, using her thumb to wipe away a lingering smudge of lipstick on his lips, just as his mother had done when he was a child. "Now enjoy the show."

"*That* was fucking unbelievable," the center said in a low voice.

"You are officially the luckiest guy in the world," the point guard added, back from his failed trip to the edge of the stage.

Adam tried to smile as his buddies clapped him on the back and roared with approval. A couple years ago, this whole scene would have been a dream come true. But he wasn't that guy anymore. Not even a hot kiss from a hot, half-naked woman could change that. The kiss just made things worse; he was ashamed to be there, because he knew *Beth* would be ashamed, if she ever found out—if she even cared.

"Woo-hoo, baby!" the center cried, waving a fistful of cash at the blond bombshell who was sliding up and down a metal pole a few feet away. "Bring it on!"

Adam sighed and closed his eyes. If he couldn't leave, he could at least pretend he was somewhere else, with someone else. He'd gotten good at pretending, lately; real life was so much easier to handle when you just ignored it.

Kaia tipped back her head to catch the last few drops of liquid in the glass, then sucked in an ice cube. She needed something bitingly cool to distract her. Sitting this close to Reed, with a table keeping their bodies apart, was driving her crazy.

She'd met him at Guido's as planned, and they were sharing a free pizza before making their escape. She of course hadn't mentioned anything about her unplanned pit stop on the way. Not because he would have had any right to know, she reminded herself, and certainly not because she felt guilty—it just wasn't worth the trouble. She'd met Powell at his apartment and used his desperation as leverage to achieve an unprecedented goal: open windows. Usually obsessively paranoid about keeping every moment of their encounter shut off from the public view, Powell had let himself be cajoled into pulling up the blinds, giving Kaia her first ever look at the view from his apartment. It was, as she'd expected, just as squalid as the apartment itself. Then came the true triumph: persuading Powell to open the sliding-glass door at the back of his bungalow and actually take her outside, if you could count a five-by-five-foot fenced-in square of weeds and gravel as "outside."

They had stood for a moment at the threshold, gazing out at the claustrophobic patch as if it were the Garden of Eden and they were considering a rebellious return, and then Powell had taken her hand and led her into the not-so-great outdoors. It was dirty and uncomfortable, and something about the fresh air or the fear of discovery had made Powell more insatiable than usual, nearly endangering her twenty minutes-and-out plan, but it had been well worth it. She'd talked him into breaking his own rules, just for the privilege of being with her, and there was nothing sweeter than that. Or at least, that's how she had felt until Reed had greeted her with a kiss, fully unaware that he was getting used goods, and her victory began to feel unsettlingly hollow.

"You miss it? Home?" Reed asked, nibbling on a piece of crust.

Kaia opened her mouth to give Reed her well-rehearsed speech on the wonders of Manhattan, from the sample sales and the galleries to the way the skyscrapers sliced into the sky on a clear winter morning, from sneaking into club openings and showing up on Page Six, to meeting up at dawn for a goat cheese omelet and bread fresh from the farmers' market before sneaking home to bed. But she stopped before she said anything.

"I don't know," she admitted—and it was the first time she'd let herself think it, much less speak it aloud. "Sometimes I miss it—I hate it here. But . . . I hated it there, too."

Another guy might have seized the moment to put on the fake sympathy, giving her a "comforting" pat on the thigh and maybe letting his hand rest there a bit too long.

Reed simply asked, "Why?"

"I don't know." And, with another guy, she would have taken this as her cue to heave a calculated sigh, designed to elicit pity or to highlight her ample, heaving chest. Instead, a small, light shiver of air escaped her as her body sagged with the energy of wondering: What was wrong with her life? "There was my mother. Total bitch. And my—I guess you'd call them my friends." She laughed harshly at the thought. "But that wasn't it. I just . . ."

Reed took her hand—and she knew it wasn't in sympathy or empathy, but out of a desperate need to touch her, because she felt it too.

"I didn't fit there. Not that I fit here," she added, laughing bitterly.

"Know what you mean," Reed said quietly, shaking his head. "But what can you do?"

Kaia didn't say anything, just pressed his hand tightly to her lips. She could never say it out loud, but she knew that, bizarrely, she did fit somewhere. Here, with him. And at least there was some comfort in that.

⸻

"Are we having a good time yet?" Harper asked snidely, wrinkling her nose after sipping a whiskey sour that tasted more like fermented lemonade. Kane had promised her a night to remember at an exclusive underground after-hours lounge at the outskirts of town. He'd failed to mention that by "exclusive" he meant "restricted to those qualified for membership in the AARP"; "after hours," on the other hand, apparently meant "after the early bird special."

"How was I supposed to know that tonight was bingo night?" he protested.

Harper stifled a laugh and glanced around. True, no one was actually playing bingo—but with half the population of Grace's senior citizens clinking glasses of stale Scotch and swapping sob stories about hip replacements and burst bunions, it seemed only a matter of time. Apparently, once a month the owner let his father use the lounge for his lodge meetings. Harper and Kane had had to sweet-talk their way in, just for the privilege of listening to the Elks, or Buffalo, or whatever they were, reminisce about the war and complain about how their children never came to visit.

It wasn't quite the pick-me-up they'd had in mind.

"So, let's hear it, Grace—what can I do to turn that frown upside down?" Kane downed his drink in one shot and rested his chin on his hands, as if overwhelmingly eager to hear her response.

"As if you could help," Harper said, but without bitterness. They'd known each other too long for her to put up a brave front—or to think that confiding in Kane would yield anything but apathy with a side of scorn. "I don't want to talk about it."

"Don't want to talk about *him*, you mean," Kane said, with a knowing smirk. "Fine, then. What about her?"

"Her who?"

"The Siamese twin from whom you seem to have had a miracle separation? Miranda—who else? Ten years, the two of you are joined at the hip, and then suddenly, in your darkest hour, she's nowhere to be found? Makes no sense," Kane complained, shaking his head. "Not unless there's something I don't know. And you know how much I hate to be in the dark."

"Get used to it," Harper snarled. "There's a lot you don't know." She could tell Kane all about Miranda's massive crush—after all, she had no reason to keep Miranda's secret when her own were spread all over school. But Harper couldn't bring herself to do it, knowing that if there was even a prayer of fixing things—and she had to believe there was—she should keep her mouth shut.

"I can't imagine that Ms. Stevens would have been so disgusted by your treatment of Adam that she would have walked away," Kane mused. "After all, she's nothing but lovely to me, and my behavior was just as . . . let's say, repulsive? Stealing my best friend's girlfriend and all."

"That's not guilt I hear, is it?" Harper asked in surprise.

Kane cocked his head. "You know me better than that. It's just honesty. I've been telling you for years, Grace, you should just embrace your dark side. You'll have more fun."

"I couldn't be having any less," Harper complained, gesturing toward the speakers that had just begun blasting out some big-band golden oldies.

"No, you must have done something *to* Miranda," Kane continued. He wouldn't stop pushing until he figured it out—but Harper wasn't about to help him along. "And if it's not about Adam, and not about Beth, it must be something else. *Someone* else—"

"May I have this dance, madam?"

Harper looked up to face a balding, pockmarked man stooped over their table and extending a liver-spot-sprinkled hand in her direction. Under other circumstances, she might have—oh, who was she kidding, *would* have—declined. But if it gave her an escape from this conversation . . .

"I'd be honored," Harper said, taking his trembling hand and rising from the table.

Kane's grin widened, and he gave her a jaunty little wave. "Have fun, Grace. Just keep those hands where I can see them. . . ."

The old man danced her away from the table, away from Kane and his nagging questions, and waltzed her across the lounge, proving to be surprisingly nimble. As soon as the song ended, another lodge member hobbled over to take his place. By the time every little old man in the place—at least the ones still mobile enough to shuffle along without a walker—had taken his turn, Kane was slouched on the table, his breathing heavy and his eyes half closed, the Miranda issue forgotten.

"Have fun?" he slurred, without lifting his head from the table.

"Actually, yes." She hadn't even minded when one of the men grabbed her ass. It was nice to be an object of desire again, even among the Viagra demographic.

"Told you so," Kane mumbled, half to himself. "Promised you a night to remember."

But Harper had done enough remembering for a while. That had been the best part about dancing in the darkness in the palsied arms of a stranger: It became almost possible to forget.

He had to congratulate himself. He'd made it through the evening without allowing his emotions to leak through, his anger to explode. She had no idea that he'd seen her, with *him*.

Hidden in the shadows, he'd watched her betray him. Even then, he couldn't help but admire her delicate porcelain skin, pale as ivory against her ink-black hair. She moved like a dancer, every swish of her arm and tilt of her head graceful and deliberate, almost as if she knew he was watching, and was performing just for him. And for a moment, he'd imagined that his hands followed hers, trailing their way across her soft, creamy skin.

But it was another man who took her hand in his. A stolen hand, a stolen touch—there should be punishment for taking something that doesn't belong to you, he thought now. There should be punishment for giving it away, as she did, to another.

He could have turned away—he'd seen enough to know the truth. But he had stayed, waited, watched. She could play with all the men she wanted, but in the end, no one knew her like he did. No one but him knew the way she moved when she thought no one was watching.

The time they spent together was tainted now by what she'd done. But when he watched her in the darkness, that was pure. She could lie to him all she wanted, but she couldn't avoid the truth: She belonged to him.

Apparently, she just needed a reminder.

chapter five

"JUMP! JUMP! REBOUND!

Make the shot!

Number 8 is hot! Hot! Hot!"

The cheerleaders flashed their pom poms, soared through the air, and led the crowd in a thundering chorus, hundreds of fans all chanting his name.

"We're the team

That's sure to win,

'Cause MORGAN always gets it in!

Morgan!

Morgan!

Morgan!"

What a rush.

Number 8, Adam Morgan, dribbled up court, his heart pounding, his feet slamming into the boards. He could feel the Weston Wolves closing in behind him, longing to pounce, but he was faster. Stronger. Better.

After weeks of playing like shit, it had all fallen into place, now, in this moment. Adam could feel his body shift into motion, a seamless connection between legs, hands, ball, net; instinct took over, driving everything from his mind but the harsh *crack* of the ball against the floor and the stinging *slap* as it rebounded against his cupped palm. He pushed himself forward, outpacing the Wolves and breaking free to a wide-open court, until, finally, he could feel this was his moment; it was a certainty that went beyond reason.

He stopped, scooped up the ball, lifted it above his head, ready to send it flying, and then, just as the ball tipped off his fingertips at the perfect angle—

A shove. Hard, from behind. Knocking Adam off balance.

And the ball bounced off the rim.

Adam barely registered what happened next: the outraged cries of his teammates, the crowd calling foul, the ref calling nothing. All he saw was his ball rolling off the rim and crashing to the floor, and the red, sweaty, sneering face of the guy who'd pushed him.

Somewhere within him, a voice urged restraint—but it was too late for that. Adam launched himself at the sneering Weston Wolf, sucker punching him in the gut and then, as the Wolf bent over, gasping for breath, kicking his legs out from under him, and knocking him to the floor.

And that was all it took.

The Wolves rushed the court to defend their man, and the Haven High Coyotes charged in to make it an even fight. Soon the court was filled with the grunts and thuds of a dozen basketball players punching and clawing one another—and the angry hoots of the crowd, cheering them on.

After all, who doesn't like a little blood with their sport?

The refs blew their whistles and the coaches rushed in to pull their players away, but they couldn't fight the chaos. And, somehow, in the confusion, after knocking one Wolf flat on his ass and barely avoiding the wrong end of a large fist, Adam found himself face-to-face with the true enemy.

Kane grinned at Adam, perhaps forgetting himself in the heat of battle. His usually perfect hair was drenched with sweat and plastered to his forehead, his eyes were wild, and a small trail of blood trickled down his face from a scratch along his temple. He smiled. And Adam exploded.

Lunging at Kane, he grabbed his old friend around the neck, pushed him against the floor, and punched him hard, in the face, where it would hurt the most, bruising his cartilage and his vanity. Adam wanted to keep punching, to feel the rhythm of Kane's head slamming against the floor as if it were the ball, even while Kane gave up fighting back and curled up tight, waiting for it to end. And, simultaneously exhilarated and disgusted by the unfamiliar bloodlust, he might have done it—but they pulled Adam off and threw him to the sidelines with the rest of his team.

He'd gotten only that first punch. Maybe, in the confusion, no one had noticed Adam turning his back on the rivals, attacking his own teammate instead. Or if someone had noticed, hopefully it would be written off as a tragic but inescapable episode of friendly fire for which no one need be held accountable.

Whatever happened next, it would be worth it for the satisfaction he'd received from the sound of Kane's head smacking against the floor and the rush of power coursing through him like a drug.

Adam wouldn't soon forget it.

And, he knew, neither would Kane.

The letters were red, almost glowing against the shiny black paint of the freshly washed BMW.

Red like blood, Kaia thought, shivering, even as she berated herself for reacting, determined not to give him—and whoever it was, it must be a him—the satisfaction.

She looked up and down the massive driveway. There was no one in sight, but that didn't mean no one was watching. The floodlights cast shadows across the grounds that seemed to flicker and shudder at the corner of her eye.

You're imagining things, she told herself. But she hadn't imagined the sound of breaking glass that had drawn her outside. And she hadn't imagined her car—the front window broken, and those letters spray-painted across its side. The floodlights cast it in a spotlight, and though she knew she should hurry inside, she couldn't turn away.

She'd take it to the garage in the morning, she decided, forcing herself to think analytically, in hopes that would stop the trembling. She'd go early so the maids wouldn't see it and report back to her father. If she told Daddy Dearest that there'd been a flat tire, he would pay as much as she asked, and she could tack on an extra hundred to ensure the mechanic would keep his mouth shut—no reason to spread her humiliation across town.

Kaia whipped her head to the left, suddenly certain she'd glimpsed a pale face peering out from the shadows. But there was no one there. She backed away from the car, edged toward her house, slipped inside, and locked the door. Then she entered in the code for her father's state-of-the-art alarm system, the one she'd always mocked him for buying when there was nothing around for miles but the occasional coyote. Even if some lunatic did stumble upon Chez Sellers and set off the howling alarm, how long would it take security to respond?

She decided it was probably best not to dwell on the emptiness outside, or the miles separating her from Grace's lackluster police department, which was largely staffed by local, part-time volunteers and closed up shop at five p.m. Instead, Kaia curled up on the couch, tucked a cashmere throw around her shoulders, and flipped on the TV. She turned up the volume, hoping to drown out the silence that seemed to hold far too many soft, rustling noises that could be footsteps, or a hand brushing up against the window.

Forget it, she told herself, peering out the window into the night. *You're being paranoid.*

But it wasn't paranoia if someone was really out to get you, right? And someone must be. Why else would he have scarred the car with his angry red scrawl, branding her with the word that kept pounding in her ears no matter how much she raised the TV volume.

WHORE.

Before Harper had trashed their friendship, Miranda had had plenty of opportunities to see Kane. Now, most of the time, her only hope was a glimpse of him in the halls or across the cafeteria. Basketball games, however, provided a two-hour stretch of uninterrupted Kane-gazing, which almost made the endless boredom and inevitable postgame headache worth it.

Tonight she was wishing for boredom. Most of the crowd seemed invigorated by the brawl, but Miranda still felt sick at the thought of Kane lying on the court, bloodied and pale. He'd pulled himself up, limped over to the bench, and sat down next to the other players penalized for the fight—he was obviously intact, she reassured herself. But still she worried, mostly about whether she'd be able to push through the crowd of bimbos at the end of the game and see for herself that he was safe and whole.

Maybe Kane dreaded the bimbos as much as she did, because ten minutes before the end of the final quarter, he quietly slipped off toward the locker room. He would probably change quickly and head for the parking lot, Miranda realized, in hopes of avoiding the crowd. She didn't let herself wonder whether he might want to avoid her, too—at this point, hesitation would just make her chicken out.

She caught up with him in the parking lot, limping toward his car.

"Kane!" she called, not quite loudly enough for him to hear. There was still time to walk away, before she risked humiliation.

But not enough time, because he'd heard her, after all.

"Stevens!" He waved and, even from a distance, she could see him wince. He brought his arm down and cradled it against his side. She trotted over, and he gave her a weak smile. Without thinking, she touched his face gently, where a large, purplish bruise had bloomed just under his eye.

"You should see the other guy," he said ruefully.

Miranda usually agonized over every word she said to Kane, striving for the perfect combination of confidence, solicitation, and flirtatious banter. But now she didn't stop to think, or disguise her concern behind her wit. "Look what they did to you," she murmured.

"It's not so bad."

"You obviously haven't looked in a mirror yet," she said, wrapping an arm around his waist. He leaned against her, and she forced herself to keep breathing. "Come on, I'm helping you to your car."

"I'm fine, I swear."

"Humor me." They made it to the Camaro, and Kane climbed into the front seat, then looked up at her expectantly. "Well?"

"What?"

"Aren't you coming? Or is your nursing shift over for the night?"

Her heart fluttering, Miranda went around to the

passenger seat and closed the door behind her. By the light of the dashboard, she could see that his face wasn't cut up as badly as she'd thought, but it still looked plenty painful. She pulled a water bottle out of her bag and dug around for a tissue. Wetting it, she began dabbing away some of the dried blood dotting his face. He squirmed away as she held the damp tissue against a cut at the edge of his lip.

"Don't be a baby," she chided him. "This'll help."

"You're good at this," he said softly.

"What? Washing faces?"

"Making people feel better."

Miranda blushed, and all her self-consciousness flooded back. "Just call me Florence Nightingale," she said wryly.

Her hand still pressed lightly against his lips. Suddenly, Kane mirrored the gesture, bringing his hand to her face and tipping her chin so they were staring into each other's eyes. "Don't joke," he insisted. The infamous Kane Geary smirk was nowhere to be seen. "I mean it. Thank you."

She couldn't allow herself to be honest, and she didn't want to spoil the moment by saying something funny. So she said nothing, and neither did he. They faced each other in silence, their faces illuminated by only the glowing dashboard and the flashing lights of passing cars pulling out of the lot.

Does he know what I'm thinking? she asked herself as she

stared at his bruised face and his swollen lips, wishing that this was about more than his gratitude. The soft, almost glazed look in his eyes made it seem almost possible. And he still hadn't taken his hand away from her face. *Does he finally see me?* she wondered. *Does he finally get it?*

And then, as if there'd been a signal that only he could hear, Kane moved away and turned the key in the ignition. "I'm headed home," he said brusquely. "Where can I drop you?"

She could go along with him, staring out the window and praying that when he stopped the car they would regain that moment of honest intimacy. Maybe things would even go further, and she'd have more than just a long gaze and a lingering touch to dream about tonight. But the moment of decision had obviously passed—and he'd decided no. Why torture herself with something that wasn't going to happen?

"Actually, I drove tonight," Miranda said, opening the car door. "So I guess you're on your own. If you think you can make it."

Kane grinned. "I'm fine, Doctor. Stop worrying." He reached for her hand and brought it to his lips in a mock-gallant gesture. Miranda hoped he wouldn't notice her trembling. "Many thanks for your services tonight."

"It was nothing," Miranda said, and she jumped out of the car before he could read the lie on her face.

⁂

Beth stared hatefully at the blinking cursor on her computer screen, the only thing marring the white wasteland of her empty document. Maybe if she stared long enough, she thought, the words would write themselves, and she could just give up and go to bed.

She'd already wasted an hour meditating on "Why Education Is Important," finding it to easy to get distracted by topics such as "Why the Principal Thinks This Is a Good Topic," "What the Odds Are This Speech Will Put the Governor to Sleep," and "How I Can Keep Harper from Ruining My Life—Again."

Beth still couldn't quite believe that Harper was going to enter, despite her threats. She could barely be bothered to do her homework most days, so how likely was it that she'd put in a nonrequired show of academic effort and produce a whole speech? But Beth had to assume that she'd go through with it, if only because Harper's desire to destroy her had so far proved unbounded. It didn't seem fair; without Harper in the race, Beth's win would have been a sure thing.

I deserve this, she told herself. She worked harder than anyone at Haven High. The rest of them were complacent, contented with their narrow, small-town lives—it was only Beth who wanted more.

She opened her browser and clicked back to the website she'd come across of award-winning essays on every topic. According to the description at the top of the page, it was supposed to serve as an inspiration for students in her position, but Beth knew what it was *really* for. She'd always known sites like this one were out there, she just never thought she'd be visiting one herself.

But her mind was so clogged with bitterness that she couldn't string two sentences together, much less compose a speech. And here they were, dozens of them—all better than anything she could have come up with, even on her best day. She could just highlight the text, cut and paste, change a few words here and there . . .

It would be wrong, not to mention risky and totally beneath her—she was supposed to be someone who, unlike Harper, actually had principles.

It would be wrong, she repeated to herself.

But it would also work.

"What do you want?"

At the sound of Miranda's voice, Harper was momentarily stunned into silence. "I . . . uh . . . didn't expect you to actually pick up." Waiting for Miranda to screen her call, then leaving a plaintive voice mail that would inevitably go unreturned had become a nightly routine for Harper. This was an unexpected break in the pattern, and now that she had an opening, she had no idea what she actually wanted to say.

"I guess it's a night of surprises," Miranda replied, almost dreamily.

"What?"

"I'm just . . . tonight was . . . let's just say you caught me in a good mood. Your lucky day. So what do you want?"

Harper wasn't sure whether she wanted to apologize yet again, or to accuse Miranda of having spread the gossip flyer and force an admission that now the two of them were even. So instead, she stalled for time. "Just to talk," she said slowly. "Just to see what's up with you."

"Same old, same old." Miranda's voice wasn't overly friendly, but it lacked that icy sheen she usually adopted when forced to talk to Harper. Maybe there was hope after all.

Carpe diem, right?

"Look, Miranda, I'm sorry," Harper said quickly, trying to spit out as many words as she could before Miranda cut her off. "I'm so sorry, you have to understand that I would never want to hurt you, or our friendship, and you know how important Adam is—was—but he wasn't more important than you—"

"Whatever," Miranda muttered.

Harper's fingers tightened around the phone. "No, really—I know you think I screwed you, but I *didn't.* I swear, if I had thought there was a chance in hell that something would happen between you and Kane—"

"Stop."

"But you need to know that—"

"Just stop." And it was back, that flat, affectless tone that belied the years of friendship between them. Whatever opening had briefly existed, it had just slammed shut. "I don't need to hear any more about how I'm not good enough for him. I already know what you think."

"Of course it's not what I think," Harper protested. "It's Kane, it's—"

"No, it's *you.* Maybe if you'd actually, oh, I don't know, *helped* me, rather than stabbed me in the back . . ."

Her voice trailed off, and for a moment there was nothing but the sound of loud breathing on both ends of the line. "Is that why you did it?" Harper asked softly. "It's really all about Kane?"

"Did what?"

"I know it was you," Harper said, trying to keep a lid on her emotions. If Miranda wanted to handle this like they were strangers, Harper would find the strength to do so.

"Is this some kind of riddle?"

"Beth couldn't have done it on her own," Harper continued. "There were things on there that no one else knew."

"So?"

"So it was you. God, Rand, teaming up with *her*? Do you really hate me that much?"

There was a long pause. "Maybe."

"Just because I didn't help you get Kane?" Harper asked incredulously.

Miranda sighed. "It's not Kane . . . not just Kane." She no longer sounded angry, or bitter, just tired. "It's you. I kept making excuses for you. Whenever anyone called you a heartless bitch, or a slut—"

As always, Harper jerked at the sound of the word. She hated the way it sounded—especially on Miranda's lips.

"I'd always say, 'Oh no, you don't know what you're talking about. *You* don't know her like *I* know her.' So congratulations," she said sarcastically, "you fooled me. But now I'm done. I'm out."

"Just like that?" Harper asked, the taste of bile rising in the back of her throat. "I'm a bitch, you're a saint, and now Saint Miranda's '*out*'?"

"That's not—well, yes."

"That's bullshit, Rand, and you know it." Harper collapsed onto her bed, staring up at the ceiling. Her voice was cold enough that Miranda would never suspect there were tears streaming down her face, or that she'd tugged a blanket over her head as if to shut out the world. "You can act like you're better than me, but we both know the truth: You're jealous."

Miranda rolled her eyes. "Of you? Right."

"Yes. *Right.*" Harper hated herself for saying it, but

Miranda wasn't the only one who could be cruel. "You hate that I get all the attention and you just have to tag along after me. You're just using this as an excuse to get away because you think that without me around, you might actually be *someone*."

"So what?"

"So think again." Harper knew she should stop—even if apologies wouldn't work, time might, if she just shut up. But it didn't matter what she wanted; her hand was glued to the phone. "At least with me, people knew who you were. You had friends. You had a life. Without me? You've got nothing." *It's almost too late*, she warned herself, but she couldn't stop. "You *are* nothing."

Harper's voice broke on the last word, but when Miranda finally spoke, she sounded perfectly composed.

"Maybe you're right," she said slowly, just before hanging up. "But I'd rather be nothing than be your friend."

Kaia almost ignored the doorbell—but that would mean she had let him win, right? Whoever he was out there who wanted to terrify her would have accomplished his goal. And Kaia refused to play that game.

"I hoped you'd be here," Reed said when she opened the door.

Hoped, or knew?

"What are you doing here?" Reed almost never showed up at her house. It wasn't his style. Instead, she would call him and they'd meet on some neutral territory. Was it possible he'd come tonight to check up on his handiwork, and see whether she'd fallen apart?

It couldn't be him, she told herself. Not Reed, the one person out here she'd grown to trust. Except—

How much do you really know about him?

Nothing.

Enough.

"Got tired of admiring you from afar," Reed said, smiling. "Figured it was time you met your secret admirer."

Alarmed, Kaia took a step back.

"Hey, it was just a joke," he said softly, taking her hands in his. "I just wanted to see you, that's all. Missed you. What's going on?"

Kaia was glad she'd turned the floodlights off before going inside, so there was no way he could have seen her vandalized car in the darkness. For a second, she considered flicking them back on and telling him everything, but she didn't want him to look at her as a victim. Or maybe she was afraid he wouldn't be surprised.

"Nothing," she said, insisting to herself that it was true. "I'm glad you came."

She forced herself to forget her ridiculous suspicions and forget the fact that the maids were out for the night and her father wasn't due back until tomorrow. And after they shared a long, deep kiss, she was almost able to do it.

Kaia led him out back to the hot tub, tossing him a pair of her father's trunks. Then she ducked into the changing room and slipped into her new bikini, determined not to let some perverted loser ruin her night.

As they let themselves sink into the churning water, Kaia knew she'd made the right decision. This was just what she needed to relax, and remind herself that Reed wasn't a threat.

"Glad I came over?"

Kaia launched herself across the hot tub and floated into Reed's arms. The nearly unbearable heat was even worse with his wet, sticky body pressed up against hers, but Kaia didn't mind. The heat was refreshing—cleansing. "Definitely."

He wrapped himself around her and then sank down farther into the seat, so they were both nearly submerged in the roiling water, with only their faces peeking out into the sharp winter breeze. He tipped his head back. "Look at that," he said reverently.

Kaia followed his gaze. The stars seemed unnaturally bright. One of them, twinkling by the horizon, had a dark, reddish glow. "I wouldn't want to be anywhere else right now," she marveled. Contentment was a new thing for her.

"Good, because you're staying right where you are," he said, turning her around to face him. Her hair floated in a halo around her, and she remembered that when she was a little girl, she had pretended to be a mermaid. She'd always thought she looked most beautiful in the water.

She inhaled deeply, burrowing her face into his neck. The water had washed away the ever-present stench of pot, the lingering grease from his tow truck and his shift at Guido's—he was fresh and clean. Just like new. "I like the way you smell."

"I like *you.*" He kissed her, roughly at first, his tongue thrusting into her mouth, tangling itself with hers, their breath loud and hurried in her ear. Then as she nibbled on his lower lip and opened her eyes, he opened his, and their movement slowed, until they were almost frozen, their lips connected, their eyes locked.

"What the hell is going on here?"

Reed flinched and thrust himself away from her, but Kaia didn't refuse to let go. She'd recognize the harsh, patrician voice anywhere—Daddy Dearest was hard to forget. She wasn't about to let him ruin her fun, not tonight. She needed Reed by her side, as a flesh-and-blood reminder that she wasn't alone.

"I should think that's pretty obvious," she quipped, finally looking up. He loomed over them, far enough back to ensure no water would touch his custom-tailored

Ermenegildo Zegna suit and Bruno Magli loafers. "What are you doing home?"

"I live here," he reminded her.

It was only technically true. Two or three nights a month he lived there. The rest of the time it was difficult to remember his existence. The maid could have warned her he was due home tonight, Kaia thought in irritation. No matter—she could be dealt with later. For now, the damage was done.

"What's the problem, Father?" she asked innocently. "I'm just making new friends. Isn't that what you wanted? I thought the whole point of sending me out here was so I could meet some new people. You know, good influences."

She tried to stroke Reed's hair, but he jerked away and pulled out of her grasp.

Her father ignored her, as usual.

"Who are you?" he asked, glaring at Reed. "Get off my daughter and out of my Jacuzzi." Reed stumbled to his feet, stepped up onto the wooden deck and, dripping, extended a hand to Keith Sellers.

Mistake.

Kaia's father looked at him as he might a wet, stinky dog who'd tried to rub up against the leg of his $1,200 pants.

"Reed Sawyer, sir," Reed said, dropping his hand when it became obvious no one was going to shake it.

"I know you, don't I?"

"He works at the garage down on Main Street," Kaia said brightly. "You probably saw him there when you took the Jag in for service."

Now Keith Sellers looked as if the wet dog had *peed* on his $1,200 pants.

"Or maybe he delivered your pizza," Kaia added helpfully, just to dig the knife in a little deeper. She knew very well that Keith Sellers *never* ordered pizza, even when he wasn't on his no-carb diet.

Her father heaved a weary sigh.

"What are you doing, Kaia?" he asked, shaking his head. "This is a lot of effort to go to, just to spite me."

"This has nothing to do with you," Kaia snapped. She climbed out of the tub and wrapped a towel around herself, handing one to Reed as well. He took it without looking at her.

"Why else would you be associating with this kind of trash?" Keith Sellers shrugged his shoulders and then strode back toward the house. On his way, he hit the lights, dropping them into darkness. Kaia could no longer see Reed's face—or guess what he might be thinking. "Get him out of here, Kaia," he called back to her, in a voice she knew better than to disobey. "I know you'll do whatever you want—but you're not doing it in my house."

It was so pathetic when he actually tried to act parental. He was just too out of practice for it to stick.

"Come on," she said, taking Reed's hand and pulling him toward the door. "Let's get out of here."

"I'm going," Reed agreed, pulling his hand away. He rested it firmly on her shoulder. "You stay."

"What? Why?" *Listen to me*, she thought in disgust, *needy and pathetic.* "Who cares what he thinks?" she asked. "I don't."

"I think you do," he said slowly, avoiding her gaze. "And that's the problem."

He walked away, and because she didn't want to seem weak, she didn't follow. She let the towel drop to the floor of the deck and in the darkness groped her way back to the forgiving waters of the hot tub.

Damn him, she thought, sinking in. Damn him for his pride, or stubbornness, or whatever had made him leave.

And damn her father. He'd been absent most of her life—was *still* absent—and despite the fact that she never asked anything of him, he kept taking everything that mattered to her. He'd taken her home, her credit cards, her freedom—and now Reed.

He wouldn't be happy until she was left alone, with nothing.

Oh wait—

Mission accomplished.

⁂

He didn't go straight to his pickup truck, but instead wandered off into the darkness, telling himself he was exploring the grounds—but the truth was, he couldn't bring himself to leave. He stopped after a few minutes, realizing that he had a perfect view of the back deck hot tub, Kaia's figure illuminated in the darkness. She was so beautiful, he couldn't bring himself to turn away. Especially since it was becoming clear that the two of them didn't belong together, not in the real world. Out here, watching, he could forget all that and just appreciate her. He could remember the way she'd felt in his arms, and forget that she was likely just playing him, stringing him along for her own purposes.

Reed sighed, resisting the urge to light up. He needed something to take the edge off. Kaia was like a drug that made everything seem too real. It was as if he lived the rest of his life in black and white. With Kaia, the world wasn't just brighter—it was blinding Technicolor.

And it was exhausting.

Reed spent most of his life hanging on the sidelines. It was his natural place, just as waiting and watching was his natural state. But with Kaia he found himself acting, rather than reacting, his normally placid mind consumed with questions: Why did she want him? Why did he want her? How would things end, and when?

Maybe it had been a mistake to get involved at all.

Reed decided to light up after all, and inhaled deeply, relishing the heat that spread through his lungs. Being with Kaia meant being in the center, under the spotlight. And he just wasn't made for that kind of hassle. He lived on the fringes. He didn't *do*. He watched.

chapter six

"THIS IS A VERY QUITE SERIOUS CHARGE, MS. GRACE." Jack Powell frowned sternly at her, and ran a hand through his floppy brown hair. "Do you have any evidence to back up these claims?"

Other than absolute certainty in the pit of her stomach? Other than nearly explicit—but undocumented—admissions from both suspects? Uh . . .

"No," she admitted. "I was hoping you could handle that. Now that you know what you're looking for."

"And why come to me with this information? Why not the vice principal, or someone else in the administration?"

"Well, I figure they must have used the newspaper

equipment to print the flyer, and you *are* the sponsor. It seemed like your department." Harper hoped it sounded convincing. She wasn't about to admit that when you're turning in your former best friend for stabbing you in the back, it's more palatable to do so with the hottest teacher in the history of Haven High. Besides, Vice Principal Sorrento had a creepy birthmark on his forehead that had already eaten most of his hair and would surely soon get started on his face. Mr. Powell, on the other hand, could have been Hugh Grant's stunt double—and pretending she was starring in one of those movies where the sassy American falls into bed with the dapper Englishman was almost enough to distract her from the task at hand.

She'd woken up that morning determined to act. Striking back was the best way to keep from obsessing over Miranda's words and what it meant that the one person who knew her best had decided she wasn't worth knowing.

"Beth Manning and Miranda Stevens are two of my best students," Powell said dubiously. "Are you sure—"

"It was them, Mr. Powell. I'm positive. Just look into it—you'll see I was right."

For a moment, Harper pictured how Miranda's face would look when she got summoned to the vice principal's office to receive her punishment, sure to be especially harsh under the new "no-tolerance" regime. But she pushed the image out of her mind.

Miranda had no regrets, right?

Fine. Good. Then neither would she.

In her backpack, Beth carried: four sharpened Dixon Ticonderoga pencils and a pale pink pencil sharpener in the shape of a rose. Just in case. One Mead notebook and one matching folder for each class, color coded. A folded-up picture of her twin brothers, stuffed into the front pocket. Two dollars in quarters, for vending machine snacks. A pack of wintergreen Eclipse gum, to help her stay awake in history class, where the teacher had a bad habit of droning on and on about his long-ago European vacation. A Winnie the Pooh wallet she'd gotten on a family trip to Disneyland and had never had the heart to replace. And today, Beth carried two neatly typed, four-page-long speeches on the subject of education, each bound together with a single staple positioned in the upper-left-hand corner.

One speech was eloquent, witty, and succinct, seamlessly shifting back and forth between heartfelt personal anecdotes and powerful generalizations. It was a sure winner.

The second speech was awkward, wordy, and nonsensical, filled with run-on sentences and the occasional misspelling. It was hackneyed and repetitive and made stunningly obvious pronouncements such as, "Without teachers, there could be no schools." It was a loser, from beginning to end.

The first speech was written by a Jane A. Wilder, of Norfolk, New Jersey. The second speech was written by Beth Manning, hastily spit out in the early hours of the morning because, at four a.m., she'd finally given up on sleep and decided that she needed a backup plan in case she decided not to let Jane A. Wilder unknowingly save the day.

As she approached the principal's office, she took both essays out of her bag. There was a box, just inside the door, marked SPEECHES FOR THE GOVERNOR. It was almost empty—but lying on top was one titled "Education: You Break It, You Buy It." By Harper Grace.

Beth resisted the temptation to pull it out of the box and read it—she'd rather not know. And she resisted the even stronger temptation to take it from the box, stuff it in her backpack, and run away.

Instead, she focused on her choice: Do the right thing or do the smart thing.

What good would it do her to be an ethical person if she was stuck practicing her ethics in Grace, California for the rest of her life, earning a junior college degree in food preparation and then working at the diner for the next fifty years until she dropped dead of boredom in the middle of a vat of coleslaw? On the other hand, what good would it be to wow the admissions committee, earning her ticket to a bright and better tomorrow, all the while knowing she was living a life that, in truth, belonged to Jane A. Wilder of Norfolk, New Jersey?

She did what she had to do.

She flipped a coin—and in the flicker of disappointment that shot through her as soon as she saw Abraham Lincoln's stern profile gazing up from the center of her palm, she realized the decision she wanted to make. She ignored the coin, and put one of the speeches back in her bag. The other went into the box.

Right or wrong, it was, in the end, her only choice.

Adam shuffled into the coach's office and slouched down in the uncomfortable metal folding chair, doing his best to avoid the coach's hostile stare. They sat in silence for a moment as Adam waited for the shouting to begin. He'd been waiting all week for the coach to summon him about the big fight and finally dish out his punishment. But that didn't mean he was looking forward to it. And he had no intention of speaking first.

"I assume you know why you're here?" Coach Wilson finally asked.

Adam nodded.

"Instigating a brawl with the whole school watching?" He shook his head. "Not smart."

Adam shrugged.

"The Weston Wolves' point guard broke his nose, and their center will be out for half the season with two broken fingers."

Adam shrugged again.

"Well?" the coach asked, his face reddening the way it did at Saturday morning practice when it was obvious half the team was too hung over to see the ball, much less send it into the basket.

"Well what?" Had there been a question in there somewhere? Adam hadn't been paying much attention. He just wanted to get this over with.

"Well, don't you have anything to say for yourself?"

Adam shook his head.

"Damn it, Morgan!" The coach slammed his palm down on the desk with a thud. "What's wrong with you? When I took over this team, all anyone could talk about was Adam Morgan, how talented he was, what a great team leader he was—and do you know what I found instead?"

Silence.

"I found you. You screw up in practice, you screw up in the games, you're surly, you're unfocused, and on the night you finally start playing to your capacity, you start a damned fight. What's wrong with you?"

Having made it this far into the meeting without

saying more than two words, Adam suddenly found the inertia too much to fight.

“I don’t know what’s going on with you, Morgan, but I don’t like it. I’ve got no use for hotheads.”

Just get to the point, Adam thought.

“I should probably throw you off the team.”

Adam searched himself for shock, despair, or any of the other reactions you’d expect at the thought that basketball, the last good thing in his life, could disappear. But he couldn’t find any. He just felt numb. And if getting thrown off the team meant he didn’t have to confront Kane’s smirk, day in and day out—maybe it would be for the best.

“But I’m not going to. You’re too good. I’m giving you one last chance, Morgan. Don’t screw it up.”

Again, Adam waited for the flood of emotion, relief. It didn’t come.

“Don’t thank me yet,” the coach continued, ignoring the fact that Adam hadn’t moved. “You know the administration is cracking down this month. Everyone involved in the fight gets two weeks’ detention—except you. As the instigator, in addition to the detentions, you’ll be suspended from school for five days.”

Suspended, while everyone else, including Kane, got off with detention? That was enough to slice through Adam’s apathy.

"Coach, the other guys were all in it, just as much as I was. I *saw* Kane Geary snap that guy's fingers—" It was a lie, but who cared?

"And *I* saw you take Geary down, so I wouldn't be throwing his name around if I were you. At least he had too much class to come in here and tattle on you like a little baby."

"Class?" All Kane had was the ability to charm any gullible adult who crossed his path. "He had it coming, Coach," Adam protested, rising from his chair. "You don't know him, he's—" But there was nothing he could say, not here. The frustration building, Adam swept his arms in a long, swift arc, knocking the folding chair off balance. It toppled over and skidded across the floor.

"I'd advise you to calm yourself down now, son," the coach warned. Adam breathed heavily through his mouth and resisted the urge to react to that single, offensive word. Son. Only his father had ever called him that, and only when he was drunk and angry—and Adam had been foolish enough to get in his way. "I'm going to forget we had this little chat, Morgan," the coach said, leaning back in his chair. "And when you come back from your suspension, you and I, we can start with a clean slate. I would advise you to use this week to take a serious look at your behavior, and find a way to get it under control. Before you get yourself into some *serious* trouble." He flicked his hand in dismissal. "Now, get out."

And, ever obedient, Adam did as he was told.

Maybe he would follow the coach's advice and spend his week off trying to relax, trying to move on and forget about the wreck Harper, Kane, and Kaia had made out of his life. Maybe he could even accept that Beth wasn't going to forgive him. Maybe he could find a way to live without the constant urge to break something.

Maybe.

Kaia used to struggle with staying awake in school; now, though it seemed like she hadn't slept in days, she arrived every morning feeling like she'd injected a double espresso directly into her bloodstream. She was too aware of every set of eyes that might be tracking her path down the hall.

She stared down at her desk every day in French class, feeling Powell's gaze resting on her from across the room. Reed was nowhere to be found, and yet it felt like he was everywhere, lurking in corners, peering out from behind lockers, sneaking glimpses of her—but disappearing as soon as she sensed his presence.

She'd had her car repainted and washed it three times, but she could still trace her fingers along the ghostly letters. They were too faint to make out, but she knew they were there, hiding under the new coat of paint, for only her to see.

So she spent her days watching and waiting, and her nights lingering in town, wandering the narrow, broken-down streets of Grace, preferring to stay away from her empty house and its loud silence. The last three nights she'd gone to a movie at the Starview Theater. The same movie was showing each night—*Clueless.* She didn't like the film very much; as someone intimately familiar with a real-world life of luxury, she didn't have much patience with the movie's shoddy impersonation. But still there was something strangely appealing about sitting alone in the dark, surrounded by strangers, watching a completely predictable life unfold with perfect symmetry on the screen.

Besides, it gave her something to do.

It was ridiculous, Kaia told herself, spinning the combination lock on her locker, all this angst over a one-time thing. It could have been a random act of vandalism—it's not like there weren't enough bored delinquents running loose in this town. There was no reason to think that she'd been a carefully chosen target.

Kaia opened up her locker, and a small envelope fell out. An envelope she'd never seen before, an envelope that couldn't have been slipped in through the vent because her locker had no vent. Just a door, and a lock. And someone out there knew the combination.

She looked up and down the hallway. No one was watching her. They were all absorbed in their own lives. Or so it appeared.

The envelope was small and light blue. And it was blank. She stuck a nail under the seam and slowly ripped it open, unaware that she was holding her breath.

She pulled out three small pieces of glossy paper. And now she breathed again, harsh and fast. They were photos.

The first, a distance shot of her buying a movie ticket.

The second, framed by her living room window, showing her curled up on the couch, eyes fixed on the TV.

The third, a close-up, her head tipped back against a wooden deck, her hair wet and plastered against her face. Her eyes closed. And there was something else in the frame, a hand, reaching down toward her face, toward the lock of hair that covered her left eyes. Proving that it wasn't a telephoto lens, that someone had been there.

Close enough to touch.

"I didn't do it." Miranda could come up with no strategy other than repeating that over and over, until they believed her.

"Ms. Stevens, we have proof. Mr. Powell found traces of your file on the newsroom computer." The vice principal nodded in the direction of Jack Powell, who stood behind his desk, stone-faced and silent. "You were the only one logged in that morning. But we do suspect you had an accomplice. Who were you working with?"

"No one," Miranda protested. "I didn't do it." She was shaking. She and Harper had gotten into plenty of trouble over the years, but never anything that had landed her here, squeezed into an uncomfortable chair, facing down the vice principal and fending off the claustrophobic conviction that the walls of his office were closing in. And she'd never gotten into trouble without Harper by her side. It was different, she was quickly discovering, when you were alone.

"If you tell us who it is, Ms. Stevens, I might consider your cooperation when deciding your punishment. What you've done is very serious, you realize. This will go on your permanent record. It could affect your entire future."

Was her loyalty to a girl she barely knew and barely liked really worth getting into even more trouble? Miranda didn't know—but she knew she wasn't a rat. Once Beth found out they'd been caught, she would surely insist on turning herself in—say what you wanted about Beth, she at least had principles—but Miranda wasn't about to make the decision for her, no matter what it cost. She lifted her head up and crossed her arms in an effort to look resolute—and to stop herself from trembling.

"I'm sorry. I wish I could help you, but I can't."

"This is a one-shot deal, Stevens. Tell me now, and I can help you. But once I've decided on your punishment—"

"I'm sorry," she repeated. "I can't."

"Very well, then." He rubbed the large brown birthmark on his forehead, then looked down at his desk and began flipping through a stack of papers, as if to signify that she was no longer worth his time. "A month of detentions, then, starting today."

Miranda got up to leave, doing her best to hold back the tears. *Harper* would never cry in a situation like this. She would just grin at the vice principal, making it clear that nothing he could do or say would affect her in the least. Miranda couldn't manage a smile, but at least she didn't cry.

"Stevens," the vice principal said as she was almost out the door, "you've made a very poor choice here today. I hope, for your sake, you don't look back on this moment and realize it was a huge mistake."

Kane ambushed her right outside the vice principal's office. She'd caught him at his weakest moment, so it seemed only fair to return the favor.

"I have to admit," he said, slipping up from behind her, "I didn't think you had it in you."

Miranda flushed and looked away, one hand flying up,

as if on its own, to check that her hair was sufficiently in place. The small gesture was all it took to confirm Kane's suspicions.

"Didn't know I had what in me?" she asked in confusion, smiling widely despite the tears forming at the corner of each eye.

"I think you know what." He jerked his head back toward the office. "What'd they give you? Life without parole? Plus a little community service?"

"A month's detention," she said ruefully. "Wait—you know, and you're not mad?"

"Mad?" Kane grinned at her, delighting in the way the blood all rushed back to her face. Not that there weren't plenty of girls falling all over themselves to have him, but Miranda was different. She'd always been a bit of a riddle, and there was something almost comforting about being able to tuck her neatly into a recognizable category. Something a bit disappointing, as well—she didn't belong with the bimbos. "Why would I be mad?" he asked, stroking his chin in deep thought. "Just because you spread a bunch of embarrassing rumors about me to the whole school?"

She raised her eyebrows as if to say, well . . . *yes*.

"I *was* mad," he allowed. But it had, after all, been such a feeble scheme. And there was almost something endearingly pathetic about Miranda's little attempt to strike back. Like a kitten trying to take down a tiger. "I *was* mad," he repeated, "but it's not a deal breaker." He put an arm around her, the way he had a hundred times over the course of their friendship—except, this time, he noticed the way she brightened up at his touch. "Besides, I'm kind of impressed. It's good to see you raising a little hell."

"I learned from the best," she said teasingly.

"Then you didn't learn enough. *I* know better than to get caught," he boasted.

She ducked her head and giggled. It wasn't a sound that suited her. She wasn't a giggler.

"How *did* you know they caught me, by the way?"

"A master never reveals his secrets," Kane swore. His network of informants depended on his discretion—and his power depended on his access to their information. "Let's just say I have my ways."

"Someday, Kane, you're going to find out you don't know everything," Miranda cautioned him.

"And someday, Stevens, you're going to find out I know even more than you think."

Do the right thing, or do the smart thing?

She couldn't flip a coin this time, not with Miranda facing her, waiting for some kind of answer. Miranda was flushed, and kept smiling and staring off into space, as if her brush with the vice principal had completely unhinged her.

"I'd never ask you to turn yourself in," Miranda said again. "I just thought you should know what was going on."

"And they didn't mention me at *all*?" Beth asked. She felt guilty for even considering weaseling out of responsibility, but she'd never been in trouble before, and the prospect of getting caught terrified her. They were huddled over a small table in the library, just across from the shelf of college guides—a vivid reminder of how much Beth stood to lose.

Maybe you should have thought of that before *you broke the rules*, a voice in her head suggested.

"No," Miranda confirmed. "They know there's someone else, but they have no idea who it is."

"A month of detentions . . ." Beth couldn't imagine it. She'd never even had one.

And it wasn't just the fear of spoiling her record—her *permanent* record—that stopped her. She worked at the diner after school. On off days she babysat for her little brothers and bounced between countless application-padding extracurriculars. She *couldn't* spend a month in detention; it would ruin everything.

"Do you *want* me to turn myself in?" Beth asked, knowing already that the ironclad rules of the teen honor code would force Miranda to say no, regardless of the truth.

"No, of course not. I mean, unless you . . ."

"I could," Beth offered. "I mean, I would, if you wanted me to. Of course."

"Oh, I know you would, of course."

"But, you know, if you don't really think it would change anything . . . ," Beth hedged.

"No, I guess . . . no reason for us both to go down, right?" Miranda said weakly. "I mean, it seems sort of silly, for you to just—out of solidarity, or something."

"But if you wanted me to—"

"No, only if *you* wanted to—"

She deserved that month of detentions, every bit as much as Miranda. But then—what was the difference?

Did she *deserve* for her boyfriend to cheat on her? Did she deserve to bomb the SATs after all her studying? To cry herself to sleep every night? To be screwed over by Adam, by Harper, by Kane, to be left alone? What had she ever done to deserve any of that?

But what had Miranda done, either, other than come along for the ride?

She opened her mouth, intending to say one thing—and then said another thing entirely.

"Okay, I guess I'll keep quiet," she told Miranda, who gave her a thin smile. "Thank you."

Beth had always thought of herself as someone who did the right thing, but now she knew the truth. She only did the right thing when it didn't cost her anything. She opened her mouth to take it back, but Miranda was already standing up and walking away. Not that it mattered: Beth didn't have the nerve, even if the alternative meant hating herself.

I'll make it up to you, she promised Miranda silently. *Somehow.*

Kaia didn't know he was there until he'd crept up behind her and laid a hand on her shoulder. She almost knocked over her coffee when she whirled around and realized he had approached her in a public place, in a coffee shop, where anyone could see. Powell was on permanent orange alert at the possibility of anyone seeing them together, and if he'd elected to throw his obsessive caution to the wind, it could mean only one thing: He was losing it.

"How did you know I was here?" she asked, wondering if he'd been following her.

"I needed to see you," Powell said, ignoring the question. He wrapped his fingers tightly around her forearm and pulled her toward a secluded corner of the deserted coffee shop. She settled into an overstuffed armchair, but he stayed standing, hovering nervously behind her.

"Sit down," she hissed, disgusted. Where was the cool

British charmer she'd pursued, the one with the icy glare and the cocky certainty that nothing mattered but what he wanted? "It'll be bad enough if anyone sees us together, but if they see you fluttering around me like a nervous boyfriend—just *sit down.*" She pointed to a chair across from her close enough that they could talk without being overheard, and far enough that he wouldn't be tempted to touch her, even if he'd truly become unhinged.

"So? What is it?" she asked, when he'd finally sat down and a minute had passed in silence. "What do you want?"

"What are you doing?" he asked, almost sorrowfully.

"What am *I* doing?" She arched an eyebrow. "Look where we are. What are *you* doing?"

"You won't return my calls. I needed to see you."

"I've been busy."

He let loose a harsh chuckle. "Busy? In this town? No such thing. No, I can guess what you've been doing."

"And what's that supposed to mean?"

"You've been with *him*, haven't you?"

"You've been watching me?" she said, pretending the realization came as a surprise.

"Of course not." He laughed, a few bitter barks of noise that contained no humor. "I've got better things to do with my time."

He seemed so honestly disdainful of the idea that she almost believed him; but then, if he hadn't been watching her, why the righteous anger? How could he be so sure?

"It's all over town, dearest. You may have some discretion, but your gutter-rat, I'm afraid . . ."

Reed wouldn't have spread anything around, he wasn't the type. But how could she be so certain, she asked herself, about a guy she'd just met? What made her so willing to trust the pizza delivery boy who drove around in a pickup truck, smoked mountains of pot, and never answered any of her questions?

"Let's say, for the sake of argument, that you're right. Let's say I was . . ."

"Cheating on me," Powell supplied helpfully. It was an odd choice of words, since cheating implied a relationship. And whatever they had—an agreement, an unwritten contract, a mutual disregard—it wasn't a relationship.

It was sex, nothing else.

"Whatever," she said, throwing up her hands in supplication. "Let's say you're right. What now?"

He looked surprised—maybe by her unruffled expression, which, she hoped, made it painfully clear that she didn't care what happened next.

"Now? Now you stop seeing him," he ordered. "We agreed—you want this, you want me, you can't have anyone else."

"Fine." Kaia shrugged.

"Fine?" He raised his eyebrows. Maybe he'd been expecting more of a fight. "You'll stop seeing him, then?"

"No." Did she have to spell it out? "I'll stop seeing *you.*" She finished her iced coffee in a single gulp and stood up. "It's been fun, Jack. See you around."

"Where do you think you're going?" he growled, grabbing her arm roughly to pull her back down. She shrugged him off. "You think you can just walk away?"

"Pretty much."

"That's not how it works, Kaia. You want to be very careful about what you choose to do right now."

It didn't sound like a desperate plea to win her back.

It sounded like a threat.

As if she'd be scared of some washed-up British bachelor who'd fallen so far, he was hiding out in the middle of nowhere teaching French to future farmers of America. Even if he was the one playing with spray paint in the middle of the night, or jerking off courtesy of his digital camera, it was a coward's revenge, and cowards didn't scare her.

"Bye, bye, Jack," she chirped, and headed for the door.

"This is a mistake, Kaia." His low, angry voice followed her out. "You're going to wish you hadn't done that."

Doubtful.

Harper had been looking forward to a nice quiet evening at home in front of the TV, hoping to lose herself in some cheesy MTV reality show—other people's misery was so much more fun than her own. But it wasn't to be. . . .

"Mind if I join you, hon?" Her mother didn't wait for an answer before squeezing next to Harper on the threadbare couch. Parents could be so inconvenient sometimes.

Harper nodded and tried to hold back a sigh. "Whatever." She upped the volume on the TV in anticipation of her mother's inevitable commentary.

"Is that the girl from that show on HBO?" her mother asked, peering at the screen. "Oh, wait, no, she has blond hair. But is she—"

"Mom! She's a real person, okay?" Harper explained, more harshly than she'd intended. "It's a *reality* show. They're all real. No actors. Get it?"

"No need to yell, dear, I'm sitting right here," Amanda Grace said dryly, raising her eyebrows. For a few minutes they watched together in blessed silence, then, "Wait, I thought she was dating that other boy? The one with the Mohawk?"

"She *was*, Mother."

"But then what's she doing with this one? And are they really going to—oh! Can they show that on TV? What are you watching?"

"It's just a show, Mom." Harper slouched down on the couch, wishing she'd chosen a different channel. Was there anything more embarrassing than watching on-screen sex with your *mother*?

"Harper, I hope that if you . . . well, if there's anything you want to talk about, you know, in that department—"

Correction: Talking about your own sex life—or, at the moment, lack thereof—with your mother was definitely more embarrassing.

"Mom, there's nothing to discuss. Trust me."

"I do, honey, it's just—" Fortunately, the scene shifted, and her mother gasped. "Is that vodka? And those two girls, what are they—? Is this really what you teenagers are doing with yourselves these days?"

"It's TV, Mom," Harper pointed out, feeling simultaneous twinges of pride and guilt that she'd been able to keep her mother so successfully in the dark.

"*Reality* TV."

Harper shook her head. "There's nothing real about any of this crap," she argued. "It's all edited to make it more exciting, and you know they're just acting up for the camera. No one's like that in real life."

Harper flipped the channel over to one of those 'All Women, All the Time' stations, hoping her mother would get absorbed by some soapy sob story and forget all about her. It wouldn't be the first time.

"I haven't seen Adam around here lately," her mother suddenly said, still staring at the TV. "Or Miranda."

Maybe she wasn't so oblivious after all.

"They're around," Harper said softly. She wasn't about to unload on her mother—last time she'd actually confided in one of her parents, she'd been barely out of diapers—but the temptation was there. There was something to be said for unconditional parental adoration, especially when everyone else you care about has decided you're worthless and unlovable.

"What's going on with you these days?" her mother asked, finally turning to her and smoothing down Harper's unruly hair, just like she used to do when Harper was younger. "You seem . . . sad."

Harper shrugged. "You know teenagers, Mom. We're a moody bunch."

"I know *you*," her mother countered. "I know when something's wrong. It might help to talk about it."

"No it won't." She knew she sounded sullen and sulky, like a little kid, but she couldn't help herself.

"Honey, I know high school can be tough—I wasn't born middle-aged, you know. But you've got to remember, it's not everything. The things that seem so horrible now, they'll pass. You'll get through it. Everyone does."

"Can we just not talk about this? Please?" *This* was why Harper never told her parents anything. They didn't get it. Harper knew her mother would probably think she just had some kind of teenybopper crush on Adam, that she and Miranda were just having a little spat that could be solved with ice cream and a smile. Having been a teenager once, a million years ago, didn't qualify her mother to understand what she was going through—and it obviously didn't give her any idea what Harper's life was like, how hard it could be.

"Of course," her mother said, lifting the remote and flipping through the channels until she stumbled upon a showing of *The Princess Bride.* "How about we just watch the movie?"

Loving this movie was one of the few things they still had in common. They'd watched it together about twenty times, and had memorized almost every line. Harper's mother switched off the light and draped a heavy blanket over both of them. Harper smiled, letting herself get carried away by the familiar jokes and the sappy but irresistible love story. If only life were as clear-cut as it was in the movies—if only you could slay a few Rodents of Unusual Size, battle your way across the Fire Swamp, slay an evil count, and get what you most desired. It would be an improvement over the real world, where danger snuck up on you and courage was so much more difficult to find.

"Harper?"

"Mmm?"

"You know your father and I love you, right?"

Of course she knew it. But it never hurt to hear it

again. She focused intently on the screen and blinked back tears as Princess Buttercup threw herself into the arms of her one true love.

"Yeah," she murmured softly, leaning her head against her mother's shoulder. "You too."

chapter seven

THE ADMINISTRATION HAD WORKED OVERTIME TO get everything ready for the governor's visit. The press—or, at least, a photographer from the *Grace Herald* and a reporter from the *Ludlow Times*—was due first thing that morning to take pictures of the school, which had been sufficiently buffed and shined for the occasion. A selection of high-achieving students had been carefully selected to speak with the reporter, and the crown jewel of Principal Lowenstein's presentation to the media was about to be unveiled.

Hanging over the front doors of the school, hidden by a white drop cloth, was the principal's pet project:

a giant billboard, labored over by the art teacher and his most talented students. It would soon welcome the governor to town—but now, in an almost as important moment, it would serve as the face Haven High would show to the world.

Principal Lowenstein allowed herself a moment to dream—thanks to the governor's star power, the local story would be picked up by the state press, perhaps even nationally syndicated. The paparazzi were everywhere, and you never knew what might excite the tabloids. She suppressed a smile, imagining her face staring back at her from the supermarket checkout aisle. She would be seen all over the country for what she truly was: a capable, zealous administrator destined for greater things.

Specifically, destined to get the hell out of this dinky town and take on a *real* school, a place where the students cared about more than football scores and truck engines, and the teachers actually understood the material they were supposed to teach.

Proud grin firmly planted on her face, Lowenstein waved to the reporters, posed for their flashes, and pulled down the drop cloth.

And because she was so intent on staring into the camera, she was the last to see it.

The art department had gone above and beyond, pulling a campaign photo of the governor riding a horse, and blowing it up so he appeared to be galloping toward the doors of Haven High. In large type, the caption beneath the image read—or was supposed to read—HAVEN HIGH WELCOMES OUR GOVERNOR—THE BEST IN THE WEST!

It was a masterpiece of administrative banality—or would have been, had someone not snuck beneath the drop cloth, pulled out their spray paint, and made a few . . . minor changes.

The governor was now truly *riding* the horse—as one imagined he might ride his wife. The new caption: HAVEN HIGH WELCOMES OUR GOVERNOR—THE BEST ^LOVER IN THE WEST!

It was juvenile, lame, inappropriate, grotesque and, all in all, a reasonably accurate representation of everything Haven High stood for.

The reporter scribbled madly, and Principal Lowenstein smiled uselessly for the camera, no longer looking forward to her front-page coverage. *Welcome to Haven High*, she thought dejectedly, *where dreams come to die.*

Everyone in school that day was consumed with the question of who had pulled the prank. Everyone except Beth, who had only one thought in her mind: Who would the winner be?

That morning in homeroom, she, Harper, and the other contenders had traipsed down to the principal's office and read their speeches into the PA system. Beth assumed no one was listening—the morning's gossip was too fresh for anyone to take a break and actually pay attention—but she still felt a tiny thrill having her voice piped throughout the school, knowing that soon people would be voting on whether or not they'd been suitably impressed.

Beth wasn't thrilled with her speech, but even in her nervousness she could tell it was better than anything anyone else had to offer. Harper's, especially—from the grammatical errors to the logical inconsistencies, to the blithe suggestion that school be made several hours shorter and students be allowed to choose their own subjects of study—Beth was sure she couldn't lose.

Still, she didn't like waiting.

The announcement came in last period, toward the end of French class. Normally, Beth detested sitting through those forty-seven minutes, feeling Jack Powell's eyes upon her—it forced her to remember the day he'd kissed her in the deserted newsroom, a moment she'd been struggling for months to forget. She could, if she allowed herself, still feel his hands gripping her body, and the flicker of fear that she wouldn't be able to push him away. It made her feel dirty, and somehow trapped, as if a part of her were still stuck there with him, in that cramped, dark room.

But today, she'd been too distracted by worries about the speech to pay much attention to Powell, and that, at least, was a blessing.

"Attention, students." As the PA speaker crackled to life, Beth looked up from her desk. This was it, she knew it. Just as she knew without looking that, three rows back, Harper was watching her.

She looked, anyway.

"Students, I'm pleased to announce the results of our speech contest," the principal announced, sounding distinctly happier than she had that morning. "All the submissions were quite impressive, but after tallying the votes, we have a clear-cut winner."

Beth held her breath. Harper continued to stare.

"The student selected should report to me after school, in order to discuss the arrangements for the speech."

Beth tucked a strand of hair behind her ear and tried to look calm, as if none of this mattered.

"And the student selected for this great honor is . . . Harper Grace." Beth felt all the breath leak out of her in a loud sigh. She felt like a flat tire, empty and ready to crumple. Behind her, she knew, Harper was still watching. Only now, she'd be smiling.

"I hope you'll all join me in congratulating Ms. Grace on her accomplishment. I know she will represent the school with honor and—if you'll pardon the pun—grace."

No one laughed. And no one applauded, or whistled, or did anything to make it appear they thought this was a big deal. Which, Beth supposed, it wasn't—except to her.

If she'd only turned in the other speech, the *good* speech, this wouldn't have happened. If she hadn't cared so much about following the rules, she wouldn't have lost. She was sure of it.

Harper, after all, never followed the rules—and she always won.

Harper caught up with her after class. "Why so glum?" she asked brightly. Beth tried to walk faster, but Harper picked up speed as well, refusing to fall behind. "Oh, don't be a sore loser," Harper chided, her voice saccharine sweet. "Your speech was good . . . or at least better than mine."

"I know," Beth said quietly, bitterly. When would Harper finally leave her alone?

"But it didn't matter, of course." Harper shook her head sorrowfully.

"And why's that?" Beth half expected her to admit she'd rigged the contest. After all, why leave things to chance? Only losers like Beth would be that stupid, right?

"It wouldn't matter if you'd written the Gettysburg address," Harper explained—and Beth would think her voice almost kind, if she didn't know better, if she hadn't seen the look in Harper's eye. "You think anyone actually cared what those speeches said? You think anyone but you was listening? It was a popularity contest. Everything in high school is a popularity contest." *And how could you get this far before figuring that out?* her look said. *I thought you were supposed to be the smart one.* "That's why I'll always win. People love me. You can't beat that."

"Not everyone loves you," Beth pointed out, amazed that, for once, she wasn't frozen and brought to tears by her anger. "Not Adam."

Harper didn't even flinch. She just smiled indulgently, as if watching a child try fruitlessly to contact the outside world on a plastic telephone.

Certain she could crack the facade, Beth pushed ahead. "None of these people have figured out who you really are. But Adam gets it—now."

"What do you know about it?" Harper asked in a perfectly measured voice.

"I know that whatever you try to take from me, you'll never get what you really want," Beth snapped. "He won't stop following me around—but he's done with you, forever."

"Nothing's forever."

"Nothing's more pathetic than watching someone chase after a guy who obviously wants nothing to do with her."

Harper shook her head. "Better watch out—this bitch

thing doesn't suit you. And it can't possibly have a happy ending."

"What's that supposed to mean?"

"Just a piece of friendly advice," Harper said, offering a cool smile, "from one bitch to another."

She walked away, leaving Beth alone in the middle of the hallway, surrounded by the surging crowd of students all with better places to be. She'd finally found the nerve to stand up for herself—and Harper had barely noticed. Maybe she didn't really care about Adam, Beth realized, or about anyone but herself. Maybe that's the kind of person you had to be to wreck other people's lives.

Yet again, Harper had stolen something from her—and obviously she'd only done it to make Beth more miserable than ever. It made her even more desperate to strike back. But how could you hurt someone who didn't have the capacity to feel pain?

She's wrong, Harper repeated silently, over and over again.

Beth didn't know anything about Harper, and she didn't know Adam as well as she'd thought, and that should be enough to make her words powerless. *Words can never hurt me*, she sang to herself, as if this were a Very Special Episode of *Sesame Street*: "B is for Bitch."

Beth was just lashing out, feebly trying to make herself feel better—and it was only an accident that she'd struck a nerve. But Harper couldn't help wondering whether that mattered. A stopped clock is right twice a day; maybe every once in a while Beth's bitter, nonsensical babbling stumbled into the truth.

She considered ditching her meeting with the principal and escaping in search of some way to clear her mind. And maybe she would have, if she'd had Miranda by her side, ready to ply her with cigarettes and chocolate chip cookies and assure her, with the certainty of someone who knew from personal experience, that soon enough, Adam would fall prey to her natural charm.

But since she was on her own, as usual, she strode down to the principal's office, her step steady and with a hint of a bounce so that no one watching would guess the truth. And the truth was that Beth's words still echoed in her mind:

He's done with you.

Forever.

And every time she thought of them, it felt like her bones were snapping and her muscles dissolving, so that it soon took all her effort not to crumple to the floor.

"Congratulations, Ms. Grace!" the principal boomed, meeting her in the doorway with a hearty handshake. "How does it feel?"

Harper returned the smile, tossed her hair over her shoulder, and looked the principal straight in the eye. "It feels great," she said, wishing they offered an Oscar for Best Performance in a High School Hallway. "I couldn't be happier."

Suspension wasn't all bad.

In fact, as it turned out, it wasn't bad at all.

Adam slept late, ordered pizza, watched TV and, in other words, did whatever the hell he wanted to do. It's not like his mother was home enough to care. She hadn't even noticed he wasn't going to school. (And, since he'd successfully forged her signature on the suspension form, there was no reason to think that she ever would.) It wasn't a bad life. And the coach was right: It gave him plenty of time to think.

That's what he did all morning, whether he was gnawing cold pizza or flipping aimlessly between ESPN and *Max and Ruby*. He thought about what had been done to him, and how he'd been wronged, and he thought about how there seemed to be no way out. And when the thoughts built up inside his head and it felt like the pressure would cause his eyes to bulge out, that's when he finally threw on some clothes and a pair of old sneakers and shambled down the street to a dark bar where they wouldn't bother to check his ID or ask why an eighteen-year-old local basketball star would want to waste his afternoon slouched over a mug of cheap, stale Bud Light.

Like father, like son, a voice in his head chanted.

After only a few days, he'd settled into a comfortable routine—and would be almost sorry when the suspension was lifted. Traipsing from class to class—facing his teachers, his ex-friends, his failures—was no match for long, lazy afternoons that turned into long evenings, hidden away in the dark, cozy recesses of the Lost and Found.

Sometimes he struck up a conversation with a regular—they were all regulars, here—and sometimes he kept to himself, his glowering expression keeping the prying strangers away.

"Hey, honey."

Today, apparently, wasn't going to be one of those days.

"What's a nice kid like you doing in a dump like this?"

Adam looked up from his beer. The pickup line was almost older than she was, though not by much. The woman who'd scraped her bar stool over toward him and was now curling a stubby finger through a lock of her platinum-blond hair was probably a couple of years younger than his mother. She wore a garish flowered blouse whose neckline plunged far lower than you might have wanted it to, and her nails were painted a bright pink that clashed with her red pants. Each had a little decal on its tip. On the nail of her index finger—which she was using to trace the rim of his half-empty glass—there was a tiny butterfly.

"How about it, hon, you got a story you want to tell?"

"Not really," Adam mumbled. But he gave her a half smile. She'd been pretty, once—and at the moment, he had nothing better to do. "How about you?"

"Oh, sweetie!" She threw back her head and laughed, and he could see the blackened enamel fillings lining her molars. "I got about a million of them. Let me tell you—"

"Here I am, Adam."

He froze as a pair of arms wrapped around him from behind, cool hands pressing his chest. Which might have been a good thing, were they not hands he knew.

"Have you been waiting long?" a too-familiar voice asked.

The older woman's face reddened—though it was hard to tell, thanks to the several layers of pale pancake and bloodred rouge. "I—I didn't know you had company. I, uh, I'll get out of your hair."

"She's not with me," Adam protested weakly as the hands traced their way up his body and began doing something unspeakably pleasurable to the tips of his ears. And the woman disappeared into the shadowy recesses of the bar—there were plenty of other men drinking alone.

"What do you want?" Adam asked Kaia dully, without turning around or pushing her away. He hated her . . . but he had never been able to push her away. "I was busy, in case you didn't notice."

"I noticed," Kaia said. She let go of him—Adam tried to feel relief, but couldn't—and pulled up a stool next to his. "So, aren't you going to thank me?"

"For what?" Now that she wasn't touching him anymore, Adam's feelings were uncomplicated. He just wanted her to go away.

"For rescuing you from"—Kaia looked off in the direction the older woman had disappeared—"that."

"I can take care of myself, thanks."

"Could've fooled me."

"Kaia, if you've got something to say, just say it. I don't have time for your games."

"Fine. You want the short but sweet version? You're screwing up."

Yeah, thanks for the news flash.

"Beating people up? Getting suspended? Walking around half-drunk all the time? It's pathetic—you've got to get it together."

"What do you care?" he growled, trying to push away her words before they could do any damage. Kaia never said anything without an ulterior motive.

She also never said anything that didn't sound at least partly true. It's why she was so deadly effective.

She shrugged.

"Good point. I don't care. I'm just telling you what I see. You want to ruin your life, that's your business. I'm just bringing it to your attention. Always good to make an informed decision." She flagged down the bartender and ordered a seltzer with lime. Adam suddenly wondered what she was doing here, in this dead-end bar in the middle of the afternoon, but forced himself not to ask. With Kaia, curiosity was just another form of weakness.

"I'm ruining my life?" he said instead, pouring on the sarcasm. "That's a good one. And I suppose you're just here for the show? You had nothing to do with it?"

"Very mature, Adam, blaming me for all your problems." She remained infuriatingly serene. Suddenly, she seemed to spot someone in the back of the bar, and she abruptly lifted her drink and stood up. "I've got better things to do than babysit you, Adam. Enjoy your beer."

"Like I really need someone like *you* looking out for me," he spit out.

Kaia looked up and down the long, empty bar, then fixed Adam with a pitying stare.

"It looks to me like I'm all you've got."

You can't go home again.

That was the line that swam into Beth's mind as she crouched behind a car in the parking lot, furious at herself for hiding like a coward, unable to find the strength to stand and show herself. She'd left school in search of Claire, or Abbie, or anyone from older, easier days, needing the reassurance of familiar faces, people to whom she mattered.

She'd found them, all right. And that, it seemed, had been the biggest mistake of all.

"Can you believe her?" Claire asked. She was lounging against the side of her silver Oldsmobile, while Abbie and Leslie perched on the hood of a boxy green Volvo. They were taking advantage of the picture-perfect weather, stretching out in the sun, and Beth would have joined them—until she heard the words that made her duck behind a parked car instead. "That speech was so pathetic. It was so *her*, though—all the little Miss Perfect crap."

"Come on, Claire, don't be such a bitch," Abbie said, in a chastising tone spoiled by the fact that she couldn't choke back her laughter.

"What? Admit it: She thinks she's better than everyone."

"Well . . ." Abbie and Leslie exchanged a glance. "Yeah," Leslie allowed. "But that doesn't mean—"

"Guys. Did you not see the way she was looking at us at the sleepover?"

"Like she couldn't wait to get away from us," Abbie mused.

"Like she was bored out of her mind," Leslie added. "And we were supposed to be honored or something that she'd showed up in the first place."

"It was kind of worth it, though, wasn't it?" Abbie asked, tipping her head back to get a full blast of sunshine. "I told you we'd get some good gossip out of her."

"Okay, but is it really worth putting up with Miss Priss for much longer, gossip or not?" Claire pointed out. "All this fake smiling's starting to hurt my face."

"Give her a break, Claire. This is Beth we're talking about—I mean, yeah, she's kind of boring and pretentious, but she was your best friend," Abbie reminded her.

Claire scowled. "*Was.* Note the tense. She's the one who ditched us—and now we're supposed to be grateful that she's come sniffing around again? Like we're some kind of last-resort rescue from total loserdom?"

"Okay, she's not *that* bad," Abbie argued. "It's not like we weren't friends with her . . . once."

"She's different now," Claire said firmly. "You know she's not one of us anymore. And I don't care how many innocent little wide-eyed smiles she gives us—she knows it too."

Maybe she had to work on her delivery. Giving someone helpful advice probably wasn't supposed to make them want to throw barware at you—but Adam had looked about ready to do just that. And the irony was, she'd actually been sincere. For whatever reason, she was tired of watching his pitiful downward spiral; but, apparently, he didn't want her help.

It was a good thing Kaia had better things to think about than the aberrant wave of consideration for her one-time mark. Reed was waiting.

"I'm glad you came," she said, when she found him slouched in a booth at the back of the bar. He was wearing a tight black T-shirt and, with his river of black curly hair and deep brown eyes, he almost faded into the shadows. She hadn't seen him—not this close, at least—since the day he'd run off from her house.

Her run-in with Powell had convinced her once and for all that if anyone in her life was a desperate perv, it was him. Reed had no motivation to torment her since she was sure he didn't know about Powell. She'd been too careful.

"I'm not doing this, Kaia." She loved the way it sounded when he said her name in his lazy, throaty voice. It sounded like honey—with a splash of tequila thrown in for flavoring.

"Doing what?" Kaia was good at acting the innocent, but in this case, she was honestly clueless. And she didn't like it.

"You and your father—I'm not getting in the middle of that."

"Of what? There is no 'that.' He barely knows I exist. And I try my best to forget he does."

"I saw what you were doing."

He spoke so slowly, as if each word did battle to escape from his brain. Usually it was sexy. Now it was just maddening. "Using me, to piss him off. I'm not doing it."

Kaia laughed. Unlike the light tinkling giggle she usually allowed herself, this was a full-throated chuckle, a mix of relief and genuine amusement. She stopped abruptly when she noticed his expression—apparently, Reed didn't like it when people laughed at him.

"Reed, did you see the look on my father's face when he went back into the house? Did you hear what he said? He doesn't care what I do. If I wanted to piss him off, I'd spill something on his white Alsatian carpeting. He couldn't care less about my dating life."

"I know what I heard," Reed persisted.

His stubbornness, usually so sexy, was going to ruin everything.

"You've seen too many movies. My father and I? It's not like that. What you heard was the same fight my father and I have every time we speak—which is about once a month. I don't care what he thinks of me, or who I'm with." She didn't say *please believe me.* Either he would or he wouldn't. "My father has nothing to do with—with whatever is happening between us," she swore. "Forget him. I have."

Reed considered her for a moment. He pushed a hand through his unruly hair, then nodded. "Okay."

"We're good?" she asked, wrapping her hands around his.

He nodded again. "We're good."

She leaned across the table to kiss him, hovering there for as long as she could, tasting his lips and breathing in his deep, musky scent. Then she stood up and laid her phone and wallet down on the table, hoping she'd chosen a clean spot.

"In that case, I'm off to find what passes for a bathroom in this place." She skimmed her fingers across his forehead—for no reason other than that she liked to touch him. "Don't go away."

Kaia had been gone for two minutes when her phone beeped. Reed could still smell her perfume lingering in the air.

The phone beeped again. A second text message. And Kaia was nowhere in sight.

The phone was lying on the table, only a few inches away. It beeped a third time, insistent, as if it were calling to him.

Reed wasn't usually a curious person. He saw as much of the world as the world wanted him to see—no more, no less. Why examine something when you could just breathe it in and enjoy?

But Kaia was different.

She was complicated and surprising. He didn't trust himself around her. And he didn't trust her at all.

When the phone beeped a fourth time, he looked quickly back toward the bathroom. There was no sign of her, so he picked up the phone and turned it face up.

See you at 8.

Wear the black teddy I like.

Or nothing.

That's even better. J

Reed had never been a big reader. And in English class—when he bothered to attend—he'd always ignored all the crap about levels and symbolism. But the message didn't require much interpretation; it said exactly what it meant.

When Kaia got through with him this afternoon, she'd be meeting someone else.

And maybe Reed was better at interpretation than he'd thought, because he was suddenly convinced that this was someone Kaia had seen a lot. "J" had certainly seen plenty—*all*—of her.

Reed wasn't usually a possessive person. A hookup wasn't a marriage proposal. People didn't belong to each other. He belonged only to himself—and his girls were the same.

But Kaia was different.

Or at least he'd thought she was.

Reed held the phone and brought his thumb toward the delete button—and then he stopped. The phone didn't belong to him. And neither did Kaia.

He set the phone back on the table next to her wallet.

And when Kaia came back from the bathroom, he was gone.

Beth didn't have the nerve to confront them in person. It was easier, safer to pick up the phone and climb into bed, swaddling herself in the fuzzy pink comforter. But, even surrounded by all the things she loved—Snuffy the stuffed turtle, her copy of *The Wind in the Willows*, her trophy from the sixth-grade spelling bee—she felt lost in hostile territory.

Claire picked up the phone after the fourth ring, just as Beth had begun to breathe an ounce easier and prepared herself to leave a message. "Claire, we need to talk," she began. "Are you . . . mad at me?" It sounded so childish—but it was all she could come up with. She couldn't reference what she'd heard in the parking lot.

"Why would I be mad at you, Bethie?" Claire asked, adopting the nickname she'd used when they were kids. "Have you *done* something? Feeling guilty?"

"You just seem . . . mad," Beth said lamely, avoiding

the question. Did she feel guilty? Had she trashed the friendship, or had they just drifted apart? What did it say that she could no longer remember?

"Beth, I'm kind of busy. Is there a point to this? Because otherwise—"

"I heard you in the parking lot," Beth blurted. If Claire hung up, Beth might not have the nerve to call back. And that would mean letting it go, returning their fake smiles and pretending she didn't know what lay behind them. "You, Abbie, Leslie—I heard what you said. About me."

"Oh."

There was a pause. Then— "You were spying on us?"

"No, I was just—it doesn't matter. I just . . ."

"What do you want me to say?" Claire asked irritably. "If you heard us, why are you even calling? What do you want from me?"

It was a reasonable question, but for all her agonizing over this call, Beth hadn't thought to come up with an answer.

"I wanted—I thought we could be friends again."

Claire laughed. "Just like that? Just because you decide, after all this time, you want to pick things up where we left off. You think it's that easy?"

"Why not?" Beth whispered.

"Because where were you, *Bethie*? Where were you when Abbie broke her leg, or got her first boyfriend?

Where were you when I almost failed precalc? When my parents got divorced—" Her voice, which had been rising steadily, suddenly broke off, and all Beth could hear were her labored breaths.

"I'm sorry," Beth began. "I wish I hadn't—"

"I don't care if you're sorry. Don't you get that? And I don't care anymore that you weren't there—I got by without you. We all did. I don't need you anymore. And I really don't care if you need me."

Claire hung up.

Beth sat with the phone to her ear for a long time, just listening to the dial tone. That was it, then. Unless she wanted to back down and forgive Adam, she was on her own.

On her nightstand, sandwiched between a stack of books and an empty picture frame (that had, until recently, held a shot from the junior prom), sat a small cardboard box. It was the size of a jewelry box, and inside it lay two yellow pills, each the size of one of her gold stud earrings.

She lifted the top and looked at the pills, examining them more closely than she had before. She even took one out of the box, just to see how it would feel in the palm of her hand. It was light, like aspirin, and it looked just as harmless.

Kane had given them to her as a Christmas present. He'd thought they could make their New Year's "*ex*-tra special"—a mistake almost as big as the one she'd made by inviting him into her life in the first place.

Still, she'd pocketed the pills, and kept them. For a rainy day? If so, this qualified, and she could certainly do with a jolt of happiness, chemical or not.

But she put the pill back in the box. She either had too much restraint or not enough nerve—she was no longer sure which. She didn't want to find out what those little pills did, no matter how wrecked she felt.

Yet, for whatever reason, she couldn't bring herself to throw them away.

chapter eight

A MONTH OF DETENTION WAS STARTING TO LOOK A whole lot sweeter. Room 246 was the same as she remembered it from her last week of incarceration: a long, gray space crammed with rows of desks drilled to the floor, the detention monitor positioned at the front with her nose buried in a book. There were just a few key differences.

First, Harper wasn't by her side to help make the hours speed by.

Second, the sign-in sheet was now yellow, rather than its former puke green.

And third, the only difference that mattered: Kane

Geary was sitting in the back corner. And he was flagging her down, pointing to the empty desk to his left.

Me? Miranda mouthed, fighting the urge to look behind her and see what tall, leggy blonde was the true target of that lazy grin.

Yes, you. He nodded, and when she slipped into the desk beside him, he patted her on the knee in welcome. It was all Miranda could do to not slide off the seat and melt onto the floor.

"Welcome to prison," he greeted her. "At least now I've got a good cell mate."

The hour passed too quickly, in a haze of whispered complaints about the monitor's hairy mole or the leaning Mohawk of the delinquent in front of them. They played dirty hangman (Miranda's winning word: "vulva"), placed bets on the number of wads of gum stuck beneath Kane's desk (seven), and, for a blissful ten minutes, Kane leaned over to Miranda's notebook and drew nasty but spot-on caricatures of the other members of the basketball team, who were seated in a hulking cluster toward the front of the room. Blissful because, to reach Miranda's notebook, Kane had to shift his body into her space and lay his arm across her desk, where it pressed, very lightly, against her own. As he stared at the page, intent on getting the point guard's dopey expression just right, Miranda concentrated on his arm, imagining that he was touching her on purpose. Knowing, even when he shifted position for a moment and his hand actually grazed hers, that he wasn't.

And then the bell rang, and it was all over.

It would be asking too much, holding out foolish hope to think that—

"See you tomorrow?" Kane asked, hoisting his bag over his shoulder and helping her gather up her scattered belongings.

"Same time, same place," Miranda replied, trying desperately for nonchalance.

Thank God Beth had weaseled out of trouble and left Miranda to face her punishment all on her own.

Miranda Stevens had spent her whole life flying under the radar and doing what other people told her to do.

So this is what you got for being a rebel?

Bring it on.

Beth felt him before she heard him. She was absorbed in her work, proofing the page layout for the next issue of the paper, and didn't hear the door to the tiny office click open. But some part of her must have registered it, and must have known whose hand lay on the knob, because gradually the words on her computer screen began to swim in front of her eyes and, unable to concentrate, she sensed a heavy quality in the air. The walls felt closer, the ceiling lower, and her muscles tensed.

He cleared his throat.

It was then she knew for sure.

"I thought we had an agreement," Beth said, trying to keep the quaver out of her voice. Her hands gripped the edge of the small computer desk until her knuckles turned white. She focused on the dull pain of the wooden desk digging into her palms. It kept her from being swept off in a wave of panicked thoughts—the room was empty, the halls were deserted, he was blocking the only exit, there would be no one to hear her scream. Yes, it was probably best to steer clear of thoughts like that, and not to even think the word "scream." Or she just might.

"You're not supposed to be in here, not while I'm here alone." It was silly, but she suddenly felt she'd made a dangerous misstep by calling attention to the fact that she was by herself—as if, otherwise, he wouldn't have noticed.

"Things have changed," Jack Powell said. He locked the door behind him and took a seat on the couch, patting the space next to him. Then he laughed at the look of horror on her face. "Oh, calm down," he said irritably. "You've got nothing I want."

Beth couldn't believe she'd once found this man adorable, fantasizing about his dark eyes and crooked smile. She had, more than once, drifted off to sleep while imagining them together in a romantic scene from a black-and-white movie. Everything about him repelled her now—even the accent seemed phony.

"Get out," she said steadily. "I told you before, I'll tell the administration what happened, what—you tried to do, if you don't leave me alone."

The last time they'd talked one-on-one and she'd unveiled this threat, it had knocked him off balance. But this time was different. He was expecting it—and more than that, he seemed to welcome it.

"Get off it, Beth. I didn't *do* anything to you. We both know that you wanted—" He cut himself off and gave himself a little shake. "Enough of that." And suddenly, his cold look was replaced by an amicable grin, the same one that made every other girl in school swoon. The sharp change, as if he'd swapped personalities with the flip of a switch, was the scariest thing of all. "That's why I stopped by," he said pleasantly, as if she'd invited him in for tea. "To tell you that the past is behind us. You won't be going to the administration, or making any more threats, and I'll do whatever it is I want to do."

"And how do you figure that?" Beth asked, forcing herself not to look away. Facing this Powell was even more unsettling than confronting him in attack mode. At least then, she knew what to prepare herself for. Now, looking at his blank face, she could only imagine what lay beneath the surface. This was the face she still saw in her nightmares.

"You made a good show of it, Beth, and I'll agree, you had something on me. Impressive. But, unfortunately, I now have something on you." He pulled a folded-up page out of his pocket. Beth knew what it was before he'd unfolded it and waved it in the air like a conqueror's flag. The bloodred color gave it away. "I've got proof," Powell said simply.

"What you did is worse," she whispered—any louder, and she couldn't trust her voice not to break.

"Maybe," he allowed. "But you've no evidence of that. My word against yours, remember? And as for this"—he waved the flyer again—"I'm afraid I've got all the evidence I need. Ask your little friend Miranda if you don't believe me. I presume you'll find her in detention." He shook his head. "Nice of you to stand up and face the music with her, by the way. That was a classy move."

Beth felt a blast of shame rise to her cheeks. "So we're even," she said, fighting against the suspicion that it wouldn't be quite that easy. "I've got something on you, and you've got something on me."

"Not quite," he stopped her. "As I see it, since I'm the only one here with any kind of proof, you've got nothing on me. Any accusation you make now is tainted. Nothing more than a pathetic attempt to get yourself out of trouble by discrediting me. No more than you'd expect from a coward who lets her partner take the blame."

She sighed. "What do you want?"

"Nothing. For now." Powell leaned back on the couch and kicked his feet up. "I just wanted to alert you that there was a new game afoot. Oh, don't look so glum," he admonished, twisting his face into a parody of her own miserable scowl. "This means we can be friends again, just like in the old days—back when you were *so* eager to help me out."

Beth remembered. It made her want to throw up.

"And if you're nice, there are things I can do for you too," Powell said.

"Like what?" she asked snidely.

"Like, for example, telling you who turned you in. Like they say, the best cure for losing one battle is winning the next. I'm sure you'd like to get even with *someone*, and since it's not going to be me . . ."

She knew it would be stupid to play any more of his games, but could it hurt to stay a moment longer, to smile and ask nicely? To get a name?

She was tired of being a victim. Maybe Powell was right: Just because she'd lost this battle didn't mean it was time to give up.

Maybe it was just time to find a better target.

And reload.

✲ ✲ ✲

She felt like a Bond girl, or a savvy spy from *Mission: Impossible*, as she snaked her way through the crowd and took position, waiting patiently to deploy her grand master plan.

We need to talk, her note had said. *Meet me on the 6 p.m. Twilight Trails train. I'll be in the front seat of the second car from the back. Beth*

The Twilight Trails company ran fake freight trains on a scenic route through the desert every day at sunset. They stopped at Grace, then continued on for an hour into the wilderness before turning around. Which meant that she and Adam would be trapped together for two hours. And unless he wanted to throw himself from a moving—albeit painfully slow-moving—train, he would be forced to listen to what she had to say.

She paid her exorbitant fee and settled into a window seat, glancing disdainfully at the scattering of passengers around her, wondering who would actually waste their money on a tour of this wasteland. She put on a pair of sunglasses—all the better to play out her interlude in espionage—and pulled out a magazine.

She didn't have to wait long.

"I was so glad to get your note—" Adam began, his voice breaking off when she turned her face from the window. "What the hell are you doing here?"

Harper tried to smile and ignore his tone—and his

disappointment. "I guess the jig is up," she quipped.

"What is this?" Adam asked, whirling around to scan the rest of the train car. "Where's Beth?"

He could be so slow sometimes . . . but, still, so adorable.

"Beth's not coming," Harper said, spelling out the obvious. "I sent the note."

He shook his head. "You're really sick, you know that?" He turned on his heel and walked back down the aisle, taking a seat toward the back of the train car.

Harper sighed, stood up, and followed him, ignoring the glare of the conductor, who cleared his throat and pointed at the large red letters ordering passengers to STAY SEATED WHILE THE TRAIN IS IN MOTION.

"It's not that big a car," she pointed out, sitting down behind Adam. If she squeezed in next to him, it might scare him away. "Do we really need to play musical chairs?" She sat on her knees and leaned forward, resting her arms on the seat in front of her. He didn't turn his face up to look at her, but if he had, her lips would still have been too far away to brush his forehead. "Train doesn't stop again until Salina," she pointed out. "You're stuck with me."

Adam closed his eyes and began to rub the bridge of his nose. "Fine. What do you want from me?"

"I want to know what you want from *me*, Ad. What can I do to fix things? Just tell me."

"Nothing," he grunted.

"You can't stay mad forever."

"Watch me."

They sat in silence for a moment. Harper watched the scenery crawl by, mile after mile of low ranging hills and straggly scrub brush. All painted in the monotonous sepia tones of desert life. *Who would search this out?* she wondered again. *Who would pay?* One elderly woman across the aisle wasn't even looking out the window. Instead, she had her eyes glued to a trashy romance novel, as if the scenery was beside the point.

"So," Harper began again, casually, "who do you think spray-painted the billboard? My money's on the sophomores—it was so lame. Reeks of some pathetic attempt to establish a rep. As if—"

"Don't do that," he said abruptly.

"What?"

"Don't act like everything's normal."

"It *can* be," she pointed out. Pleaded.

"No."

She'd tried being patient and giving him his space, but that just wasn't her. She couldn't just wait—she needed to *act*. She refused to let Beth win, and she was physically incapable of just letting him go. If it meant sacrificing her precious dignity and making him understand how much she needed him, then that's just what she would do. And so she'd formulated her plan, and now she just needed to push through his anger and pride, and uncover that piece of him that still loved her.

"Adam, you want Beth to forgive you, right?"

"Don't talk about her."

"I know you do. Everyone sees you running around school after her and—"

"I said, *don't* talk about her."

"Okay, fine. I just . . . I just don't get it. How can you expect . . . some people to forgive you, but you won't forgive me?"

"It's not the same," he snapped.

"But, why? Okay, I lied—so did you. I screwed up—so did you. And I still love—"

"It's. Not. The. Same," he repeated.

"You're right, because what you and I had together, it's nothing like you and Beth. It's so much more—"

"You really want to know?" he asked, loudly enough that the woman across the aisle looked up from her book in alarm. He whirled around to look at Harper, who resisted the urge to sink back into her own seat and turn her face away from his expression and what it meant.

"Of course I do."

"No, you don't."

"*Yes,* I really do." Though she wasn't sure it was true. "Tell me. Why can't we just get past this?"

"Because it's not what you did!" he yelled, as if he'd been holding the words in for weeks and they had finally battled their way out. They were all looking at her now: the old woman across the aisle, the mother with two squirming kids who kept shooting her a sympathetic smile, the preteen girls two rows ahead who couldn't even be bothered to disguise their eager eavesdropping. Harper knew exactly how pathetic she must look, but she forced herself not to care what a train full of tourists thought of her. Today only one person's opinion mattered.

It's not what you did. Then . . . what?

"It's who you *are*, Harper," he said, more quietly. This was how a doctor's face must look when he's telling someone the patient died, Harper realized. Adam was pronouncing their relationship. Time of death, 6:09.

"I don't get it," she said, but that was just another lie. After all, hadn't she already been treated to this little speech? Hadn't she already been informed of what a horrible, irredeemable piece of trash Harper Grace had become?

"Look, with Kane, what he did? It was shitty, but . . . no big surprise. I knew better than to trust him. But you?" Adam sighed. "I always trusted you. Out of everyone, you were the only one . . ."

"That's what I'm saying, Ad," Harper begged. "It's

different between the two of us. You can't let one screwup ruin everything."

"It's not just about that," Adam said. "It doesn't matter if I forgive you. I can't be with someone like you. Or be around someone like you. Not someone who'd do what you did."

"Someone like me?" Harper cried. "Someone who's been your best friend since you were eight years old?"

He shook his head.

"You're not that person. I thought you were, but . . . something's different. You're . . ."

"What?"

"I don't know."

"*What?* Just say it."

"Wrong. Okay? Something in you, it's like . . . it's gone bad. Rotted."

Harper just looked at him, her eyes watering, her hair falling down over her face. Surely he would look at her and see that she *was* still the same person, that however much of a bitch she could be, it didn't define her. She'd done the wrong thing, she conceded that—but it didn't mean there was nothing right left in her. It wasn't fair for him to think that. It wasn't right for him to say it.

And when he saw how he'd hurt her . . .

But he did look at her, and his face didn't soften; in fact, his mouth tightened into a hard, firm line. And then he turned away and settled back into his seat.

"I told you that you wouldn't want to hear it," he said, and his voice was casual, almost sneering, as if he couldn't hear her collapsed onto the seat behind him, choking back her sobs. But of course he heard; he just didn't care.

"Want some?"

Beth shuddered. She'd come out here hoping to be alone. No one used the playground this time of night, and she figured there'd be no one to see her huddled under a tree, her knees tucked up to her chest and her eyes filled with tears. Fleeing from Powell, she'd needed to go somewhere safe, and for Beth, the playground felt like home. All the more reason to be displeased when some stoner in a weathered leather jacket and torn black jeans slumped down beside her, waving a joint in her face. (At least, Beth assumed that's what it was—she'd never seen one in real life, not this close.)

She shook her head and laid it back down on her knees, hoping that if she closed her eyes and ignored him, maybe he would slink away.

"I just figured, you know, your eyes are going to be all red, anyway," the guy explained. "So, might as well take advantage of it."

She didn't say anything.

"Pot joke," he said. "Not funny, I guess." He paused,

and she could hear him inhale deeply. "Look, you sure you don't want any? You look like you could use . . ."

Beth looked up then, and faced him with a fierce expression, silently daring him to finish the sentence. That's all she needed to hear right now, some burnout telling her that she was an uptight Miss Priss who could use a little fun in her life. She didn't know whether he was trying to insult her or pick her up, but either way, she wasn't in the mood.

"A break," he concluded, blowing out a puff of smoke. "Bad day, huh? Me too."

"I'm sorry, I really don't want to be rude, but I don't even know you, and—"

"Reed," he said, raising the joint as if to toast her. "Rhymes with weed."

She rolled her eyes.

"Another joke," he added. "Still not funny?"

It suddenly occurred to Beth that she was alone on a deserted playground with this guy—anything could happen. But whether it was his amiable expression or her exhaustion, she didn't feel threatened, just worn out. "Like I was saying, I came here to be alone, and I'm sure you're a nice guy and all, but—"

"I'm not trying to pick you up," he said suddenly.

"What?"

"Too much trouble." He leaned back against the tree,

staring up at the sky. “Girls. Women. Whatever you call yourselves. I’m out.”

“Uh, congratulations?”

“Damn right.” Reed closed his eyes and took another hit.

“So what do you want, then?”

“World peace? A Fender Stratocaster?” he grinned. “How ’bout a warm breeze and a good buzz?”

“What do you want from *me*?” Beth clarified, not sure whether to be annoyed or amused. “If you’re not trying to pick me up, what are you doing?”

“You were crying,” he said, as if that explained everything.

“And?”

“And I wanted to make you stop. Which you did.”

“Oh.” Beth blushed, feeling a little silly for having assumed some dark ulterior motive.

“But if you want to be alone . . .”

She realized that was the last thing she wanted. “No, stay—I mean, you can. If you want.”

Reed shrugged. “Whatever.” Raising his eyebrows, he tipped the joint toward her again. She waved him away. Not that tuning out didn’t seem like a pretty good idea right about now, but it wouldn’t solve anything. And it’s not like Reed looked particularly cheerful himself.

"I'm Beth," she blurted, blushing again. He hadn't asked for her name, probably didn't even care.

Reed shifted away from the tree, lying flat on his back with his arms splayed out to his sides. A slow smile broke across his face. "Beth Manning. Yeah, I know."

"What do you think you're doing?" Kaia hissed as soon as Powell picked up the phone.

"Right now? Grading papers and trying not to vomit over the sad state of secondary education in this country."

"Don't be cute. I assume you were there." She hoped her voice wasn't betraying how much this pervy stalking routine was freaking her out. So she focused on her anger—it gave her clarity.

"*Cute* is not something I aspire to be at the moment. Enlightened might be a better goal to strive for. Care to fill me in on what's got you so hot and bothered?"

"I got your text message, Jack—and so did he, just like you intended."

"He? He who?" He sounded so genuinely clueless that Kaia was certain it was an act; nothing about Powell had ever been genuine.

"Drop it. You know I was with Reed. I know you saw me with him. You probably followed me there." Kaia could almost see it—his figure, waiting in the dark, coldly weighing his options, delighting in his view. She shivered.

"Are you actually admitting that you were with someone else?" Now his tone shifted from innocence to outrage. "And I'm supposed to feel *guilty* because my intimate message somehow fell into the wrong hands? Seems like the only guilty party here, *mon amour*, is you."

"I'm supposed to believe it was just a coincidence?" Kaia laughed bitterly. "Right. Just leave me alone, okay? This is it. We're done."

"I don't think that's your decision to make," Powell said, his voice low and steady. "Only one thing is done here, and it's your little dalliance with the Sawyer boy. I warned you before to keep your hands off."

"Or what?" Kaia struggled to keep her voice as calm as his. "You'll keep following me around until I realize you're the only man for me?"

"Oh, Kaia." Powell sighed, and took on a patronizing tone that suggested he was delivering wisdom from on high to a silly little girl. "Stalking is a coward's game. Hiding in bushes. Peering in windows." He laughed humorlessly. "Now does that really sound like me? No, when I want something, I take it."

"Not everything's yours to have," she snapped.

"Not everything, true. But you are."

"You're pathetic," she spit out.

"Now, now, that's not very nice. And as I've already suggested, you should be rather nice to me. Or do you *want* to fail your senior year? Get thrown out of school? Let's remember who's in charge here."

Enough.

"I am," Kaia snapped. "You know what will happen if I go to the administration and tell them how you've been forcing yourself on poor little me."

"Your word against mine," he said simply. "And once I'm through with you, your word will be worthless."

"Your word against mine and *Beth's*," she reminded him. "Or have you forgotten I know about that little misstep?"

"Beth's been taken care of," he said shortly. "I think you'll find she won't be much interested in joining forces with your little campaign. It's over, Kaia. No more leverage. But I'm a bighearted man. If you're ready to apologize and come back to me—"

"Dream on."

"Have it your way," he said agreeably. "But I think you'll change your mind soon enough."

"Just leave me alone."

"I'm afraid I can't do that, Kaia." He chuckled again. "You know, I once suggested that you stick to playing with boys your own age. Looks like you should have taken my advice."

chapter nine

"GET OUT."

The girl rolled over and snuggled up against him, her blond hair brushing against his lips. Kane spit it out, pushed her away.

"I said, get out." He climbed out of the bed and began gathering up her clothes, then packed them into a ball and threw them at her.

"It's so early," the girl whispered sleepily, burrowing deeper into the covers. "Come back to bed."

It was early, just past sunrise. *Time to take the trash out*, Kane thought, but chose not to say. If she wouldn't leave, he would. He couldn't stand to look at her anymore. That silky blond hair and those cornflower blue eyes had looked so appetizing the night before. Now they just looked . . . like Beth.

He slammed a fist against the wall. Damn it. Her again. He'd driven her out of his mind and now, here she was—or a pale imitation of her—in his bed.

"I'm going out," Kane growled, pulling on a T-shirt and pair of sneakers. "Be gone when I get back."

"Kane," the girl whimpered, "what did I do?"

Let's see, thought Kane. *You went home with some guy you met at a party, before he even knew your name. You were insipid and sloppy drunk. You were easy.*

But that wasn't really it, was it? He made two fists, digging his nails into the fleshy heel of his hand to force the thought away.

You weren't Beth.

He despised himself for his weakness. It was a part of himself he hated, and he'd thought he'd rooted it out years ago.

Beth was like poison to his system, corroding its works. This had to stop.

He didn't want her forgiveness.

He didn't want her back.

He wanted her gone.

Gone. But not forgotten.

The card was unsigned.

When the doorbell had woken her just after sunrise, Kaia had hoped it would be Reed. And when she'd opened the door to a delivery man with a long, white box of flowers, she'd hoped it would be a gift from Reed. Maybe he'd decided to call a truce and forgive her.

Hope springs eternal.

Twelve long-stemmed roses.

Each one dyed an inky black.

And that card.

Gone. But not forgotten.

She hadn't dropped the box in horror—she'd hurled it away from her. Roses painted the color of death flew through the room, their black petals fluttering through the air like locusts.

It would have been bad enough if she'd been absolutely sure it was Powell.

But she wasn't—and that was worse. Reed and Powell both thought she'd betrayed them; one of them was too cowardly to face her, and too obsessed to walk away.

It wasn't fear that made her hands tremble or her heart slam in her chest, she told herself. It wasn't fear that made her pace across the room, unable to sit down or stay still, made her check and double-check that she'd locked the door.

It was anger.

No one did this to Kaia Sellers.

No one had power over her like this. Kaia was the one

with the power—nothing happened unless she wanted it to happen.

Hadn't she already proven that?

After all, she'd *made* him want her.

Now she could make him go away.

She could make him sorry.

He'll be sorry. They'll all be sorry.

Harper awoke with a gasp, the words still pounding in her ears. *They'll all be sorry.* For a moment, caught in that foggy zone between sleep and waking, the sentence had no meaning.

And then it all came flooding back.

Beth.

Miranda.

Even Adam, who had turned his back on her.

She only remembered flashes of what she'd dreamed—the screams, the silence at the end, and the feeling of satisfaction.

A cold sweat dotted her brow. As the disjointed memory of the nightmare crowded back into her mind, Harper lay still, flat on her back, staring at the cracks in the ceiling and trying not to be afraid.

She could still hear the screams.

It felt like a beast lay deep inside of her, waiting for her to relax control, so it could awake and unleash its wrath.

Harper liked to believe she was in charge. Everything she did, she did by choice.

But there were Miranda and Adam—the two people who knew her best—and they didn't think she had a choice.

You can't help it. You are who you are.

They thought she couldn't help but spread her poison.

And remembering the rage that had coursed through her as she slept, Harper couldn't help but wonder: Maybe they were right.

I was right. I knew *I was right.*

Miranda stuffed the last Hershey's Kiss into her mouth and checked the clock. Six thirty a.m. She'd now officially been up all night—and had the empty bags of candy to prove it.

She'd actually gone to bed early, craving those moments before sleep when she was free to think about anything she wanted, and she could let her mind wander to Kane. In the dark she could indulge her wildest fantasies about what he might say, and how they might be together.

But her mind kept veering away from happy thoughts. It took her back toward Harper—and all her lies.

He says he just likes you as a friend.

Forget him, he's an ass.

You'll never have him—just move on.

It's for your own good.

All those months, Miranda had assumed Harper was just avoiding the obvious, ugly truth: Miranda wasn't good enough. Kane was out of her league. She'd even thought Harper was being *sweet.* Such a good friend, she'd thought, to soften the blow, obscure the truth.

As if Harper knew anything about truth.

She'd taken away the one guy Miranda had ever truly wanted and handed him to Beth. She'd excused herself with one lie after another, enjoying everything she'd ever wanted while Miranda was left feeling worthless and ugly.

But now that the lies were finished and Miranda had Kane all to herself, she was certain: It wasn't hopeless. There was something between them, even if it was only a kernel of possibility.

And what was she doing about it? Scheming and strategizing how to satisfy her deepest desires? Funneling her empty rage into a plan that would finally put Harper in her place?

Of course not.

She was eating her way through a pound of candy. She was disgusting herself.

Suddenly, Miranda felt the lump of chocolate within her transform itself into a volcano, about to erupt. She needed to purge herself of the calories and, along with them, the helplessness that must have announced to the world, *I'm nothing. Walk all over me.* She had to purify her body and herself, and then, as the sun rose, she would be ready to face the new day. Face Harper. Take care of business.

Taking care of business. Adam gritted his teeth at the memory. That's what Kane used to say before he went out with a girl he was planning to dump.

And then he would smile, as if it really were a business transaction. As if it were nothing.

And here I am, Adam thought, *dwelling and agonizing and analyzing. Like a girl.*

So which of us is the freak?

He'd forgotten to shut his blinds the night before, and this morning the sun had woken him. Not that he was getting much sleep these days, thanks to her.

His blood still boiled at the thought of the wasted hours sitting on that train in stony silence, pretending he couldn't hear her weep behind him.

She brought this misery on herself, he reminded himself.

She wasn't his problem anymore.

He didn't care.

He shut his blinds and, when that didn't make a satisfying enough sound, slammed his fist into the wall.

It hurt so much, he did it again.

No more, he thought. No more dwelling on Harper, letting the anger drive him through the day. And, while he was at it, no more Beth. No more mooning, following, begging, pleading. She didn't want to forgive him? Fine.

He had his dignity, and it was time Beth understood that.

Forgetting how early it was, he called—for the last time, he told himself. It rang and rang.

"I know you're screening," Adam said harshly after the voice mail beep. "And don't worry. I won't be bothering you anymore. If you want to be a bitch about all this, fine. I'm out."

He hung up.

He'd called her a bitch.

It felt good.

And, then, a moment later, it didn't.

"Look, I'm sorry about what I said," he began gruffly, after the beep. "You've just got to know, the way you're acting—" No, that wasn't right. He hung up again. Climbed back into bed and closed his eyes.

But he couldn't go back to sleep.

Unfinished business and all.

"I know it's crazy, calling you again, but how the hell else am I supposed to talk to you? You're so damn sure that everything—" He hung up again, almost threw the phone across the room. This was humiliating. He hated himself for doing it. Hated her for putting him through it. And yet—

"Beth. Look, I'm sorry. Please, just call me back. I—I love you. Please."

I love you. He'd never said the words aloud. But with Kaia, he'd thought . . . not that he did, of course—not now, not yet. But maybe someday. Or so he'd imagined.

Just goes to show he must be even stupider than people thought.

Reed pushed the pedal to the floor and the speedometer edged up to 55. The truck couldn't go any faster. It was a piece of shit, just like everything else in his life.

What had he been thinking, to imagine a girl like that would take him seriously? Her life was like a Ferrari—and his was a clunker that couldn't even hit the speed limit.

The night before, he hadn't cared. A few drinks, a few joints, and nothing mattered. But this morning, neck and back sore from sleeping on the guys' couch, it was all he could think about. He'd been stupid enough to forget who he was and ignore who she was, and he'd let himself get burned.

His guitar rattled around in the back and, suddenly, Reed made an abrupt U-turn, his tires screeching as the truck veered around and headed off down the highway, away from town and into the desert.

He would find a quiet, empty spot and play until his voice went hoarse and his fingers bled. And maybe then he would be able to purge her from his system. Or at least purge the reckless surge of anger that shot through him every time he thought of her and what might have happened.

If only he hadn't picked up her phone.

If only the truck would go faster.

If only he hadn't used up all his stash.

Things were easier when you didn't have to think.

When you didn't have to feel.

I feel nothing, Beth thought, watching the tiny red light flash on her phone. *I see his name flash up on the screen, again and again, and I feel . . . nothing.*

It was just after dawn and she was at work. These days she was always at work, she thought bitterly, plunging the first batch of fries into the deep fryer and switching on the coffeemaker. She couldn't complain too much; it's not like she had anywhere else to be.

The phone rang again—she stuffed it into her bag.

It was easy to hide out in the diner, losing herself in the mechanics of wiping down the counters and mopping the floors. Sometimes, she even thought she'd reached some kind of Zen state, where she could accept whatever happened and move on.

The phone rang a third time and, without warning, the wave of rage swept over her. It beat against her, pummeling her with the whys she couldn't answer. *Why me?*

That was at the top of the list.

She pictured Adam rolling around in bed with Kaia, while they were still together. She pictured Kane and his lying smile, touching her, stealing her trust. She pictured Harper whispering poisonous nothings in Jack Powell's ear. It wasn't fair, she raged, stomping from one end of the kitchen to the other.

And when another part of her responded: *Life isn't fair*, it only fueled her anger.

Beth began refilling the ketchup jars, wiping off the lids. And she instructed herself to calm down. She'd never felt like this before, so helpless and so powerful at the same time, and she didn't know what to do with it, or how she was supposed to get herself under control.

Maybe deep breaths.

Counting to ten . . . or a hundred.

Closing her eyes, sitting down, forcing her body to chill.

It all might have worked—but instead, she tightened her grip on the ketchup bottle, and then, without thinking, flung it across the room. It shattered against the wall, spraying glass through the air and leaving a garish smear of red dripping down the stained tile.

Beth should have felt horrified or panicked, afraid of herself—or for herself.

But she didn't.

She just felt better.

chapter ten

REED WAS ALL ABOUT AVOIDING THE HASSLE. School sucked, but it's not like there was anything you could do about it, right? So he floated along, attending the occasional class, lying low, sneaking out for a smoke when it all got too much. He stayed under the radar. That would have been his motto, if he'd ever bothered to formulate one.

That, also, was too much effort.

So when they pulled him out of class, he was stumped—and also a bit stoned, which wasn't helping matters. He hadn't done anything. He never did anything. So why haul him down to the vice principal's office and stick him in front of the administrative firing squad?

Best not to speak until spoken to. More words to live by.

So Reed slouched in the low-backed wooden chair and stared at them: the principal, the vice principal, that French teacher all the girls were so hot for. They didn't scare him.

And then his father stepped into the office.

Shit.

"If you admit what you've done, I may be inclined to go easier on you," the vice principal finally said.

He'd done nothing, so he said nothing. And he tried not to look at his old man.

"Mr. Powell found the evidence," the vice principal continued. "You can't just weasel out of this one, Mr. Sawyer. Just tell us why you did it. And who helped you."

Reed laced his fingers together and put them behind his head, sliding down in the chair. He didn't have to speak out loud for them to receive his message: *Get to the point.*

"Does this look familiar?" Vice Principal Sorrento dropped a can of spray paint onto the desk. "Mr. Powell received a tip that led us to search your locker. Imagine our surprise when we found a number of these." He pursed his lips, as if it pained him to continue. "It's obviously what you used to doctor the billboard."

"I don't know anything about that." Damned if they were going to pin that lame stunt on him. As if he'd waste his time. If Reed wanted to say something, he'd say it—he wouldn't need to hide behind an anonymous prank. And if he had nothing to say, he'd shut up.

"Are you denying that we found these cans in your locker, young man?"

Reed snorted. "For all I know, you found them up your ass."

"If they're not yours, perhaps you have an alternate explanation to offer?" the principal jumped in, before Sorrento could lose his shit.

Reed shrugged.

"Maybe you've been framed, is that it?" Sorrento suggested sarcastically. "Someone's out to get you, right? And who might that be?"

Reed shrugged again. "For all I know, it was you."

That's when his father spoke for the first time. "That's enough! For God's sake, boy, just tell them you did it and that you're sorry, and we can get out of here."

Reed was sorry, but only that the school had bothered to drag his father out of work for this. His father usually didn't care what Reed did—but he *did* care about missing his shifts. And, like everything else, this would somehow become all Reed's fault.

He would have been happy to speed things along, even if it meant sucking it up for a parental lecture, but he wasn't about to admit to something he hadn't done.

Bring it on, he thought, staring at the vice principal. *You don't scare me.*

Sorrento couldn't threaten Reed, not with anything that mattered, because you could only threaten someone who cared.

"Mr. Sawyer, I hope you realize that your son is putting us in a very difficult situation here," Principal Lowenstein said. "I simply can't have this brand of . . . disruptive element polluting my student body."

Reed's father took off his cap and rubbed his bald spot, looking distinctly uncomfortable. Reed wondered what kind of memories this office held for the old man, who'd been a proud Haven High dropout, would-be class of '88.

"I understand, ma'am, you gotta do what you gotta do," Hank Sawyer said, and Reed winced, hating the way his father talked to the people who ran his life. "You wanna suspend him for a week or so, I'll put him to work, set him straight. You don't have to worry."

Not his life, Reed vowed to himself, not for the first time. *Not for me.*

"I'm afraid you *don't* understand me, *Mr.* Sawyer." It seemed to physically pain the principal to address Hank with even the barest term of respect. "If Reed here refuses to take responsibility for his actions—his very serious actions, I might add—we might be forced to take harsher measures. As I always say, if a student truly doesn't want to learn . . . well, I'm afraid sometimes there's just nothing we can do."

"I'm not sure I get what you mean," Hank mumbled.

But Reed got it. He wasn't as thick as people thought.

"She means if we can't settle this to our satisfaction—if we see no signs of . . . remorse, it may no longer be possible for Reed to attend Haven High School," Sorrento explained with a barely hidden smile.

Hank Sawyer looked dumbfounded.

Lowenstein looked apologetic—or rather, what she thought a suitably apologetic expression might be.

Sorrento looked triumphant.

Powell looked satisfied.

And Reed looked away. Whatever happened, he'd still have his job. He'd still have his band. He'd still have his buddies, and his stash.

There was nothing in this place he wanted or needed, so maybe Sorrento, for once in his miserable tight-ass bureaucratic life, was right.

Maybe it was time for Reed to go.

"I know I said I'd do the lab for you, but don't you think you should at least *pretend* we're working together?"

"Sorry, what?" Harper looked up from her doodles to discover her geeky Girl Friday had put down her beaker, turned off her Bunsen burner, and was waving the lab instructions in Harper's face.

"I *said*, how about you actually help me out here, before Bonner catches on?" The girl jerked her head toward the front of the empty room, where their robotic chem teacher was nominally supervising them.

Harper had cut class again today, unable to face Miranda across the lab table, but that meant a makeup lab—and *that* meant a big fat zero unless she could find someone to do the work for her.

Enter Sara—or was it Sally? Sandra? whatever—a Marie Curie wannabe who always aced her labs and whose semester-long services could apparently be bought for the price of an outdated dELiA*s sweater and a setup with debate team captain Martin somebody the Third.

"Trust me, you don't want my help," Harper said, laughing..

"But it's easy," the brainiac argued. "If you just balance the equation and calculate the molarity of solution A, then you can estimate . . ."

Harper tuned out the droning. Back in the old days, with Miranda doing their labs, she hadn't been subjected to any of this chemistry crap; instead, Miranda had just measured and stirred and poured, all the while keeping up a running commentary on Harper's latest rejects or the possibility that the Bonner was naked under her ever-present lab coat.

Miranda had always known the perfect thing to say; she was never judgmental, patronizing, or—the worst crime, in both Harper's and Miranda's minds—boring. Harper had taken her for granted—and driven her away.

She got that now. Miranda and Adam were right: They'd been too good for her. Maybe she was lucky it had taken so long for them to realize it. And maybe she still had time to change.

"Thanks for your help, Marie, but I'll take it from here," she said suddenly, grabbing the lab instructions.

"Uh, my name is Sandra?" the girl pointed out, sounding slightly unsure of it herself. "And I'm not sure you want to do that. We're at kind of a delicate stage, and last time you—"

"I *said* I've got it," Harper said, accidentally sweeping one of the beakers off the table. Both girls jumped back as some of the solution splashed through the air.

Young Einstein pushed her glasses up on her face and began backing away. "Sure. Okay. No problem. I'll just get out of your hair then, uh . . . good luck!" She turned and raced from the room.

No one's got any faith in me, Harper thought in disgust. No one realized that she could be diligent and virtuous if she set her mind to it. Hadn't she managed to manipulate and connive her way to the top of the Haven High social pyramid? *That* took strategy, brains, and forethought. Compared to that, being a good person would be easy.

Harper sighed. Okay, maybe not easy. But it wasn't impossible; she was just out of practice. Whatever Miranda and Adam thought, she had it in her. She'd prove it to herself, and then she'd prove it to them. "Okay, what've we got here?" she mumbled.

Step 3: Combine 10 ml of your titrated acid solution with 10 ml of water. Record the pH.

What had Marie Curie Jr. said about balancing the molarity and calculating the equation of the solution? Or was it estimating the equation and balancing the solution? And what was a titrated acid, anyway?

Harper threw down the work sheet. She didn't need to get a perfect score on her first try, right? The important thing was making it through the lab on her own. So all she needed to do was concentrate and—

CRASH!

Oops. Hopefully that wasn't the beaker of titrated acid that had just smashed to the floor.

"Everything all right back there, Ms. Grace?" the Bonner asked nervously, too nearsighted to see for herself.

"Just fine, Ms. Bonner," Harper chirped. "Don't worry."

Harper picked up something that might or might not have been her titrated acid solution and dumped some into the remaining beaker. Then she spotted a test tube filled with a clear liquid. Marie must already have measured out the water; now, all she had to do was dump it in and . . .

A huge puff of smoke exploded out of the beaker, blasting past Harper before she had the chance to move out of the way. "Ugh," Harper moaned in alarm, "what's that—?"

The Bonner looked up in alarm, wrinkling her nose as the stench wave hit her. "Harper!" she cried, pinching her nostrils together and backing toward the door. "What did you do?"

"I don't know!" Harper waved away the foul greenish smoke, trying to hold her breath and escape the noxious combination of rotten eggs and raw sewage. She dumped the beaker into the sink, grabbed her backpack, and ran out of the room, joining the Bonner in the hallway.

"Oh dear oh dear oh dear," the Bonner was muttering to herself. "I'll have to contact the principal, I'll have to have the room fumigated, I'll have to—" She caught sight of Harper, or rather, caught *scent* of Harper. "Smells like we'll have to get *you* fumigated too," she said, stepping away.

Harper took her hand away from her nose and breathed in deeply, her eyes widening in horror. She smelled like she'd gone swimming in a toilet.

The Bonner shook her head sadly and pulled her lab

coat tighter around herself, as if it would offer some protection from Harper's cloud of stench. "Ms. Grace, I'm afraid I'll be forced to give you a zero on this lab."

Harper looked down at her soiled clothes and back at the lab-turned-toxic-waste-dump, took a big whiff of her new eau de sewer, and nodded. "Zero sounds about right," she muttered. Apparently, these days, that's all she was worth.

When Kane had coaxed Miranda out for a post-detention aperitif, he hadn't intended a torture session at the Nifty Fifties diner. But when Miranda had suggested it, her face flushed with pleasure, he'd said yes almost instantly.

Not that there weren't plenty of good reasons to stay away from the diner, even above and beyond those the local health inspector published in the town paper every year. He could have cited the watery milk shakes and five-alarm chili, aka heartburn-waiting-to-happen. He could have reminded Miranda of the grating Chuck Berry anthems piped through tinny speakers, punctuated by scratches, squeaks, and the high-pitched whine of a grimy waitress announcing "order's up." Then there was the burned-out neon, the scratched faux-leather bar stools, the vintage movie posters peeling off the wall, and the Route 66 junk clogging the counter, longing for impulse buyers to give them a new home.

But all of those would have been excuses, skirting the truth of why he'd hoped never to set foot inside the dilapidated diner again. It was Beth's turf, and he didn't want to face her there. He'd spent one too many long afternoons lingering over a greasy plate of fries, waiting for her to finish her shift, and he could do without the flashback to happier days.

But when Miranda had raised the idea, he hadn't hesitated before agreeing, "Shitty Fifties it is." His own reluctance was reason enough to go; he wouldn't let Beth's presence scare him away from anywhere, especially one of Grace's few semi-tolerable dining establishments. Reluctance stemmed from fear, and fear was a sign of weakness, to be attacked wherever it appeared. Better to do it yourself, Kane believed, than wait for someone to do it for you.

He and Miranda kept up a steady stream of banter as they settled into a booth and waited for their food to arrive. She was so much easier to be around than most girls, neither boring nor demanding, just . . . there. Like one of the guys, only with a better ass.

"You sure you don't want some?" he asked, waving a spoonful of ice cream under her nose.

"You're a growing boy, Kane—I can't take food out of your mouth."

He shrugged and swallowed another mouthful of the flavorless vanilla.

"Not quite Ben & Jerry's?" she asked, grinning wryly at his expression.

She was okay, he supposed—physically, probably even a seven, thanks to her long, slim legs and model's body. The chest was a little flat for his tastes, but she compensated for it with a tight ass. Her long, thin face wasn't complemented by the long, thin hair—but it wasn't bad. It was the rest of her that brought the total package down to a five: the way she never quite looked you in the eye, the plain white T-shirts, boxy jeans, the fight-or-flight reflex on overdrive, and, most problematically, the way she seemed so content to fade into the background.

She was a fixer-upper, basically. The raw materials were all there. It would just take some effort—a project best saved for a rainy day.

Beth, on the other hand, was fully formed, and a perfect ten. She'd have to be, for Kane to be giving her a second thought. As Miranda longingly eyed the milk shake he had insisted she order—and from which she'd yet to take a sip—he eyed Beth. Her long blond hair was pinned back from her face, and her full lips glistened with a see-through gloss.

He still wanted her, he realized. Despite everything, he missed her.

It only made him more determined to wash her out of his system for good.

"Waitress," he called loudly, "we need you over here." He'd sat in this section deliberately, knowing how much she hated to be watched at work. That was the thing about being in a relationship, he'd discovered: You learned people's weaknesses.

It was why he planned never to get ensnared in one again.

"What are you doing?" Miranda hissed, as Beth approached. She clucked her tongue. "Play nice."

"Do you need something else?" Beth asked thinly. "Or just the check."

"I need you to clean up this spill."

"What spill?"

True, the table was clean. He'd have to remedy that. Kane took a sip of his Coke, and then, with a slow and deliberate turn of the wrist, dumped it out all over the table. The sticky brown liquid spread across the metallic tabletop, spattering onto her white sneakers. "Oops."

Beth took a deep breath, then tossed a filthy dish towel in his face. "Clean it yourself."

"Excuse me?"

"Kane, drop it," Miranda said sharply.

He glanced at her in surprise, raising his eyebrows questioningly. *What? What did I do?*

"Can you, just for once, not be an asshole?" Miranda asked, as if genuinely curious to hear the answer.

"Now, where's the fun in that?" he drawled, waiting for the inevitable smile.

But Miranda's face was indecipherable, her lip twitching slightly, as if choosing between potential expressions. Finally, she settled on a scowl. "I'm going to the bathroom," she announced, standing up and throwing down her napkin. "I'll be back, maybe. Try to behave yourself."

She hadn't walked out on him, Kane thought with pleasure; he disliked melodrama of all kinds, unless he'd created it himself. But she hadn't egged him on, either, or sat there with an adoring look the way the bimbos all did, chastising him with their words while rewarding him with their eyes. No, the original go-along-to-get-along girl, Miss Gumby herself, had actually taken a stand—of sorts.

He could apologize later; for now, Beth still stood over him, fuming, and he found that he couldn't stop himself from pushing just a little harder.

"I know this isn't the finest of dining establishments," he drawled, "but didn't they bother to teach you that the customer is always right?"

"I guess you're the exception that proves the rule," Beth snapped. "I always knew you were special."

"Oh Beth, just give it up," he said, suddenly raising his voice to ensure that it would carry to the table of eavesdropping juniors a few feet away. "We're *not* getting back together."

"What?"

She was so smart in some ways—and so pathetically dumb in others.

"I'm glad it was good for you," he continued loudly, "but it just wasn't for me. I'm sorry—you're just . . . not very good."

"Shut up." Her pale face was turning a bright red. "Stop."

"You keep saying that, and yet you just keep coming back. It's a little embarrassing."

"*You're* embarrassing."

What a snappy comeback.

Kane smiled serenely and handed back the dish towel, now sopping with Coke.

"I'm serious about one thing," he said more softly. "Stop pretending this is all some game you can win."

"I thought everything was a game to you."

"That's because I know how to play." He gestured toward the giggling juniors who kept sneaking looks before turning back to their huddle and bursting into laughter. "As you can see. When you're a born loser, it's better to just stay out of the game altogether. Just a helpful piece of advice, from me to you."

"You—I can't—what—"

"Spit it out," he sneered, trying to convince himself he was having fun.

"Go to hell." And she picked up Miranda's untouched milk shake, gave him her sweetest Beth smile, and dumped it over his head.

It was juvenile, but effective—and very, very cold.

He smeared a finger across the icy goop sliding down his cheek, stuck it in his mouth, and sucked, hard.

It was sweet, but not as sweet as what came next. An overweight, under-showered man lumbered up behind Beth and, in a voice choked with anger, uttered the three little words that every bitter, milk shake–covered ex wants to hear:

"Manning? You're fired!"

Kaia hadn't known where to look, not at first. She didn't even know where he lived, she realized. It was just one of the many things she didn't know about him.

It should have been a warning, she thought now, disgusted with herself. She'd been so eager to believe in Reed that she'd ignored the possibility that his sleazy, pothead, criminal-in-training exterior wasn't just a veneer.

She still couldn't quite believe that someone who'd kissed her the way he did could have tormented her the way he had. How had he touched her so gently, and then branded her a whore? It didn't seem possible, but the evidence didn't lie. They'd found the paint in his locker: two cans, both red, like blood.

As soon as she'd heard the truth, she'd gone looking

for him. She'd searched the dingy Lost and Found, his father's garage, and Guido's Pizza, but had no luck at any of them.

Then she realized that she knew exactly where he'd be.

She drove slowly down the highway, savoring the roar of the BMW's engine and the clatter of the gravel kicked up by her tires, trying to enjoy the dusty billboards:

AIRSTREAM TRAILERS FOR SALE!

GET MARRIED QUICK—GET DIVORCED QUICKER!

LIVE! NUDE! GIRLS!

She was dreading the encounter, yet hungry for it, eager to finally have an end to the uncertainty and an outlet for her rage. She arrived at the mines, and his truck was pulled off onto the shoulder of the road, just as she'd expected. Reed was standing at the mouth of the abandoned mine as if wondering whether to disregard the fading DANGER signs and step inside.

"What's wrong with you?" she asked, keeping a few feet of distance between them.

"Excuse me?"

"Forget it. I don't even care. I just came here to tell you to stay away from me." She didn't touch him, or look at him, just stood next to him, facing the gaping hole at the head of the mines. The industrial processing complex stood several yards away. This entrance must have been a remnant from an even earlier era, one of pickaxes and rickety wooden machinery. It had once been boarded up with plywood and barbed wire, but the wood had rotted away, and the torn, frayed strands of the jagged wire climbed haphazardly over the entrance like vines. It would be easy enough to slip inside.

"What the hell are you talking about?"

"I heard what they found in your locker," she snapped. "You think I'm too stupid to see what that means?"

"You think that crap was mine?"

"What else am I supposed to think?"

Reed shrugged. "Whatever. Do what you want. Get out of here. I won't follow you."

He began to walk away, toward the entrance to the mines. The dark, hulking mouth of the tunnel loomed over him. It reminded her of a carnival haunted house, but with no safeguards to stop the roof from crashing down.

"Where are you going?" she asked, grabbing his shoulder. "Are you crazy?"

"Maybe." He turned back to her. "What do you care?"

"I don't."

"Hey—" He grabbed her shoulders, and she felt a moment of panic but resolved not to let it show. "I don't know what's going on with you or what's got you so mad, especially when you're the one who . . . I know there's some other guy, and—"

"And that's it, right?" She tore out of his grasp and

started hitting at his chest. "I cheated on you, and that makes me a slut, right? A *whore*? Go screw yourself. You don't scare me." Her voice was rising, but she couldn't help herself. "Do you hear me? You. Don't. Scare. Me."

He grabbed at her hands, and she swatted him away until finally he grasped them both and held them still. "I don't want to scare you," he said softly, intensely. "Look at me. *Look* at me," he insisted as she stared resolutely over his shoulder.

Finally, Kaia gave in and met his dark eyes. She shivered, still feeling the irresistible pull to give in, to fall against him and forget herself. She leaned in, hating herself, but hating him more. Then she stopped, just before their lips touched. He was so close that when he spoke, she could feel the movement of his lips even before she heard his words.

"I need you," he whispered. "I need you to believe me."

Remember the car, Kaia told herself, *remember the flowers, and the photos.* She breathed in and out, aware only of his strong hands wrapped around hers, and the dark locks of hair framing his bottomless eyes. She wanted things to be different; but Kaia had given up on fairy tales long ago—you couldn't make something true just by wishing for it. You couldn't turn a frog into a prince just by giving him one last kiss.

"I'm sorry," she whispered back, pulling away. "I can't."

He didn't say anything as she walked away, nor did he follow. She got into the BMW and leaned her head back against the cool leather headrest. Maybe now it could finally be over.

Reed had turned his back on her, and was striding toward the entrance of the mines. Kaia sat behind the steering wheel, one hand on the ignition key, one hand clenched into a fist, unable to stop watching as he swung one leg over the barbed wire, then another, then ducked beneath the rotted wooden boards and disappeared into the dark.

"Sorry about before," Kane said as they walked out of the restaurant together.

"Before? Oh, you mean when you pulled off that great magic trick, turning into a giant asshole before my very eyes?" But Miranda asked the question without rancor; she knew she should have been disgusted by Kane's treatment of Beth, and was a bit disgusted with herself for not caring more. Instead, she'd made excuses for him: He'd been hurt, was just lashing back—and the saddest thing of all was that the prospect of him still harboring feelings for Beth was what upset her the most. Someone else might have mistaken his cruelty for anger, but Miranda recognized it for what it was; and if he still felt that way about Beth, there seemed no hope he'd ever look in her direction. No matter how much time they spent together, it suddenly seemed likely that Miranda was only imagining the possibility it could ever be anything more. Just because you talked yourself into believing in something didn't make it true.

"Actually, I was apologizing for stepping on your foot back there," Kane said, laughing, "but let's say it covers the asshole thing too. And, since I spoiled our afternoon, let me make it up to you." He led her to the car and opened the door for her.

"And how are you going to do that?"

"A little fun in the sun," he said cryptically, getting behind the wheel and pulling out of the lot. Miranda wrinkled her nose in confusion, but said nothing as they followed a familiar route, finally pulling back into the school parking lot.

"Didn't you say something about fun?" she asked as they came to a stop.

"Trust me." He got out and went around to the back of the Camaro, pulling a basketball out of the trunk. Miranda gaped at him in horror.

"No. No way. Are you kidding me?"

"Stevens, I am about to do you the biggest favor of your life," he promised, grabbing her hand and pulling her toward the rickety outdoor court set up on the opposite end of the parking lot.

Miranda hated sports. She hated everything about them: the running, the jumping, the sweating, the terror when she caught the ball, the humiliation when she missed it. The last thing she wanted to do was subject herself to all of that in front of Kane, object of her deepest and darkest desires.

But he was tugging her along and giving her that boyish grin she couldn't resist. He was holding her hand.

"I'm not sure I see where the favor part comes in," she said skeptically as he began bouncing the ball against the concrete pavement. "Unless you're about to clue me in on how to get out of gym for the rest of my life."

"Better." He tossed the ball casually toward the basket, turning away a moment before it swooshed through the net. "Stevens, I'm about to show you the surefire way to any guy's heart." He grabbed the rebound and tossed it toward her; she hoped she didn't look like too much of an idiot when it slipped out of her hands and rolled away.

"*Basketball* is the key to any guy's heart?"

"Basketball, baseball, whatever—no guy wants some girlie-girl who's going to get all mushy when it comes to sports," Kane explained, chasing the ball and tossing it back to her. This time, she caught it. "Football works, too, though." A slow smile spread across his face. "Especially the tackling."

Miranda threw the ball toward the basket as hard as she could—it arced back down to the ground long before coming anywhere near the net. "So this is all for my own good?" she asked.

"Yup."

"You're just helping me out of the goodness of your heart?"

"Shocking, isn't it?"

"And it's got nothing to do with the fact that you missed practice today and you're just looking for an excuse to get out on the court?"

Kane stopped dribbling and turned to stare at her, an unreadable expression on his face. "You think you've got me all figured out, don't you?"

Miranda shrugged. "Pretty much."

Kane jogged over and handed her the ball. He placed both hands on her waist, turning her around to face the basket. Miranda tried to keep her breathing steady and ignore the fact that she could feel his breath on the back of her neck. He reached around her, arranging her hands into a shooting position while murmuring soft instructions in her ear.

"Like this . . . no, a little higher . . . use your right hand to balance it . . . bend your knees . . ." When she was set up exactly as he wanted, he stepped away, instructing her to freeze in position. It wasn't too difficult; Miranda hoped never to move again, the better to remember every place he'd touched her.

"Most girls wouldn't do this, you know."

"What?" she asked, forcing herself to stay focused on her bent knees and straight posture and *not* on Kane's reedy voice or laughing eyes.

"This, here. All of it."

Miranda suspected he'd have no trouble getting most any girl in school out on the court, especially if it meant some physical contact with Haven High's resident Greek god. But all she said was, "I'm not most girls."

"Tell me about it," he said as she launched the ball into the air, holding her breath as it sailed closer and closer to the basket . . . and bounced off the rim.

"Told you I suck." She rolled her eyes and began walking toward the sidelines, but he grabbed her, drew her back to the center of the court.

"Okay, you *do* suck," he agreed, retrieving the ball and slipping it back into her hands.

"Nice. Very nice."

"But you've got a great teacher." He moved behind her again, and this time, as he grabbed her arms, she leaned back, ever so slightly, so that her shoulders grazed against his chest. She could feel him breathing. "See? That was only your first try and you hit the rim. It's a start."

Of what? she wanted to ask, playfully but meaningfully. Of course she didn't have the nerve. So she closed her eyes, feeling his chest rise and fall, his voice soft in her ear, and let him guide her body into position. It didn't mean anything, she knew that. He didn't realize what it felt like, his fingers wrapped loosely around her forearms, caressing her hips, her lower back, her thighs—for him, this was just another day on the court.

But even though she knew it was silly, Miranda allowed herself a moment of let's pretend: *What if* he spun her around and pulled her into his arms, for real? *What if* this was all just foreplay, and the real game was about to begin? *What if* he wanted an excuse to touch her just as much as she longed to be touched?

And then he let go again and, perfectly lined up for the shot, she let the ball fly off the tips of her fingers. It sailed toward the basket, rolled around the edge of the rim, again and again, before finally tipping away and toppling to the ground.

She'd missed. Again.

But it was a start.

It was pitch black inside the mine. But Reed didn't need to explore. When he was a kid, he'd spent hours blundering around in the dark, holding a flashlight up to his head like an old-time miner. He could've gotten himself killed.

This time, he just stepped far enough inside the

darkness to make everything disappear, then sat down, his back pressed against the cool, dank wall.

What did she want from him?

Why did he even care?

His father wanted him to confess, and had already made it clear that he'd throw Reed out of the house if he got expelled.

Then what?

Reed wished he could light up a joint, since that was the best way to drive the questions away. A few puffs and he could sink into the worry-free zone and forget it all. But you didn't sneak into an old mine and light a match—not if you cared about staying alive.

There were other ways to forget. Reed closed his eyes—though there was no light to shut out—and leaned his head back against the wall. He could almost hear the sounds of an earlier time: pumping, clanging, chugging, grunting, rhythmic grinding of steel on steel. That was why he liked it here: The place was full of ghosts, and it was easy to imagine you were one of them, fading into the past, all your problems long solved, your decisions made, your life lived.

Reed knew he'd eventually have to get up, walk out, and *do* something. He couldn't just hide there in the dark, waiting for his problems to pass. But it was tempting to imagine the possibility, just for a while.

He'd never been afraid of the dark, just like he'd never been afraid of dying. As far as he was concerned, darkness was easy. Leaving it all behind was a piece of cake. The hard part came when you turned on the lights and had to face the day.

chapter eleven

KAIA WASN'T SURE SHE OWED POWELL AN APOLOGY, and she hadn't decided whether she wanted to give him another chance or whether the time had come to make a clean break from both of the men in her life. All she knew was that she needed to see him, and didn't know why.

The uncertainty had driven her straight to his doorstep.

"Kaia, *ma chérie.*" He swung the door open before she had a chance to knock. "I've been expecting you."

The last time Kaia had been in the cramped bachelor pad—*every* time, in fact—she'd headed straight for the bedroom, which was large enough to fit Powell's sagging mattress and not much else. This time, she sat on the futon. It was burnt orange, inherited from the previous tenant. Powell squeezed in next to her, and Kaia willed herself not to inch away.

There was one question answered: She didn't want him back. His pathetic threats had twisted Kaia's attraction into an instinctive repulsion.

"I knew you'd be back," he leered, fondling a strand of her hair.

She slapped his hand away. "I didn't come here for that," she informed him.

"What, then?"

"It's over," she told him. She was certain now of what she wanted, but uncertain about too many other things—like why she'd felt so safe with Reed, even knowing what she knew, and why, sitting here on this familiar futon with her horny but harmless ex, she felt a shiver of danger.

Powell sighed. "Haven't we danced to this song before?"

"Don't be—"

"Cute. I know." He tried to put an arm around her, and she jumped up off the futon, unsure why she felt so jittery, but willing to trust her instincts. "What? Are you still going on about that stalking thing? I told you, not my style."

"No, I know it wasn't you . . ."

"And you can't seriously still think the Sawyer boy is a reasonable option—not after what happened yesterday."

"How do you know about—"

Powell shook his head, his eyes twinkling. "I was there when they tossed him out of school. Very sad case, that. So tragic to see a young man just throw his life away, and all on a nasty little prank."

Now Kaia sat back down again, taking Powell's hands in her own and trying to smile. This had all worked out a little too well, especially for him. "Jack, tell me something." She raised a hand to his temple and wound a finger around one of his chestnut hairs, curling it idly as she spoke. "How did you know about me and Reed, really?"

"I told you, *ma chérie*, I just knew. I could tell."

She leaned toward him, brushing her lips lightly against his cheek, trying not to gag on the overpowering scent of his cologne. "You were watching, weren't you? It's okay, you can tell me. It's kind of a turn-on."

"Well, since you put it that way . . ." Powell traced his fingers down the side of her face and began lightly massaging her neck. Kaia tried not to jerk away. Then his fingers closed down on her skin, pinching her shoulder. He pushed her away from him, holding her in place like a vise. "What kind of an idiot do you take me for? 'Oh, Jack,'" he simpered in imitation, "'tell me all about how you love to watch me when I'm alone, how you've been following me, how you love to see me weak and scared.

Tell me everything, Jack, it's *such* a turn-on.' If you want to know something, Kaia, just ask."

"You took the photos," Kaia said. It wasn't a question.

"No point in lying now, is there?"

"And the car."

"Mea culpa."

"You planted the spray paint in Reed's locker," she realized, the pieces all falling into place.

"A master stroke," Powell preened. "And yet you waltz in here ready to toss me away anyway, still loyal to that piece of scum no matter what he does. 'Stand by my man' really doesn't become you, dear."

"You're going to fix it—you know that, right?" She couldn't let them throw Reed out of school, especially now. The memory of pushing him away the day before rose in her like bile. "You're going to get him out of trouble."

"Or what?"

It was funny. Yesterday, when she'd thought she'd learned the truth about Reed, she'd felt empowered. But now, confronting the real threat, it was all she could do to force herself not to flee. "Or I sic my father on you. At school, it may be your word against mine, but if Daddy Dearest finds out that some perv has laid a finger on his darling daughter, what do you think he'll do?"

"Come at me with a baseball bat?" Powell sneered. "I'm trembling."

"Come at you with a team of lawyers," Kaia corrected haughtily. "Get you fired, deported, jailed—he'll get whatever he wants. He's just like me that way."

"Is he really ready to drag his baby girl's name through the mud?"

"Wouldn't be the first time. Though I doubt he'll have to, once his team figures out how you ended up in Nowheresville, USA, in the first place. We all know it wasn't by choice. What are you willing to do to keep that skeleton safely hidden in the back of your closet?"

Powell flinched, and Kaia suppressed a smile. Her hunches were never wrong. Jack Powell had obviously stuck his hands somewhere they didn't belong—and gotten burned.

"You really care about this loser so much?" he asked.

"I think the real question is, do you?" Kaia stood up. "Are you willing to risk it all, just to screw with him?"

"I'd rather screw with you," Powell said. "It would be a much more pleasant way to handle this. You stay here with me now, and in the morning, I'll smooth things over for your little playmate."

Kaia darted her eyes toward the bedroom. "You're suggesting . . . ?"

"Don't play coy, *mon amour*. You know exactly what I'm suggesting. Just think of it as—what's that they say here? 'One more for the road.'"

It would be nothing she hadn't done before . . . and it *would* be a much easier way of getting Reed out of trouble than involving her father, who was sure to make a huge deal out of everything, but—

Even the thought of touching Powell again filled her with revulsion. She couldn't whore herself out like that, even for Reed.

"Thanks, anyway, but I'll pass." She grabbed her purse from the couch, but he curled his fingers around it as well, suddenly yanking it toward him and pulling her off balance. His other hand clamped down on her wrist and pulled her back down to the futon, onto his lap.

He leaned over and kissed her, mashing their lips together and thrusting his tongue against her teeth, which were gritted together so hard, she thought they might snap.

"I *told* you to be nice to me," he growled, his breath sour and hot on her cheek. "I gave you every opportunity."

They wrestled for a moment, Kaia squirming and pulling, Powell's hands locked tight on their prey, his muscles—the ones she'd so admired, compact, but like steel—forcing her down on her back, knocking the back of her head against the metal bar of the futon, pinning her arms behind her head.

"One more for the road," he repeated as an unfamiliar sensation swept through her. Panic. "I think I deserve that much."

Adam did his best to behave himself at basketball practice—but once practice ended, he was ready to step out of bounds. Forget trying to earn back a certain someone's trust—he was done with women.

Correction: done with relationships. They'd done nothing but cause him pain, and all because he'd been thinking of other people when he should have been thinking about himself. He'd been slow to learn his lesson, but he'd learned it well.

Look out for number one—and right now, number one wanted some fun. Lucky for him, practice had been pushed back two hours since half the team was stuck in detention all afternoon. That meant missing dinner—but it also meant sharing the court with the cheerleaders. And now that he was back on the market, he was already their top priority.

Time to make someone's day, Adam thought. The inner voice, cocky and cruel, didn't sound like him. It sounded like . . . Kane. So much the better, Adam resolved. Kane was happy. Kane didn't lie awake nights cursing the way his life had turned out. And Kane, his only previous competition, was mysteriously absent from practice.

More for me.

As the coach blew the final whistle, Adam scooped up the ball and dribbled it down toward the bouncy bimbos, who had just finished their last tumbling routine. He heard a few hoots of encouragement from the guys before they headed into the locker room.

"Adam, you were playing so great out there today!" one of the new cheerleaders gushed. She was cute, with an almost frighteningly wide grin, and seemed vaguely familiar.

"Totally awesome!" another chimed in. She, too, seemed familiar, but he couldn't place her. "We almost screwed up our cheers because we were so busy watching you. Oh—" Her face turned red, and she burst into giggles. "I mean . . . we were watching the team."

It was the "we" that gave it away. Individually, they had cute but totally forgettable faces. Together, Adam would know them anywhere as the joined-at-the-hip sophomores who'd been following Harper around all year, worshipping at the feet of their goddess of cool. Harper claimed to detest them, and refused to learn their names, instead, dubbing them Mini-Me and Mini-She. Adam had always suspected that she loved the attention they lavished on her, vapid and giggly as it might be. They were her clones, her property—

They were perfect.

"Glad you liked the show," Adam said. *Smile*, he instructed himself, struggling to dig up the flirting skills he'd once had, before Beth. His mother had always told him he was a charmer—though she'd never made it sound like a good thing. He'd put that part of him up on a shelf somewhere for two years, but now it was time to dust it off, get back in on the action. "But you know, it's a team effort."

"Oh, the team would be nothing without you!" Mini-Me gushed. (Or was it Mini-She?)

"You're the *star*."

Adam sighed. Something about this felt wrong. *You're just out of practice*, he assured himself. After all, he'd thrived on this kind of attention for years before meeting Beth; there was no reason he couldn't turn back the clock and enjoy some meaningless fun. Or, at the very least, there was no reason he couldn't go through the motions and pretend he was enjoying himself—sooner or later, it would have to turn into the real thing, right?

"So . . . I guess since you girls go to all the games, you must see all our mistakes," he said, flashing a modest smile.

"No way!" Mini-She protested.

"You guys rock!" Mini-Me swung her pom-poms in the air, as if that should decisively settle the point.

"Still, I bet you could give me some pointers—you

know, as objective observers," Adam said. "How 'bout I treat you both to some pizza and you can tell me what you think?"

"Us?" the Minis gaped at each other.

"*You* want to take *us* out?"

"*You* want to hear what *we* think?"

"Now?"

"Both of us?"

Adam nodded. Two girls—double your pleasure, double your fun, right?

(*This isn't you*, a small voice inside him pointed out. *Shut up*, he told it.)

"I'll go get changed and meet you back outside the school in fifteen minutes, okay?"

They nodded, too dumbstruck to say anything. Then, simultaneously, they turned and raced toward the girls' locker room, ponytails and pom-poms flying out behind them.

Adam trudged back toward his own locker room and tried to think eager thoughts. But all he could think of was the looks on Harper's and Beth's faces if they saw what he was doing.

Beth would be disappointed.

Harper would be disgusted.

By the time he'd showered and changed, Adam was both—but it was too late to back out now. He wasn't the kind of guy who made a date and disappeared, even if it was a date his kind of guy should never have made in the first place.

They were already there waiting for him when he pushed through the front doors, each dressed in a tight-fitting skirt he was sure he'd seen Harper wear and discard a few months earlier.

"We were afraid you'd changed your mind!" Mini-Me chirped, her face lighting up when she spotted him.

"Ready to go?" he asked weakly. Mini-Me linked her arm through his.

"Three cheers for pizza!" Mini-She squealed, and grabbed his other arm.

Too bad Adam had lost his appetite.

Beth fidgeted in her seat by the corner of the stage, fuming. When the principal had asked her, as a special favor, to participate in the governor's assembly even though her speech hadn't been chosen, she'd figured it was a decent enough consolation prize. Some prize.

It turned out that "participate" had meant "introduce Harper and tell the school what a wonderful girl she is."

Upon realizing that, Beth had been too horrified to back out—she'd just frozen, bobbing her head up and down in response to the principal's babbled comments about poise and eloquence.

There wasn't enough poise in the world to pull this off, Beth thought, glancing to her left, where Harper was playing with a long thread fraying off the pocket of her jeans. The principal had insisted on having a run-through before the main event—and it wasn't like Beth had anywhere else to be. After all, work wasn't an issue anymore.

Get out, her manager had said. *Take off your uniform, leave your time card, and get out.*

All those months of sucking up to him, with his bad breath and greedy comb-over, all those late nights and double shifts, all wasted in a single, fatal failure of her impulse-control system. She'd trashed everything just because Kane Geary couldn't leave her alone and, for once in her life, she couldn't just grin and bear it.

Part of her believed it had been worth it, just for the look on his face—at least, the patches of his face visible beneath the dripping milk shake. But the other part of her knew she needed the job: for her family, for college, for keeping herself on track, and sane.

Still, it had felt good.

"Beth?" the principal called. "You're up."

"Good luck," Harper whispered.

"What's that supposed to mean?" Beth snapped.

"Just . . . good luck," Harper said with no trace of a smile. "I'm, uh, sure you'll be . . . great."

Beth stared at her, waiting for the punch line, but

there wasn't one. Harper had never said a friendly word to her—not without an ulterior motive—and there was no reason to think she'd start now. "Don't talk to me," she hissed. "I don't want to hear it."

Beth walked slowly toward the podium at the center of the stage, thinking that something was wrong here. It should have been Harper delivering the saccharine opening lines, forced to stroke Beth's ego and choke on her words. It should have been Beth welcoming the governor, awing the auditorium of students and faculty and media with her stunning prose.

For a moment, Beth wondered: If she tried hard enough, could she wake herself up to find that she'd fallen asleep in Adam's arms three months ago, and all this was just a bad dream, brought on by pre-SAT stress?

"Ms. Manning? Any day now will do," the principal said dryly.

If it was a nightmare, it wasn't ending anytime soon.

Beth unfolded the small sheet of paper she'd brought with her, a two-paragraph intro she'd jotted down the night before. She took a deep breath and faced the sea of empty seats. "Thank you, Principal Lowenstein. And thank *you*, Governor, for visiting Haven High School. We're all so honored to have you here." *Pause for applause*, Beth told herself. But she was just delaying the inevitable.

"I'm now pleased to introduce one of Haven High's most distinguished students, someone who deeply cares—"

Beth stopped. This was a joke. As if Harper Grace had ever deeply cared about anything except herself.

But they were just words, she reminded herself. Lies, yes, but not important ones. She just needed to talk fast and get it over with.

"Who deeply cares about the future of this school. As everyone knows, Harper Grace—"

She stopped again. She may not have had the nerve to speak the truth, but she didn't have the stomach to tell the lie.

"Are you okay, Beth?" Harper called from the side of the stage. At the sound of her voice, Beth only felt weaker.

Principal Lowenstein walked over to the podium and put a hand on Beth's shoulder. She flinched away. "Is everything all right?"

No.

When was the last time the answer hadn't been no?

"I'm just not feeling very well," she said softly. "I think . . . I think I need to go, if that's all right."

She fled before the principal had a chance to respond, and before she could see the jeering look on Harper's face.

Every time she thought she'd scored a point, it seemed like she just got kicked down into the mud again, trampled and humiliated. Everything she tried to do blew up in her face, while every move Harper made was flawless—and deadly.

Beth still had the moral high ground. She had all the principles in the world on her side. But Harper had the strength, the will, and the ruthlessness. Which meant Harper had the power, and maybe she always would.

Miranda had heard the rumors.

That Rising Sun Casino was a desert oasis, filled with bronzed guys and buxom blondes, high-roller tables and penny slots, drama, intrigue, adventure, a twenty-four-hour buffet and all the cocktails you could stomach. And they didn't card.

It seemed an unlikely setting for bacchanalia, Miranda thought, as the silver Camaro pulled into a space by the entrance of the casino. A few neon lights flickered on and off, and an old man lounged in the doorway smoking a cigarette. It didn't scream intrigue so much as infection.

But at least some of the rumors were true, Miranda discovered, as Kane held the door open and she walked down an aisle lined with withering potted palms. The cocktails were abundant, as were the buxom blondes ferrying them around the casino floor.

And indeed, they didn't card.

"You like?" Kane asked, sweeping his arms wide to encompass the place as if it were his handiwork.

Miranda couldn't help but wrinkle her nose. "It has a certain . . . charm." To her right, a line of older women looked up from their slot machines, their hands fixed on the levers with a death grip. (And they seemed determined to stay there until "death grip" became a literal description.) Eventually, having ascertained that neither Miranda nor Kane looked likely to infringe on their turf, they looked down again, back at the buckets of coins and spinning dials that always came up one short of the jackpot.

Kane laughed. "Never brought a girl here before," he admitted. "But, somehow, I thought you'd enjoy it."

Miranda flushed with pleasure. When he'd proposed the impromptu road trip after detention, she certainly hadn't worried about her curfew, or asked where they were going or when they'd be back. She'd just basked in the glow of his attention.

"So what's first?" he asked. "Blackjack? Slots? Maybe you want me to teach you a little poker?"

Miranda and Harper had been playing poker late into the night since junior high. They used M&M's and Vienna Fingers for chips, then ate their winnings. She shook off the memory and grinned up at Kane. "Please. Point me to the poker table. I'll kick your ass."

And she would have, too, if he hadn't pulled out a straight flush at the last second.

It was hard to tell when he was bluffing.

After a full circuit around the casino floor, it was clear: Kane couldn't lose—not at games of skill, not at games of chance.

They eventually ended up in the gift shop. Kane had declared they needed a souvenir to commemorate the occasion. "How about this?" He held up a teddy bear in a bright blue shirt reading I ❤ POKER.

"Congratulations. That may be the tackiest thing I've ever seen."

Kane clucked his tongue. "Oh, Stevens, you're not trying hard enough. Just look around us—this is a cornucopia of crap."

Miranda had known Kane for a decade, and had studied his every move for almost that long. She'd seen him sardonic, sarcastic, sullen, supercilious—but never quite like this. Never silly.

"Okay, then, how about this?" She lifted a pair of earrings, holding them up against her lobes; the bright orange and green feathers dangled so low, they brushed her shoulders.

"Gorgeous. Now all you need to finish off the look is . . ." He selected a heavy chain of oversize, garishly painted beads and fastened it around her neck. She shivered at his touch, and his hands paused. She looked up at him and, for a moment, it seemed like—

"Not my style," she said, ducking out of the necklace, and out of his reach.

What is wrong with me? Her heart was pounding, her breaths too fast and too short, and she backed up a step, almost knocking over the shelf of commemorative shot glasses. "Careful, Stevens." He took hold of her arm to steady her. "You break it, I buy it."

Breathe, she instructed herself. *This could be it.* But it was as if her body was rejecting the good luck as too alien for her system. She'd imagined this moment so many times, and now that it was here, she didn't know what she was supposed to do or say. She couldn't get her hands to stop shaking.

Probably, she was just imagining the sudden shift between them. Nothing was going to happen, she warned—or maybe reassured—herself. To Kane, she was just a buddy; why would he suddenly see her differently?

It must be the double vodka martini, she realized. It had made her forget herself.

She'd also forgotten that he was still holding on to her arm. Or perhaps he'd forgotten to let go.

"Problem, Stevens?" He smirked, and it was almost as if he could tell what she was thinking.

"I'm fine," she claimed. "But the martinis in me seem to be a little clumsy."

"I don't think it's the martinis." He guided her toward the back of the gift shop, against a wall of "Guaranteed authentic!" Native American dreamcatchers. They were hidden from the rest of the store by a shelf of tourist guides to the Southwest. "I think you're nervous."

"Why would I be nervous? Were you playing with loaded dice?" she teased. "Think they're onto us?" She shook her head in mock disappointment. "I should have known you'd only gamble on a sure thing."

"You know me too well." He was close enough now that she could smell the alcohol on his breath. How drunk was he? she suddenly wondered. How much of this amazing afternoon was him, and how much—"That's what I love about you," he said softly.

"And here I thought you only loved yourself." She kept her voice hard and bright, hoped he wouldn't see how that word affected her.

Kane grabbed her hands and pressed them to his chest. "Stevens! You wound me! Here I am trying to be all sensitive and all you have for me are insults and innuendos?"

He was joking—or, at least, she hoped he was. Miranda had a nasty habit of blurring the line between flirtatious banter and cutting dismissals. But this time, she felt relatively safe, and so she played along.

"So sorry, Kane," she gushed fakely. "However can I make it up to you? I'll do anything!"

"Anything?" He arched an eyebrow.

"Anything your devious little heart desires."

He smiled then, the same smile he'd given her at the

poker table just before laying down his hand: *I win, you lose.*

"Then kiss me already."

And there, between the dreamcatchers and the tourist guides, swaying to the scratchy, easy-listening remix of an old Céline Dion song, Kane gently cupped her chin in his warm hand, tipped her face toward his, closed his eyes, and slowly brought their lips together.

Technically, it wasn't her first kiss—but, in a way, it was. Because always before, it had been about the mechanics: the teeth scraping, tongue swirling, saliva swishing. Miranda had always focused on her breathing and where her hands should go, on the sucking and popping noises her lips made, silently wondering, *Is this it? Can this be all there is?*

Now she had her answer: no. That was nothing. This was—this was Hollywood, this was *Gone With the Wind*, Bella and Edward in *Twilight*, Elizabeth and Mr. Darcy in *Pride and Prejudice.* This was every amazing kiss she'd ever imagined, with sparks and fireworks and a shock of pleasure exploding through her body.

This was Kane Geary caressing her cheek, sucking on her lip, moaning softly, pressing her against the gift shop wall. And this was her, forgetting herself, and how she might look or whether she was doing it right, forgetting to worry about what it might mean, how far it might go, if they'd be caught.

This was pure. This was passion.

And, most impossible of all—

This was real.

Would everyone in the audience hate her, Harper wondered, gripping the sides of the podium. Would all those hundreds of faces watching her be hoping for her to fail, or maybe just wondering what the hell she was doing up there in the first place?

She'd tried to stay true to her resolution to be a better person. She'd even been nice to Beth, much as it had twisted her stomach. It hadn't done much good. Beth didn't want her to change, that was obvious; Beth wanted her to be the unredeemable bitch, someone she could blame all her problems on, so she wouldn't have to take a closer look at herself. Harper knew the feeling.

But Harper couldn't avoid looking at herself now. She looked out at the sea of empty chairs and grew certain that tomorrow's audience would see right through her surface, down to her rotten core. And what was her reward for all this self-examination? Clammy hands, sweaty brow, pounding heart, lockjaw. She didn't need WebMD to diagnose herself. It was a textbook case: stage fright.

Harper fixed her eyes on the top line of the speech. She opened her mouth.

Out popped a squeak, and nothing more.

Her lips were dry, and her tongue suddenly felt too large for her mouth. She needed water. She needed air—in bigger and bigger gulps.

She needed to get away.

"Ms. Grace?" the principal asked, probably suffering from her own case of déjà vu. "Everything all right?"

Yes, she tried to say. *It's fine.*

But nothing came out.

And Harper Grace didn't do speechless.

There isn't even anyone watching, she told herself angrily. But it didn't seem to matter. It was all those empty seats, all that space, all the pressure—

"I have to get out of here," she mumbled, finally able to speak now that she'd given up the fight. She left the copy of the speech on the podium, waved weakly at the principal, and ran off stage, feeling sick.

She'd always been proud to be Harper Grace, with the distinguished name and the impeccable rep—everyone wanted her life.

They could have it.

Is this what it feels like? Kaia asked herself dimly in the small, faraway place she'd retreated to in her mind. She pushed Powell away, twisted, turned—but wasn't it all a bit halfhearted? Wasn't there a piece of her wondering, *Is this really happening?* She couldn't believe, couldn't force herself back down into her body, where it would be real. It seemed like something she was watching on TV, like one of those interchangeable Lifetime movies where the damsel always finds herself in distress. As if the scene would play out the same way no matter what she did.

Kaia had always thought that, in a real emergency, life would be clearer, the picture sharper. You wouldn't coolly wonder whether those self-defense classes had been a waste of money, you wouldn't be as cold and calculating as you were in everyday life. You would recognize the need to act. Instinct would take over.

You wouldn't wonder, *Should I scream? Will that seem foolish? Am I overreacting?* You wouldn't wonder, coldly, curiously, *What's wrong with me? Why don't I scream?*

And then she heard the low purr of the zipper, felt it scrape against her skin, and then she did scream. She stopped thinking and wondering because it *was* real—he was on top of her, heavy, unmovable, and she screamed and spit and bit and tore at him, and still his hand clenched both her wrists and forced her arms down though her muscles screamed in pain, and when she slammed her forehead up into his, he barely moved, barely noticed, so intent was he on holding her down, shifting into position, wriggling out of his khakis with one hand while gripping her wrists with the other—

Her knee came up, hard. And connected. He dropped her wrists, grabbed his groin, doubled over with a soft sigh, and she sat up and punched him in the Adam's apple. Twice, for good measure. Grabbed her purse—not her shirt, though, because he was on top of it, half sitting, half lying on the futon, grunting with pain. But before she could escape, he pulled himself up and lunged toward her. She darted away, but not fast enough, and he slammed her against the wall, the edge of the futon digging painfully into her lower back. He grabbed her hair, tugged her head back, his laughter hot against her skin.

One hand pinned between their bodies, her other flailed behind her, waving wildly through the air, then fumbling across the coffee table until she felt the head of his tacky marble copy of Rodin's *The Thinker*. It was solid and heavy in her grasp, and in a smooth arc she hoisted it into the air and slammed it into the back of his head.

There was a surprisingly quiet thud, and he fell limp against her, the small statue slipping out of her trembling fingers and crashing into the floor. A splash of blood lit up the stone face.

Kaia pushed Powell's inert body away, and it toppled to the floor, facefirst. She didn't check to see whether he was breathing, or wipe the blood off the statue or her fingerprints off the doorknob. She didn't cry, didn't scream, didn't hesitate.

She just left, fumbling with the lock, slipping out the door and stumbling on her way to the car. She pulled out of the driveway fast, without looking, and sped down the road into the darkness, away from town, away from people, turning up the radio and rolling down the windows to drown the night in cold air and loud music.

She blew through three red lights and hit open highway before realizing: She had nowhere to go.

chapter twelve

"HELLO?"

At first there was no sound on the other end of the line, then a harsh, rasping breath. And another. "I'm hanging up now," Reed warned, and was about to, when—

"Wait. Reed, please . . ."

"What, Kaia?"

It was her, unmistakably. And yet somehow, not her—not cool, contained, a voice dripping icicles.

Reed was stoned, and had been zoned out for hours lying on his bed, strumming along to an old Phish album. But through the haze, he began to feel the beast creeping toward him. Trouble. But was she in it, or looking to cause it?

"Kaia, what is it?"

"I shouldn't have . . . I didn't mean—"

"What's going on? What do you want?" *She's just mocking you*, he told himself. Nothing between them had been real, why should this be anything but a cruel joke?

But she didn't sound cruel. She sounded . . . broken.

"It's all my fault."

"What is?"

No answer.

"Kaia?"

"Kaia?"

Disconnected.

Another mistake. Kaia threw down the phone, cursing herself. She couldn't do anything right.

Great idea. Call Reed for help. Throw yourself on his mercy. It was almost as brilliant as going to Powell's house in the first place.

She was shivering.

So she pulled off onto the side of the road. No longer afraid of jackals or coyotes, or whatever lost and angry souls might be wandering the desert at night. What was left to fear?

She had no shirt. It was cold, a cloudless winter night, and she was curled up in the front seat of the Beamer, her cheek pressed against the smooth leather, wearing only her jeans and a black bra.

She wasn't crying. She must have been, at some point—her face was wet, sticky against the leather seat. But she couldn't remember. Could barely remember how she'd gotten there. The night was fading, the details blurring. She remembered only shards of moments: his hands on her wrists. The sound of the zipper. His body, limp and still. The blood. Driving faster and faster, the top down and the frigid air burning her face, roaring in her ears. Reed's voice as she hung up the phone.

I have nowhere to go.

I have no one.

The road was dark, the only traffic an occasional truck thundering by.

She could get out of the car, stick out her thumb. Someone would pick her up, take her as far away as she wanted to go, leave everything behind. And, after all, there was nothing to leave.

Or she could turn the key in the ignition, drive back to her father's house, slip inside and tear off her clothes, immerse herself in a scalding shower, cleanse herself of it all. Wash away his touch from her skin.

But instead she got out of the car, walked over to

the highway emergency phone. She couldn't use her cell, not for this call. She leaned against the cool steel, fingers hesitating over the receiver.

He didn't deserve her help.

And maybe it was already too late.

But she lifted the receiver and, in a dull monotone, gave out the necessary information. No names, no circumstances, nothing that would connect her to the sordid mess. Just an address. Just, "Hurry."

And when the ambulance arrived? They'd find her all over the apartment, wouldn't they? Her shirt, her fingerprints, her hairs . . . his blood. If he woke up, who knew what he'd say. And if he never did . . .

She crawled back into the car and wrapped her arms around herself for warmth. She was so tired. Cold. Finished. Later there'd be decisions to make, consequences to bear. But for now, she couldn't. Couldn't go home, couldn't go to the cops, couldn't disappear on the open road. She was tired of fighting, of moving. She just wanted it all to stop. Just for a while, just long enough that she could get her bearings.

Long enough that she could stop trembling.

She was frozen, unable to do anything but curl up in a ball in the front seat, hug her knees to her chest, close her eyes against the darkness surrounding her.

She was spent.

She was tearless.

And she was on her own.

Miranda was grounded for two weeks.

And she'd never been happier.

When she'd strolled—more like floated—in the door at half past ten, her mother was waiting. Miranda had forgotten to pick her sister up after dance class, had skipped dinner, had disappeared without a word, had apparently worried everyone half to death.

She'd just smiled through her mother's tirade, and her father's gloomy silence. She'd ignored her sister's pestering questions, waiting impatiently for the moment she could flee upstairs, shut herself in her bedroom, and relive the day, minute by minute.

She climbed into bed without changing out of her clothes, at first not wanting to admit that the day had officially ended. But then, thinking better of it, she wriggled out of her shirt and jeans and kicked them onto the floor, relishing the feel of the comforter against her bare skin. It reminded her of Kane's hands.

She could still remember everywhere he had touched her. When she closed her eyes, she imagined the pressure of his fingers on her hip and the light, tickling touch of his nail tracing its way up her back, down her collarbone. She lay in bed replaying it, lightly touching her own lips, as if to evoke a shadow of how it had felt.

She imagined what it might be like to have Kane lying in the bed with her, his strong arms wrapped around her and his chest pressed against her naked back. Would she lie on top of his arm, she wondered. Or would that cut off his circulation? Would he instead tuck one arm under the pillow beneath her head, use the other one to pull her close, and twine his fingers through hers as they both drifted off to sleep?

Miranda had never shared a bed with anyone, unless you counted family vacations when she and her sister squeezed together on the lumpy cot next to their parents' bed. So she was unsure of the logistics.

But now, finally, she could at least be sure of what it felt like to have her body come alive at someone else's touch.

They had left the casino and wandered away on foot into the desert, where they had explored each other. After years of worship from afar, Miranda had been certain she'd known every inch of Kane, but she'd been wrong.

They had done little more than kiss before Miranda had gotten nervous and pulled away. She was fearful that would be the end of it, but not fearful enough to push forward in spite of herself. Kane had only smiled, nodded, stopped what he was doing, or about to do, and went back to the kissing—it seemed to go on for hours.

Suddenly, more than anything, she wanted to call Harper. In her dream scenarios, the romantic night always ended with a triumphant call to Harper, who would shriek and then listen in disbelief as Miranda described every moment.

Even as they'd kissed, Miranda had at times found herself silently narrating, as if preparing herself to tell the story.

I couldn't believe he was touching me, she had thought, as Kane's tongue explored her mouth and her hands brushed his silky hair away from his face. *And I couldn't believe how natural it felt. Isn't that weird?*

She hadn't admitted it to herself, but she'd been talking to Harper that whole time. She had spent so many hours listening to Harper bleed details of her own innumerable conquests—and always, Miranda had listened, waiting for the day when she would have her own story to tell.

Miranda considered it. She even lifted her phone, pulling Harper up in her contacts, as if rehearsing. She needed to tell *someone* what had happened. Somehow saying it out loud would make it real and save her from the fear that when she woke up in the morning, all this would prove to have been a dream.

But too much had gone wrong between them.

So Miranda put the phone back down and rolled over

on her side, throwing her arm around a pillow and pretending it was Kane. Like a warm blanket, she tucked the memory of him around her—the laughing look in his eyes, the current between them when he first put his hands on her chin, when she knew for certain that everything was about to change.

Then kiss me already, she whispered to herself. She didn't need a witness. She remembered. Her body remembered. *It really did happen.*

It was their space.

It was sacred.

So what was he doing out there without Harper?

What was he doing out there with not just another girl—but *two*?

Harper pressed herself against the window of her dark bedroom, hating to watch yet unable to turn away, as Adam guided the girls to the large, flat rock—their rock—and lay down between them.

These weren't just any girls.

They were the sad, worshipful sophomores who wanted to have everything that Harper had—and now they were one big step closer to accomplishing their goal.

Harper could barely breathe as Adam took one of their hands. Her own hand made a fist, as if trying to clutch something that was no longer there.

The figures lay flat on their backs, side by side, and Harper wondered what they could be talking about, and whether Adam could be thinking about anyone but her. It seemed impossible; and yet, if he thought about her at all anymore, how could he bear to involve himself in something so sordid, in *their* place? How could he ruin the final thing they had between them and expect her to bear it?

Adam turned over to face Mini-Me, propping himself up on his elbow, and their heads moved toward each other. Mini-She rubbed his back, one of her legs crossing over and entwining itself with his. Harper thought she might throw up or pass out. But, instead, she just kept watching.

The scene unfolded in slow motion. Adam's face drew closer and closer to Mini-Me. And then, just before their lips touched, Adam froze and turned his head away, up, toward Harper's window.

He knows I'm watching, she realized. *He wants me to see.*

It was too dark to make out his face, but Harper imagined him to be sneering. He couldn't possibly see her, a dark figure in a dark window, but even so, it felt like their eyes were locked, and Harper willed him to see the person he needed her to be.

But he saw nothing but the darkened window, and after a moment, he looked away, back down to Mini-Me, and then he kissed her.

⁂

It was the perfect plan. But Beth didn't know if she had the nerve. It would humiliate Harper, dealing a crushing blow to that reputation she was oh so fond of. It would be the picture-perfect revenge for the way she had gone after Beth, systematically destroying everything that was important to her.

Beth held the small box in her hand and wondered: Did she have it in her? And could she do it right?

The old Beth had no experience with this kind of thing. She lacked the strategic-planning skills, the devious imagination. But the last few weeks had taught her a few things. She'd done a lot wrong, but this time, perhaps she'd finally get it right.

No one would be hurt. No property would be destroyed. And certainly no one would ever think to trace it back to kind, appeasing Beth, pure as the driven snow.

She hated the person she had been—the weak, meek girl who'd let anyone hurt her. But she missed her old self, as well, particularly her assumption that life was, despite what they say, fair. She had always believed that if she worked hard enough and long enough, she'd get what she wanted.

She'd been weaned on platitudes:

Early to bed, early to rise . . .

A bird in the hand . . .

Revenge is a dish best served cold.

That one was just as wrong as the rest of them—she didn't have the patience to wait for the perfect moment to arrive. She'd have to create it. It would, of course, have been preferable not to adopt the tactics of her enemies. It would be nice if turning the other cheek would get you anywhere in life. But it wouldn't. Harper had proven that.

Beth put the box in the outer pocket of her backpack. She wished that something would happen the next day that would allow her to forget it was there, and that the need for revenge would magically disappear.

She'd learned the platitudes from her father, who was full of them. His favorite: *If wishes were horses, beggars would ride.* And now Beth finally got it: Wishes weren't worth much. You couldn't just close your eyes and hope things would turn out right. You had to make things happen. Harper had taught her that, too.

Harper had been a good teacher this year—and, of course, Beth had always been an eager student.

Tomorrow would be the final exam.

She was ready.

"I didn't know who else to call," Kaia said apologetically, when Harper met her in the parking lot and handed her the shirt she'd requested. Kaia slipped it on. "Thank you."

"Dare I ask what . . ."

Kaia shook her head. "Better not to. Sorry I had to drag you out here. It's late, and—"

"Trust me, I could use the diversion," Harper admitted. She looked more closely at Kaia, who seemed normal on the surface—but that surface was somehow thinner, more fragile than Harper had ever seen it. She gestured toward the coffee shop they were parked in front of. "I don't know about you, but I could use a drink."

"No." Kaia ran a trembling hand through her hair. "I have to"—she looked at her watch, looked at the road, the car, anywhere but at Harper—"I just have to go."

"Not like this," Harper said firmly. "One drink. Just some coffee. We'll talk."

"I don't need—"

"Not for you," Harper said, only half lying. "For me. It's been a crap night. I could use some company."

As if too tired to fight, Kaia nodded. As they walked toward the door, Harper cautiously attempted to put a hand on Kaia's shoulder—in comfort, she thought. Kaia flinched away.

Inside Bourquin's, they nestled in two comfy overstuffed armchairs in front of a roaring fire. Each sipped a steaming cup of coffee, black.

"You sure you don't want to talk about it?"

Kaia shook her head again. "There's nothing to—"

"Come on."

"Okay, there's plenty to tell. But it's not like I'm going to—" Kaia stopped herself, and Harper recognized the look on her face. She'd worn it enough times herself, when she was about to say something catty and caught herself just in time.

"You talk," Kaia said instead.

"About what?"

"About anything, I don't care. I just want to . . . sample someone else's problems for a change. So just talk. What's going on with you?"

Harper couldn't stop herself from laughing.

"What?" Kaia asked, annoyed.

"It's just . . ." How to say it without sounding rude? Then again, who cared how she sounded? "My life is totally fucked up, everyone's gone, and—let's just say I never thought I'd be pouring out my problems to *you.*"

Kaia lifted her mug in a mock toast. "Right back at you," she said, forcing a grin.

Harper sighed and slumped against her chair. She'd hated Kaia, once, and then they'd been cautious allies, brought together by circumstance. And now? Harper still didn't trust her. But she somehow felt that she knew her—or maybe that Kaia knew Harper. It was the one person she'd thought she'd never let see her vulnerable; but these days, Kaia seemed like the only one with whom she could drop the act.

"Where should I start?" she asked, rolling her eyes. "Adam's probably screwing some other girl in our backyard, as we speak. Or two of them."

"Two girls? *Adam?*"

"Don't ask. Meanwhile, Miranda hates me. I've got to give this shit speech tomorrow and"—this time, her laughter took on a twinge of hysteria—"turns out I've got stage fright."

"Well, at least that one I can help you with." Kaia dug through her purse and pulled out a tiny pink case, then opened it up and slipped two pills into Harper's hand.

"And this would be . . . ?"

"Xanax," Kaia explained. "Mother's new little helper. I snagged her stash before they shipped me out here. Take a couple before you go on. You'll be fine." She let forth an almost manic giggle. "I might have a few myself tonight."

Harper slipped the pills into her pocket and sank back into her seat. "One problem down. Too many to go."

"Feels like everything's closing in on you?" Kaia asked—and was that sympathy in her voice?

Harper nodded.

"Like you don't belong anywhere and you don't deserve to?"

She nodded again.

"Like everyone thinks they know you, but no one really does?" Kaia took a deep breath and surreptitiously wiped the corner of her right eye. "Feels like maybe you'd be better off if you just took off one night and never came back?"

"Run away and leave it all behind?" Harper asked, surprised—because she'd just been staring out the window imagining how good it would feel. "If only."

"Yeah. If only."

It wasn't their kind of thing. But it was a nice fantasy.

There was silence between them for a moment, comfortable enough that Harper found the courage to speak. "Have you ever . . . done something that you wished you could take back? You know, just go back in time, do it all over again, the *right* way?"

Kaia dipped her pinkie into the coffee mug and stirred it around the dark liquid. "Maybe."

"It just seems like it should be possible to fix things," Harper said, thinking of the look on Adam's face when he'd thought Beth was cheating on him. He'd crumbled, totally destroyed. All because he trusted Harper and she'd used that trust to ruin him. "One bad decision, one screw-up, that shouldn't be it. You shouldn't have to feel guilty forever, right? There should be *something* you can do."

"What, like atone for all your sins?" Kaia asked. She shook her head. "No. Sometimes, maybe. But sometimes . . ." She shrugged and closed her eyes for a long moment. "Sometimes you make the wrong decision and that's just . . . it. Everything changes. You can't go back."

"You really believe that?"

"I don't know if I really believe anything."

Harper nibbled on her lower lip. "I don't buy it," she said finally. "No second chances, no hope. That would be hell."

"Look around you," Kaia drawled, gesturing to the tacky, faded, over-stuffed and over-ruffled coffee-shop decor, the darkness that lay beyond them. "We're *in* hell."

"You really hate it here, don't you?"

Kaia shivered, though the coffee shop was almost overly warm. "More than anything," she said, almost too softly to hear. "More than you know."

Harper almost envied her. For Kaia, this was all temporary—she had somewhere to go back to, a happy memory and hope for the future to keep her warm. For Harper, this was it. Life in Grace was all there was. And she'd destroyed everything that made it bearable.

Kaia could dream about waking from the nightmare, going back to New York, moving on with her life.

But for Harper, this was permanent reality. There was no escape.

chapter thirteen

"CHECK IT. I THINK IT'S A SECRET SERVICE AGENT!"

"No way."

"No, look, he's got a wire leading up to his ear, and—"

"Nice try, but I think that's the janitor and his new iPod."

"Whatever, they must be here somewhere, since he's coming soon and—"

"Do you think there'll be a limo?"

"Or, like, a whole motorcade, with cops and shit?"

"Are those sirens? Adam, you hear that?"

"Adam?"

The pale cheerleader hanging off his shoulder was

staring at him, waiting for some kind of answer. Adam didn't have one for her. He'd checked out. It was the only way he was making it through this whole big-man-on-campus act. Hanging out in front of the school with his buddies and three hot cheerleaders—one of whom, he'd discovered the night before, could do this thing with her tongue that . . .

It should have been awesome. A walk in the park. Instead, Adam was just zoned out, waiting for the bell to ring. If he was going to be bored and miserable, better to do it inside a darkened auditorium, where he could slouch in his seat and stare off into space, undisturbed. Better than here, where something was expected of him. He mustered a smile.

"Who cares?" he asked. "It's just the governor. Big deal. You aren't even old enough to vote."

"God, Adam, did you wave *hasta la vista* to your brain?" Mini-She gave him a gentle push, and he guessed he was forgiven for chickening out the night before after a couple kisses and a little over-the-sweater action. The whole double-your-pleasure angle had seemed so appealing in theory, but in practice, it had been too seedy, too sordid, too much.

And he had his doubts whether he could have handled even one of them; much as he hated to admit it, he was no longer into the one-night-only thing. Not that he'd admit it to the guys—or even to the girls, at least these girls.

But he wanted something more, something better; he just didn't think he'd ever have it, not again.

"He's not just the governor," Mini-Me protested. She snuggled up again him, shoving Mini-She out of the way. "He's—"

"Here!" Mini-She shrieked, as the sirens blared and a full motorcade pulled up in front of the school. A fleet of Secret Service agents—and they didn't disappoint, dressed in black suits, sunglasses, cocking their heads to the side as commands issued from their earpieces—swarmed out of the fleet of black SUVs, pushing the gawkers back to create a perimeter for the figure emerging from the long black limo.

It was really him, he'd actually shown up. This was officially more excitement than Grace had seen since the eighties, when a movie crew had shown up, along with the requisite stars, trailers, and paparazzi—and then turned around and left a week later, sets built, extras hired, and funding vanished.

Adam waited to feel some excitement now that the big moment had arrived, but he felt nothing.

Let this be the biggest day in Haven High history.

So what?

For Adam, it was just another crappy day.

Kaia had driven all the way to school before allowing herself to consider whether or not to go inside. She'd scanned the local paper that morning, but there was no mention of a lone British bachelor found unconscious in his apartment. Not that you'd expect the *Grace Herald*'s crack reporting staff to be on the case so quickly, not when said staff included only two reporters, one of whom worked from his "office" in the Lost and Found, and the other who restricted herself to items on gardening or fashion (preferably both). And though she'd lain awake all night, listening for approaching sirens, an impatient rapping at the door or even a late-night phone call, nothing had happened.

But Kaia had watched too much TV to be fooled into thinking she was in the clear. No, either Powell had woken up and elected not to tell anyone his twisted version of what had happened, or . . . he hadn't woken up at all. And maybe wouldn't.

Kaia couldn't decide which option she preferred. She wouldn't even allow herself to consider the question, since every time her mind strayed to the image of Powell lying there, his blood on her hands, she froze. And she couldn't afford to do that anymore, not while time was running out.

She could turn herself in, tell the truth, engage in the inevitable he said–she said, and hope things swung her way. She wasn't stupid—she knew that was the responsible thing to do, probably the smart thing to do. But she didn't feel very smart right now, and she'd never been a big fan of responsible.

She could waltz into school as if nothing had happened. Maybe Powell wouldn't remember, or wouldn't want to implicate himself, or wouldn't . . .

There were any number of ways this could come out okay and she could slip away from the whole thing unseen and unsuspected, if only she could get it together and put on the right show.

Or she could get back in her car, drive away, and make a new life for herself somewhere. It was the dream option—the impossible one.

The alternatives were all shitty, and so instead of choosing one, Kaia leaned against her car and pulled out her phone. There was one thing she was sure she needed to do, even if it was too late.

The voice mail picked up on the fifth ring, which gave Kaia enough time to collect herself and plan her words.

"Reed, I don't know if you want to hear this, but I need to tell you that I'm sorry. I was wrong, about everything. I'm sure you don't want to talk to me, but I need to talk to you, to explain and . . . just call me back. Please. Because I—" She paused, wishing she could bring herself to say more. "I'm sorry."

Showtime. The art room was serving as a greenroom for the presenters as they waited for the governor's entourage to settle themselves on stage and the student body to filter in.

Everyone was buzzing about Powell's "accident" the night before—thanks to a cryptic announcement, they all knew the dreamy French teacher was in the hospital, but for what, and from what, no one had any clear idea. Fragments had spread, phrases like "stable condition," "unforced entry," "open investigation," and "mitigating circumstances" floating through the grapevine courtesy of the sons and daughters of doctors, cops, nosy receptionists, and taciturn administrators. But no one had been able to piece together the full story, and no one could let it go, wondering: Was his pretty face still intact? Was it a bitter student? A jilted lover? Would French be cancelled? Would the perpetrator strike again?

Beth didn't care about any of it. She sat off to the side, alone at one of the large drafting tables, watching Harper across the room. Even from a distance, Beth could see her fingers tapping compulsively against the side, her knees jiggling, and, like Beth, she was steering clear of the huddling gossipers, locked in her own thoughts.

She looked nervous—*but not as nervous as I am*, Beth thought, clutching one of Kane's little yellow pills in the palm of her hand. She'd done some research the night before and decided one should be enough. And, according to her calculations, it was time. You had to give it some time to kick in, after all.

Beth felt like the room was watching her, but she

forced herself to take a deep breath and make her move. Two cups of coffee—the lukewarm instant crap courtesy of the faculty lounge. One for her—and one for Harper, with a little something *ex*-tra mixed in for flavor.

Harmless fun, Beth told herself. That's all it was. No one would get hurt. Beth would get even.

"What are you staring at?" Harper asked sullenly, when she realized Beth was hovering over her desk. "Just thought you looked a little nervous," Beth said. "Thought this would help." She offered Harper a cup, making sure to give her the right one. Harper took a sip and put it down on her desk. Then she lifted it again and took a long gulp.

There's still time, Beth told herself. *I could knock over the cup before she drinks any more. I could forget the whole thing.*

"Thanks, I guess." Harper frowned. "As long as you're here, there's something I need to say."

Here it came. Beth steeled herself. "Yeah?"

"I . . . I wanted to tell you . . . well, about . . . I'm really . . ." Harper closed her eyes, and a series of expressions flickered across her face as if she was having an in-depth conversation inside her head. Then, all at once, she shook her head and her features relaxed into a familiar sneer. "Just don't screw up, okay?"

Forget turning back.

Beth smiled sweetly.

"Uh, thanks. Good luck to you, too." Beth backed

away, retreated to the other side of the room—but she snuck enough glances to spot Harper downing the cup.

Beth checked her watch. It should take no more than twenty minutes. She couldn't believe she'd actually done it. She didn't know how she was going to wait.

At least this time she wouldn't have any trouble choking out her introduction. The more lovely things she had to say, the higher the audience's expectations rose, the harder Harper would fall.

Beth checked her watch again. Only a minute had passed. This was maddening. But there was nothing left for her to do now, nothing left to worry about.

All she had to do was wait it out—and then sit back and watch the show.

Play it cool, she'd told herself all night.

Play it cool, she'd insisted this morning as she wolfed down a bowl of cereal, eager to get to school to see him.

It was time to face facts: Miranda wasn't cool.

For years now, she'd borrowed cool from Harper, but that was over now. There was no one to tell her to keep her mouth shut and go with the flow. And there was no one to calm her down when Kane gave her a casual smile and quick wave as they passed in the hall—then kept going.

Was that it?

Was the whole casino trip a one-time deal? Or was

he just keeping it casual, waiting to see what she wanted? Or—

Miranda couldn't sift through the possibilities like a rational human being. They buzzed around her, worst-case scenario piling on top of dreamscape, misery and ecstasy mixing together, and all the while, she was only half present to begin with, thanks to the chunk of her mind still dedicated to preserving the memory of his touch.

She hovered in the entryway of the auditorium, watching the students file in. No Kane.

No surprise—this wasn't his thing. When Miranda was certain he wasn't there, she waited until the faculty had turned away to view the main event, then slipped out herself. She knew she'd find him in the parking lot, half hidden behind a utility wall, enjoying a cigarette.

She wasn't usually the kind of girl who could confront a boy—not someone like Kane, at least, who'd cowed her into silence for years. But the not knowing was even more overwhelming than her fear. So she spurred herself into action, and found him just where she'd expected.

One problem: She didn't know what to say. She hadn't planned that out, and could only hope that once she started, he would finish.

This is a bad idea, she warned herself, knowing that Kane wasn't the type to react well to being pressured; he *was* the type to do things without thinking and then hope never to speak of them again. *A very bad idea.* Still, she couldn't help but be a little impressed with herself. Who knew Miranda Stevens could ever be this brave?

"Hey."

He looked up and smiled as if he'd been expecting her. "Want a smoke?"

She waved away the pack. The way she was feeling now, the nicotine buzz would put her over the edge.

"So . . . get any flak when you got home last night? You know, for disappearing and—" She broke off at his laughter. *Stupid*, she berated herself. Of course *Kane* wouldn't get in trouble. He probably did this kind of thing all the time. *Nice job letting him know you're a loser with overprotective parents.* Still, she'd raised the subject. It was a start.

"So," she continued, in a small voice—her stomach was clenched, and it felt like there was no air left in her lungs. "About last night . . ."

"Yeah, it was great, wasn't it?"

Miranda beamed, and some of the tension leached out of her.

"You know, if you were any other girl, I'd be so screwed right now," he continued.

"Why?"

"Oh, you know how it is—have a little fun and the girl gets all lame and clingy. Wants to know what it all means, where it's all going, crap like that." He took a long drag on the cigarette. "You know, girl stuff."

"Yeah," Miranda echoed weakly. "Girl stuff."

"But not you."

No, not good ol' reliable Miranda. No girl stuff here.

"You know me, and you're cool with it. And just because we had a great time yesterday, you're not, you know, freaking out and wondering where we'll go on our honeymoon."

The Italian Riviera. Or maybe Tuscany.

"It's what I've always liked about you, Stevens." He punched her lightly on the arm. Like she was one of his teammates. "You're not like other girls."

Uh, thanks?

Miranda clamped her teeth together, afraid otherwise they would clatter, and her lip would start to wobble uncontrollably as always happened when she was about to cry. She had to get away before it happened.

"Whatever, Kane." She forced herself to laugh. "As if I'd go all gooey eyed over you. Please. Could your ego get any bigger?"

"Well, I *am* working out." He offered her the pack of cigarettes again. "Come on, join me. It's rude to let some-one smoke alone."

"Much as I'd like to join you on the road to lung can-cer, I think I'll pass," Miranda said, trying not to meet his eyes. "I just came out here for a little fresh air. So that would kind of defeat the point." She checked her watch. "Anyway, I should probably get back inside. If someone notices I'm gone . . ."

"Who's going to—"

"Later, Kane." She had to leave now, fast, before he talked her into staying—and she so wanted to stay. Every moment she was around him was a moment of possibility. That *something* would happen. But it would kill her if something didn't.

And it wasn't going to.

"Suit yourself, Stevens." Kane tilted his hand back and puffed out a perfect smoke ring. "I'll miss you."

It's just a line, Miranda told herself as she slammed back into school and trudged down the empty hallway. *He doesn't want you.*

And all her fantasies, all the lies she'd told herself, came crashing down, because that was the truth.

Play it cool.

Play it cool.

But the halls were empty. There was no one left to appreciate the act. So Miranda dropped it. And, letting out a ragged breath, she finally allowed herself to burst into tears.

He doesn't want me, she moaned to herself, chest heaving. She ducked into an empty classroom and closed the door, slumping down to the floor behind it and curling up into a tight ball, rocking back and forth.

She'd always thought that if she could just get him to notice her, just for once get him to see her as an object of desire, that he wouldn't be able to resist.

Well, he'd seen her. He'd gotten the best of her, in every way. He'd hung out with her, he'd flirted with her, he'd kissed her, and after all that?

He'd passed.

It's not that she was invisible.

It's that she was unworthy. Unappealing.

And now she couldn't even retreat into her fantasies, because everything had happened exactly as she'd hoped and it still hadn't been enough.

There was nothing left to hope for.

It was over—and she was done.

chapter fourteen

HARPER STEPPED UP TO THE PODIUM, AND IT WAS SO warm and light under the spotlight, all the people beaming up at her with love in their eyes. It was such an amazing view with all the lights and colors and sounds so strange as if she could see them shimmering through the air, glittering filaments streaming toward her ears.

My turn, she thought and she took out her speech, but then it seemed so dull and colorless. She was so tired of keeping everything inside tight bottled up pressing against her insides. There was so much pain and now here today she could let it out.

Harper crumpled up her speech and tossed it away.

Thank god for Xanax, she thought, thinking fondly of the two pills she'd popped before stepping onstage. If she'd been nervous before, she now knew that was silly, ridiculous, there was no reason to worry, she was warm, she was loved, this was her moment, and she began to speak.

"I don't know you," she said, sweeping her arms out at the sea of people. "I know you, and I know you"—she pointed—"but not all of you, and you don't know me. You think you know me, but not the me inside, you know? Not Harper Grace. Who am I? It's like . . ." Train of thought vanished, because there was his face, glowing golden in the middle of the room. "*He* knows me. He loves me, but he won't admit it. He thinks he hates me. But you can't hate me, Adam, because you need me, we're like one person, you and me, together. Remember when we were together for the first time?" She sighed and ran her hands up and down her body and moaned because for a second it was like his hands were her hands, no, like her hands were his hands—whatever it was, it was better than being alone, which is all she ever was anymore, and someone was trying to make her shut up to go away but she pushed him away and kept talking because she'd been silent for so long. "You couldn't and then you could, and we screwed and—and then you left me all alone. Why would you do that, Adam? Why would you leave me when you said you'd never leave me?

I'm so sorry, I'm sorry for everything and everyone and I was just so scared to say it, but I'm weak, I'm weak and bad terrible evil I know, but you said *forever*, Adam. Why would you do that to me? Why would you lie?"

And the principal was pulling at her dragging her away and she gripped the podium because it was too important, she needed an answer, but she'd lost sight of his golden face and now there were only strangers, and their laughter looked black and felt like knives, and then Harper, who had been feeling no pain suddenly felt it all and she broke from the principal's arms.

Get away, that was all she could think, all she could do.

Must get away.

Adam slumped down in his seat, jaw wide open, eyes squeezed shut. Whatever she was on—and it must have been something—she'd humiliated herself. Not to mention him. He couldn't stand to watch. And it just kept going, forever. *When will they drag her away?* he kept thinking as the horror stretched on, and on. *When will they make her stop?*

Now she was gone, and they were all staring at him instead. He was a part of this freak show, like it or not, and he hated her for dragging him down with her.

And yet—inside, his stomach twisted into a tight, painful knot at the thought of her up there, broken, for all to see.

Did I do that to her? he wondered.

And he couldn't help but care.

Maybe she really did love him, in her twisted, fucked-up way. They had dragged her off the podium as she flailed about like an animal—and wouldn't stop screaming his name.

He should go to her. But then everyone would see him get up, walk out, and everyone would know he was a part of this. After all she'd done to him, he was supposed to forgive and forget, just because she had a public meltdown?

For all he knew, this was just another strategy to win him over, and playing into it would just make him look like an idiot, again.

Yes. No. Stay. Go. He froze up.

And by the time he finally made his choice, it was too late. She was gone.

If only life were DVRed, and she could rewatch the moment again and again.

I did that, she thought, watching Harper flee the stage, not sure whether she felt triumph or nausea. *I won.*

Of course, Harper could never know what Beth had slipped into her drink, or that she'd finally been bested by the one whom she'd looked down on the most. But it hardly mattered—after that performance, Beth suspected it would be a long time before Harper was able to look down at anyone.

Beth had expected it to feel better, sweeter. But all she felt was a sense of finality, as if this had ended things, with a fittingly sordid coup de grâce.

As she'd watched Harper self-destruct, her anger toward Kane and Adam had fallen away. As Harper ranted, and the laughter of the crowd grew louder and crueler, Beth decided that this was it.

She'd taken her revenge—and it had been necessarily brutal, but now it was over.

This is what they called "closure," she supposed. It was a good word, because the past few months now felt like a tedious story she'd plowed through, pitting herself against the pages that mounted up with no end in sight. She'd made it through, and now she would shut the book forever. She would throw it away.

Beth was different now—thanks, she supposed, to Harper, to all of them. She was stronger. Harder.

There were four months till graduation, and she would spend them alone and miserable. But she would deal. She had let Harper turn her into the kind of person she'd always despised, and maybe there was no going back from that. But she could go forward.

Kaia made her decision. She would call the police, tell her story, take responsibility. She was in the right, after all. She was no criminal, and no victim, either. She had just done what had to be done, and that's just what she would do now. Not because it was what her parents would have wanted, or what a million Lifetime movies would have advised, but because she just knew it was the right thing. She'd let Powell make her feel weak—but now that was over, and this was the way to be strong.

And then Harper ran out of the school, past a smirking Kane, past a zoned-out Secret Service guy, across the parking lot, and straight toward Kaia. It was like a sign.

Harper stopped a few feet away, her breath ragged, tears streaming down her face. "Kaia?"

"What's going on? What's wrong?"

"I don't—" She furiously rubbed at one of her eyes, her hand curled into a fist and tucked into the cuff of her sleeve. "Nothing. It's fine. Nothing. Let's just go, okay?" she said, her face lighting up like a child's.

"Go where?"

"Away. Just away." Obviously upset, the words were spilling out of her almost too quickly to follow, but they made sense. "Like you said before, let's be gone. Jump into your car. Go. Out."

Kaia didn't stop to think. Get away, just drive—not forever, not for more than a few hours, but it would be enough. She could clear her head, gather her strength, and prepare for the coming storm. It was just what she needed; given Harper's unexplained meltdown, just what they both needed. And when they came back, she would go to the cops, she promised herself. She would take care of everything.

Harper grabbed the keys from Kaia's hand and jumped into the front seat. "Where to?" she asked. "We can go anywhere, I just want to feel the road beneath me—you know, drive and drive until it's all behind us—"

Kaia opened the passenger door and hopped in, glad not to be stuck behind the wheel, so she could just relax, watch the world stream by through the window, lose her focus, and let all her worries escape. "Anywhere," she agreed. "I don't care. Let's just go."

She'd barely gotten the door closed when Harper shifted the car into gear and peeled out of the lot, pulling a sharp U-turn and speeding down the road, heading out of town.

"Harper, slow down!" Kaia gripped the dashboard as they flew over a speed bump.

"I can never go back there," Harper was saying, pushing the car faster and faster. They whipped around a sharp curve and Kaia gasped—but at least now they'd passed through the town limits and were out in the open, where speed was exhilarating, not deadly.

Kaia's apprehension mixed with her stress and exhaustion, and through a strange alchemy, she suddenly found herself smiling, pressing the button to lower the top on the car. Suddenly, the speed *was* exhilarating. Like a roller coaster. And just as she used to do before she got too old for such things, Kaia raised her arms and screamed into the wind.

"We're getting out!" Harper cried, and Kaia closed her eyes, letting the wind thunder in her ears, the sun warm her face. Whatever had happened, whatever would happen, they had this one moment.

And in this moment, they were finally free.

He didn't see them until it was too late.

They came barreling over the hill out of nowhere, swerving from lane to lane as if they owned the road. He'd been up all night, driving across the state. His reflexes maybe weren't what they should have been, and the van was hard to maneuver.

He veered out of the way as soon as he spotted them—but it wasn't soon enough.

The scream of the metal as his van sliced through the body of their car—it was a sound he'd remember for the rest of his life.

It was a long, slow, grinding whine, a high screech, a sickening crunch.

The van was big, tough. And when it was over, the van was pretty much intact.

The BMW wasn't as lucky. The force of the impact

had knocked it off the road, flipped it over, crushed it.

It barely looked like a car anymore. And whoever had been inside—

He looked away.

Not my fault, he assured himself. *Not my problem.*

The van was dented, but still running. And he had a long drive ahead of him. Better to start now.

Someone else would come along, eventually.

They always did.

It hurt to open her eyes. It hurt to move.

She did neither.

There may have been sirens, in the distance. Or maybe it was just the loud whine in her head. Or maybe she was screaming. Still screaming. She remembered—

What?

Horns.

Squeals.

And then she had been weightless, flying.

Darkness.

She could hear her breathing, ragged and slow. And she could feel pain. Everywhere.

Alive, she decided. *I hurt, therefore I am.*

There was something missing, though.

She could hear her breathing—but nothing else.

She remembered her screams—but nothing else.

She opened her eyes. All she saw, at first, was the bright white blazing sky. Then, slowly: tangled metal. Smoke. Licks of flame. Dirt. Rivers of red. And . . .

A body. Still.

She tried to open her mouth and call out. But no sound came. And in the wreckage, nothing—no one—moved.

She tried to reach out, to crawl over, but she was swept up in a wave of pain. It sucked her down, deep, back into the darkness, and she closed her eyes again, and let it drag her under.

Help was on the way.

And, eventually, it showed up.

Two ambulances tore off toward town, one speeding down the highway, lights blazing, sirens blaring. The other took its time, stopped at traffic lights, observed the speed limit. Its lights were dark, its sirens silent.

There was no hurry.

There was no one left to save.

Turn the page for a sneak peak at

seven deadly sins

VOL 3.

"Sloth"

"I'M IN HEAVEN," HARPER MOANED AS THE MASSEUR kneaded his supple fingers into the small of her back. "You were right, this is exactly what we needed."

Kaia shooed away her own masseur and turned over onto her back, almost purring with pleasure as the sun warmed her face. "I'm always right."

"I wouldn't go that far," Harper snarked, but there was no venom in her tone. The afternoon sun had leached away most of her will to wound—and a half hour under Henri's magic fingers had taken care of the rest. "Mmmmm, could life get any better?"

"Yoo are steeel verreee tense," Henri told her in his heavy French accent.

"And yoo are steeel verreee sexeeeee," Kaia murmured, in an impeccable accent of her own. The girls exchanged a glance as the hunky but clueless Henri smoothed a palmful of warm lotion across Harper's back.

"Zhees weeel help you reeelax," he assured her. As if anyone could relax with a voice like that purring in her ear. "I leave you ladies now. *Au revoir*, *mes chéries*."

"*Arrivederci*, Henri!" Harper cried, giggling at the rhyme.

"That's Italian," Kaia sneered. "Idiot."

"Who cares?" Harper countered. "Snob."

"Loser."

"Bitch." Harper narrowly held back a grin.

"Slut." Kaia's eyes twinkled.

"Damn right!" Harper pulled herself upright and raised her mojito in the air. Kaia did the same, and they clinked the plastic cocktail glasses together. "To us. Good thing we found each other—"

"—since no one else could stand us," Kaia finished, and they burst into laughter.

It was the kind of day where the clouds look painted onto the sky. The scene was straight out of a travel brochure—five star all the way, of course. Storybook blue sky, turquoise ocean lapping away at the nearby shore, gleaming white sand beach, and a warm tropical breeze rustling through their hair, carrying the distant strains of a reggae band. The girls stretched out along on their deck chairs, their every need attended to by a flotilla of servants.

"I could stay here forever." Harper sighed. She let her leg slip off the chair and dug her bare toe into the sand, burrowing it deeper and deeper into the cool, dark ground. "I wish we never had to go back."

"I don't know about you," Kaia drawled, "but I don't *have* to do anything."

"Right," Harper snorted. "The great and powerful Kaia Sellers, with the world at her fingertips. As if you can ditch real life and just stay here in paradise."

"I can do anything I want. Haven't you figured that out yet?" Harper rolled her eyes.

"Why not?" Kaia continued. "What do I have to go back for? What do you? Isn't that why we came out here in the first place, to leave all that shit behind?"

Harper sighed. "You're right. And it worked. I can barely even remember what we were escaping from, and—" Her eyes widened. "You're bleeding." A small trail of blood trickled down Kaia's temple; Harper raised her hand to her own face, as if expecting to feel a similar wound.

Kaia frowned for a moment, dabbing her head with a napkin. "Just a mosquito bite," she said with a shrug. She took a closer look at Harper, whose face had gone pale. "You were totally freaked, weren't you?"

"No," Harper lied. "It's just gross. All these bugs . . ." She swatted at a mosquito that had just landed on her bare leg, then another whizzing past her nose. "They're everywhere."

"Easy way to fix that." Kaia stood up, her bronze Dolce bikini blending seamlessly into her deep tan. "Come on." Without waiting to see if her orders were followed—after all, they always were—she bounded toward the shoreline, kicking up a spray of sand in her wake.

Harper raced after her, and they reached the ocean's edge at the same moment. Harper stopped short as a wave of icy water splashed against her ankles, but Kaia didn't even hesitate. She waded out, the water rising above her calves, her knees, her thighs, and then, submerged to her waist, she turned and flashed Harper a smile. It was the eager, mischievous grin of a little kid sneaking into the deep end even though she's not quite sure how to swim. Harper waved, frozen in place, unable to force herself to go any deeper into the churning water, unwilling to go back.

Kaia took a deep breath, closed her eyes, and dove under the surface, her arms slicing through the water, pulling her into the deep. She resurfaced, gasping for air, and leaned back into an easy float, the salt water buoying her body, the gentle waves bouncing her up and down. Harper's shouts, dim and incoherent, blew past with the wind, but Kaia dipped her head back and the roaring water in her ears drowned out the noise.

Harper stood in the same spot, the tide carving deep rivulets around her feet as the waves washed in and back out again. The wind picked up, but the sky remained clear and blue. Harper stood, and Harper watched, and Kaia floated farther and farther out to sea—

And then she woke up.

She'd hoped the dreams would stop once she weaned herself off the Percodan. They hadn't. Just like the phantom pains that still tore through her legs when she tried to sleep, they'd outstayed their welcome.

For a long time, the pain had kept her awake.

Ambien had helped with that, the little pink pills that carried her mind away. But when sleep came, so did the dreams. They weren't always nightmares. Sometimes they were nice, carrying her away to somewhere warm and safe. Those were the worst. Because always, in the end, she woke up.

It was better just not to sleep.

But she needed her strength, they were always telling her. *For what?* she wanted to ask. For tolerating her disgustingly bubbly physical therapist? For avoiding phone calls and turning away visitors? For limping from her bedroom to the kitchen and back again? For zoning out through a *Little House on the Prairie* marathon because she was too lazy to change the channel? For turning two weeks of recuperation into four, inventing excuse after excuse until she no longer knew how much of the pain was real and how much was just expedient?

Maybe they were right. Because her strength had finally given out. She'd run out of imagined excuses, and the big day had arrived: back to school.

She'd already picked out the perfect outfit: an eggplant-colored peasant top with a tight bodice and sufficiently low neckline, a tan ruffled skirt that flared out at the bottom, and, just for added panache, a thin, gauzy black scarf woven through with sparkly silver.

After a long, too-hot shower, she slipped into the outfit, certain it made the right statement: *I'm back.* She brushed out her hair and mechanically applied her eye shadow, mascara, a touch of gloss, barely looking in the mirror; it was as if she went through the routine every morning, and this weren't the first time she'd dispensed with her cozy gray sweats since—

Since the accident. Since what had happened.

It still hurt her to say the words. It hurt to think them. And that was unacceptable. She couldn't afford to indulge in that kind of frailty, especially not today, when everyone would surely be staring at her, the walking wounded, waiting for a sign of weakness. So she'd been practicing. Every day, she forced herself to think the unthinkable, to speak the hateful words aloud. She whispered them to herself before she drifted off to sleep, in hopes of forestalling the dreams. She murmured them while watching TV, while waiting for the doctor, while pushing her untouched food around on the plate—she had once shouted them at top volume, her stereo turned up loud enough to drown out her voice.

Speaking the truth didn't make it seem any more real. In fact, it sounded just as strange, just as surreal, each time it trickled off her tongue. And it always hurt. But she was hurting *herself*, and that gave her power. It made her feel strong, reminding her that there was nothing left to be afraid of. She said them to herself now, as she hovered in the doorway, gathering her strength to face the day. The first day. She ran a hand through her hair, willing it not to shake. She zipped up the new boots that rose just high enough to cover the bandage on her left calf. She applied a final layer of Tarte gloss, then practiced her smile. It had to look perfect. Everything had to look perfect.

She took a deep breath and held herself very still. And then, softly but firmly, she said it:

"Kaia is dead."

And with that, Harper Grace was ready to go.

"Haven High! Haven High! Haven High!"

Beth Manning did her best to hold back a sigh at the roars of the crowd. When she'd volunteered to organize Senior Spirit Week, she hadn't taken into account the fact that it would require so much . . . spirit. That meant mustering up some kind of enthusiasm for the place she was most desperate to leave. But that was her penance, right?

She forced herself to smile as she handed out the carefully crafted info packets to the rest of the Senior Spirit team. Too many tasks and not enough people meant Beth had been up for two days straight pulling things together; despite a morning espresso and a late-morning Red Bull, her energy level was still in the toilet.

"Let's hear it for the senior class!" she shouted now into the microphone, tossing back her long blond hair and aiming a blazing smile out at the crowd. She pumped her fist in the air, trying to ignore the embarrassment creeping over her. So she sounded like a cheerleader. So what? "Are you ready for an awesome end to an awesome year?" she cried.

College apps were in. Decisions were pending. Grades were irrelevant. And, as tradition dictated, the senior class was treated to a whirlwind of activity: a senior auction, a community service day, a school spirit day, student-teacher sports challenges—day after day of celebration, kicked off by this inane afternoon rally. An official Haven High welcome to the beginning of the end, capped off by a very unofficial blow-out party.

There'd be a lot of hangovers in the next couple weeks.

And a lot of girls weeping and guys manfully slapping one another on the back as the realization began to sink in: High school came with an expiration date. It couldn't arrive soon enough, Beth thought, as she announced the schedule of upcoming activities in the perkiest voice she could muster.

Once, she would have enjoyed all of this. Even the marching band's off-key rendition of the school song. Even the cheerleaders firing up the crowd and the jocks preening under the spotlight. Especially the jocks—one of them in particular. Beth had been eager for college; she'd spent half her life preparing—studying, working, saving, dreaming—but she hadn't been eager to leave behind everything and everyone she knew. She would have mourned and celebrated with the rest of them, cheered and shouted and wept and hugged until it was all over.

But that was before.

As she stepped away from the microphone to let the student council president make his speech, Beth's gaze skimmed across the crowd—until, without meaning to, she locked eyes with Harper. Only for a second. Then a lock of curly auburn hair fell across Harper's face, hiding it from view, and Beth looked away.

One glance had been enough to confirm it: The queen was back. Her lady-in-waiting Miranda hovered dutifully by her side, and in the row behind them, fallen courtier Adam, angling to get back into his lady's good graces. It was as if nothing had ever happened, and from the self-assured smile on Harper's face, Beth could tell that was just the way she liked it. Surely it would only be a matter of time before Harper and Adam picked up where they left off—

Stop, she reminded herself. She was done with all that bitterness, anger, and—she could admit it now—jealousy. She was better than that. And she owed Harper the benefit of the doubt, even if her former rival could never know why. She owed everyone the benefit of the doubt; that's what she had decided on that day last month. When you've screwed up everything, not just stepped over but set fire to the line, you needed all the good karma you could get. When you can't apologize for what you've done, and you can't fix it, all you can do is forgive others, and try to make everything better. And Beth was trying, starting with herself.

Even when it was hard; even when it seemed impossible.

After the accident, things are strange for days. Silent, still, as if a loud voice could break through the fragile frame of reality that they were slowly trying to rebuild. Eyes are rimmed with red, hands tremble, empty spaces sprinkle the classroom—absent faces who couldn't bear to stare at the chair that will stay empty forever.

Beth wants to stare at the chair in French class, but she sits in the front. So all she can do is tune out the substitute and imagine it behind her. And in her imagination, the seat is filled.

I'm not responsible, *Beth tells herself. It has become her mantra.* Not my fault. Not my fault.

But that feels like a lie. A comforting lie, supported by cool logic and endless rationales, but a lie nonetheless. There are too many what-ifs. What if Harper had been in the school, rather than in the car? What if Kaia had gone inside, rather than drive away? What if Harper hadn't had such a reason to escape?

Step one to being a better person: Forgive. She sees Adam every day at her locker, and on the fourth day, she talks to him.

"I'm not angry anymore," she says, wishing that it were true. "I don't hate you. Life's too short."

And it is. But when she looks at him, all she can think about is his bare body on top of Kaia's, the things they must have done together. And when he beams and hugs her, she can't forget that he pledged his love, then betrayed her. He slept with Kaia. She can't forgive that, not really.

Of course, she forgives Kaia, she reminds herself. Of course.

Next up is Kane.

"Apology accepted," she says, although he never apologized. He wrecked her life—tricked Adam into dumping her, fooled her into turning to Kane for comfort, trashing her reputation when the truth came out—and he walked away unscathed. Kaia helped. Not because there was anything in it for her; just for the fun of it. Just to see what would happen.

"I hope we can be friends," Beth says, hoping she never has to speak to him again.

Kane nods and walks away. He knows a lie when he sees it.

Beth smiles as she closes her locker. She smiles as she waves at someone across the hall. She should start smiling more, she decides. Being a better person is supposed to feel good; she should look the part.

A round of applause snapped Beth back to the present, and she realized it was time to step up to the mic and wrap things up. "Welcome to senior spring," she announced, her voice nearly lost amid the cheers. "Let's get ready for the best time of our lives!"

"Is everything okay?" Miranda asked again.

Harper nodded, shifting her position on the narrow

metal bench. The bleachers couldn't be very comfortable for her, Miranda suddenly realized, feeling like an idiot. Her leg was still healing, and with a sore neck and back . . .

"Do you want to take off?" Miranda asked. "We don't have to stay if you don't—"

"I'm fine," Harper said quietly. She stared straight ahead, as if mesmerized by Beth's ridiculous speech. A few months ago, the two of them would have been soaking up every absurd word, adding ammunition to their anti-Beth arsenal. Later Miranda would have them both cracking up over her Beth impersonation, complete with bright smile and frequent hair toss. Or more likely, they would have skipped the rally altogether, snuck off campus to gossip and complain, then drunk a toast to their high school days drawing to a party-filled close. Instead, Harper had insisted on attending. It was her first day back, and maybe she'd been looking forward to the crowds and excitement, or maybe she'd just wanted to get it over with; Miranda didn't know. She hadn't asked.

"Do you need anything?" she asked instead. "I could get us something to drink, or—"

"No. I'm fine."

"Are you sure?"

"Miranda, *I'm fine*" Harper snapped. "Can you give it a rest?"

"I'm sorry, I—"

"No, I'm sorry." Harper shifted in her seat again, rubbing her lower back. Miranda successfully resisted the urge to comment. "Really." Harper smiled—and maybe someone who hadn't been her best friend for almost a decade would have bought it. "I'm just . . . can we talk about something else? Please." It wasn't a request. It was an order.

No problem; Miranda was used to talking about something else. It's all they'd been doing since that first day, when Harper had finally agreed to visitors. Miranda had been on her best behavior; and she'd stayed that way.

Among the questions she knew better than to ask:

How do you feel? What's it like? Do you miss her? What were you on, and why, when you humiliated yourself in front of the whole school? Why did you get into the car? Where were you going? What really happened?

It had been a long month of unspoken rules, and Miranda was almost grateful for them, as if they were bright flags dotting a minefield, warning her where not to step.

They never spoke Kaia's name. They never talked about the fight, the betrayal that Miranda had forgiven the moment her phone rang with the news. It made things easier. Like now—Miranda knew better than to mention the last time she'd been in this auditorium, shivering in an upper row of the bleachers while student after student somberly spoke of Kaia's grace and fortitude. Her beauty, her wit, her style—they never mentioned her cruelty or her penchant for causing misery, the way she thrived on other people's pain. They never mentioned the rumors swirling around her relationship with a certain former French teacher, lying in a hospital bed of his own, Kaia's fingerprints found at the scene of the apparent crime.

A wreath of flowers had lain at the center of the court, right where the Haven High mascot was currently doing cartwheels to rally the crowd. An enormous photograph of Kaia, bundled up in cashmere with windblown hair and rosy cheeks, had stood behind the podium, where Beth now raised her hands and clasped them in triumph. Kaia's father had already left town, maybe for good; Harper was still in the hospital. Miranda had sat alone, trying to force her mind to appreciate the tragedy of wasted youth, to force herself to weep or shake like all those girls who'd never even spoken to Kaia, who knew her only as the newish girl with the Marc Jacobs bag—unlike Miranda, who'd shared drinks with Kaia, shared a limo with Kaia, shared a best friend with Kaia.

Kaia, who was now dead. That should mean something. It should be a turning point, one of those moments that make you see the world in a new way. But everything had seemed pretty much the same to Miranda, except that now the second-tier girls had a new strategy for sneaking onto the A-list; they'd been unable to befriend Kaia in life, but now there was no stopping them. She'd thought instead about Harper, who, she'd been told, was in stable condition and recovering well. No visitors allowed, patient's orders.

She'd thought about how strange it was to see her math teacher cry. She'd thought about whether her chem test that day would be cancelled. And that was about it.

"So I've decided I hate all my clothes," Miranda said now, plucking at her pale blue T-shirt that had been washed so many times, she could no longer tell when it was inside out. "We're talking serious fashion emergency—and you know what that means. . . ." Harper didn't say anything.

"Shopping spree," Miranda chirped. "You, me, Grace's finest clothing stores, and, of course"—she patted her purse—"Mom's gold card."

A faint smile crept across Harper's face. "I could use some new . . ."

"Everything?" Miranda prompted.

"You know it." She rolled her eyes. "Not that anything in this town would be worth buying—you know Grace."

"It's a total fashion—" Miranda cut herself off just in time. *Train wreck*, she'd been about to say. "Wreck" was too close to "collision." Accident. And that was another thing on the list of what they couldn't discuss. "Wasteland," she said instead. "I guess if you want, we could drive down Route 53 and pick up some swank duds at Walmart. . . ."

Harper laughed, and it actually sounded real. "I'll pass, thanks. Hopefully Classic Rags will have some good stuff, and we can check out—oh."

"What?"

"It's nothing." Harper glanced off to the side. "It's just, I'm supposed to go to physical therapy this afternoon . . . but it's totally stupid. I can just blow it off."

"No!"

Harper's eyes widened, and Miranda softened her tone. "I just mean, no, you should go. We can shop anytime. You have to take care of yourself."

"It's really no big deal," Harper argued. Her fingers tightened around the edge of the bleacher seat.

"But you really should—"

"I guess, maybe. . . ."

"Unless there's some reason you actually want to—"

"Forget it." Harper stood up, wincing a bit as she put weight on her left leg. "You're right, we can shop another time. I'll see you later, okay?"

"Where are you going?" Miranda jumped up from her seat. "I'll come with you."

"I've got some stuff to do," Harper said, already walking away. "You should stick around here."

Once again, it wasn't a request. It was an order.

"Where are you taking me?" the redhead giggled as Kane Geary led her, blindfolded, down the empty hallway.

"That's for me to know"—he kissed the back of her neck, then ran his fingers lightly down her spine, relishing the burst of shivers it caused—"and you to find out. Come on"—Sarah? Stella? Susan?—"babe. Time to make your dreams come true." He pulled her along faster.

"I can't see anything," she reminded him, squeezing his hand. "I'm going to trip."

"I'd never let you," he assured her. "Don't you trust me?"

She laughed. "I'm not that stupid."

Kane begged to differ. But not out loud.

"How about you take off the blindfold and just tell me where you're taking me?"

"Where's the fun in that?" Kane shook his head. "I've got a better idea." He hoisted her over his shoulder. Once she stopped wriggling and giggling, she lay pressed against him, her arms wrapped around his waist and her lips nuzzling the small of his back.

"All the blood's rushing to my head, Kane," she complained, "so hurry." But he stopped. A month ago, Kaia's locker had been transformed into a makeshift shrine, with a rainbow of cards and angel pictures adorning the front, above an ever-growing pile of flowers and teddy bears. There were notes, bracelets, magazine cutouts, candles—an endless supply of sentimental crap—but no photos. None of the mourners had any pictures of Kaia; none of them even knew her.

Even Kane had no pictures. Back in the fall, he, Kaia, and Harper had staged an illicit photo shoot, a faux hookup between Harper and Kane captured on film—and later doctored to make it appear that Beth was the one in his arms.

Kane still had the original images stored away for a rainy day; but Kaia had stayed behind the lens. And Kane's mental picture was blurry. He remembered the way she'd felt, the one night they spent together—he remembered her lips, her skin, her sighs. But the room had been dark, and she'd been gone by morning. For the first few days, there had been a strange zone of silence around her locker—you dropped your voice when you passed by, or you avoided it altogether. But then it faded into the background, just one of those things you barely noticed as you hurried down the hall.

Even Kane, who noticed everything, had successfully blocked it out after a few days of cringing and sneering. He'd almost forgotten it was there. And now it really wasn't.

The collage of cards and pictures had disappeared, with only a few stray, peeling strips of tape to remember them by. The pile of junk was gone—only a single teddy bear and a couple of votive candles remained, and as Kane watched, they too were swept up by the janitor, deposited in a large bin, and wheeled away.

Now it was just any other locker. Reduce, reuse, recycle.

"Kane, what is it?" the redhead asked, tickling his side. "Are we here? Wherever we are?"

"No, we're not here," he said, still staring at the locker. "We're nowhere."

It's just a locker, he told himself. *She doesn't need it anymore.*

He put the redhead back on her feet, tipped her blindfolded head toward his, and gave her a long kiss. Then he put his arm around her shoulder and guided her away from the locker, down the hall, toward the empty boiler room, where he'd prepared his standard romantic spread.

"We're two of a kind," Kaia had once told him. Meaning: icy, detached, heartless. Winners, who didn't need anyone else's approval to be happy, who sought out what they wanted and took it. Who didn't look back.

Wouldn't it be a fitting tribute to prove her right?

ABOUT THE AUTHOR

ROBIN WASSERMAN is the author of *Hacking Harvard*, the Seven Deadly Sins series, the Cold Awakening trilogy (*Frozen*, *Shattered*, *Torn*), *The Book of Blood and Shadow*, and *The Waking Dark*. She lives in Brooklyn, New York.